R0201546918

10/2020

W9-AQH-025

SORCERY OF A QUEEN

ALSO BY BRIAN NASLUND

Blood of an Exile

SORCERY
OF A
QUEEN

BRIAN NASLUND

A TOM DOHERTY ASSOCIATES BOOK
NEW YORK

SORCERY OF A QUEEN

Copyright © 2020 by Brian Naslund

Map by Jennifer Hanover

A Tor Book
Published by Tom Doherty Associates
120 Broadway
New York, NY 10271

www.tor-forge.com

Tor® is a registered trademark of Macmillan Publishing Group, LLC.

The Library of Congress Cataloging-in-Publication Data
is available upon request.

ISBN 978-1-250-30967-9 (trade paperback)
ISBN 978-1-250-30966-2 (hardcover)
ISBN 978-1-250-30965-5 (ebook)

Our books may be purchased in bulk for promotional, educational, or business use. Please contact your local bookseller or the Macmillan Corporate and Premium Sales Department at 1-800-221-7945, extension 5442, or by email at MacmillanSpecialMarkets@macmillan.com.

First Edition: August 2020

Printed in the United States of America

0 9 8 7 6 5 4 3 2 1

For Jess

Himeja

PAPYRIA

SOUL
SEA

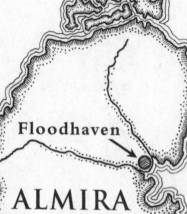

Floodhaven

ALMIRA

Deepdale

THE
HEART

JUNGLE NATIONS

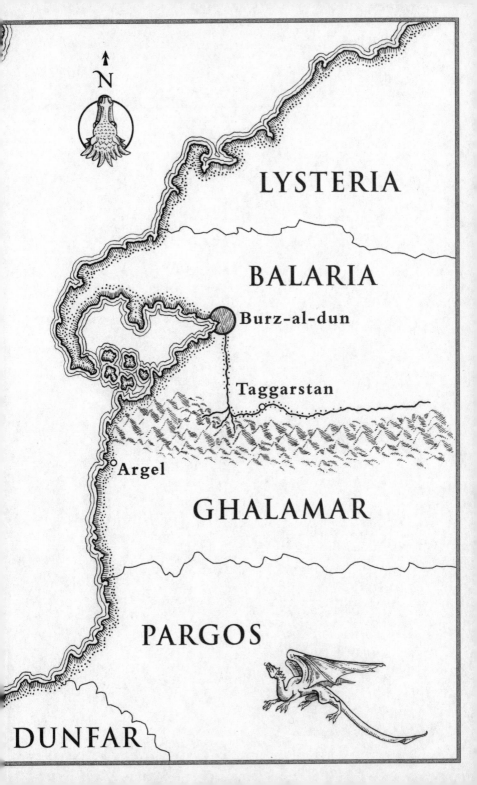

PART I

The peacefulness of nature is an illusion. A trick played on untrained eyes.

—Ashlyn Malgrave

1

BERSHAD

Realm of Terra, the Soul Sea

After the goatfuck at Floodhaven, Bershad, Ashlyn, and Felgor sailed north to Papyria.

A good sailor with decent wind could have made the journey inside of a fortnight, but their wind was shit and the weather was all sharp rain and heaving gusts that blasted their sails to tatters. After twenty-seven days at sea, they'd barely made it to the Broken Peninsula, which was a stretch of small, rocky islands that marked the halfway point between Almira and Papyria.

But on the twenty-eighth day, the skies cleared and they finally started making good progress. For the first time in almost a moon's turn, it seemed like luck was tipping over to their side of things.

Everyone on the ship relaxed. Bershad sat with Ashlyn at the stern of the frigate, watching the sky above, where a thinning line of dragons winged eastward. Blackjacks. Needle-Throated Verduns. Thundertails. Red Skulls. Greezels. There were even a few Gray-Winged Nomads, soaring at a much higher altitude than the other breeds. These were the final stragglers of the Great Migration. There was a victory in watching them and knowing they'd find a safe place on the far side of the Soul Sea. A place that he and Ashlyn had created for them.

So there Bershad was—basking in his achievements, sipping rice wine, and thinking about breakfast—when five Red Skulls broke off from the swarm and hurtled toward their ship in a hunting formation.

"Oh, shit."

Bershad leapt up from his spot by Ashlyn's side and started tearing through the gear on deck, looking for a weapon. The dragons encircled their lonesome ship, screeching aggressively and snapping their jaws in hungry anticipation.

"I need a spear."

"None aboard," growled the ship's captain, Jaku. He and his crew had rescued Bershad and Ashlyn from the battle of Floodhaven. He waved at the pile of fishing tack. "Best I got is one o' them orca harpoons over there."

All around him, the crew was cursing in Papyrian and cranking their crossbows.

"Forget the crossbows, they'll just piss the bastards off," Bershad growled, sifting through the gear. He picked up a harpoon with shit balance, but a point that was sharp enough to cut glass.

"You going to kill five Red Skulls by yourself, Almiran?" Jaku asked.

"No," Bershad said. "Not by myself."

He turned to Ashlyn. She was already unwinding the dragon thread on her wrist. In the back of his head, there was an idiot-brained warden telling him to rush her belowdecks before the dragons attacked, but Ashlyn had toasted two armies with that scrap of Ghost Moth spinal tissue. She was going to be the main factor in their survival, not him.

"Silas and I will deal with the dragons," she said. "Everyone else get belowdecks."

The Papyrian sailors didn't need to be asked twice. Even Jaku retreated down the hatch without a fuss. But Felgor, Hayden, and the rest of the Papyrian widows remained on deck. They were sworn to protect Ashlyn from any danger, dragons included.

"You can't help," Ashlyn said to Hayden. "But you can hurt by being in the way. Go."

Hayden's body tensed with uncertainty, but widows were nothing if not pragmatic, and Ashlyn had spoken the truth. Hayden gave a curt nod, then followed the sailors below, taking her sisters with her.

Felgor shrugged. "Well, fuck me if I'm gonna stick around trying to look brave when even the widows have run for shelter." He scrambled over to the hatch. "Try not to die!"

Bershad scanned the sky. The Red Skulls were increasing speed and drawing closer with each rotation around the ship. It was a hunting pattern unique to their breed, and it always preceded the same behavior.

"Two of them are going to break off and attack together from opposite sides," Bershad said.

"I know," Ashlyn responded. "Which side do you want?"

"Whichever one comes with the smaller dragon, witch queen," Bershad said.

"Don't call me that," Ashlyn said, then ripped her hand down the length of the thread, sparking a crackle of lightning that she cupped in her hand as if it was a perfectly sized river stone she was preparing to throw at an easy target.

Bershad took the final scrapings of Gods Moss that remained from Floodhaven and ate them. His stomach turned hot, and a familiar, unnatural strength coursed through his muscles.

Two of the dragons careened from the gyre. Both females. Both enormous.

"Perfect," Bershad muttered, moving starboard. Ashlyn went in the opposite direction, raising her lightning-wreathed fist.

Bershad lined up with his Red Skull. She was twice the size of the one he'd killed outside of Argel—massive wingspan heaving, tail lashing through the air. Eyes burning down and focused on him. He focused right back. Gripped the harpoon tight. Waited until she was about a hundred strides away.

"Now!" he yelled.

Bershad threw the harpoon. Ashlyn threw her lightning. His spear connected but he couldn't tell exactly where. The dragon whooshed over his head in a blur of scales and a rush of wind. He heard a high screech and a thundering snap, then something hard bashed him in the back of the head, knocking him face-first into the deck and turning his vision white.

The fall broke his jaw and nose. His skull was cracked, too, judging from the searing pain. But there was enough Gods Moss in his system to repair the injuries. He popped his jaw back into position with a hard jerk before the bone healed crooked. His vision began to return, so he struggled to his feet. Ashlyn was standing. Unharmed. Looking around. The mast of the ship was sheared off at the middle and both dragons were in the water. The one that Bershad harpooned had a blooming cloud of red water around her head. Ashlyn's was belly-up and floating like a dead fish.

"Huh." Bershad dabbed at his skull wound, which was almost gone. "That went well."

"Sure. If you subtract the broken mast and the fact that those three are still circling." Ashlyn pointed at the dragons with a smoking finger. They all lilted to the left in unison, their crimson skulls flashing in the bright afternoon sun.

"They're about to attack," Ashlyn said.

"Yeah."

Bershad grabbed another harpoon from the wreckage of the deck. There wasn't anything to do but hope they got lucky a second time.

The problem with Red Skulls was that they were just as smart as they were vicious. They saw what happened to their fellow huntresses and switched up the pattern—breaking in three different directions, each one approaching with as much distance between themselves as possible.

"This isn't good," Bershad said, trying to decide when and where to throw his spear.

"Just try to get one of them," Ashlyn said, ripping her hand down the thread to create another crackling charge. "I can bifurcate the lightning and get the other two. Maybe."

"Maybe?"

"It's theoretically possible, I just need to manipulate the balance and . . . wait . . . fuck!" The hiss and snap went quiet.

"Ashlyn?" Bershad turned around. There was smoke around her arm, but nothing else. Ashlyn ripped her hand down the cord again, sparks spitting and flying, but she couldn't seem to summon more lightning.

Bershad looked back at the closest dragon, cutting through the sky toward them. After all the intentional dragon encounters he'd survived, getting killed in a random lizard attack at sea seemed about right. Bershad just wished Ashlyn wasn't coming down the river with him.

The closest Red Skull dropped her claws. Opened her horrifying mouth.

Bershad moved closer to Ashlyn. Took her hand. "I love you, Ashe. Always have."

A shadow fell. Something slammed the Red Skull into the sea.

It took Bershad a moment to register the smoke-colored hide and hulking creature for what it was: an enormous Gray-Winged Nomad.

The Nomad roared—loud and booming—then tore the dragon apart in her claws, blasting a spray of blood and organs across the waves. Her wingspan was so long that she made the Red Skull look like a stunted swamp lizard. The two remaining Red Skulls pulled up from their attack and scattered, their aggression replaced with rabbits' terror.

Bershad kept his harpoon raised, thinking the Nomad might attack the ship next. But she ignored them, and instead scooped the front half of the divided Red Skull into her claws and carried it to the nearest island, which was only a few hundred strides away. Then she buried her snout deep and came up chewing. Maw covered in gore. Ashlyn watched, too. Enthralled and silent. The others came up from belowdecks while the Nomad was enjoying her kill.

"What happened?" Felgor asked.

Bershad shrugged. "The Nomad killed the Red Skull."

"What, that dragon owe you a favor or something?" Felgor asked.

"Don't think it works that way."

They all watched the dragon eat. When she'd had her fill, the Nomad turned back to their ship for a moment—glowing blue eyes sharp and aware. Then she raised her wings and snapped into the air with a few quick beats—salt water and blood dripping off her smoke-colored belly. Once she was a few hundred strides up, the dragon caught an ocean thermal and rode it in a wide gyre until she was a coin in the sky, shifting in and out of sight between the clouds.

"That is the biggest fucking dragon I have ever seen," Jaku said, shielding his eyes from the sun.

"Yeah," Bershad said, watching her. She was the largest he'd seen, too. And Bershad had seen more than most. Their ship meandered northeast in the sea's current. The Nomad's gyre followed their movement. "And it looks like she's planning on sticking around awhile."

"Um, what're you gonna do about that?" Felgor asked.

"Long as she stays up there, not a fucking thing," Bershad said.

"I'm less worried about the dragon and more worried about how we're going to get moving again," Ashlyn said.

"Aye, that'll be an issue," Jaku said, pointing at the broken mast. "Gonna need to cut ourselves a replacement."

Ashlyn pointed to the island where the Nomad had eaten the

Red Skull. Along with the dragon carcass, it was pocked with tall cedar trees. "There."

"Aye," Jaku agreed, then called to his men. "Looks like we got some carpentry in our future, boys. Get the saws out of storage."

———

For eleven days, they sailed north through the Broken Peninsula.

The weather had remained clear, but their journey was still slowed by the time it took to replace the mast, and—now that the skies were devoid of storms and dragons—the new and constant threat of being discovered by Linkon Pommol's navy.

Three times, they'd spotted a Papyrian frigate—now flying Linkon's turtle banner—patrolling the Almiran coastline. As far as they knew, Linkon Pommol believed Ashlyn was dead, and was simply flexing the strength of his navy to ensure the small lords of the Atlas Coast behaved. But they couldn't risk a confrontation, so they'd been forced to sail into the chaotic interior of the Broken Peninsula for cover. The peninsula was all tiny islands and surging currents that threatened to beach them on sharpened shoals. Every time they went inland for cover, they got lost in the mess of islands and it took days to get back out to the open sea.

The Nomad had circled them the entire time. Never landed. Never strayed course.

"Doesn't it need to rest at some point?" Felgor asked, squinting up at the gray dragon.

"I've told you before, that dragon is a *she,* not an it," Ashlyn said from her spot on the stern, where she was sketching the dragon using a piece of charcoal and a scrap of storm-ruined sail. "And Nomads have the longest range of any dragon in Terra. They can remain airborne for a moon's turn before exhausting themselves."

"Doesn't it, uh, *she* get hungry though?" Felgor asked.

"Not soon," Bershad said. "She ate half that Red Skull."

Bershad couldn't explain it, but he could feel her full belly, somehow. A pressure that hung in the sky, but was tied to his guts, too.

"So, you're saying it's normal to have a dragon follow you all the way across the Broken Peninsula nonstop like a street urchin tracking a sausage cart and hoping for scraps?" Felgor asked.

Ashlyn stopped drawing. Rolled her bare shoulders in small circles, which caught the attention of a few Papyrian sailors. The battle at Floodhaven had left a jagged series of blue scars on her skin that started on her right wrist and ran up the flesh of her arm and across her chest, mapping her veins with sawtooth lines.

"No. It's unusual," she said.

Bershad looked up at the dragon, too. Raised a hand to shield his eyes from the sun. She was riding the western wind—wings fully expanded, the webbing aglow in the midday sun.

"Normal events are in short supply these days," he said.

Truth was, the Nomad's relentless focus on them wasn't the strangest thing about her, it was the fact that he didn't feel the bone tremor that usually came with a proximity to dragons. Instead, there was a gentle pull that was twisted up in both their pulses. The connection was intimate and tight—he could feel a surge in his balance and bloodstream anytime she rose or dipped, lilted closer or farther away.

Bershad didn't understand it. But he was used to things happening to him that didn't make any sense. He'd learned to ignore the deeper implications.

"Unusual or not, she is screwing with our fishing," Captain Jaku said, locking the ship's wheel into place with a worn loop of leather and coming over. "Generally, we'd be pulling marlin and tuna outta these waters easier than a heron pulling frogs from a clear pond. But that Nomad's spooking everything with gills for leagues. This rate, it's gonna be hardtack all the way home."

"How much longer's that gonna take?" Felgor said, scratching his ear. "Because those biscuits are detrimental to the normal routine of a man's bowels. My last proper shit is a distant memory at this point."

Jaku spat over the gunwale. "We keep getting the turtle lord's ships pulling on our ass hairs and sending us into the Shattered Shithole, it'll be a month, best case."

"A month," Felgor muttered. "By Aeternita, I may never shit again. You know, it's not healthy getting all backed up like this. I knew I guy back in Burz-al-dun who stole a massive crate of persimmons off the docks, then proceeded to eat them for damn near every meal until they were gone. Afterward, he went *three* weeks without a shit and wound up—"

"Gods, Felgor. I will get you a fucking fish if you just stop talking," Bershad said. He looked up at the dragon. She'd scare away the fish during the day—even the creatures that lived beneath the waves knew to watch the skies of Terra—but under the cover of darkness, things would be different. "I'll do it tonight."

———————

"Has a dragon ever followed you like this before?" Ashlyn asked when they were in the privacy of their own cabin.

"Well, I missed my pass on a Blackjack a few summers ago and got chased through about fifteen leagues of swamp before the thing lost interest. Had to wait until his blood calmed down the next day before I could settle things."

"Don't be cute. I'm not talking about a dragonslaying gone wrong."

Bershad sighed. "No," he admitted. "It's new."

Ashlyn chewed on that for a moment.

"The way your body heals. That dragon overhead. There has to be an explanation for it all."

"Sure. I'm a fucking demon."

"Very funny. Osyrus Ward didn't say anything about dragons following you?"

He shook his head. "No. But that crazy old man was pretty light on specifics."

After they'd escaped Floodhaven, Bershad had told Ashlyn about Osyrus Ward and the dungeon amputations he'd endured. But he hadn't told her what Osyrus Ward had said: that the strength in his blood would eventually kill him. And he didn't plan to. He was used to death sentences. Throwing another one across his shoulders didn't move him much.

"What are you holding on to, Silas?"

She was studying him with her careful, scrutinizing eyes.

"Nothing."

"Liar."

He shrugged. Knew he was keeping the secret because of stupid, stubborn instinct, but he also knew Ashlyn. If he told her he was doomed, she'd go chasing after answers, no matter where they took her. He didn't care if a dragon was following him, so long as she stayed in the sky above, which he had a feeling she'd do. He wanted whatever time he had left to be quiet and peaceful. Lived out on some empty Papyrian island where nobody could bother them. So little of his life had been like that. A week. A month. A year. He didn't care how much time he got, so long as he shared it with Ashlyn.

"You know I'll figure it out eventually," Ashlyn added when he stayed silent.

"Maybe. Or maybe some things are truly unknowable, witch queen."

"Stop calling me that."

"Make me."

Ashlyn scoffed. "Very well."

She crossed the cabin and grabbed him by throat and jaw. Then slowly pushed him down onto his knees.

————

After Ashlyn had fallen asleep, Bershad slipped out of the tiny cot in their cabin and climbed above deck. Took a few moments to breathe in the salty night air. He nodded at the only sailor on duty, who had tucked himself as deep as possible into the little pilot's nook, and was clutching his crossbow as if it was a long-lost lover.

Bershad considered reminding him that shooting that crossbow at the Nomad was about as useful as attacking a fully armored warden with a toothpick, but resisted. These days, comfort was hard to find, even if it was a false one.

He dug through the equipment on deck until he found a deep-sea fishing line and a large silver hook. Cut the line with a knife, baited the hook with the freshest herring he could find—which wasn't very fresh at all—and headed for the stern.

Bershad cast the line into the sea, letting the ship's wake do most of the work for him. Their escape from Floodhaven had been filled with long periods of downtime—waiting in a hidden cove or behind a rocky island for ships to pass—but he hadn't spent any of it truly alone. He was either with Ashlyn in their cabin, killing dragons, or on the deck listening to Felgor prattle on while everyone watched the Nomad from the corner of their eyes.

He took some time to savor the solitude. The events of the last year swam through his mind. Crossing the Razorback Mountains. Losing Rowan and Alfonso in Taggarstan. Killing the emperor of Balaria. The horrific torture he'd endured under the hands and hatchets of that crazy bastard, Osyrus Ward.

Getting back to Floodhaven. Seeing the things Ashlyn had done to survive.

A low blanket of fog covered the stars and prevented Bershad from seeing the Nomad. But he knew she was there. He could feel her.

An hour or so later, the fishing line jerked hard in Bershad's fingers.

He wrapped the line around his forearm with a quick loop, straining to stop himself from being pulled into the sea. Then he started hauling whatever he'd caught toward the boat. The line dug deep into his flesh with each yank, but the pain felt good in a way. Focused him on the task at hand. When you were battling a huge fish that could pull you into the water at any moment, there wasn't much room to worry about cursed blood, clingy dragons, lost kingdoms, or magical threads. Bershad liked that.

After ten minutes of fighting the fish, Bershad hauled up a red-finned tuna the size of a pony. The fish's panicked pulse thrummed against his fingertips with a manic sensitivity. He drew the knife from his belt and killed it with a quick stab to the brain.

The smell of fish and blood filled his nostrils—the scents far sharper than they should have been. A feral urge compelled Bershad to crouch over the fish, cut a swath of raw, bleeding meat from its flank, and take a juicy bite that was full of briny tang.

Bershad ate his fill, propelled by instinct and hunger. When he was done, he wiped some of the blood from his mouth. Looked down at the massive fish. There was plenty of meat left for the crew, and more than enough to unlock Felgor's clogged bowels. But the dragon hadn't eaten anything since the Red Skull, which was weeks ago. Bershad didn't know why she was following him, but he knew that he was responsible. He looked over his shoulder. The lone sailor was still huddled in his cabin and hadn't noticed the tuna.

Bershad yanked the hook free and slid the fish back into the water.

Nothing happened for a while. The tuna stayed afloat, scales shimmering as it lolled in the ship's wake. Just as Bershad was starting to think he'd wasted a perfectly good fish, a smoky flash careened through the fog line and snatched the tuna from the water. Ascended back into the fog a moment later.

Bershad felt the Nomad swallow the head in one bite, then the rest. The same briny flesh that sat in his stomach sat in hers, too. He nodded, then headed back up the ship.

"Heard a ruckus," the sailor said. "You hook anything?"

"Yeah. But it got away."

Belowdecks, Bershad dug up a jar of Crimson Tower moss and wiped it across the cuts in his palm and forearm from the fishing line, then wrapped it all with clean bandages. The wounds would be gone by morning. Then he crawled back underneath the scratchy sheets. Pressed up against the warmth of Ashlyn's body. Tried to focus on her smell and her heartbeat. But he could still feel the dragon above.

Bershad went to sleep thinking that maybe they'd finally seen the last of Linkon Pommol's ships, and with the Great Migration complete, they could enjoy clear skies and peaceful days the rest of the way to Papyria.

He was wrong on both counts.

2

JOLAN

Almira, Dainwood Province

Jolan saw the vultures an hour after dawn.

He'd been foraging in the southern warrens of the Dainwood for two moon turns. Almost all of the dragons of Almira had flown across the Soul Sea for the Great Migration, so he'd taken full advantage of the clear skies and forest to explore every cramped ravine and secret cave. His backpack was bulging with valuable and rare ingredients—six vials of Kelarium mudfish scales, seven jars of Iondril root tendrils, three Daintree fox livers, two pounds of glowing solarium caps, five pounds each of Spartania and Crimson Tower moss. All of that alone was enough to start his own apothecary, if he hadn't been expelled from the Alchemist Order. But it paled in comparison to his true haul.

Two pounds of Gods Moss, harvested from the roots of a gnarled tree deep inside an ancient warren. He'd tried to find other trees like it to harvest more, but in all his spelunking and exploration, this was the only one he'd encountered.

The Gods Moss was worth thousands of gold coins. If Jolan wanted, he could ride to Floodhaven, sell it off to a merchant magnate, and then live for the rest of his life off the profits. But Jolan wasn't interested in a lazy life of luxury and riches. He planned to rent a cottage somewhere near Glenlock and start running careful experiments on the Gods Moss until he discovered the secret of what he'd seen that morning in Otter Rock last spring. The secret of the Flawless Bershad.

But first, he had to trek out of the wilderness.

It had been two rough moon turns filled with hard work, and Jolan was looking forward to returning to civilization. He was walking along a shallow stream—daydreaming about spending a small portion of his earnings on a long bath, several big mugs of rain ale, and a feather bed—when the vultures caught his eye.

There were at least a score of them, all circling a clearing in the forest about half a league to the north. Part of Jolan wanted to press on—vultures weren't a sign of peaceful events—but after watching them for a while, he decided to check it out. If there was a wounded animal, he might be able to use the poor thing as his first Gods Moss test subject. The Alchemist Order always stressed that experiments should begin with small insects and move upward in size from there, but he was willing to jump ahead if an injured rabbit or deer crossed his path.

Jolan reached the edge of the clearing, stifled a gasp, then dropped to the ground and ducked underneath some ferns.

There were three wardens. All wearing masks and full armor, and carrying weapons. The biggest of the men was sitting on a tree stump, leaning against a greatsword that was nearly as tall as Jolan. The others were crowded around him. But the living men weren't the most alarming aspect of the scene.

It was the ten dead ones at their feet.

Jolan took a moment to let his heart rate slow down. When it refused, he began to slowly crawl backward. If he could just return to that stream unnoticed, he could follow it to Glenlock without a problem.

Something metallic clicked behind him.

"Whaddawe got here?" someone asked. He had a thick Dainwood accent. "A hiding turtle?"

Jolan didn't move. Or speak.

"Whoever you are, you're gonna have a crossbow bolt through your skull if you don't speak up soon."

"I'm just a boy," Jolan said, raising his hands off the ground a little, doing his best to appear harmless.

There was a silence. Then boots tromping through grass. A shadow fell on Jolan's face. He looked up to find a fourth warden with a crossbow pointed at his face. Jolan nearly threw up.

"A boy, is it?"

"Y-yes."

"Well, get up, then."

Jolan did as he was told. On instinct, he turned away from the crossbow, as if that would make the weapon disappear.

"Cross the clearing. Over to the others."

Jolan started walking, unable to get the image of a crossbow bolt going through his brain out of his mind.

"Look what I found crawling around in the ferns!" the warden called to his comrades. They all looked over. Now that Jolan was closer, he could see that all of them were wearing jaguar masks.

That made them wardens of the Dainwood.

"Another turtle?" asked the tallest of the wardens. His jaguar mask was painted blood red except for a black line down the middle. He stood up from the stump, but leaned on his sword as if it was a crutch.

"Nah, just some kid."

"Huh. Come closer."

When Jolan was within five paces of the wardens, the big man put up a hand.

"That's far enough." He glared at Jolan. "Who are you?"

"I . . . um." Jolan's palms were coated in sweat. His mouth was dry. "Um."

"Um is not a name, boy. Spit it out."

"Jo-Jolan," he managed.

The man pointed a meaty finger at Jolan's backpack. "What're you carrying, Jolan?"

"Supplies."

"What kind of supplies?"

"Healing ingredients, mostly."

The warden who'd found him stepped forward. His jaguar mask was blue and white, but he pulled it off, revealing a narrow face with a huge chin. "Healing. Like cock rot and such? 'Cause I got a nasty situation brewing down south."

He jerked his belt a few times, which made the two war hatchets he carried rattle.

"Well," Jolan said, thinking, "my Cedar Finger and Spartania moss should take care of it if I mix it with—"

"Forget your cock rot for a second, Willem," the red-masked man interrupted. Then he raised his arm and shifted his body so that Jolan could see a broken arrow protruding from a seam in his armor along the rib cage. "Can you remove this bastard without sending me down the river?"

When he'd been an apprentice, Jolan had only seen Master Morgan do one arrow extraction. A hunting accident. And the truth was he hadn't been able to see the procedure very well with all the blood and thrashing limbs that were involved. But judging from the wardens' stern faces and closely clutched weapons, refusing wasn't an available option.

"I can try."

While Jolan disinfected his pincer-tongs in boiling river water, he wondered to himself how many injured killers he was going to run into in the middle of the woods during his life. At this rate, the number was going to be significant.

The red-masked warden—whose name he learned was Cumberland—had removed his armor and shirt while Jolan got everything ready. The man was in his forties, with wild, black hair full of tangles and silver rings. Cumberland reminded Jolan of the Flawless Bershad, except this man wasn't quite as tall as the legendary dragonslayer.

Jolan checked the tongs. "Almost ready," he said.

Cumberland gave a weary nod, then picked up a stick and moved to put it in his mouth.

"You won't need that," Jolan said.

"You ever had an arrow pulled out of you, boy?"

"No, but after I put this in the wound, I could saw off three ribs and cut out your stomach, and you wouldn't feel a thing." Jolan produced a glass vial full of blue, viscous liquid.

"Is it safe?" Cumberland asked, frowning.

"Everyone always asks that," Jolan said. "Fighting in a battle isn't safe, but you did that anyway."

"Fair point. But I need an answer all the same."

The tonic was a new variation of the same numbing agent Jolan had given to Garret before removing the dragontooth in his arm last spring. It was derived from the poison-dart frogs of the Dainwood, but Jolan had reduced it with the liver and heart of a massive, warren-grown koi fish, which would make the numbness last far longer. That was good, because the arrow had broken two of Cumberland's ribs on the way into his body. This wouldn't be a quick extraction.

"It's safe," Jolan said. "May I begin?"

Cumberland grumbled, but eventually nodded.

An hour later, Jolan had extracted the shaft, the arrowhead, and three splintered arrowhead fragments. Then he'd closed the wound with seven perfect stitches, packed it with Spartania moss, and bandaged the whole thing with silk.

Jolan had considered using some of his Gods Moss, but he was afraid one of the wardens might know what it was—and how much it was worth—in which case they would most definitely steal it. Probably kill him while they were at it.

Jolan didn't know much about people. But he knew better than to trust valuable commodities with men who made their living ending lives.

Cumberland examined the work. "Not bad. Last arrow I caught took some drunken butcher half the night to pry out. Knee still aches every time it rains, too. Which is every fucking day in the Dainwood."

"This one will heal fully," Jolan said, packing up the last of his materials. He swallowed, then said, "That'll be three gold pieces."

Cumberland looked up from his ribs. "Is that a fact?"

"That's just the value of the ingredients that I used," Jolan said. "My labor is free."

"Oh, and to what do we owe this generous discount?"

Jolan kept his body straight and refused to break eye contact. "I know who you are. The Daintree Jaguars are fearsome and vicious and they pay little heed to the laws of the wider world. So I will settle for breakeven, but no less. I do not work for free."

Not anymore, anyway.

Cumberland glanced at his comrades, who'd been drinking and

playing dice around a fire while Jolan worked. "You got some balls on you, boy."

Jolan shrugged. "I need to make a living in this world. Same as you."

"Hm." Cumberland considered that. "Well, we seem to be fresh out of spare gold pieces, seeing as there's a war on and all."

"War? What war?"

"You been living in a cave all summer, boy?"

"Yes."

Cumberland cocked his head. "Well, you missed a lot. Cedar Wallace laid siege to Floodhaven like the warmonger that he is. And if the stories are to be believed, Ashlyn responded by incinerating his entire fucking army with some kind of demoncraft, but got herself killed in the process."

Jolan frowned. "If Ashlyn is dead, who rules Almira?"

"That's a matter that's up for debate." Cumberland kicked one of the dead men with a boot. He was wearing a mask carved in the shape of a turtle. "But this bastard's liege lord has got the bulk of it."

"Linkon Pommol?" Jolan said.

"Yup."

Jolan looked between the men. For the time being, they didn't seem eager to kill him. And he clearly needed to catch up on current events if he was going to find safe haven in Almira to work on the Gods Moss.

"Why is the Jaguar Army fighting a war against Linkon Pommol?"

"Because Linkon Pommol is an asshole," said Willem, laughing.

Cumberland laughed, too. But then his face got serious.

"You know who we are. And you know that we're dangerous. But what else do you know about the jaguars, boy?"

"I know you used to be Bershad's men. And you never changed masks, even when you served Elden Grealor."

"Do you know why?"

Jolan shrugged.

"Men of the Dainwood go their own way," said one of the wardens. He was the only one who hadn't taken his mask off yet. It was painted green and yellow. His body was wiry and lean—a stark contrast to the other wardens, who were all built like bulls.

"Always," Willem murmured. His face turned serious. Everyone else nodded.

"After things went bad for Lord Silas in Glenlock Canyon, we didn't have much choice but to put up with Elden Grealor," Cumberland continued. "A bunch of good men got the bars for their part in that mess, and Hertzog Malgrave was just itching for an excuse to snuff the last of us jaguars out by way of blue tattoos. So, we behaved. But seeing as the whole of Almira's lost its fucking mind, we figured it was about time to write our own fate for a stretch."

"And Linkon Pommol ain't crossing the Gorgon and sticking his prick in the Dainwood while I've got warm blood in my veins," Willem added. "Bastard'll cut more Daintrees down than the Grealors did."

"Who's in charge, though?" Jolan asked. "I mean, who commands your army?"

"Carlyle Llayawin," Cumberland said. "He's a high-warden who served Ashlyn Malgrave up in Floodhaven and somehow survived that mess, along with some of his men. Now he's the head o' the Jaguar Army. And now that we've dealt with these bastards"—he motioned to the dead turtle wardens—"we're heading back to Umbrik's Glade to rendezvous with him." Cumberland gave Jolan a clap on the shoulder. "And you're coming with us."

Jolan hesitated. "Um, I was heading to Glenlock."

"You were," Cumberland agreed, as if he'd help Jolan make his travel plans personally. "But Timult was the only warden we had with a passing familiarity with healing arts, and that's him over there."

He pointed to the headless body of a warden about twenty strides away.

"Speaking of, you found his head and given him the shell, Willem?"

"Yeah, yeah. He'll get to the sea. No problem, boss."

Cumberland nodded. "Even if Timult wasn't heading down the river as we speak, if he'd been running the show, all this with my ribs would have involved a far larger portion of screaming and cursing. You got a treasure trove in that pack and head of yours, boy. I aim to keep both nearby for the foreseeable future. There's a lot more injury-prone work to be done before this deal with Linkon Pommol is finished."

Jolan looked at Cumberland's stern face, then the other wardens. They'd all stopped dicing and were now glaring at him. Jolan became very aware of the rather large number of weapons these men carried among them.

"I suppose my travel plans could be somewhat flexible."

"Good!" Cumberland said, as if he'd given Jolan a choice. "Quick introductions, then. You already know the cock-rot-ridden Willem. The one to his right with the frying pan for a face is Sten."

"I take offense to that," Sten said. Although once Jolan took a look at the man's round, pock-scarred face, the comparison made pretty good sense.

"Uh-huh." Cumberland continued, "Last one's Oromir. Take off your fucking mask, will you, Oro?"

The warden in question had been staring up at the sky, watching a hawk. But he jerked to attention at Cumberland's bark. He pulled off his mask.

Oromir couldn't have been older than sixteen. He had black hair and sharp features. Pale blue eyes. "I like my mask."

"That's 'cause you've only had it for two moons," Sten said. "Wait'll the thing's got a decade of sweat and blood soaked into it. You'll pull the bitch off soon as the fighting's done."

Oromir shrugged. "It's good to meet you, Jolan."

Cumberland gave a nod. "All right, we all know each other, then. Great. Loot the bodies. Fill every mouth with a seashell. Then we move. Need to get to Umbrik's Glade in four days."

"What's the rush?" Willem asked. "If Linkon Pommol's navy got toasted by dragons like that traveling merchant told us the other day, the skinny king can't have much fight left in him."

"The merchant didn't say it was dragons," Oromir said. "He said it was flying ships made from dragon bones and gray metal."

"Well, that's obviously impossible. But some stray dragons from the Great Migration deciding a navy didn't need to exist so much? I can see that happening. I mean, this is Almira. Our dragons can tell when a navy belongs to a bastard."

"Only morons believe the stories of traveling merchants," Cumberland said. "Their lies are just grease meant to open and then empty purses. Till my eyes prove otherwise, there aren't any flying ships, Linkon Pommol's fleet is strangling the coast, and we got a damn war to win. Now let's move out."

Jolan started packing up his supplies, then noticed that Willem was standing over him. He scratched his crotch once. Gave a sheepish look. "Little help before we get to walking?"

"Oh, right." Jolan reached into his pack to get a salve. "Drop your pants. Let's get a look at that cock rot."

3

BERSHAD

Realm of Terra, the Soul Sea

"So, you promised me a fish," Felgor said, holding a piece of hardtack in one hand. He tapped it unhappily with a finger. "You were all confident and dismissive, which is the way you always get when there's something to do that everyone thinks is impossible, like kill a dragon or regrow your own foot. But here we are, the next morning, and there is no fish for Felgor."

"I never promised anything."

"You did though. It was an implied guarantee."

Bershad gave Ashlyn a look.

"There was a bit of an implication," she admitted.

"Thanks for the loyalty, Queen."

"Blind loyalty hurts everyone, dragonslayer."

"I could give a shit about loyalty," Felgor said. "I want a fish! At this rate, we'll sail across the whole of the Soul Sea and I won't have dropped a single bowel movement. It's extremely uncomfortable to go this long without—"

"Quiet," Jaku hissed. "We got bigger problems than your shit schedule."

He pointed south. There were three green-sailed Papyrian war frigates hauling their way up the coast with full sails and dropped oars.

"Black skies," Hayden cursed. "Not again."

The captain started barking orders to his crew, who flew into a frenzy of activity—climbing up masts and dropping sails, tying lines, and cranking shafts. Jaku adjusted their course with a grim look.

And Felgor, without orders, decided to cut a heavy barrel of hardtack free from its spot on the deck and roll it overboard.

"What the fuck are you doing, Balarian?" Jaku growled.

"Reducing weight, obviously. We gotta slim down and increase speed to escape."

"Can you restrain your idiot friend?" Jaku said to Bershad. "They have the better wind. And do you see the dozen oars popping out each side of their frigates? There's a full crew of rowers in the belly of those ships. Dropping our food in the sea'll do about as much good as pissing in the harbor in an attempt to raise the tide."

"Well, let's get Silas working our oars. He's strong."

"Nobody's that strong," Bershad replied.

"And we don't have any fucking oars," Jaku added.

Everyone looked back at the ships. They were still three or four leagues away, but closing the distance with a noticeable and alarming alacrity.

"How're they moving so much faster than we are?" Bershad asked.

"I told you, they have the wind." Jaku scanned the coast. "No coves. No good channels into the Broken Peninsula where we might lose 'em. Shit. They're gonna catch up with us, and if they have a full crew of wardens to go with their oarsmen, we are going to be in a particularly tight spot."

Hayden and her widows had already drawn their slings and blades. "We are used to fighting Almirans under poor odds."

Bershad eyed the ships, which were breaking into an attack formation—two in the lead, one trailing a few hundred strides behind. He could see the outlines of wardens on the decks. Swords and spears gleaming.

"Think we're gonna need some more of your demoncraft, Ashlyn."

But instead of unwinding the thread at her wrist, Ashlyn pointed to a cloudy stretch of sky above the frigate.

"What is that?"

Everyone followed her gaze. There was a dark mark in front of a white cloud—flying high but shedding altitude.

"Another dragon?" Jaku asked.

"No, its wings aren't moving," Bershad said. He squinted as the object got closer and the details clarified. His stomach dropped.

"That's a ship made from dragon bones," Ashlyn said, seeing the same thing as Bershad.

What Jaku had mistaken for wings were actually long struts jutting out from the ship's hull. Leather sails were lashed to the bottoms of the struts and filling with wind. Instead of a proper mast and sails, there was a massive, bloated sack strung above the deck. Hundreds of cords and wires connected it to the hull, which was made from a strange union of steel and dragon bones.

"Impossible," Jaku muttered. "Ships ain't sparrows."

"If a ten-ton Red Skull can fly, so can a ship," Ashlyn said.

"Seems like faulty logic," Felgor said, trying to cut another barrel of hardtack off the deck despite what Jaku had said.

"It's a simple transitive property," Ashlyn said.

"Transa-what?"

"Leave the logic of it alone," Bershad said, watching the ship. "I'm more concerned with what it's going to do, not the particulars of how it does it."

They all watched. The wind died down, causing an eerie quiet and calm. Their sail flapped listlessly against the mast. One of the Papyrian sailors was clicking the safety catch of his crossbow on and off in nervous succession.

The flying ship lined up with the trailing frigate. As it passed, it dropped an orb.

"Did it just take a shit?" Felgor asked.

A heartbeat later, the frigate exploded. Splinters and sail scraps and flaming bodies were blown across the surf like a handful of pebbles thrown into a lake. There was a flurry of desperate hand paddling from the wardens who'd survived the blast, but they'd been wearing armor in anticipation of a violent boarding. Nobody stayed above the water for very long.

The two remaining frigates veered in separate directions, but they might as well have been actual turtles running from a hungry Naga Soul Strider. The flying ship descended, then flew directly between the two frigates, raining arrows onto both of them as it passed between. Another torrent of flames erupted from the ships—not as powerful an explosion as the orb, but plenty of damage to sink both frigates.

"Explosive arrows," Ashlyn muttered. The smell of burning dragon oil wafted across the open sea.

The flying ship rose again. Adjusted course so that it was cutting a line directly through their wake.

"Ashlyn, you need to—"

"I'm aware." She was already rolling up her sleeve and moving to the stern. "All of you need to step back. Way back."

The flying ship was about two leagues away. Ashlyn ripped her hand down the thread in a practiced and slick motion. She winced as the crackles of lightning swarmed around her hand, then settled in her palm. Snapping and hissing with power. She waited until the ship was about a league away, then raised her palm and released the charge.

The current sawed through the sky and connected with the prow of the bone ship, but it was absorbed into the hull. No damage. And no change to its course.

"Black skies," she hissed, turning around. "I need Gods Moss to strengthen the charge."

"None left," Bershad said. "Ate the last of it dealing with those Red Skulls."

They all watched the sky for a few heartbeats.

"Make the dragon attack it!" Felgor said, pointing to the Nomad, who was shadowing the flying ship from the coastline.

"What?" Bershad asked.

"We all know it's following you, Silas. Tell it to attack or something."

"It's not my fucking pet, Felgor."

"Well, you got dragon blood in your veins or whatever. You could at least try it," Felgor muttered.

Dragon blood. That wasn't right, but it wasn't entirely wrong.

He motioned to Hayden, who was gripping her short sword as if she planned to throw it at the flying ship when it got in range. "Give me that."

Bershad snatched the offered blade and ran it across his palm.

"What are you doing?" Ashlyn asked.

"Transitive property, Queen," Bershad said, letting the blood pool in his hand. "That thread of yours lays waste to armies when you throw some Gods Moss on it. And my blood has a relationship with the moss that we all know about."

"Regrows your fucking feet," Felgor muttered.

"So, let's find out what happens when we mix my blood with your thread."

He held his palm up. Saw the doubt in Ashlyn's eyes.

"Or we can all die in the next minute."

"All right," Ashlyn said, holding up her wrist. "Do it."

Bershad crossed the deck and spread his blood down the length of Ashlyn's forearm. As soon as he made contact, a quiver of energy ran through his body—made his blood and bones hum.

Ashlyn's hand crackled with a new, stronger spark. But it didn't stop there. The charge cascaded up her arm and encircled her body, making her hair writhe.

"Gods," she whispered as the power enveloped her.

Bershad stepped back. Watched as the thread on Ashlyn's wrist turned white hot, like a piece of steel that had been left at the bottom of a blacksmith's furnace for hours. The skin around her thread sizzled and burned. He could smell her flesh cooking.

"Ashlyn?" Bershad asked.

She ignored him. Mouth open in a mixture of pain and ecstasy. Eyes glassy and far away.

The ship was two hundred strides away.

"Ashlyn!"

Her eyes snapped back into focus and she raised her palm again. Pointed it at the ship. Released.

There was a flash and a thundering boom. Bershad's vision went white.

Then there was a great, echoing snap—as if the entire world was made of wood, and someone had broken it in half.

When Bershad's vision returned, the flying ship was engulfed in flames and plummeting toward the sea.

The lightning that had radiated from Ashlyn's body disappeared like a snuffed candle. She collapsed. Bershad caught her as the burning ship crashed into the surf. A moment later, a massive wave hurtled over their gunwale, soaking everyone on the deck.

"Ashlyn." Bershad touched her face. Watched as the cold seawater evaporated off her sweltering skin. "You all right?"

She opened her eyes. Swallowed. Winced. Touched her throat. "I'm fine. Throat just hurts."

Bershad motioned to Hayden, who produced a canteen and passed it over. Ashlyn drank, greedy and long.

"Did I get it?" she said when she was done.

Bershad glanced to his left, where an enormous hunk of blackened dragon bone was smoking as it sank.

"You got it."

"Any others?"

Everyone searched the sky. Empty except for the Nomad, which was still following them, and seemed unperturbed by the lightning from Ashlyn's arm and the destruction of the flying ship.

"We're clear."

Ashlyn pushed herself up and looked out over the steaming wreckage. Eyes narrowing as her mind churned. Bershad looked at her arm. The thread had sunk into her skin and was charred black like a piece of burned meat.

"We need to get that off you."

"I'm not sure that's possible, and even if it was, there's no time." Ashlyn touched the charred skin near the edge of the ruined thread. Winced. "Just get me a bandage. We need to salvage that wreck before it sinks."

"Why?" Jaku asked. "It's destroyed."

"I seriously doubt that was the only flying ship filling the skies of Terra right now," she said. "But that *was* the last time I'll be able to destroy one with this thread. I need to learn more about them."

By the time Jaku and his crew had fished out enough scrap from the skyship to satisfy Ashlyn, it was nearly dark. She carefully selected certain pieces from the pile and took them down to their private cabin. Spent almost two hours examining them in silence.

"This is Balarian made, but the complexity goes far beyond their clocks and pulleys and plumbing machinery," she said to Bershad, running her hand down a slat of carved Thundertail rib with steel bolts running through it. Next to that piece, there was a hollowed-out skull that was covered in scorch marks and attached to scores of small gears and pistons. "Far beyond anything Mercer Domitian ever designed. Who could have done it?"

"If I had to guess, I'd say it was the same asshole who made the ballistas for him, and cut off both my legs in that dungeon."

"Osyrus Ward." She nodded. "That makes sense."

Bershad wasn't eager to dredge up that experience. "What else can you tell about the machinery?" he asked.

"Well, the apparatus is powered by dragon oil," she said. "These pipes here and here, they're conduits that must have been connected to an engine—you can see the dragon-oil residue on the interior of this one, then steam damage on the other. The system is doing an incredible amount of work to keep those ships airborne. And the propulsion seems to burn a huge amount of dragon oil. But that's not my biggest concern."

"What is?"

She turned back to the bones. "He's using dragon bones for the structural elements of the skyship because they're probably the only material in Terra that is light enough to fly, but can also handle the stress that the engine puts on it in the air. But I have no idea how he preserved them on such a massive scale. The only example of preserved dragon bone I've seen is that dagger you used to carry." She looked at him. "How did you really forge it?"

Ashlyn had asked him that same question last spring, before he'd left Almira to kill the emperor of Balaria. He'd lied to her then because he didn't want to tell her what he really was, or what he could do. But there was no point holding on to that secret anymore.

"I used my blood," he said. "A Gray-Winged Nomad bit me in the stomach. Tooth got stuck in my belly. Rowan pulled it out and threw it in a sack while he dealt with the wound. The tooth soaked in my blood for a few days. When I took it out, I saw it had softened, but hadn't gone to rot. So, I cleaned the blood off and sharpened it. It hardened after that and hasn't taken a scratch since."

He paused, thinking of Rowan, and then, inevitably, of the bastard who'd killed him, Vallen Vergun. The same bastard who had the dagger now.

"Your blood preserved a Nomad's bones. And now you've got one following you across the Soul Sea."

"Always did like the Nomads," Bershad said. "Guess they like me, too."

Ashlyn didn't laugh. Just frowned a little more. "Blood explains the method, but not the volume."

"What do you mean?"

"Look at all this." Ashlyn motioned to the bones. "I can't imagine that Osyrus Ward stabbed someone like you through the stomach each time he needed another dragon bone for his ship."

Bershad shrugged. "I wouldn't put it past the crazy bastard. He's not afraid of hurting people. And he did say there were others like me. Called us Seeds."

"But there can't be many, otherwise the impact of Gods Moss on your body would be more common knowledge. If almost nobody knows about the phenomenon, then it must be extremely rare. But from the looks of it, he's preserved dozens of dragons. Maybe hundreds." She paused. Put her head down. Closed her eyes and rubbed her temples. "It doesn't seem possible."

"Go back ten years. Did you think it was possible to shoot lightning out of your hand using a piece of Ghost Moth spinal tissue?"

"No. But that doesn't help me down here, in the hold of this ship, surrounded by metal gears and bones, trying to figure out how that ship got built."

Ashlyn blew out a breath. Put a hand on her bandaged arm. Winced.

"How does it feel?" he asked, trying to bring her down from the rafters of her own head.

Ashlyn turned away from the pile of metal and dragon bones, then unwrapped the bandage. The thread was dug into her flesh like the roots of a thousand-year-old Daintree gripping deep into the earth. The skin around the blackened thread was red and blistered, but the rest seemed pink and healthy.

"Like I have a foreign object fused to my bone," she said, digging a fingernail into her skin at the seam where the thread met flesh, which drew a little blood. She wiped the blood along a blackened edge of the thread and flexed her hand a few times. Nothing happened. "There's no way to get this off my arm. But there's also no more lightning."

"So my blood broke it?" Bershad asked, pouring her a cup of chilled rice wine and handing it to her.

"Not broken. Altered." Ashlyn studied her wrist. "The thread doesn't produce lightning anymore, but I can still feel its energy rooted deep against my bones. A warmth. Which makes sense."

"How does that make sense?"

"The threads exist in Ghost Moths to heat their blood. That's why they can roost in the northern reaches of Terra during the winter. Nagas manage it, too, but they burrow into the earth where it's warmer and hibernate. Their blood turns to jelly while they sleep."

She paused. Traced one of the sawtooth scars that followed the blood vessels of her forearm. Near the place where it intersected with the thread, the blue scar tissue had turned black.

"If this had happened two days ago, I'd have been relieved. The things I did in Floodhaven . . . thousands of people murdered in moments. And killing that Red Skull. Even if it saved our lives, nobody should have that much power. But now, with those flying ships out there? I need the thread more than ever, and I don't have it."

They both went quiet. Above them, the dragon caught a gust of cold, rough wind and struggled to rise above it. Her sudden jerk tugged at Bershad's stomach lining. Made him wince.

"You all right?" Ashlyn asked.

"It's not me. It's the Nomad." He motioned to the ceiling. "Windy up there. She's working hard to stay on us, but she won't quit."

Ashlyn narrowed her eyes. "Look. I was going to entertain your tendency toward deception for a while, because getting information out of you that you don't want to share is like pulling teeth from a goat. But I need to know everything that Osyrus told you in that dungeon, and I need to know right now."

"Why?"

"Because it's all connected. Your blood preserves dragon bones. We were just attacked by a flying ship made from more preserved dragon bones than anyone's ever seen before. And Osyrus Ward is somehow at the center of it all. I need to know what he knows. Help me."

Bershad hesitated. Being followed by a Gray-Winged Nomad had barely loosened his grip on the dream of finishing out his life with Ashlyn on some remote, peaceful island. But this was different. If there were more skyships—and Osyrus Ward controlled them—his quiet plans were properly fucked.

"Like I said, the old man was light on specifics."

"Be unspecific, then."

Bershad took a sip of rice wine. "Osyrus called me a paradox.

The creator and destroyer of dragons." He shrugged. "I thought maybe I'd turn into one eventually."

"No, that's wrong."

"How do you know?"

"Because dragons are reptiles. They mate, they lay eggs, they hatch, and the cycle continues. There's no room for some obscure human transmogrification. It's not how nature works."

"You asked for information, then shit on the kind I provide."

"I want to know what *Osyrus* said. What else?"

Bershad tightened his jaw. "You're not gonna like it."

"All the same, I need to know."

Bershad sighed. "He told me that the same power that's kept me alive all these years is eventually going to kill me. I don't know how. Just that it's painful and inevitable and you don't want to be nearby when it happens."

Ashlyn blinked. Looked away. Cleared her throat. "What else?" she asked, voice strained.

"Nothing helpful. After that, he mostly just hacked off body parts and took notes."

"That is helpful, though. Your body's reaction to pain plays some part in all this."

"Yeah. It's gonna kill me someday."

"Oh. Silas."

She stepped toward him.

"Don't do that," he said. "The day you go soft and emotional is the day I know I'm truly fucked."

"You're not fucked."

"How do you know? You don't know what's happening to me."

"Because back in Almira, when I was first working with the thread, I used to feel like a little girl in a tide pool who was pretending she understood the ocean. I felt overmatched. But not anymore. I may not understand every system in this world, but I've learned how to pluck out their secrets, one strand at a time." She paused. "I'm going to find a way to help you, Silas. I promise."

Bershad's instinct was to say it didn't matter. He was ready to go down the river whenever the current came for him. That was how he'd carried his first death sentence for all those years. But the truth was, now that he was back with her, his interest in catching a few more seasons in the realm of Terra was gaining momentum.

So instead, he kissed her—long and soft, tasting rice wine and sea-water on her breath.

"I believe you, Ashe." And he really did. Bershad ran his hands down her shoulders and settled on her hips. "But I'm thinking before we deal with my corrupted blood and black fate, we're gonna need to deal with those flying ships."

She stopped his hands from drifting any lower.

"Like I said. They're all connected."

4

VERA

Balaria, Burz-al-dun, Imperial Palace

"Ganon, are you alive?" Kira called pleasantly.

By a way of response, the emperor of Balaria retched into his porcelain toilet for the third time that morning.

"I think he needs a few more minutes," Kira said, moving away from the privy door and returning to her cushioned chair by the window. She stirred her cup of tea with a small spoon made from dragon bone. Took a sip. Then she returned to reading the stack of papers in front of her.

Vera scanned the doors and alcoves of the royal chamber while they waited. She timed her shifting gaze by the pulsing clock on the inside of her wrist. In general, Vera did not care for the myriad of Balarian inventions that filled the city. Most of them brought noise and steam and the smell of burned dragon oil. But the synchronized bracer clocks of the military were useful tools—allowing hundreds of soldiers to stay in harmony across the city, and the empire.

The only problem was the ticking noise, which Vera could not abide. Far too easy to give away your position by accident. But when she complained about it to Osyrus Ward, he had returned a week later with a custom-made clock that was completely silent, and marked the passing time with a gentle pulse against her skin.

Vera had been trained never to rely on a specific tool to perform her duties, but she had to admit this one was helpful.

"Do you ever stop looking for trouble?" Kira asked, turning a page.

"No, Empress."

"But it's just us in here."

"You think that it's just us," Vera said. "You are not certain."

She adjusted the sword on her back slightly. Bershad's old blade. It was an impractical weapon for the narrow hallways and confined rooms of the palace, but Vera had found she liked the sword more than her pulsing bracer. The Papyrian design reminded her of home.

Plus, she still had her daggers—*Owaru* and *Kaisha*—for work in confined spaces.

Ganon retched one more time, cursed, spat, then yanked down on the mechanical pulley that flushed the toilet. He exited the privy a moment later.

The emperor's eyes were bloodshot. His skin was pale and clammy. His hair was mussed up and wet with cold sweat. Despite his hangover and retching, there was no denying that Ganon Domitian was an uncommonly attractive man. His aquiline nose and pale eyes carried a graceful symmetry that made an average man's face seem deformed by comparison.

But Vera's first few months in Balaria had quickly taught her that for all the raw, exterior beauty the man possessed, the character beneath his skin left a great deal to be desired.

"I'm going back to sleep," he said, heading to the massive bed in the middle of the room and wrapping himself in the thick blankets.

"But the war council is starting shortly," Kira protested. "There's news of the armada's foreign operations."

"There will be another war council next week. There's always another council. Bloody things are as reliable as Aeternita yanking the sun and moon across the sky each day."

Kira took another sip of tea. Pressed her lips together as she swallowed.

"This one is rather important, Ganon. I was hoping to send you with several inquiries."

Kira had matched Ganon drink for drink the night before—even goaded him forward on the last few—but unlike her husband, Kira's face was fresh and her eyes were clear. Kira never required more than a few hours of sleep and a cup of hot tea to recover from a night of revelry. She had woken at dawn and spent three hours reading through the stack of pages that had been delivered along with her breakfast.

"No more inquiries. Leave that crap to Actus. That's what I appointed him for." Ganon cracked open a bloodshot eye. His lips spread into a lecherous grin. "You should come back to bed. You know how I get when I'm hungover."

"I do," Kira said. "You get selfish and lazy and I don't get anything."

His smile disappeared.

"Shall I attend the council in your place?" Kira offered.

Ganon hesitated. Kira had been sending her husband to government meetings with lists of questions and issues for weeks—she was trying to get a feel for the movements of the bureaucracy. He typically returned with nonexistent or—at best—incomplete answers, but Kira had never pushed him. And she had never asked to attend a meeting until today.

"Actus won't like it," Ganon said.

"Actus Thorn works for you, not the other way around." She stood. "Speaking of him, I don't understand why you gave the man so much power in the first place. You could remove him and we could—"

"Bother me again with removing Thorn, and I will throw you into the sewers."

Kira's back straightened at that threat, but otherwise her frustration was invisible.

"Noted, my dear husband. But there is still the matter of the council meeting."

Ganon sighed. Burrowed further into the bed.

Kira crossed her arms. "Well?"

"Fine. Go play empress. Just don't fuck about, yeah?" He paused. "And tell a servant to bring me a tonic on your way out. Something with ginger." He paused again. "And juniper liquor."

"Will you quit it with the shadow routine?" Kira said to Vera as they made their way around the palace. "Walk next to me like a normal person."

"I am not a normal person," Vera said. "I am your widow."

"In the great and rich history of your order, has any widow besides you been to Burz-al-dun?"

"No."

"And has any half-Almiran, half-Papyrian princess ever married a Balarian emperor?"

"No."

"Well, seeing as we are both pioneers of our stations, I think we can afford to break the molds of tradition a bit when it comes to traversing hallways."

Vera begrudgingly matched pace with her charge. They passed a gangly engineer with ink stains on his fingertips. An assistant rushing along behind him with a bundle of papers in his arms. A group of lavishly dressed ministers muttering in low voices from an alcove. Then two Horellian guards—the elite sentries of Balaria—running their endless patrol around the palace rim. Both carried a spear and sword, and both gave her a disapproving glare as they passed. Nobody likes competition.

"You do not hide your disdain for Ganon very well," Kira said after a while.

"That is the third time this week he's been too hungover to get out of bed."

"You think I made a poor choice in husband?"

"I think you deserve a lover with self-control."

"Self-control is boring. And Ganon can be such a delight when he's feeling good. I've never met someone who can make me laugh like he does."

Vera didn't say anything, but she also didn't think a good sense of humor outweighed Ganon's numerous and glaring character flaws.

"Anyway, look on the bright side," Kira continued. "If Ganon was a stern and responsible emperor like his older brother was, you and I would not be on our way to the war council right now. It's exciting."

"Speaking of the meeting, what was in those pages you were reading all morning?" Vera asked. Kira had a sharp mind, but she rarely used it to consult ledgers and reports. She was far more interested in palace gossip and intrigue.

"Oh, nothing that interesting. Ration and food distribution lists from the Ministry of Agriculture. I had to flirt with some junior minister for almost an hour last night to get them brought up. Those skinny-armed bureaucrats keep an awfully tight guard on their papers. Such a hassle."

"Then why bother with it?"

"You'll see," Kira said, flashing a devious smile.

"Be careful around Actus Thorn," Vera warned. "Ganon has given him an immense amount of authority by making him Prime Magnate."

"Have you ever known me to be reckless in front of powerful men?" Kira asked.

Vera couldn't help but smile. "Never, Empress."

"Don't worry, I will be the pinnacle of propriety." She paused. Her face twitching with the suppressed happiness that Vera knew from experience generally coincided with the birth of a devious scheme. "But I would like to put them on their back foot a bit. Nothing too drastic. An aggressive entrance from my infamous widow should do the trick. Are you up for that, do you think?"

"Is that really necessary?"

"The more frightening you appear, the less threatening *I* need to be."

Vera sighed. There was some logic to that notion.

"Very well, Empress. Aggressive entrance it is."

———

Vera burst through the door of the council chamber with a purpose, making the five Horellian guards that ringed the big table move hands to blades. There were four men sitting at the table: Prime Magnate Thorn, War Minister Lox, Agriculture Minister Cornelius, and Osyrus Ward, the enigmatic royal engineer who had built the Balarian armada of skyships.

Actus Thorn glared at Vera, jaw and fists tightening. His thick limbs and chest had never lost the meaty strength of an infantryman, despite his rise to the highest rank in the Balarian army, followed by the highest rank in the empire's government.

Vera scanned the room with a careful eye. She didn't like the high number of Horellian guards, but Actus always traveled with a large amount of protection. Nothing to do but watch them carefully.

"Prime Magnate Thorn. Ministers. Empress Kira Domitian has arrived."

Vera moved one pace to the right so that Kira could enter the room. As soon as Kira passed her, Vera followed—two paces behind and one to the right. Widows were trained to stay to the left of their charge because most swordsmen were right-handed, and she could better intercept an attack from that angle. But Vera knew for a fact that Actus Thorn—the closest, and most dangerous, man in the room—was left-handed.

"You'll have to excuse Vera, she takes my protection very seriously," said Kira, taking the empty seat that was meant for her husband. "What have I missed?"

Minister Cornelius cleared his throat. "Empress Domitian, forgive me. But I believe your husband was—"

"Ganon is too hungover to join us today. I have come in his place. And even if I hadn't, it does not appear that you were waiting for him, anyway." Kira smiled. "So, please. Continue."

War Minister Lox gave Actus a glance, asking for permission. The prime magnate begrudgingly motioned for him to proceed.

"We were just reviewing the combat report of the skyship armada's first engagement with the Almiran navy."

"Good. I am eager to hear the results."

"The operation was a great success," War Minister Lox said, beaming with pride. "Linkon Pommol was using the fleet that he stole from your sister to patrol the eastern coast of Almira. The skyships flew the coastline and turned every ship they encountered to cinders. The longbowmen in particular were valuable—the range of their explosive arrows was simply a marvel. Even the swiftest of ships was unable to escape."

"I see. Any Balarian casualties?"

"One skyship failed to return," Lox admitted. "But it was the vessel we sent to the Broken Peninsula, where the weather becomes dicey. We believe they hit an early-autumn storm and, unfortunately, crashed. The skyships are powerful, but vulnerable to atmospheric conditions. Still, to have lost only one skyship out of thirty, whilst in return the entire Almiran navy was annihilated. Well, Empress, this is a truly unprecedented victory."

"It was also an unprecedented expense," Actus Thorn added, face grim. He turned to Osyrus Ward, who had been looking out the window, watching the Kor Cog churning its slow and relentless circle through the heart of the Imperial Palace. "Ward, can't you curb the amount of dragon oil the skyships require? They burn through it like starving pigs chewing through slop."

Osyrus turned back to the meeting and considered General Actus for a moment, looking at him with the cold disdain of a snake deciding whether a rat was too large to swallow.

"Anything is possible, Prime Magnate. But since Mercer Domitian had enacted plans to inject a nearly unfathomable amount of dragon oil into the Balarian economy, building a more efficient engine was not my priority. I focused my recent efforts on a more stable placement of the levitation sack—above the entire ship, versus beneath the wing struts. That design improvement is the reason that only a single ship was lost in the incursion, rather than the entire fleet."

"Mercer Domitian is dead, as are his plans." Actus leaned forward. "At this rate, those ships will begin falling from the sky halfway through their next operation. A better engine *is* your priority now."

"Very well." Osyrus rubbed his knobby hands. "As it so happens, two of my spies have recently returned from Floodhaven with information that will help me construct a more efficient model."

Kira cleared her throat. "Floodhaven. Did your spies return with any news about Ashlyn?"

Actus Thorn bristled at the distraction, but Ward's face softened when he looked at Kira. Vera had noticed that while Osyrus Ward was more than happy to boil the blood of Actus Thorn and his ministers, he had been uncommonly kind and patient with Kira, despite her relatively limited amount of power and influence. The discrepancy bothered Vera.

"They did, Empress. By all accounts, Ashlyn Malgrave was killed in the battle at Floodhaven. There have been no reports to the contrary." Osyrus bowed his head. "I am sorry, Empress."

"Pity," Kira said. She chewed her lip. "Did she really destroy Cedar Wallace's entire army with demoncraft? That was the rumor at the gala last night."

"*Demoncraft* is a crude and unspecific term," Osyrus Ward said.

"But she did use some new kind of power," Kira said. "Do you know what it was?"

Osyrus Ward smiled. "I have an idea, yes. And as I said, my informants were able to obtain some of her research. But her work was extremely complicated, and will take time to decipher." He turned to Thorn. "If my laboratory was returned to me—and new specimens provided—I could move faster."

"That wasn't a laboratory," Thorn said. "It was a horror show. Half of my custodial workers refused to go back in there after the first day of cleanup from the fire. I cannot believe Mercer allowed such things on palace grounds, even if they were in the deepest sublevels."

"He allowed them because he knew they led to progress. This is the problem with soldiers and bureaucrats. You enjoy the fruits of my work, but turn your nose up when you glimpse the mess that creation requires. If you want a better engine, return my resources and let me work."

Actus ground his teeth. "Explain to me how the things that you did to those creatures in the darkness will lead to a skyship engine that burns less oil in the sky."

"They won't. They will eventually lead to an engine that burns *no* dragon oil. I am not sure how Ashlyn Malgrave created such a formidable energy source on that battlefield, but it was extremely clean. Almost . . . pure."

Osyrus said that last word with an edge of jealousy that surprised Vera. The royal engineer spoke of most people with imperious disdain.

"If it was so formidable, how was she defeated?" Thorn asked.

"Some say the power itself consumed her. Turned her to ash. But the truth is far less fantastic. After she won the battle, Linkon Pommol betrayed and killed her. His wardens have been bragging about it in the streets."

"All the more reason that we should celebrate the destruction of his fleet," Lox interrupted, trying very hard to remain relevant in a conversation that was getting away from him.

"But the destruction of that fleet has made an enemy of Almira," said Kira. "I wonder if such an aggressive move was prudent?"

"Empress, you have no authority to question my decisions," Actus Thorn said, voice barbed. He leaned forward. "Your husband has imbued me with absolute control of the government and military. I will run operations as I see fit."

"Of course, Prime Magnate. I wouldn't deign to question your military acumen and wisdom, I am simply trying to understand things a little better. Perhaps you could enlighten a young and uninformed empress?"

Actus Thorn retained his aggressive posture for a moment, but eventually leaned back in his chair.

"The attack was necessary for two reasons. One. Almira needed to be punished for their assassination of Mercer Domitian. Pommol might not have ordered the killing himself, but his new fleet paid the cost of Ashlyn's aggression. Two. The skyships required a low-risk combat test before deployment in Lysteria."

Everyone had been talking about the Lysterian rebellion, which had broken out as soon as word of Emperor Mercer's death reached the north. Seven garrisons had been sacked and an entire Balarian legion was missing. It had most likely been annihilated, just like Linkon's fleet.

"That's a very succinct explanation, Prime Magnate Thorn," Kira said, ignoring his demeaning tone. "Thank you. Your actions make much more sense now. When will the skyships head to Lysteria?"

"That depends." Thorn turned to Osyrus. "When will the new uniforms be complete?"

"I am still perfecting the cold-weather insulation that is required for the skyship crews to operate in the high-altitude temperatures of a Lysterian winter," Osyrus said. "The intricacies take time and precision and—"

"Just get it done," Thorn snapped. "I want to crush this rebellion as soon as the skyships return from Almira."

"There are still skyships in Almira?" Kira asked.

"Yes. There is a little more work to be done in your homeland, Empress. You are aware of the food shortages, yes?"

"I spoke with a minister at the gala last night who mentioned something about a wheat blight in Ghalamar," Kira said, pronouncing the last few words slowly, as if she was unfamiliar with their meaning.

"The problem extends far beyond poor wheat yields," said Agriculture Minister Cornelius.

Vera liked Minister Cornelius because, unlike General Actus and Minister Lox, he'd never held a weapon more dangerous than a dinner knife in his life. That being said, if he did make a move

on the empress, Vera was standing at the perfect angle and distance
to throw a dagger into the main artery of his neck.

"How much farther?" Kira asked.

The minister cleared his throat before speaking.

"The eighth and ninth merchant districts of Burz-al-dun are
supplied with grain rations from the Portsmouth Province of
Ghalamar. However, that province had an especially hard time
with the famines this year. Their annual shipment came up sig-
nificantly short of their quota." Cornelius licked his lips. He spoke
with much more authority now that the conversation had moved
away from war and toward crop quotas. "They've delivered
enough to last a month. Maybe."

"One moon's turn?" Kira said, slipping into her native Almiran
tongue for a moment. "Did Mercer not know about this?"

"The late Emperor Mercer Domitian was aware of the issue.
And I informed Emperor Ganon as soon as he was coronated. But,
um. Well. He didn't . . ."

Cornelius trailed off. Glanced at Kira, then at Vera. She knew
that her presence made the bureaucrats of Balaria nervous. She
liked it. Intimidation was better protection than a suit of armor if
it was used properly.

"Cornelius, you can relax." Kira gave him a warm smile. It was
the same smile she'd used at countless feasts and celebrations in
Almira to befriend half the court, and it melted Cornelius as if he
was a stick of dragon fat dropped in a burning hearth. "We can all
be honest about the situation. My husband is not interested in being the emperor of Balaria. That is why he is not here today. And
that is why he appointed Actus Thorn as the prime magnate to rule
as his proxy. But I *am* interested. We must find food for our people.
Perhaps we can divert rations coming in from one of the other
Ghalamarian provinces?"

Cornelius cleared his throat again. "Empress, I'm afraid the situation is the same—and in some cases worse—across all of Ghalamar."

"What about Lysteria?"

"Even if Lysteria wasn't in open rebellion, I'm afraid we would
find no food there, either."

"That is why they have rebelled to begin with," Actus said,
impatient. "The truth is, there is simply no place left in our empire
from which we can source adequate rations for all of our people."

"No place left in *our* empire," Kira repeated. "I see. So there was a third reason for sending the skyships to Almira. You're going to raid the Clear Sky harvests."

"Correct," Actus said. "Now that the skies of Almira are temporarily devoid of lizards for the Great Migration, the muddy farmers of your homeland will produce a crop yield that is ten times the size of a normal season. I have ordered the armada to collect those yields by force. Commandeering Almira's harvest isn't a permanent solution, but it should get us through the year."

"I don't understand why we don't just conquer Almira now," Cornelius said absently.

"That is because you don't understand war, you moron," Thorn snapped. "Almirans might be muddy-haired savages, but their wardens are the best soldiers in Terra. You ever tried to kill a man who's spent his whole life learning the best ways to kill you, instead?"

"No," Cornelius said softly.

"Well, I have," Thorn said. "Thirty years ago, in the Almiran Incursion, I saw a warden with half his guts dropped out his stomach defend a hill for hours. Most Balarian grunts would have curled up and begged for their mothers, then died uselessly in a heap of their own crap. That bastard kept cutting down Balarian soldiers like they were made of chaff. Every single valley and hill and castle will be full of killers like that. Do you feel like now—with no food and an open rebellion in the north—is a good time to attack those men's homes?"

Cornelius's face turned blood red with embarrassment. He didn't respond.

"We will conquer Almira," Thorn continued. "But we will do it when the time is right. For now, we procure the food, and leave one skyship to guard the western coast against a naval landing by the Papyrians."

"Do you truly think that Okinu will throw her hand into the war so overtly?" Lox asked.

"Given the ties she's built in Almira over the years, it's a possibility. And if she does want to enter this war, the western coast of Almira is the door that she will use. I prefer to keep it closed." He turned to Osyrus. "If this new engine of yours is more efficient, it will be a valuable tool for this purpose."

"I agree," Osyrus replied.

Kira cleared her throat. "General Thorn, I am the rightful heir to Almira. Couldn't all of this be accomplished with diplomacy?"

"Diplomacy is a wise course of action. So wise, in fact, that Emperor Mercer Domitian already tried it. He risked life and limb to access Almira's rich natural resources through a trade agreement with Ashlyn Malgrave. And then you and Ganon began your little love affair, an action which had the equivalent effect of taking a wet shit overtop the entire thing."

Vera took one step forward. Moved her hands to her daggers on instinct. The Horellian guards behind Actus did the same.

"Mind your tongue, Thorn."

"Spare me, widow. If you draw one of those little blades in anger, you and the empress will both go for the long swim directly afterward." He motioned to the Horellians behind him, then turned back to Kira. "The less involved you are with important matters, the more likely they are to succeed. I will get the harvest from Almira, and then I will deal with Lysteria. You can go back to your feasts and your moon orgies. Leave this work to the people who know what they're doing."

"Well, Actus, I admit that elements of your plan have merit," Kira said, her tone changing. Turning serious and cold. "However, you still have a problem. Assuming you're able to steal the Almiran harvest, half of it must go to the soldiers you're sending to Lysteria. And the remnants won't feed all the mouths in Burz-al-dun. Not nearly. You'll naturally prioritize the merchant and government districts with rations, but you'll have to deprive the slums."

Actus Thorn didn't respond, but the guilty looks exchanged by the other ministers made it clear that Kira was correct. The empress saw it, too.

"I wonder how long the slum districts will put up with empty bellies before they start to riot in the streets?" Kira continued. "Order in Burz-al-dun has always been predicated on three hot meals a day for every citizen. What happens when the food runs out? We will quash the Lysterian rebellion only to find a fresh one boiling up behind the walls of Burz-al-dun."

"Maybe. Maybe not. Have you come here today simply to suggest hypothetical problems and dangle them across our eyes?" Thorn asked.

"No, I have come to prevent them from becoming a reality."

"And how are you going to do that?"

"You don't want me in these meetings, stumbling over military strategy. That's fine. It is not my strong suit. A woman like me is far better suited to more domestic and ceremonial tasks. I can keep the people of Burz-al-dun happy, despite the wars and famines and growing hunger in their bellies. And I only need one thing from you to do it."

"Which is?"

"A skyship of my own."

Actus Thorn grunted. "You're joking. There is no way I'm giving you a war frigate."

"No, certainly not. But Osyrus Ward has recently completed the plans for a new design. One that is more suitable to my needs."

"Are your ears too packed with mud to hear what's been said? We've got no fucking dragon oil to spare. Whatever oil the skyships don't require must be earmarked for the Kor Cog. There is barely enough oil to keep the thing running for the next year. Do you know what happens if that cog stops? The checkpoints lock down and this city turns into a nightmare. Even the few days it was down over the summer were catastrophic. It took a month to quell the riots in District Eleven."

"I don't need an engine," Kira responded. "Just the ship."

"What?"

"I don't need my skyship to fly," Kira said. "So, no engine. No fuel."

"What value is a ship that cannot fly?"

"Anticipation is a powerful tool, Prime Magnate. The grand unveiling of my royal ship gives the people something to look forward to. A wedding would be better, but my marriage was sadly rushed due to circumstances outside of our control. Still, the skyship will work nicely. The military frigates were built in secret, and they're intimidating, not inspiring. But if we were to show them a different kind of ship—one that is beautiful and sleek, outfitted in vibrant and soft colors instead of cold, military black and gray—we can capture their imaginations, and their hearts."

"Empress, I do not think that the people of the slum districts will forget about their food simply because you show them a colorful skyship," said Minister Lox.

Kira turned to him. Smiled. "That is because you lack vision, Minister." She paused. "Even if the distraction doesn't work, the project would keep me quite busy. I would be forced to stop intruding on meetings like this one."

Actus chewed on this. Eventually, he turned to Osyrus.

"You can guarantee the materials for this ship of hers will not deprive the fleet of resources?"

"Yes. I have built the Balarian armada of skyships in the image of dragons. The empress's ship will be a sparrow in comparison."

"Fine." Actus dismissed the idea with a wave of his hand. "Have your ship. But once it is complete, if you come asking me for an engine and dragon oil, I will light the useless thing on fire." Actus stood. "We're done here."

Osyrus cleared his throat. "Actually, Prime Magnate, there is still the matter of my laboratory, and my request for specimens."

Actus took a long look at Osyrus Ward. "Your personal projects are disgusting and foul. I have no reason to tolerate them. Build me a better skyship engine with the resources that you do have, and then we'll see. Fail me, and I'll have you beaten from the city."

Osyrus held Actus Thorn's gaze for a long time, but eventually conceded defeat with a small nod. "At the very least, I need more parchment. Most of my notes were destroyed in last summer's fire and I cannot work without a way to record my progress."

"Paper? Fine. But nothing else until I have my engine."

Actus departed the room with the urgency of a battlefield commander returning to the front lines, the Horellian guards close on his heels. The ministers followed behind, giving sheepish bows.

The doors closed. Only Osyrus Ward remained in the room.

"What a deeply unpleasant man," Ward said cheerfully.

Kira started laughing.

"Right?" She turned to Vera. "You told me to be careful around Thorn, then you practically threatened to kill him!" she squealed, then scrunched her face into an artificial frown. "Vera, Vera, Vera. I'm very disappointed in your lack of self-control."

"He should not have spoken to you that way," Vera said, still gripping her daggers and glaring at the door through which Actus Thorn had departed.

"Maybe not, but if we get caught up in petty insults and poor manners, we'll never get anywhere. This was a good first step."

"First step to what? Why do you want a skyship so badly? This unveiling is likely to do more harm than good—hungry people don't want to hear about the lavish toys of their rulers."

"Of course they don't," Kira said. "I'm not a moron. I asked for the ship because the unveiling preparations will give me an excuse to take more meetings with important members of the government. I cannot challenge Actus Thorn's authority yet, but I can start building my own influence, one step at a time. Everyone wants something, Vera. Often, the things that they want don't even need to be given to them, just dangled in front of their eyes, slightly out of reach."

She paused. Looked out the window at the Kor Cog.

"That was my sister's problem. She understood dragons and plants and ledgers, but she didn't understand people. That is why she is dead. I won't repeat her mistake. Instead, I'll build a base of power and control from within the government, and then I will use it to remove Actus Thorn myself."

Vera glanced at Osyrus Ward, then back at Kira.

"Don't worry about Osyrus. He wants the same thing that we do."

"Why is that, exactly?"

The old man began twisting two strands of his greasy beard together, forming a glistening rope of dirty hair.

"I spent many years enjoying the fruits of a mutually beneficial arrangement with Mercer Domitian. I created the tools he needed to rule his empire, and in return he provided me with unlimited access to the materials I required to conduct my experiments."

Vera didn't like the ways in which Thorn had described Osyrus Ward's laboratory. And she didn't like how vague the old man was about his work.

"Materials. Define those."

"Oh, dragon oil, for one. Precious minerals from the kilns. Exotic imports from beyond Taggarstan—rare insects and birds and such." He paused. Smiled. "You can never have too many specimens, Vera. Never."

He released his beard. Blew out a sigh.

"Sadly, I do not enjoy the same relationship with Actus Thorn. He has taken my armada, which is expected. But he gives nothing back to me in return. And when I do inevitably provide him this new engine, I have no confidence that he will suddenly become more generous. He is a taker. He knows no other way to behave. I would prefer a different arrangement with the ruler of Balaria. And I know that Kira will remember who her friends are once she has achieved her goal."

"This amounts to treason," Vera said. "We could all be put to death because of this conversation alone."

"True." Kira shrugged. "But if it goes to shit, you and I will simply fly away on the skyship that Actus Thorn just gave us permission to build."

"What?"

"Of course, I plan to use my skyship for joy rides once the people of Balaria are fed and Actus Thorn is dealt with, but if the presence of an escape craft will stop you from being such a pest while I work, then I embrace the dual purpose."

"How will we fly away on a ship with no engine?"

Osyrus swatted the question away. "We'll use the new engine I plan to build. For all of Thorn's irritations, he was correct. We cannot rely on dragon oil alone to power the skyships. We need a new type of Kor—one that is more compact and powerful than the massive Cog in the middle of the city. The research that has come back from Almira has given me what I need to build one. The only uncertainty is time, but I expect it will take no more than a . . . *moon's turn*." His Almiran accent was perfect. "The new engine will be far more efficient, especially on the smaller ship I am building for the empress."

Vera narrowed her eyes. "You said the prototype engine would go to Almira."

"One of them will. I have the resources to build two. I didn't feel it necessary to share this information with Thorn, of course."

"What about fuel?"

"Do not worry. Not only will Kira's skyship be a spectacle to behold, but in comparison to the oil-hungry engines of the current fleet, it will require mere sips of the substance to stay in the air."

"And in smaller amounts, dragon oil can be acquired in many ways," Kira added. She turned to Osyrus Ward. "Tell Vera about the black markets of Burz-al-dun that we were discussing the other day."

Vera tightened her grip on her dagger. She did not like the idea of Kira and Osyrus meeting alone to collaborate—especially when they were exploring criminal ways to undermine one of the most merciless and jingoistic military leaders in the realm of Terra.

Osyrus Ward stirred from the corner, moving to the main table. Vera moved as well, so that she could nick the old man's jugular with a flick of a wrist if he attempted to touch Kira.

"Nobody in the energy ministry likes to admit this fact," Osyrus Ward explained, "but the Kor Cog's monthly output of refined dragon oil is not always consistent with expected yields. For example, last month, the Kor's output was one point two percent less than projected. The month before, it was point seven percent lower. Emperor Mercer attributed these discrepancies to mechanical inefficiencies of the machine because the alternative—that small amounts of oil are being systematically skimmed and smuggled out of Balaria—would have meant his supposedly perfect checkpoint system was imperfect. The man was a visionary, but arrogance was his critical flaw. It clouded his vision. Now that he is gone, the problem remains because Actus is too preoccupied with the Lysterian rebellion to care about a little oil missing from the ledgers."

"One point two percent," Vera repeated. "How many barrels is that?"

"About three hundred. And, as requested, I'm building Kira's ship to be an explorer's vessel. Extremely lightweight when compared to the hulking monstrosities that Actus Thorn is taking to war. Fifty barrels will be enough fuel to keep her in the air for weeks."

"See?" Kira turned to Vera. "All we need to do is rob some criminals and we'll have all the dragon oil that we need for you to stop acting like a scared mother hen."

"Why rob anyone? If we need oil, surely we can purchase it legally through back channels of some kind."

"Not anymore, I'm afraid." Ward massaged his knuckles. "Actus Thorn is stockpiling every documented barrel of oil for the skyships. The night lanterns have been running on pine-scented tubes of goat fat for weeks now. For appearances. But I assure you, the only way to acquire the amount of dragon oil that the ship requires is to steal it from someone who has already stolen it."

He turned to Kira.

"I must warn you, Empress, that procuring oil from the criminal underbelly of Balaria will not be easy. We cannot use customs agents—many of them are working for one of the crime syndicates of Taggarstan. And if we used soldiers from the regular army, Actus Thorn would simply take whatever we found for himself."

Kira frowned.

"But do not lose heart," Osyrus continued. "I have recently been informed that a local merchant of fine silks is one of the principal procurers of contraband dragon oil in Burz-al-dun. And he is preparing to send a rather large shipment to Taggarstan on the next full moon."

"Why the full moon?" Vera asked.

"That is typically the best time for the ships to navigate the Bay of Broken Clocks," Osyrus said. "I am told he has overextended himself quite a bit with the size of this shipment, and can only afford a comparatively light crew of hired killers guarding it." Osyrus smiled. Turned to Vera. "If a certain highly trained and capable individual were to lend her assistance, I believe we can take this oil for ourselves."

"Highly trained individual," Kira repeated. "Vera, yes. That's perfect. What does she need to do?"

"The first step is finding out exactly who this silk merchant is. Thus far, he has been able to conceal his identity, despite my inquiries. In time, I am sure I could discover him, but if we wait too long, we'll lose our chance to steal this month's shipment. I am told that he has been using a tavern in the fourth district called Aeternita's Grace to run his expanding black-market operations. If Vera were to visit this tavern and . . . compel a name from one of the patrons, that is all I will need to suss out the location of his oil stockpile."

"What does a name get you that you don't already have?"

"Names are powerful tools in Burz-al-dun. They appear on property records. Land deeds. Dock leases. And the seal system makes it difficult to use a fake name for anything meaningful. This explains why this smuggler values his anonymity so highly."

Vera chewed on that. The logic made sense, but somehow that made her more uneasy. Osyrus Ward had plotted all of this far in advance. Vera got the feeling that she and Kira were both cogs in whatever larger machine he was building. And now they were beginning to spin. She did not like it.

"Kira. Robbing from oil smugglers is not the type of work that—"

"This is an excellent plan," Kira said, interrupting her. "Vera will retrieve the name tonight. That will be all, Osyrus. We'll speak more later."

The royal engineer stood. "Finding smugglers and depriving them of oil is relatively straightforward, Empress. But your part in this coup is mired in the swamp of Balarian politics. If you'd like, I can arrange to have a number of salient tomes brought to your chambers that might provide some insight and . . . inspiration as to how Actus Thorn might be removed."

"That will not be necessary."

Ward frowned. "We have no army. Toppling a military dictator like Actus Thorn through political maneuvers alone will be a complicated endeavor."

"Politics are complicated. People are simple. Do not worry, Osyrus. I know what I'm doing."

Osyrus bowed. "Very good, Empress."

Kira waited until Osyrus was gone before speaking again. "Please don't give me another lecture about what a widow does and doesn't do."

"If I felt you understood the scope of my duties, I wouldn't keep explaining them to you," said Vera. "I am here to protect you, not serve as your personal enforcer."

"Oh, please. My Papyrian aunt is infamous for using her widows as assassins. Don't pretend it's not true. I've heard the same stories about Shoshone Kalara Sun that you have."

"I am not Shoshone. And you don't need to follow in your aunt's bloody footsteps."

"Yes, I do." Kira's face turned serious. "Look, Vera, a bodyguard may have been all that I needed in Almira, safe behind the walls of Castle Malgrave, doing nothing but feasting and drinking and screwing third-born sons of minor small lords. But things are different here. I want to do more than just . . . *exist*."

"You can't do more than exist if you're killed while I am stealing dragon oil, and unable to protect you."

"I don't need more protection," Kira continued. "There are a hundred Horellian guards in this palace alone who are dedicated to keeping me alive."

"They're men," Vera said. "That means they can't be trusted."

"You trusted Silas Bershad."

Vera scowled. Kira wasn't entirely right about that, but she wasn't wrong either.

"I needed his help to get to you," she said. "And speaking of Silas, he murdered eight Horellian guards before killing Mercer. They're hardly invincible."

"And you would have stopped him, I suppose?"

"If protecting Mercer had been my responsibility, I would have avoided the situation entirely."

"Listen, Vera. I appreciate your perspective and your advice. You should always feel free to bring your misgivings to me. But I did not escape from Almira just to be shoved into another silk prison by Actus Thorn. I am going to take control of my life, one way or another. You can disagree with me, but you cannot talk me out of it. I know there are risks, but I am going to take them."

Vera gave her a resigned look.

"You're disappointed in me," Kira said.

"I want you safe, Ki. What you're planning. What you're doing. It is the opposite."

"Would you rather I go back to all the drinking and screwing? Become the perfect partner to Ganon and his life of debauchery, then die a couple of decades from now in a puddle of my own juniper-liquor-soaked vomit?"

"There is a middle ground between drinking yourself to death slowly, and getting yourself executed tomorrow for treason."

"There is no middle ground for what I'm trying to accomplish."

"What is that, exactly? You say that you want more power for yourself. But what will you do with it once it's yours?"

Assuming we don't get killed in the process, Vera thought to herself.

Kira stared at Vera with her icy turquoise eyes. Her face turned serious.

"I thought Almira was a broken country," she said. "A bunch of muddy roads doing a shit job of connecting a bunch of savage warlords who brutalize commoners in order to finance the next raid on their neighbor's land so they can afford more debauched orgies inside their decrepit castles. Meanwhile, the commoners hunker down, praying to forest gods and poorly made mud totems to grant them one more day of survival in their dragon-surrounded hovels. Of course I led a miserable existence. How could anyone be happy in that kind of place? In my heart, I believed Balaria would be better."

She sighed.

"But now that I'm here—surrounded by running water and ticking clocks and flying ships—I've realized that this place is no better. The only difference between a Balarian minister and an Almiran warlord is that Balarians wash their hair more frequently and they bend the wills of their subjects with taxes instead of swords. Almira isn't broken. The entirety of Terra is broken. And I am going to fix it."

"Fix every country in Terra?" Vera asked. "How?"

"One step at a time."

"That is not an answer."

Kira turned back to the Kor Cog. "I know what I'm doing, and removing Actus Thorn from power is the first step. But look, if you don't want to get the fuel, don't. I'm more than happy to proceed with my current resources. You're the one who's so concerned about the consequences."

Vera let out a long, slow breath. Recognized in Kira's tone that she wouldn't be able to talk her out of this. And she had made the mistake of positioning herself as a source of discipline once before—all it had accomplished was a missing princess and a murderous trek across Terra. She wouldn't make that mistake again. They were in this together, no matter what.

But beyond her widow's duty and her loyalty, Vera had never heard Kira talk this way. And in all her years perched in the hallways and chambers of kings and queens and emperors and lords, Vera had never heard any of them point out the flaws of a system that benefited them. Even her sister, Ashlyn, had been focused on using the Almiran government—fractured and corrupt as it was—to further her own goals. She had no desire to change the system. Maybe Kira was different. Better.

"I will help you, Ki."

"Good." Kira stood up. "You should leave soon—the checkpoints to District Four take forever."

5

JOLAN

Almira, Dainwood Province

"Where you from, boy?" Willem asked, stuffing a wad of the chicken into his mouth. They'd had chicken for breakfast each morning, three days running.

Jolan struggled to swallow the meat in his mouth, which was so dry it might as well have been wood. Sten—the group's cook—was not very good at his job.

"My name's Jolan," he said, after finally getting the bite down his throat.

"Jolan. Boy. Whatever. Where are you from?"

"Otter Rock."

"Never heard of it."

"It's a village on the Atlas Coast," Oromir said. Somehow, he'd already managed to finish his portion of the scorched chicken. Jolan suspected that he might have hidden it somewhere out of sight. That was the only explanation for how quickly he consumed the awful food. "About two days west of Black Pine, at the fork of the Atlas's northern tributary."

"That's right," Jolan said, surprised.

"How the fuck do you know some tiny village that far up north by name?" Willem asked.

Oromir shrugged. "I like maps."

"Likes maps," Willem repeated. "You're an odd one, Oromir."

"I know."

"My father died at Black Pine," Cumberland said, eyes on the embers of the fire.

"Mine, too," said Sten, who was busy making a totem out of clovers and leftover chicken bones. "Along with all my uncles. Cedar Wallace got the glory and the stories about his vanguard charge. Nobody mentions the Dainwood wardens who spent all night crawling through the woods on the Balarian's flank so they could launch an attack at the same time he charged."

"That was important for the battle?" Jolan asked.

Morgan had made him study the histories of Almira—and the realm of Terra—but he'd glossed over the logistics and details of military strategy. They were irrelevant to an alchemist's work.

"Hitting their flank split their forces. Turned the battle. But afterward, the Dainwood men were cut off from the main army." Cumberland dug into his own totem pouch. Handed Sten a small, blue rock. "Every warden with a jaguar mask who fought that day got shoved down the river by the clock-worshippers."

"Cedar's charge at Black Pine will probably get mentioned less and less now," Jolan said without really thinking. Everyone turned to him. "After Floodhaven and all."

"Yeah," Cumberland said. "Getting toasted by a witch queen tends to take precedence when it comes to fireside stories."

Jolan was still trying to puzzle out what truly happened at Floodhaven. None of Cumberland's men had been there, but they all seemed to agree that Ashlyn Malgrave had killed Cedar Wallace during a duel by expelling lightning from her hands. Afterward, she'd massacred his army with sorcery. That was obviously inaccurate—Almirans labeled anything they didn't understand as sorcery, including the work of alchemists. But Jolan couldn't figure out what natural phenomenon was at the core of the story. A man getting struck by lightning in the middle of a duel seemed statistically unlikely to the point of being impossible. And even if there *had* been a lightning strike—or, somehow, multiple strikes within a short time—that still didn't explain the decimated army. So, what happened?

Given the available information, there was no way to know. The farther Jolan traveled looking for answers, the more questions he seemed to find.

"Back to Umbrik's Glade today, then?" Willem asked, wiping his mouth with his sleeve. "There's a baker there named Elandra with some very pretty freckles, and I owe her a visit. Now that Jolan's taken care of my, uh, situation, we'll have lots to do together."

"We're not going directly," Cumberland said. "Need to stop at a mill to the east, first."

"How far to the east?"

"Ten, maybe fifteen leagues."

"C'mon, boss! Why didn't you tell us sooner? I haven't been laid in weeks. A man starts building plans up for himself on a certain timeline. Now I have to readjust."

"That grieves me."

Willem sighed. "Collecting more Papyrian pigeons, is it?"

"Correct."

"I don't get it," Willem complained. "Why's some island empress half a world away helping us fight Linkon Pommol's men?"

"Dunno," Cumberland said. "But the only reason we got the drop on that last group of turtles is 'cause a Papyrian bird told us where they'd be. The paper lashed to those pigeon legs is keeping us in this war, and Carlyle said that mill's got the next message."

"We ain't seen Carlyle in weeks. How'd he know where the next bird'll show up?"

"Don't know that either." Cumberland sucked some meat out of his teeth, then tossed a chicken bone over his shoulder.

"They're using homing pigeons," Jolan said. "But they're only trained to go to specific places. So when the empress of Papyria sends one letter, she probably also says where the next one's going to show up."

"Huh. Why don't they just train the birds to fly back and forth between two places?" Willem asked.

"I'm pretty sure that's impossible," Jolan said.

"Yeah, but if you really tried to, I bet—"

"I'm not gonna sit here all morning while you scholars argue about pigeons," Cumberland interrupted. "We have walking to do."

Everyone started preparing their weapons and gear. Jolan took one last look at his remaining portion of chicken, but decided the effort to chew it wasn't worth the reward and threw it into a blueberry bush.

Tomorrow, he would volunteer to do the cooking.

———

There were seven wardens in turtle masks outside the mill. Five were crowded around the door and two were running a loose patrol around the mill itself—keeping an eye on the different points of approach. Most of their attention was focused on a stone bridge set over the river that powered the mill.

"Seven demons in a fucking tree," Sten muttered, looking down on the mill from the ridge. Jolan and the wardens were all on their bellies, hidden from view by the thick ferns that carpeted the forest. "What're Pommol's men doing here?"

"Unknown," Cumberland said. "But they are in our way."

Cumberland shifted, wincing a little and touching his rib. Jolan was a good healer, but he couldn't make an arrow wound disappear after just a few days. Not yet.

"Is seven a lot for you to fight?" Jolan whispered to Oromir, who'd slid up so close to Jolan that their shoulders were touching. Jolan knew ratios of tonics and properties of herbs, but he had no idea if four against seven was decent odds for a fight, or suicide.

"More than manageable if we get the drop on them," Oromir whispered back.

"Why didn't they bring more men?" Jolan asked.

"We've been bleeding any large groups that stumbled into the Dainwood for months. Took them a while, but they finally learned to travel small and inconspicuous. Same as we do. The northerners are thick-skulled, and they lack creativity when it comes to warfare, but they do eventually learn."

"What's the plan, then?" Willem asked Cumberland, voice impatient.

"Wait a spell. See what they do."

"So, nothing?" Willem said.

"For a spell." Cumberland settled into the ferns and focused on the mill.

Three of the wardens went inside the main building. Two stayed outside to guard the door, and another two started making lazy laps around the perimeter. Willem looked at Cumberland expectantly, but the older warden ignored him.

Sten started pinching together another mud totem. Once he'd formed the figure, he pressed a few rusted chinks of mail into the body, then added black river stones for the eyes.

Ten minutes later, a warden burst out of the mill's door. He lifted his mask to spit, then cinched it back into place.

"Give me good news," said one of the men by the door.

"There's a nest and shit up top, but we didn't find no bird or paper."

"What's the miller got to say?"

The warden motioned to his knuckles, which were split in several places. "He's kinda stubborn."

"Well, stop punching him and start taking away things he'll miss. Everyone squeals eventually. Orders were to kill all the pigeons, and come back with all the paper."

The warden with the cut knuckles hesitated.

"Gods, but you're a thin-blooded bastard." The other warden drew a knife from his belt. "I'll show you how. Key is to start by taking an eye before you even ask a question . . ."

They both went back inside, leaving one man at the door and the other two running a patrol.

"Time to move," Cumberland said, hauling the two-handed greatsword off his back. Oromir and Sten drew their swords. Jolan shivered at the whisper the steel made leaving its scabbard. Drawn weapons reminded him of Garret.

"Oh, now it's time to hurry up and get to work, is it?" Willem said. "Maybe if we hadn't wasted so much time ogling the whole fucking—"

"Close your mouth," Cumberland said flatly. "And crank that crossbow."

Willem stared at him for a moment, then loaded a bolt into his weapon and tightened the mechanism with a few quick pulls on the machinery.

"Me and Sten'll take the door. Willem and Oromir deal with the two wanderers soon as we get started."

They all gave short nods of understanding, then slipped their masks over their faces.

"What about me?" Jolan asked.

Cumberland looked down at him. "You do not move from your present spot until I come back for you." He grabbed Jolan's shoulder and squeezed it so hard Jolan almost yelped. "And be warned, boy, I can follow your footprints from here to the jungle nations. If you force me to chase you down, I will be a lot less polite about things moving forward."

Jolan swallowed. "Got it."

"Good. I'll call for you when we're done."

Cumberland and his men moved with the predatory confidence of wolves surrounding an elk. Willem and Oromir strafed to the right and ducked beneath the bridge, then waded across the water under the bridge's shadow. Cumberland and Sten went left and took cover at the edge of the field. Once the patrolling men passed them, they bolted across the open field with their bodies hunched low until they reached the unguarded wall of the mill. Cumberland snuck along the wall and stopped just short of the southern corner. Crouched low. The man guarding the door was only a few paces away, but couldn't see him. Sten moved to the far side of the same wall and peered around the opposite corner, eyeing the patrol. He put one arm up. Cumberland watched him.

They stayed like that while the two patrolling men wended their way around the bridge. Screams started from inside the mill. But the jaguar wardens remained still as statues.

When the two patrolling men were three strides past the bridge, Sten dropped his hand.

Cumberland darted around the corner and decapitated the man guarding the door with a brutal hack.

Before his head hit the ground, Oromir and Willem were out from behind the bridge.

Oromir rushed the two men at a sprint while Willem raised his crossbow and took careful aim. He fired a bolt into the left side of one turtle's back—straight through his heart. The warden fell face-first into the mud.

The other one turned around and raised his sword into a guard, but Oromir was on him. They exchanged a flurry of strikes and parries. Oromir steadily beat the man backward, blade moving so fast Jolan could barely keep track of it. Jolan blinked, and suddenly Oromir's sword was jammed through the man's heart. His arms and head went slack. Oromir removed his blade and the man crumpled to the ground.

Without missing a step, Oromir rushed toward the mill. Willem shouldered his crossbow, drew the war hatchets from his belt, and followed. Cumberland was already coiling his body and getting ready to break down the door. One hard pound from his boot was all it took to blast the wood off its hinges.

All four jaguars rushed into the mill. Jolan heard steel beating against steel. Shouting. Cursing. Then screaming. He kept his eyes fixed on the door—mouth dry, heart racing. In the back of his head, Jolan told himself he should run. There were a dozen ways to lose a man in the Dainwood. But he was so scared he couldn't even stand up.

A minute later, Cumberland appeared in the doorway. There was blood all over his mask.

"Jolan! We need you."

For some reason, Cumberland's shout broke Jolan's trance. Maybe because his bark had the same urgent bite as Master Morgan's voice. Jolan stood, grabbed his pack, and ran to the mill.

The broken door led to an open living area. There was a kitchen, a cast-iron stove, and a large straw mattress in the corner. The turtle wardens were spread around the room, all of them killed in various ways. One had his entrails spread across the kitchen counter. Another had a massive vertical gash from collarbone to stomach and was bleeding all over the bed.

The miller was tied to a chair in the middle of the room. His face swollen and battered. One of his eyes was missing. He was pulling ragged breaths.

"Fix him," Cumberland said, in a tone that made it sound simple for a half-trained alchemist runaway to brew a tonic that would regrow the lost eye.

Jolan nodded and came over to the man. Examined the wounds. His nose was broken. Someone had jammed a thumb into his eye and pressed it against the socket, turning it to mush. Jolan would need to remove the ruined remains along with any errant nerves that would cause him pain, clean the area, and make him a patch.

"Get me some fresh water from the creek," Jolan said, already opening his pack to get the ingredients he'd need. "Boil it, let it cool, then I'll tell you what to do next."

———

Two hours later, Jolan had removed the ruined eye, flushed the wound with a disinfectant solution, and covered it with a healing poultice. He fitted the miller for an eyepatch made from deerskin leather and gave him a week's worth of tonic that would dull the pain and reduce inflammation. Cumberland was the only one who'd stayed for the entire thing—the others had opted to wait outside.

"Drink one of these vials in the morning, and another right after your dinner. It will help ease the pain."

"I'm grateful," the miller said. He'd withstood the painful surgery with very little fanfare—gripping the arm of the chair was the only indication of discomfort. Jolan noticed he had plenty of scars on his hands and forearms. He did not think this man had always been a miller.

"I wish I could have done more," Jolan said.

He'd added a small pinch of Gods Moss to his standard herb poultice. The same thing he'd done to Bershad's leg back at Otter Rock. Then he added two mudfish scales, which were used to intensify the reaction of several different chemical processes. He was half hoping the eye really would grow back, but nothing extraordinary happened. Just a cleansed wound that wouldn't get infected, even if the miller rubbed dung in it.

One experiment done. A few thousand more to go.

Cumberland came over and squeezed the man's shoulder as Jolan was packing up.

"Godrick," he said. "I hate to ask, but . . ."

"The bird is safe. And the message. One moment."

Godrick stood with a grunt, then moved to his stove and bent over behind it. He pried a brick out of the wall with a fire poker, dug around in the little hollow behind it, and came out cradling a dark blue pigeon. The bird's head bobbed as it scanned the room.

Cumberland gave a sigh of relief. "Good. Good."

Jolan studied the bird. It looked like an ordinary carrier pigeon. "What's so special about her?" he asked.

"She's one of the last of Ashlyn Malgrave's birds that can reach Papyria," Cumberland said, taking the bird in his massive hands. "My orders are to bring this pigeon and her message to Umbrik's Glade. Carlyle says there'll be a widow waiting for it."

"It true they wear sharkskin armor?" Godrick asked.

"Yeah."

"There's a storm rolling in from the south," Godrick said. "You and your men are welcome to the barn."

Cumberland nodded. "Appreciated, old friend."

"Don't think you're getting off that easy." Godrick went over to the kitchen and produced a jug of liquor from a cabinet. "Seeing as

I'm injured and we're old friends, best get drunk and tell some lies to each other. You can blow smoke up my ass about how heroic I was in the old days. How I taught you everything you know."

Cumberland bowed his head. "Of course."

Willem, Sten, and Oromir had monopolized half the barn with their weapons and armor. They were sharpening and oiling their blades. Replacing chain-mail links in their armor. Willem had disassembled his crossbow into five pieces and was cleaning the recurved limbs with a rag. They muttered little jokes and jabs at each other while they worked.

Jolan dropped his pack on the far side of the barn, lit a candle, and started unpacking his supplies and organizing his thoughts for the next experiment.

There was already a known list of Gods Moss concoctions—all of them extremely valuable. And because of that, nobody in the Alchemist Order had looked for new ones for hundreds of years. But Jolan believed there was more. Some mixture that Master Morgan had discovered, but not revealed—Morgan had been an extremely secretive person, always sending and receiving mysterious note from Pargos. Jolan was determined to re-create the recipe.

The first step was to start ruling things out. He decided to begin with Canallum roots.

They were a rare warren root, and were often used as an acceleration agent in blood thinners. Maybe they could have other, undiscovered properties. Jolan spent ten minutes purifying a flask and preparing the two ingredients. He sliced the roots, measured his moss, and then used a steel rod to flatten the mixture against the bottom of the flask.

The early-autumn storm howled at the walls of the barn—rattling the wood slats and making his candle shudder. This was a far cry from the quiet, perfectly insulated apothecary where he used to conduct experiments, but it was all he had.

Jolan filled the flask with a warm brine made from spring water and Atlas Coast salt. Sealed the top—careful to prevent contamination—and set it aside. It would settle overnight, and ferment over the course of several weeks. Jolan watched the cloudy mixture swirl. Started thinking of other combinations he could try.

"Where did you learn all of that?"

Jolan twitched, surprised. Oromir had come over while he was conjuring imaginary healing tonics in his head.

"I used to be apprenticed to an alchemist."

"Truly?"

"Yes. I became Master Morgan's apprentice when I was ten years old. I lived with him at the apothecary after that—gathering and measuring ingredients for hours each day. Setting up the anti-venom experiments for the red-shelled snail pestilence that plagued the area. And I assisted with all the field surgeries."

"Field surgeries? How many could there have been in Otter Rock?"

"Needle-Throated Verduns like those foothills. There were a lot of attacks over the years. Even a few dragonslayings."

"Ah. I see. I guess dragonslayers make for good practice. No harm screwing up the stitches on a dead man."

"No," Jolan said softly.

"But you're not an alchemist anymore?"

He shook his head. "I'm working on this for myself."

"What's it going to do?"

Jolan shrugged. "I'm not sure yet, actually. I'm trying to find something new. It's hard to explain."

Oromir picked up on Jolan's apprehension. "Well, I'll leave you to it, then."

The young warden turned back toward his side of the barn.

"Where did you learn to fight so well?" Jolan asked, stopping his departure. His experiments could wait, and after two moons alone in the jungle, he craved conversation.

Oromir gave him a look, then a devious smile. His tone changed. "What makes you say I fight well?"

"I saw the way you moved by the bridge. You're faster than all the others."

"Twice as quick, half as strong!" Sten shouted from his spot.

Jolan looked down at his feet, suddenly feeling foolish. "Well, I was impressed by the way you moved. You were very graceful."

Oromir's face softened. "Sword work is like any trade, you practice it every day—and practice hard—you get good at it. Same as a seamstress or a cook. Or a healer." He stared at Jolan with his bright green eyes for a moment, then pulled a flask from an inner pocket of his jacket. Took a sip.

"Brandy?" he said, offering the flask to Jolan. "It's from Deepdale, cost two silvers."

Jolan remembered the pleasant buzz he'd gotten from rain ale when he'd visited Deepdale with Garret. After the things he'd seen and done that day, he could use something to help him relax.

"Sure. Okay."

Oromir gave Jolan the flask, then sat down next to him. Once again, he was so close their shoulders were touching. Jolan took a sip and did his best to pretend it didn't burn the back of his throat and make his eyes water. He'd have preferred rain ale.

"It's good."

"Only the best for you, Jolan."

"And Oromir makes his move," Willem muttered from across the barn.

"Just keep it down this time, will you?" Sten added. "The storm ain't loud enough to drown you out."

"What's he talking about?" Jolan asked.

"Ignore those two. They're just bitter they have to wait for a woman to get a little intimacy."

"I don't understand."

Oromir smiled again. Took the brandy from Jolan. "He thinks we're gonna screw."

"Oh." Jolan's stomach whirred. He didn't know where to look, so he wound up giving the rafters a very careful examination.

Oromir drank, then laughed. "Relax, Jolan. I'm a little too tired for that kind of thing after all the walking and killing today." He made a show of sniffing his armpit. "Little too ripe as well."

He offered the brandy back to Jolan. He took it.

"But since we're on the topic, which way do you prefer it?" Oromir asked.

"Prefer what?"

"Screwing. Do you like men or women? Or is it both?"

Jolan hesitated. Master Morgan never brought up sex outside of academic pursuits. Jolan mostly associated intercourse as a necessity for reproduction or the cause of unpleasant illnesses he'd needed to treat over the years, like Willem's cock rot or the pubic lice outbreaks back in Otter Rock. But that didn't seem like the right thing to say in that moment.

"Well, I've never . . . done it with anyone."

"But you must have a preference. Weren't you sweet on anyone back at Otter Rock?"

"Um, it was a small town. And . . ." Jolan struggled for words. His mind was churning like a hurricane but seemed unable to produce coherent thoughts or words.

"Okay, okay, don't have a seizure," Oromir said. "No crushes. Got it. When you touch yourself, what do you think about?"

Jolan was fairly certain his face could not get any redder than it was in that moment.

"Don't tell me you've never done that before, either!" Oromir half shouted.

"Of course I've done it," Jolan hissed, trying to quiet him down. He didn't know what Willem and Sten would contribute to the conversation, he just knew he didn't want them to do it. "But I don't . . . I don't think about anyone specific."

Oromir raised his eyebrows. "Really? That's weird."

No, this was now as red as Jolan's face could get.

"I'm sorry, I didn't mean it like that," Oromir said quickly. "I just always think about someone, that's all." He took a nip of the brandy. "So, if it's not a specific person, what do you think about?"

Jolan hesitated. By that point, the brandy had seeped into his blood just enough for him to have the courage to keep talking. "I think about the warmth of someone else's touch. Their hands moving . . . you know, all over. I've never been touched that way by someone else. So just thinking about my skin against someone else's is enough, I guess."

"Mmm, that's sweet, actually." Oromir took a long sip of brandy and stared at the ceiling for a few moments. "For me, it was this warden named Lok. He would take his shirt off and chop wood in front of his house every evening as the sun went down. Gods, but those arms." Oromir released a long breath. He held out the brandy. "One last sip before we call it a night? It'll be another long day of walking tomorrow."

Jolan nodded. Took a sip without looking away from Oromir, who watched him the entire time, too.

"Don't worry, I've got plenty more for another time," Oromir said. Then he went back to his corner and curled up under a blanket. A minute or two later he was snoring.

Jolan tried to go to sleep, too. But the thunder and rain and thought of someone else's skin against his kept him awake.

6

VERA

Balaria, Burz-al-dun, District Four

Aeternita's Grace smelled of copper and eucalyptus. The barkeep must have added some aromatic oil to his keg's centrifuge, so that each time he filled a mug, the steam that hissed free from the opened spigot was laced with the natural scent.

Burz-al-dun was full of machines whose work was masked by manufactured whiffs of nature. Vera hated it. She longed to return to the overgrown wilderness of Almira, or the clear, cold, and salty air of Papyria.

But Kira was here. And so was she.

She headed for the long bar on the far side of the room, passing copper tables ringed with patrons. Most had the wrinkled foreheads and saggy midsections of merchants who spent their days squinting at shipping ledgers from plush chairs, but two men sitting at a table in the far corner had broad shoulders. Careful eyes. They also had short swords tucked beneath their long black jackets. The grips of their weapons were corded with white thread that had been blackened by frequent use.

Hired security.

Even the least savvy of Burz-al-dun's politicians understood that the soldiers of Balaria were ultimately loyal to Actus Thorn, not them. So private mercenaries were common in the villas and manses of wealthy ministers and merchants. But it was rare to see them in a tavern. Most public establishments relied on the strict checkpoints and the Balarian soldiers who operated them to keep the peace.

About half the patrons stared at Vera as she crossed the room. She'd kept her widow's armor on, which always attracted attention, but the fact that she had Bershad's sword slung across her back attracted far more. She'd considered leaving the big weapon in the palace and dressing in a courtesan's silk robe and cloak in an attempt to blend in and run subtle reconnaissance. But her dark and smooth Papyrian features stood out against Balarians' sharp noses and pale complexions like a black heron in a snow-covered field—there was no hiding her nationality or her nature in this city, so she amplified it, instead.

Plus, subtlety took time. She did not want to be gone from Kira for any longer than absolutely necessary.

Vera swung the sword off her back and placed it on the bar in front of her. From the spot she chose, there was nothing behind her except a wall, and she had a good view of both the main entrance and the secondary supply door behind the bar. Vera had checked the tavern's floor plan and surrounding area in the imperial records before leaving the palace, and that second door made her nervous. It led through a small pantry and then into a narrow alley that snaked north for almost a league before it dead-ended against the district wall, which was seventy strides of sheer marble. That was all normal for Burz-al-dun, but that league of alley connected to twenty-seven undocumented basements. Those could lead anywhere. Or be filled with anything.

Vera remembered what Felgor had told her as they snuck into the Imperial Palace using the sewers—there were entire communities of criminals living below the surface of Burz-al-dun. And she'd seen how dragon oil and opium changed dirty hands in the covered docks of the city, moving from Balaria to the smugglers' nest of Taggarstan. That was how she'd gotten into Clockwork City to begin with.

The capital of Balaria presented itself with aromatic and clean skin, but the meat and bones beneath were black and rotten. In her memories, Himeja was a different kind of city. Quiet and honest and clean. But Vera's memories of Papyria were more than a decade old. She wondered what she would think of her homeland now, after all the dark things she had seen and done on foreign soil.

"Your order, mistress?" the barkeep asked, raising an eyebrow, which he'd oiled into a point. He worked very hard not to glance at the sword Vera had placed onto the bar. "We have fine bubbled wine. Juniper spirits—"

"Just ale."

"A most excellent choice, mistress. We use hops from the free nations of Juno for our brew, one of the few taverns in this district with a steady supply."

"Wonderful." Vera leaned forward. "Is there anything else this tavern might have a unique and steady supply of?"

"Not sure what you mean, mistress."

"Dragon oil, for instance."

The man barked out an uncomfortable laugh. "That's a good one. I'll get your ale."

Vera scanned the room from her vantage point while the bartender poured. There was a group of three soldiers drinking near the main entrance. Their purple cloaks were pinned to their armor with silver clasps shaped like arrows. Longbowmen. Two of them were visibly drunk. The third just seemed tipsy. Probably not a threat, but worth keeping an eye on.

When her drink arrived, Vera took a long gulp. Then she waited.

She'd barely finished half of her ale before the least-drunk longbowman came to the bar. He sidled up next to Vera, despite a huge swath of the bar being empty.

"Nice sword."

Vera glanced at him. He was about thirty years old, and had the pale eyes and long nose of a Balarian, but his features were rougher than the palace froth Vera was used to—sun-weathered skin and a few small scars on his forehead and cheeks that looked like they'd come from some kind of shrapnel. Even with his armor and cloak on, it was easy to tell that he had powerful shoulders and a broad chest. A trait all longbowmen shared. It was the only way they could draw their massive weapons.

"Thanks."

"I'm Decimar Baurus, lieutenant of the seventh platoon of the Royal Longbow Legion."

Vera didn't say anything.

"What's your name?" Decimar pressed.

Vera gave him a long look. "You know my name, Lieutenant."

He smiled, relaxed and confident. "I do indeed. It's an honor to meet you." He glanced over his shoulder. "I'm glad I have those two with me. They may be drunk, but they're still witnesses. Otherwise, nobody back at the barracks would believe me when I said I shared an ale with Vera the Papyrian widow."

"We're not sharing ale, though."

"Not yet," Decimar said, flagging over the barkeep and ordering a fresh ale for Vera, in addition to another round for his comrades. "So, what brings you to Aeternita's Grace?"

"I should ask you the same thing," Vera said. "Soldiers below the rank of major are only given access to districts five through ten. What are you and your men doing here?"

"I'm surprised a foreigner like yourself has such command of the district policy."

Vera had memorized maps of the fifteen districts—along with the access requirements to each—within a week of arriving. In Balaria, laws were enforced by the seals, and she couldn't do her job if she didn't understand the rules.

"Answer my question."

"Very well. The longbowmen have been granted special travel privileges for the night—our seals switch back to their regular codes at two in the morning." He checked his clock, which was embedded into the bracer on his right wrist. "So, we have time to share one round, at least."

Longbowmen weren't part of the regular army. Their tactics and equipment differed so much from standard infantry that it didn't make sense to lump them in with the grunts. Plus, longbowmen had to start training when they were little boys—ten or eleven—so they'd be strong enough to draw the enormous bows they used by the time they were eighteen. In many ways, the longbowmen reminded her of the widows. They both traded their childhoods to become lethal adults.

"What did you and your comrades do to earn such generosity?" Vera asked.

"Classified, I'm afraid," Decimar said. "But it was a good day."

He had no way of knowing that Vera was well aware of exactly why they were celebrating. Nothing like reducing an entire foreign navy to cinders to earn the men a drink.

Behind them, Decimar's two comrades burst into laughter over some private joke.

"Beware of a soldier's delight," Vera said. "They tend to portend violent times."

Decimar cocked his head. "Where did you learn to speak Balarian so well?"

"I speak every language that might come out of an enemy's mouth."

In truth, Vera's Balarian had been weak when she arrived, but Kira had drilled with her for hours each night until she could understand and reproduce most of the local idioms. Some of the gutterspeak still got past her, though.

"I see. Any enemies in this tavern tonight?"

The barkeep came over with their drinks, pretending not to eavesdrop as he slid the mugs forward.

"Oh, I wouldn't call them enemies," Vera said. "A few smugglers perhaps, but that's all."

The bartender's pointed eyebrows flicked toward the ceiling, surprised and alarmed. He hid the reaction a moment later, but was too late.

"Sounds serious," Decimar said, raising his mug to his lips.

"Not for very long."

"Why is that?"

There were many ways to hunt an animal. For rabbits, you used a trap. For deer, bait. But for boar, you simply found their lair, flushed them out, and trusted yourself not to miss when the beast attacked.

This was a boar hunt.

"Because I've come down here tonight to kill them," Vera said, raising her voice just enough so that the bartender—who had turned his back and was pretending to clean a glass—would have no trouble hearing.

Decimar froze, mug halting a finger's width from his lips. He put it down again without drinking. "So, it's true what they say about widows."

"I'm not sure." Vera took a drink. "What do they say about widows?"

"That you're not to be fucked with."

"Most people come to regret it," Vera said, looking past Decimar and watching the movement of the barkeep, who'd scampered down to the edge of the bar and said something to a squat man in a white silk robe while passing him a glass of bubbled wine. That man, in turn, had moved to the two patrons with careful eyes and poorly concealed weapons. Relayed something to them. The taller of the two departed using the front door of the tavern, but something about his posture and the way he gave the merchant a little nod on his way out told Vera that he'd be back soon.

"What about the man who took your finger?" Decimar said, gesturing to the missing pinky on Vera's left hand.

"Who said it was a man?"

Vera stared at Decimar until he gave a helpless shrug.

"Relax, Lieutenant. I'm just giving you a hard time. The man responsible died in the Razorback Mountains. The man who actually cut it off is . . . gone."

Vera had tried to piece Bershad's fate together as best she could, but the intelligence coming from Almira was both fragmented and filtered through Osyrus Ward's spies, which made it untrustworthy. As best Vera could tell, Bershad and Felgor snuck out of Burz-al-dun on a stolen schooner, then disappeared. There were unconfirmed reports he'd been spotted with Ashlyn during the battle of Floodhaven, but the truth of that mess was impossible to glean from the far side of the Soul Sea.

The only certainty was that nobody had seen Bershad, Ashlyn, or Felgor alive since the battle. Vera knew they were probably dead, but in the back of her mind she remembered watching Bershad's body knit itself back together in the hold of that ship after he'd taken a dozen wounds that would kill a normal man.

If Bershad truly had lost his life, it hadn't been taken easily.

"Come on, soft star!" one of the other longbowmen called. "Stop flirting with the Papyrian and bring that next round over!"

"Soft star?" Vera asked.

Decimar took a sip of his drink. "You need good eyes to join the longbowmen. And you need to start young if you're going to build the strength to work one of our bows. So recruiters trawl the slums on clear nights, look for boys with strong arms, and have 'em look up at the stars. Tell 'em what they see. Anyone who can spot four of the six stars that make up the Falling Ghost Moth constellation gets a chance to join."

"How many did you see?"

"Seven."

"I thought you said there were six?"

He nodded. "The seventh star is the furthest away, and so difficult to see it's not even considered a part of the constellation."

"The soft star," Vera repeated, understanding. "I suppose that means you have good eyes."

"Better than most, anyway."

Vera didn't say anything.

"So, you know how I got my nickname. How'd you come by such a big sword?" Decimar continued.

Vera turned away, scanned the room again. Decimar had served his purpose, and now she needed him to leave.

"You should return to your friends, Lieutenant. They sound thirsty."

Decimar gave a defeated shrug, then left. His two friends slapped his back when he returned to their table, laughing and taking gulps from their fresh drinks.

Vera ignored the rest of her ale. She needed to keep her head clear. Instead of drinking, she spent the next hour staring at the merchant who'd relayed the message to the hired thugs. He squirmed under her gaze, but was clearly waiting for something specific to happen before he moved. When Decimar and his friends left, Vera pretended not to notice. Just kept staring at the merchant.

Eventually, the tall man returned. Sat down at the table with his partner, giving the merchant another nod. Very subtle. The merchant dabbed his sweaty forehead, revealing a disgustingly damp and yellow armpit. He downed the last of his bubble wine and moved to leave. But he headed for the pantry door, not the front.

Vera slid a Balarian copper onto the counter, picked up her sword, and followed him. She didn't bother checking to see if the hired thugs came, too.

She knew they would.

The alley was poorly lit and dominated by sprawling copper pipes that hissed and rattled as if large rodents used them as transportation tunnels. Steam leaked from the pipe seams, creating a hazy mist. The merchant had turned left and scurried deeper down the dead-end passageway. As Vera followed the pale flicker of his robe, she slid the sword off her shoulder and held it next to her left hip, where it would be easy to draw.

Vera turned a few corners, letting the merchant stay about fifty paces ahead of her, just barely in sight. She counted the basement hatches as she passed them. Counting things always kept her calm.

After passing the twenty-third door and turning a corner, the merchant was gone. Replaced by three men with drawn short swords. They wore leather jackets that were probably reinforced with steel shanks, but were otherwise unarmored.

"You're not very subtle, Papyrian," said the man in the center. He had a neatly trimmed black goatee and hazel eyes.

"I wasn't trying to be." Vera angled her shoulders so she could quickly check behind herself. The other two were approaching, also with their weapons drawn. "But if all of you were trying to spring a surprise attack, you did a piss-poor job of it."

"Uh-huh. I'm sure you meant to get yourself surrounded by five men in a narrow alleyway where the closest Tick-Tock Grunt is half a league away."

"Who hired you to guard Aeternita's Grace?" Vera asked.

"We're the ones asking the questions," responded the man with the goatee.

Vera shrugged. "Ask them."

"Who tipped off the Madman's spies?"

Vera knew who they meant. Even among the ministers who frequented the palace, the Madman was a perfectly acceptable and well-known term for Osyrus Ward.

"You'd have to ask the Madman."

"So, he is the one who sent you here. Why?"

Vera smiled. There was no reason to mince words at this point.

"Because selling dragon oil on the black market is illegal."

"It is. But since when does the empress's widow get sent to deal with that kind of thing?"

"My duties are expanding." Vera opened and closed her right hand. "There's no reason to make a mess of this. If you give me the name of the merchant who hired you, that'll be the end of it."

"Who, Trovis?" The man with the goatee smiled. "Everyone in the fourth district knows who that sweaty weasel is. Wasn't no need to get yourself cornered down here to learn his name."

Vera assumed he was referring to the merchant in the white robe who'd disappeared.

"Not Trovis. The man Trovis gets his orders from. You know, the silk magnate who's stockpiling dragon oil and preparing to send it to Taggarstan on the next full moon?"

The man's smile disappeared. Vera did not trust Osyrus Ward any more than she trusted a Red Skull dragon, but in this case his intelligence was clearly accurate.

"Oh," Vera said. "Was that supposed to be a secret?"

"If I were you, I'd be less concerned with *that* man's name, and more concerned with the orders he gave regarding *you,* widow." He motioned to his men. "We're to make sure your trip up the alley only goes the one direction."

Vera tapped her thumb against the guard of the sword. She was willing to carve answers from this man's hide, but once steel was drawn things became unpredictable. Gold was a more reliable method for getting questions answered.

"How much do you get paid to follow that order?" she said. "Might be there's more coin to be made as a friend to Empress Domitian."

The man with the goatee shook his head. "No chance."

Oh well. Worth a shot.

"Very well," Vera said. "Let's do it your way."

The man nodded. Then stalked forward, slipping into a low guard. The two men behind him followed.

Vera waited until the man with the goatee was between steps, then she darted forward and rammed the pommel of her sword into his teeth, turning them to splinters. He fell on his ass. With her left hand, she drew the scabbard off her sword and threw it at one of the thugs behind her, forcing him to bat it away with his sword. Then Vera hurled the sword itself like a spear and skewered the man through the heart.

She followed the momentum of her throw, ducking a clumsy swipe by the second thug from the tavern. She drew *Kaisha* and ran the blade in and out of the side of his neck, severing both of his main arteries.

The other two were on her, but they moved like turtles. She dodged a sword jab, which went past her and into a copper pipe that released a spray of hot steam onto the man's arm. He howled in pain but was silenced when Vera slashed his vocal cords apart.

The last man tried a sideswipe. Vera stopped it by stabbing him through the forearm. When he recoiled, he took the dagger with him, so Vera drew *Owaru* and rammed it through the bottom of his jaw and into his brain. She pulled her daggers out of the dead man before he fell to the ground, then stalked toward the man with the goatee. He was still on the ground and shuffling away from her like a crab, blood pouring from his broken mouth.

Vera kicked him between the thighs hard enough to make him curl his legs and moan, but not so hard she made him vomit or pass out. There was a thin line between those two results, but Vera knew it well. Her widow's training had involved several weeks focused solely on the unpleasant things you can do to someone's manhood to produce a desired behavior. Right now, she wanted him to start telling secrets.

She squatted in front of the man.

"Let's try this one more time," Vera said. "Who hired you?"

7

JOLAN

Almira, Dainwood Province

Jolan and the wardens traveled across the northern rim of the Dainwood for a day and a night. They walked in a loose formation—alternating between game trails and streambeds to stay off the main roads. Jolan passed the time by foraging for mushrooms and trying to make his loose orbit around Oromir appear natural and casual. But every time he came close to the young warden, a lump formed in his throat and his pulse quickened. He couldn't stop thinking about what they'd talked about in the barn.

"What day is it?" Willem said, switching the shoulder that he was carrying the pigeon cage on. Each warden had taken a turn carrying the bird through the backcountry. "We're not gonna miss the Clear Sky markets, right? Umbrik's Glade has a good one."

The Clear Sky markets only came every five years, during the autumn after the Great Migration. While the dragons were mating

in the eastern warrens, the farmers of Almira enjoyed an entire
season of clear skies. Without the looming threat of lizard attacks
to interrupt their harvests, the reaping was far more bountiful and
rich than other years. All the big cities in Almira—Umbrik's
Glade included—ran a special market for the occasion.

"Don't worry yourself," Sten responded. "It'll be running
strong for another week, at least. They're probably still bringing in
all the crops. Pineapples. Bananas. Oranges. And the Glade always
has the best salt pork you can find."

"Gods, but I love Dainwood pineapples," Willem said. "Need
to get myself some more preserves this year. Miscalculated on the
last Clear Sky and my stock was spent before the first winter solstice."

"How are you going to carry around jars of preserves with a
war on?" Sten asked.

"I'll bury 'em somewhere. That's obvious."

"I'll take three-to-one odds whatever jars you bury, you can't
locate the following morning. Forget lasting until the next solstice."

"Fuck yourself, Sten. My memory for buried caches is rock
solid."

"Spend a lot of time burying things besides your own turds?"

"Maybe I do," Willem said cryptically.

"Willem the squirrel," Sten said. "Kind of has a ring to it."

They reached a ridge that looked down on a wide valley. From
their vantage, they had a nice view of the entire settlement.

Umbrik's Glade was a new town that had sprawled around an
ancient holdfast. The small fortress was made from heavy slabs of
dark granite, but the mortaring had decayed in some places and
been repaired, giving it an unbalanced and vaguely unsettling
look. In contrast, the town's houses and shops and taverns had all
been cut from fresh lumber and roofed with expensive red slate.
They spread out from the holdfast in five concentric circles. The
innermost road that ringed the holdfast was packed with massive
crates of different food: corn, beans, wheat, rice, and dozens of different fruits and vegetables. It was enough to feed the city and surrounding countryside for weeks. Hawkers stood in front of the
massive crates, shouting and bargaining and selling to buyers.

"I see a pineapple pile!" Willem shouted, pointing at a mountain of fruit. "Still plenty left."

A coffee plantation dominated the eastern hills. To the west—where the Dainwood forest thickened in earnest—there were half a dozen lumber mills and wide roads leading into the dark forest. A team of oxen was hauling a long, flatbed wagon filled with freshly cut lumber out of the forest and into the town.

"Fucking Umbrik." Cumberland spat. "Bastard's still running his mills."

"Of course he is," Oromir said. "With the Grealors dead and the jaguars in rebellion, there's nobody to come collect taxes from this operation. It's pure profit."

"It's a fucking disgrace," Cumberland said, turning to Oromir. "You're too young to remember what it was like before, when the Bershad lords ruled and there wasn't a single mill in all of the Dainwood." He looked off into the distance. "It was beautiful. The heavy fog of the early morning. Jaguars napping in the trees. Bird songs thrumming down from the canopy like a swelling storm."

"There are still birds," Willem said.

"It's not the same."

"Those annoying motmots have been following us all day," Willem said.

Jolan listened for a moment. Frowned.

"I don't hear any motmots," Jolan said.

Everyone went silent. Listening.

"You're right," Sten said. "They went quiet. When did that happen?"

"Not interested in when so much as why," Cumberland said, scanning the trees, then the sky.

A long shadow fell over the valley. Despite the season, instinct told Jolan it was a dragon, but instead of the quick flicker of a Blackjack or a Verdun, this shadow dropped over the valley and stayed there. Lumbering and slow. A cloud?

Jolan looked up and saw something that he didn't understand.

At first, he thought it was some strange species of undocumented dragon. Twice as large as a Naga Soul Strider, but with black and gray coloring and a massive hump on its back.

No. Not a hump. It was a massive, bloated sack made from a

patchwork of dark leather. Hanging beneath it was the unmistakable shape of a ship's hull that was made from dragon bones instead of oak. But that was impossible. Nobody could have preserved so many remains of a great lizard. At that size, it would have taken dozens of cobbled-together dragons. Maybe hundreds.

"It's a flying ship," Jolan said, not quite believing the words coming out of his mouth. Steel support beams and copper cables ran along the belly of the flying object like the twisted roots of a messy winter garden. The sound of metal hammering echoed down from the ship, as if a hundred blacksmiths were inside, pounding away on blades. The piney smell of burning dragon oil filled Jolan's nostrils.

"Demon's breath," Sten muttered, gaping up at the ship as it cut across the sky. Jolan glanced back to the city. People were leaning out of windows. Pointing. Shouting. One man had dropped his haul of raspberries and rice and fled toward the tree line, leaving his two small boys to fend for themselves.

The ship lilted, turned, and then stopped above the holdfast. A square hatch at the bottom of the ship opened. Scores of black cables dropped to the ground.

Cries of fear from the citizens of Umbrik's Glade rose above the mechanical din of the flying ship. Now they all fled in a panicked mass—rushing down side streets and alleys, heading for the cover of the jungle. The man who'd reacted first had already disappeared into the gloom.

Armored men started sliding down the cables. When they reached the ground, they scattered around the market, hooking those same cables to the massive crates of food.

"I know that armor," Cumberland muttered. "Those are Balarian soldiers."

"Clock fuckers?" Sten asked. "What are they doing here?"

Nobody responded. Nobody knew. But less than a minute later, it became obvious.

The soldiers jumped onto the crates of food. There was a shout, and the cables started retracting upward, carrying the men back to the ship, along with the entirety of Umbrik's Glade's Clear Sky harvest. They disappeared into the ship's hull, but the hatch remained open. The ship hovered in the sky.

A steel orb the size of a horse dropped from the hatch and landed in the square. There was a mechanical box on top of the orb that was sprouting copper wires and pipes that ran in and out of the orb's innards.

"Is that a clock?" Willem asked.

"Dunno. Never seen anything like—"

There was a blinding flash that forced Jolan to shield his eyes. Then, an earsplitting boom. It was as if a hundred bolts of lightning had struck the city at the same time.

When Jolan opened his eyes—blinking to regain sight—the holdfast was gone. In its place, there was a smoldering crater of rubble. Any building within a hundred strides of the crater was on fire.

Everyone gaped at the ruination, unable to believe what they'd just seen.

A mechanical roar boomed from deep inside the ship. It flew east at a fast clip. Before long, it was just a black dot on the horizon.

"The merchant's stories were true," Willem muttered. "I didn't believe them. Not really. Gods."

"We move," Cumberland said, starting down the ridge.

"What if it comes back?" Willem asked.

Cumberland didn't answer. Just picked up his pace.

The first body they came to was a woman in a yellow dress. Half her face was untouched, but the rest was blackened and burned beyond recognition. On instinct, Jolan knelt and shrugged his pack off. Started pulling out ingredients for a burn tonic.

"Leave her," Cumberland growled.

"But she needs a tonic for the—"

"She needs a seashell, boy. But there will be others you can save. C'mon."

Jolan took a closer look at the woman. Saw that she was dead. Sten was kneeling beside her and fishing out a seashell from behind his breastplate. He muttered some words as he placed it in her mouth.

They moved down the main street, which was still half mud from the storm two days earlier. Eventually, they reached the square. The air was cloudy with soot. Jolan could taste copper and smell scorched flesh. Four unplucked chickens that had been hung outside of the butcher shop were smoldering. All their feathers singed black.

There was a crash from inside the shop, and a moment later a man in a dirty apron stumbled out. He was holding both hands over his face. Blood streamed from between his fingers. He collapsed in the road.

Jolan started to run over to him, but saw another man across the square lying on his side. One of his legs was gone, the other torn to shreds. And a dozen paces away there was a woman kneeling over a child, pressing down on the girl's stomach to try and stop the bleeding of an abdominal injury.

You can't run from person to person, Jolan realized. *They're too far apart. You need to make a plan before you act.*

Jolan had never worked a battlefield, but he'd read all fifteen volumes of *The Alchemists' Field Guide to War Contracts*. He knew what to do. He'd just never done it before.

Focus. Work smart.

Jolan unslung his backpack and started removing supplies.

"I'll set up my treatment center here," he said, pulling on Master Morgan's sealskin gloves. "Bring everyone to me. If someone is too hurt to be moved, break down a door, gently roll them onto it, and drag them over. Arrange them so those with the most serious injuries are the closest to me."

Jolan looked up. The others were frozen in place. Overwhelmed with the destruction.

"Hey!" Jolan shouted, breaking their trance. "They need help. *Bring them to me!*"

———

Five hours later, Jolan had done everything he could.

Sixty-three were killed by the explosion. Another twenty-nine died while Jolan was treating them—or while they were waiting for their turn. Twenty-two had critical burns and probably wouldn't live out the week. Nineteen had severe wounds but would probably live. Fifty-three had minor injuries and would make full recoveries.

"Keep this on for three days," Jolan said, as he finished packing a Gods Moss poultice against a man's shoulder, which had been scorched in the explosion. "It will prevent infection."

"Thank you," the man whispered. "For everything."

Jolan had used half of his Gods Moss. He knew that he'd given away a fortune, but many of the burn victims were just children.

Some were babies. Even if they died—and the Gods Moss was wasted—he couldn't live with himself if he didn't give them the best possible chance at survival.

When the man was gone, Jolan sat back on his haunches. Closed his eyes. Blew out a sigh. It was almost dark.

"That was incredible."

He looked up to see Oromir standing in front of him. One hand on the hilt of his sword.

"Not sure *incredible* is the right word," Jolan said. He motioned to the line of bodies. Sten and Cumberland were giving them shells. "So many dead. So many that I couldn't save."

"There would have been far more heading down the river if you hadn't been here." Oromir squatted in front of Jolan. Took his hands. "You have a gift, Jolan. The way you stayed calm in all the chaos. The way your hands move so fast when you're mixing tonics and stitching. Doing seven things at once without screwing any of it up. It was amazing. Truly."

Oromir looked down at Jolan's palms. Squeezed them.

"Thanks," Jolan said. He'd never been praised like that. If Master Morgan had been here, all he would have done was give Jolan a curt nod and an extra cup of coffee the following morning.

Oromir opened his mouth to say something else, but stopped short. His hand moved back to his sword as he stood and looked to the left.

A woman had appeared. She had jet-black hair pulled into a tight bun and was wearing a strange kind of black armor with rivulets and grooves across the surface. There was a forked scar along her face and a meat cleaver in her hand.

"Who is in charge here?" she asked with a thick Papyrian accent.

"Who's asking?" Oromir said, voice guarded.

"My name is Shoshone Kalara Sun. I am here to help the Jaguar Army."

"Help us do what?"

She motioned to the sky. "Deal with the Balarians."

Oromir brought Shoshone to Cumberland. Cumberland decided they should all take shelter in a cobbler's workshop to talk. It was one of the few structures that hadn't been damaged by the explosion.

"The skyships came from across the Soul Sea and launched a coordinated attack on Almira," Shoshone said.

"Show me," Cumberland said, spreading a map out on the floor of the workshop. Dozens of half-finished shoes were hanging from the ceiling.

"They hit Glenlock first, then moved along the northern rim of the Dainwood and through the Gorgon Valley," Shoshone said, moving her gloved finger along Cumberland's map of Almira. "Here. Mudwall. Vermonth. Greenspur."

Jolan found himself unable to stop stealing glances at Shoshone's weapons. She had left her meat cleaver unsheathed, and also had a longer dagger with an orca-bone hilt on her opposite hip.

"So, they hit the Dainwood and the Gorgon valley hard. What about Floodhaven and the Atlas Coast?" Cumberland asked.

Shoshone shook her head. "My intelligence says those areas were spared."

"Balaria allied with Linkon Pommol?" Sten asked.

"Unlikely. His entire fleet was destroyed by these same ships three weeks ago."

"I told you that was true!" Willem said, from his spot in the corner. He'd found a jug of rain ale and was taking large swigs. "Nobody believed me."

"You admitted that you didn't believe the merchant, either," Sten said. "Remember?"

"Oh. Right."

"Why pass over the capital and the coast, then?" Cumberland asked. "They're closer to the sea."

Shoshone shook her head. "Food was their priority. And the rich harvests of the Dainwood and Gorgon Valley are more bountiful."

"There are a lot more wardens on the Atlas Coast, too," Oromir said. "Floodhaven is still bursting at the seams with all the warriors that Ashlyn called behind the walls. But most of the Jaguar Army is spread out across the jungle—it was just luck we were nearby to see the attack. And the Gorgon Valley is practically empty after what happened to Cedar Wallace's army at Floodhaven."

"The boy makes a good point," Shoshone said.

"I'm not a boy," Oromir said, voice clipped. "I've earned my mask and my place."

Shoshone considered him. Smiled joylessly. "I meant no offense, tree cat."

"Jaguar."

"Jaguar," Shoshone repeated. "Right."

There was a moment of tension, but it passed. Oromir relaxed his shoulders and turned back to the map.

"They only dropped a score of men onto the ground, too," he said. "Enough to steal the harvest, but not nearly adequate if the townspeople had swarmed them. Might be they correctly assumed the flying ships would scatter everyone, but they couldn't have known that for sure." He looked at Cumberland. "I don't think the Balarians have that many soldiers to spare."

"Agreed," Cumberland said. "We can use that to our advantage."

"Advantage?" Jolan asked. "Am I the only one who saw what happened today? That was a flying ship, and it destroyed half the town in five minutes." He lowered his voice. "Killed all those people."

Shoshone turned to Jolan. He found her cold gaze extremely unsettling.

"This one is a boy though, correct?"

"Child, more like," Sten said.

"Green as a fruit frog," Willem agreed.

Oromir didn't chime in. Instead, he gave Jolan an apologetic shrug.

"He is to become a warrior someday?" Shoshone asked, frowning. "If so, this cat has a very tall tree to climb."

"We're not tree cats," Oromir said again. "We're—"

"Jolan is our healer," Cumberland interrupted. "And we are getting distracted. I got a lot of questions for you, widow. First, how is it that you know so much about these ships so soon after they left?"

"The Balarian ships fly fast," came a man's voice. "But so do Ashlyn Malgrave's pigeons."

Everyone turned. When Cumberland saw the face of the man standing in the doorway, he stood up.

"High-Warden Llayawin," Cumberland said, bowing his head. "It's good to see you."

When the others heard his name, they straightened up a little, but overall the jaguars did not seem to take the presence of an officer with a huge amount of ceremony.

"Fuck off with my titles and my family name," he said. "You called me Carlyle when you were pounding me to dust in the Deepdale training yard. Or shit heel, more often. No need to stand on ceremony just because I'm currently in command of this mess."

Carlyle's voice was clear and precise. Jolan could tell he was a man who'd spent time at Floodhaven court—it had a way of sharpening the edges of a backcountry man's words.

"If you didn't want to get put in charge, you should have thought twice before starting the rebellion," said Cumberland.

"Just couldn't stomach bowing to that asshole after what he did to Ashlyn, and what I know he'll do to the Dainwood." Carlyle sighed. "When it was just turtle wardens to fight, we had a chance. But now we've got these flying ships to deal with."

"I know how to deal with them," Willem said. "Pack up all our shit and head into the deep gloom of the Dainwood, where the canopy'll keep us outta sight o' those atrocities."

"You gonna live your whole life in the gloom?" Sten asked.

"I was born in the gloom. Got no real problem going back and staying there."

"Maybe you don't," Carlyle said. "But there are thousands of people living in the Dainwood's cities and valleys and farms. It's not feasible to hide everyone in the deep jungle forever. We need those ships gone from our skies, or our way of life will be gone, too."

Willem thought on that. "Any chance you can shoot lightning outta your cock like Ashlyn Malgrave? 'Cause that'd go a long way toward resolving this predicament."

Carlyle gave Willem a look. "First of all, seeing as Ashlyn doesn't have a cock, that isn't where her lightning came from."

"Naw. For her, I figured she blasted the demoncraft out of her—"

"Second," Carlyle interrupted. "Whatever demoncraft Ashlyn did or didn't have, it died with her after that battle. We'll need to destroy those ships another way."

Everyone was quiet. Willem cleared his throat. "Begging your pardon and all that dragonshit, but that doesn't seem possible."

Carlyle gave Willem a measured look—somewhere between a frown and a suppressed smile.

"Here's the situation: We have reports of six flying ships that came to Almira. Five stole the Clear Sky harvest, bombed the city, and disappeared over the Soul Sea. But the sixth ship stayed in Almira and took control of Black Rock."

"Cedar Wallace's old city? The fuck is it doing all the way out there?"

"Black Rock has the second-largest harbor in Almira, and the best place for Papyria ships to land an army. The Balarian ship alternates between hovering over the city at night, and patrolling the western coast during the day. We think that skyship is guarding the coast to prevent Okinu from coming to Almira's aid."

Cumberland turned to Shoshone. "Is Okinu planning on sending an army to Almira?"

"The Eternal Empress of Papyria likes to keep her options open," the widow said.

"Uh-huh." Cumberland didn't sound impressed. "So, you want to destroy the lingering skyship?"

Carlyle smiled. Came all the way into the room finally, picked up a fallen chair, and sat down in it.

"Anyone here know the history of the Gorgon Valley Autumn War?"

Willem spat on the floor. "Naw, m'lord. See, while you were in some library reading about wars, we were in the fucking jungle fighting them."

Carlyle gave that weird expression again. "I like the younger generation of jaguars," he said. "They haven't learned to conserve their energy yet."

"Younger? There's no way you've seen more than five summers I haven't."

"Five summers can bring an awful lot of experience, depending on how they're passed." Carlyle paused. Pulled on a nail that was half-buried in the arm of his chair. When it refused to budge, he abandoned it. "Anyway, the reason I bring up the Autumn War is because that was the first time any Almiran brought one of those crossbows to battle." He pointed at the weapon slung over Willem's back. "They're carried by plenty of wardens now, but they're a Balarian invention."

Willem shifted in his boots, clearly uncomfortable with the news that he was hauling a Balarian weapon around and hadn't known it.

"This was before the Balarian Invasion, when trade lines with the clock fuckers were still open. It was a Gorgon lord who bought a few hundred of the machines from across the Soul Sea. And when the next bunch of jaguars came charging onto his lands, they got turned into porcupines. The jaguars hadn't taken a beating like that in decades. They were forced to retreat into the gloom with their tails between their legs." Carlyle glanced at Willem, then went back to his work on the nail. "Turned out that in all the commotion of the retreat, one Dainwood man with a sharp mind had grabbed one of the weapons and run with it. Now, times being what they were, most of the jaguars took the hunk of metal and wood to be a demoncraft weapon. They'd never seen gears or levers or a bolt that could punch through steel armor like cheese. So they wanted to destroy it. Sacrifice it as an offering to the forest gods for good fortune in the next skirmish. But someone in that room with a little extra sense—or a little less superstition than most—had the idea to take the thing to an alchemist, instead, and copy the design. Find a way to make more of them."

Willem cleared his throat. "Due respect, Carlyle, but why the fuck are we getting a history lesson about crossbows?"

"Anyone?" Carlyle asked.

"The skyships are the same thing as the crossbows," Jolan said. "A new weapon. A new technology. Something that could be copied, if we saw how they worked." He paused. "You don't want to destroy the skyship . . . you want to steal it."

"Sharp kid, that one," Carlyle said. "That's exactly what I want you to do."

"Boss," Cumberland said. "I appreciate the historical context and the logic, but I'm a soldier. Got no mind or experience for plucking ships out of the sky."

"Neither do I." He turned to Shoshone. "But she does."

"They train widows to steal flying ships nobody knew existed, do they?"

"They train us to hurt our enemies."

"Thought you all were just a bunch of scary bodyguards."

"No."

Cumberland weighed that. "How many with you?"

"Just one. Iko. She's outside."

"Really?" Willem looked over his shoulder, as if he'd find a widow in the shadow behind him. "I didn't hear anyone."

"That is because your ears are clogged with mud," Shoshone said. "Iko is my finest. But we do not know this country. We need a guide to Black Rock. From there, the two of us will steal the ship on our own."

"So we're just tour guides through the backcountry?" Cumberland asked Carlyle.

"Yes."

"Feels wrong, us heading west on some ill-advised caper while there's a war to fight in the east."

"I have three thousand men in this forest. Four extra soldiers will not help me win this war. But a skyship of our own will. I want you for this job because you're reliable."

"Not sure *reliable* is the word I'd use for my crew," Cumberland said. "Just managed to keep shells out of our mouths a little longer than most."

"I won't force it on you. The rest of us are marching north to deal with the remnants of Linkon Pommol's turtles who crossed the Gorgon without permission. You can come with us if you want."

"Saying we did that, who'd help the Papyrians?"

"Olrick's crew."

"They all took the long swim two weeks ago at White Crow's Hill," Sten said.

"Vullon's, then."

Cumberland winced. "That bastard could get lost walking to the shithouse in his own backyard." He paused. "We'll take you."

Shoshone nodded. "Good."

"Um, not to be an asshole, but have you widows given any thought to the fact that if you're gonna steal a skyship, someone's gotta fly it?" Oromir asked.

"We will compel the crew into cooperation," Shoshone said.

"Two of you will manage that?"

Shoshone smiled. "We would accept help, if it's on offer. But we are prepared to complete the task alone if necessary."

Cumberland glanced at Carlyle, a question in his eyes.

"It's your call," Carlyle said. "An escort through the backcountry is one thing. Stealing a skyship made of bones is another. I won't force that aspect of it over your shoulders."

Cumberland chewed on that for a few moments.

"We'll escort the Papyrians to Black Rock. Beyond that, we'll just have to see."

"That works," Shoshone said. "How long will it take to get to Black Rock?"

"Three weeks, give or take."

The fearsome widow nodded, satisfied.

"What will you do while we're on our little hike?" Cumberland asked Carlyle.

Carlyle stared digging at the nail in the chair again. "Oh, once we boot Linkon's men back across Grealor's Bridge, I figure they'll move on the eastern bridges again. I plan to let them cross in force so that they stretch their supply lines deep into the jungle. Then I'll sever them. Spread the turtles out and pick them apart."

"A good plan," Cumberland said.

"This war with Linkon is just the start of things. If the Dainwood is going to stay free, we need one of those ships." Carlyle finally got the nail free. He stood up and—for reasons that were unclear—put it in his pocket. "I'm counting on you. All of you."

Carlyle gave each man a long look. Even Jolan. Then departed.

"I will need that bird from you." Shoshone motioned to the caged pigeon they'd taken from the mill, which Oromir had brought into the cobbler's workshop with them. "The empress requires an update."

"All yours."

Shoshone picked up the cage. Calmed the bird with a surprisingly tender series of coos. But her face and voice were steeled when she turned back to Cumberland.

"Iko will arrange mounts and supplies. We'll meet you in the apple grove outside the village at dawn tomorrow."

"We'll be there."

Shoshone collected her weapons and disappeared into the night.

Cumberland rolled up his map. Surveyed his men.

"I saw a dining hall down the street that wasn't entirely destroyed," Cumberland said, eventually. "Sten, Oromir, Willem, see about some food and get a good night's sleep."

"What about Jolan?" Oromir asked.

"He and I need to talk."

Oromir hesitated, but Sten and Willem guided him out of the workshop. Jolan listened to their footsteps—wet and thick from the mud—until they faded to nothing.

"The world is changing," Cumberland said eventually. "For a long stretch, war was about training men to fight, keeping 'em healthy, and moving your crew faster than the enemy can move his. Now we're chasing flying ships made from dragon bones." He stared at his hands. "This is the problem with living too long."

Jolan didn't know what to say.

"You don't have to come with us," Cumberland said.

"I don't?"

Cumberland grunted. Studied the shoes hanging from the ceiling. "I know I pressed on you pretty hard—all the business at the mill about tracking you through the jungle if you ran off. That was just pushing hot air, by the way. No way I'd have bothered chasing some kid through the gloom when there's a war on."

"Oh."

"But I won't pretend I can't use you, either. Dunno what's in store at Black Rock, but the odds of needing a healer along the way are pretty good. Damn near certain, I'd say." He turned back to Jolan. "But you've got your own life to lead. I'm not going to take that away from you. You want the door, there it is."

He motioned toward the darkness.

Jolan thought about it for a long time. He thought about the plans he'd made when he left the warren, and how far he'd already strayed from them. He thought of the people he'd saved today, and then all the people that he hadn't. The woman in that yellow dress on the outskirts of town. All the children in the middle of it.

And he thought of Oromir's hand squeezing his own.

"I'll go with you."

Cumberland raised an eyebrow, surprised. "Why?"

"My master taught me that progress and technology was a good thing. For alchemists, it leads to better cures and tinctures and procedures. Better lives for people. But what we saw today . . . all those people hurt and killed." Jolan trailed off. Chewed his lip for a second. "I am not sure that technological progress in warfare is a good thing for Terra. But it is inevitable. Change always is.

But the effect of change must be balanced. If I can help the Dain-wood stand against those ships—even if my part is small—I have to play it."

Cumberland nodded. "A good reason, so far as they go. But I'm thinking there's another one."

"I'm not sure what you mean."

Cumberland clapped him on the shoulder. "'Course not, boy. 'Course not. I forget what it's like to be your age. Nothing makes sense and nothing's certain. Wait till you get older. The fog clears, but your fucking knees hurt all the time. So, it's a trade. C'mon. I'll walk you to the dining hall."

When they reached the spot, Cumberland motioned to it with his meaty hand.

"Head on in and tell the others we're rallying at dawn."

"You're not coming in?"

"Thing about leading a crew, boy, is that sometimes you gotta piss off to keep things level. Everyone needs a chance to unclench their asshole, you know?"

"I guess."

"And tell Willem not to get too drunk. He won't listen, but maybe he'll skip the last few rain ales."

————

Willem, Sten, and Oromir had taken a table in the back corner of the dining hall. The proprietor and all the guests seemed to have fled, so the wardens were helping themselves to a massive keg of ale, the top of which had been broken open by a falling support beam.

"Ho!" Willem called when he saw Jolan. "The alchemist decided to stick it out. You got bigger stones than I thought. Figured we'd seen the last of you once Cumberland gave you a chance at the door."

Willem was already slurring his words. Jolan decided the best time to tell him not to drink too much had already departed.

"Aye," Sten said. "For a smart kid, heading to Black Rock with us is a pretty stupid decision."

"Don't listen to them," Oromir said, motioning for Jolan to take the spot across from him. "Here, I saved you a drink."

Oromir pushed a mug of rain ale across the table—the frothy head had a mouth-shaped hole in it.

"Willem tried to steal it," Oromir explained.

"Yeah, yeah. Whatever." Willem took a huge gulp from his own ale. Burped. "So like I was saying, why're the Papyrians helping us so much? This ain't their war."

Oromir shrugged. "High-Warden Carlyle was close with Ashlyn back in Floodhaven. If I was the empress of Papyria and my niece had been murdered by some Almiran lord who's calling himself the king now, I'd probably prefer he didn't control the whole country, too."

"And now Oromir, amateur political strategist, arrives," Willem said. "Been a while."

Oromir shrugged. "Well, whatever reason they have, you can't argue the advantage of having the widows on our side of a fight."

"No, you cannot," Sten muttered. "Gods but they are murderous women."

"Speaking of the dark-haired devils . . ." Sten jerked his thumb to the door.

A Papyrian woman wearing black armor had come inside. She had a half-full saddlebag slung over one shoulder.

"Must be the other one," Oromir said. "Iko."

Despite the fact that they were the only other patrons in the room, Iko ignored the wardens. She hopped over the counter and fiddled with a stove back there—getting a pot of water boiling with practiced efficiency. While the water warmed, she started rooting through cabinets and drawers—taking whatever bits of dried meat and hard cakes were still available.

By the time the kettle started whistling, Iko had filled the saddlebag to bursting with food. She produced a small ceramic mug from her pocket and tapped a vial of green powder in the bottom. Then she filled the mug with hot water and took a spot on the far side of the hall. Began sipping from the ceramic mug in silence.

Willem smiled at Jolan. "You should go introduce yourself. Offer her some of your ale."

"Uh, no. I don't think that's a good idea."

"Fine, I'll do it then," Willem said, lurching up from his seat and heading over to the keg for a refill. He dunked his mug into the top of the broken keg rather than pouring from the spigot. "If we're gonna travel together, best get to know each other."

"This'll be good," Oromir muttered.

They all watched as Willem stumbled over to the table and offered up his mug. She eyed the drink as if it was a dead rat.

"I do not drink ale," she said in a thick Papyrian accent.

"No?" Willem asked. "Too bad, this is decent stuff."

He went to take a sip, but spilled about half of his remaining ale on the sawdust-covered floor.

The widow turned back to her mug.

"I'm Willem, by the way."

"Iko."

"Nice name. It got a special meaning or anything?"

"No." Iko blew on her tea, then took a sip.

"So, what's that beverage you got there?"

"*Oricha.*"

"Ori-ka?" Willem repeated, butchering the pronunciation. "Any good?"

Iko ignored him. She seemed to have forgotten that he was there. The widow took a few more sips of her tea, then dumped the dregs on the floor, shouldered the heavy saddlebag, and left without a word.

Willem lingered for a few more moments, swaying. Then returned to their bench.

"Appears you charmed her tits off," Sten said.

"Was just trying to be social," Willem murmured into his mug. "She don't drink ale though. Just some Oriki shit. Whatever that is."

"Jade-leaf tea," Jolan said. "It's good for you."

"You speak Papyrian?" Oromir asked.

"A little."

"Huh," Willem said. "Does this, uh, leaf thing get you drunk?"

"No," Jolan said. "But it helps with blood circulation and—"

"Then I don't give a shit about it. Who's for another round?"

The wardens raised their glasses in unison. Willem turned to Jolan. Frowned.

"Don't go soft on me now, kid. Drink with us."

"Uh, yeah. Sure. Just one more, though. Cumberland said that we shouldn't have too much."

"Cumberland says, does he? Best slow it down then." Willem drained his mug and dunked it into the keg again. "Can't go wandering away from Jon Cumberland's advice."

By Jolan's estimations, Willem drank about half the keg of beer by himself.

He looked like he was on the verge of needing a seashell when Cumberland kicked him awake the next morning. Jolan made him a tonic derived from Dainwood beets and ginger, but the hungover warden vomited the whole thing up almost immediately.

"That'll be three silvers," Jolan said.

"Fuck yourself."

Shoshone and Iko were waiting on the western edge of town. Shoshone was adjusting the bridle on her horse when they approached. Iko was eating an apple.

"Morning," Cumberland said.

Shoshone gave a nod of acknowledgment.

"We have horses for each of you," Shoshone said. "Fully rested and outfitted."

Apparently, Iko had been busy that night. Everyone's mount had a full saddlebag of provisions.

"Appreciated. Been a while since we put leagues underneath anything besides our own heels."

"What's the closest crossing?" Shoshone asked Cumberland.

"Grealor's Bridge is closest, but that don't make it the best option. Elden Grealor hired a bunch o' Balarian-trained architects to build the massive thing so as he could move more lumber out of the Dainwood. Those gray-eyes took their work to heart. The bridge has more fortified checkpoints and towers than Castle Malgrave, and Linkon's men control them all. No way we make it across there." He paused. "We'll use the Devil's Confluence—two weeks' ride west."

"Two weeks?" Shoshone asked. "I saw many viable bridges on the map."

"No bridges. Too many turtles on the far side of them."

"I know a place we can cross due south of Mudwall," Jolan said. "I've done it before."

"You've crossed the Gorgon out in the middle of nowhere?" Cumberland asked.

"Yeah. On a raft."

"I thought the boy was a healer," Shoshone said.

"You don't need to train under an alchemist to build a raft. We crossed due south of Mudwall."

"I know that stretch of river," Cumberland said. "You took a raft across it?"

"Yeah . . ."

"How is it that you didn't get eaten by a River Lurker?"

"I actually pointed that out to the person I was with, and we did see one! But we also made it across."

"Well, I'm apparently not as crazy as you, Jolan. We're not messing with any rafts along the warmest section of the Gorgon, where we're more likely to find a gold nugget in our next shit than survive the crossing. Plus, I know every road and path and passable drainage in the Dainwood. North of the Gorgon, not so much. We're better off staying in familiar territory for as long as possible, which means we'll ford at the Devil's Confluence, then skirt west of the Cragnar valley villages on the way into Black Rock." He looked at Shoshone. "Or, you're welcome to find your own way through Almira. But you'll do it alone."

Shoshone reacted to the ultimatum with a long, cold stare.

"Your route is acceptable, warden," she said eventually. "We leave in five minutes."

"Hey now," Sten said. "I need to properly outfit my horse before we take off."

"As I said, the mounts are ready to go."

"The nags might be saddled, but I like my tack done a specific way. And I guarantee that you widows didn't do it right. I need twenty minutes at least to get her perfect."

"Gods you are a pain about your horses," Oromir muttered.

"We ain't all young and spry like you, kid," Sten responded. "Day'll come when you can't just hop onto anything with hooves and speed off, either."

"Enough," Shoshone said. "Ten minutes. Then we go."

8

BERSHAD

Realm of Terra, the Soul Sea, Papyrian Coast

Bershad squinted at the Papyrian coastline, which was shrouded in a low fog that hung among the branches of massive cedar trees. There was a small city on a peninsula, but it was difficult to see—only the roofs and edges of buildings poked through the gray haze. On the other hand, it was easy to make out the half-dozen warships that had dropped oars, raised sails, and started digging toward their lone ship as soon as they'd come within view of land.

"Does the fleet generally move into attack formation like that when you return home?" Bershad asked Jaku.

"No." Jaku spat over the hull. "Not generally."

"What should we do?"

The captain chewed on that for a moment.

"Drop sails. Stay put. Hope they give us a chance to explain before sinking us."

"What are the chances of that?"

"Depends on the captain." He paused. "One o' them mud totems you Almirans like isn't a bad idea."

"What's wrong?" Ashlyn asked, coming up from belowdecks.

"Bit of trouble coming our way, my queen," Jaku said, pointing to the warships heading them off.

Ashlyn crossed the ship. The Papyrian sailors who'd been pointing and cursing about the warships went silent as she passed. Several of them appeared to suddenly remember an urgent task elsewhere on the ship, judging by the speed with which they moved away from her. It had been like that ever since she sank the skyship. The weight of what they'd seen Ashlyn do hung like a dirty secret everyone knew, but refused to say out loud.

The men were in awe of her. She'd saved their lives, after all. But they were scared of her, too.

Bershad studied the approaching ships with Ashlyn. He figured each one could fit two scores of troops in the hull and another dozen archers in the tower nests near the stern. They were hopelessly outnumbered if it came to a fight, especially with Ashlyn's dragon thread ruined.

"The empress will have heard about the fate of the fleet she sent south," Ashlyn said, eyes on the ships. The ocean wind whipped her dark hair around her face. "She's most likely ordered her navy to attack every returning ship on sight."

"Seems awfully hostile," Bershad said.

Ashlyn scoffed. "Hostile is a good way to describe Empress Okinu when it comes to outlanders."

"Got to agree with the queen on that one," Jaku said.

The warships swarmed around their lone vessel. Once their escape was cut off, two ships broke formation and headed straight for them, not unlike the Red Skulls' hunting pattern. Just slower. Their hulls were covered with black iron that had been forged into a pattern of roiling waves and jumping orcas. As soon as they were in range, a score of bowmen appeared on the rail. Crossbows cranked and loaded.

"Ho!" called a man from the deck of one ship. "The fuck are you thinking, bringing that warship back to Papyria unannounced?"

"Didn't have a method of announcement other than showing up," Jaku called, moving toward the gunwale.

"We got orders to sink any ship returning from Almira."

"Why're we still floating, then?"

"'Cause of my discretion." The other captain squinted down at Jaku. He had a shaved head, but his beard was all wisps and empty patches. "Don't believe I know you."

"Captain Jaku."

The man grunted. "Heard the name."

"Who're you?"

"Captain Po."

Jaku gave a nod and a firm, Papyrian salute. "Heard of you as well. My old first mate, Tomkin, did a few turns under your command. Said you knew your business well enough."

"Where is Tomkin these days?" Po asked.

"Swallowed a seashell three summers ago." Jaku paused. "As to why we sailed up on you unannounced, you'll understand when you get a look at my cargo."

Jaku motioned to Bershad and Ashlyn.

Po scanned the ship's deck, lingering on Bershad's tattooed face and then Ashlyn's grim stare. "Who the fuck are you two, then?"

"That's Ashlyn Malgrave, queen of Almira and niece to the Eternal Empress Okinu." He paused. Spat. "And that's the Flawless Fucking Bershad."

"Huh," Captain Po said, beard twitching a little. "Show me your arm, lizard killer."

Bershad stepped forward, attracting the aim of at least a dozen crossbows. He pulled off his jacket, then unbuttoned his shirt and yanked at the sleeve until his flesh was exposed. His arm was covered with sixty-six tattoos of the dragons he'd killed during his fourteen years in exile. More than any other dragonslayer in history. Po licked his lips, eyes fixed on the legend drawn with ink.

"Fuck me."

"Uh-huh," Bershad grunted.

"So?" Jaku pressed. "How about you tell your men to stand down and let us through? We have news from Floodhaven, and it isn't good."

"Aye," Po said. His men's bows stayed exactly where they were. "Word from Floodhaven's arrived ahead of you on a pigeon sent by the widow Shoshone. We know what happened in the muddy capital."

A shadow fell across the ship. Po looked up into the sky.

"Is that a fucking Gray-Winged Nomad?"

Everyone looked up. Jaku cleared his throat.

"It's been following us for a spell. Hasn't caused any trouble."

"It's a dragon. Trouble is all they cause."

"Gray-Winged Nomads aren't typically aggressive toward men," Ashlyn said in fluent Papyrian. She stepped forward. The aim of several crossbowmen moved with her.

Po spat. "I don't know much about dragons, but I know they don't generally heed the declarations of deposed queens." He looked at Bershad. "Might be I should get you a spear and make you deal with it."

"I don't do that anymore."

"No? Restricting yourself to emperors these days, instead?" He pointed at Bershad. "You got a Balarian bounty on your head the size of a fucking whale for murdering Mercer Domitian."

"I set his palace on fire, too."

"Forget the dragon and the Balarians, Captain," Ashlyn pressed, trying to refocus things. "We have urgent news. Let us take it to Himeja."

"Not so fast. Along with the pigeon, we've also had a bunch of merchant galleys coming through who've talked about the battle. They had a little more room for color in their stories, which included tales of Ashlyn Malgrave being a witch who incinerated Cedar Wallace's army with fireballs shot from her mouth."

"Do I look like a witch to you?"

"Being honest, I don't know what a witch is supposed to look like. But I don't know what Ashlyn Malgrave looks like, either." Po scanned the ship a moment. This time, he stopped on Felgor, who was sitting on a barrel, picking at his fingernails with a splinter of wood. "You. I *do* know your face. You're Felgor the Brothel Burner."

"That nickname's not really fair. All I did was char up an attic."

"Let me get this straight. Sitting on this ship, we have a stranger who claims to be a witch queen. An emperor-killing exile. And a notorious thief. In what realm would I bring the three of you within ten leagues of our Eternal Empress Okinu?"

"That's a fair question," Ashlyn said. "But if Shoshone sent that message, she would have also said that I might have escaped Flood-haven on a Papyrian frigate. And Empress Okinu would have given you a way to confirm my identity in the event someone claiming to be me arrived."

Po paused.

"Aye, that she did." Po frowned, clearly concentrating to remember something specific. "The empress asked that any alleged Ashlyn Malgraves tell me the best way to stop an outbreak of bloody runs in a small mountain village."

Ashlyn smiled. "The key is the water sources. In the near term, treat every well, twice daily, with a ten-gallon mixture of equal parts mashed warren apples and Crimson Tower moss. In the long term, any affected village needs a new water source, preferably transported to a single cistern from raised aqueducts that are fed by a spring at high elevation."

Po's expression tightened as he listened. He was clearly hearing the expected information, but wasn't happy about it.

"Aye, all right. My orders are to take you to Nulsine." He motioned to the fog-shrouded city on the peninsula. "The empress will see you there."

"We're not going to Himeja?" Ashlyn asked, frowning.

"No." He looked at Bershad, then back at Ashlyn. "And you'll see the empress alone. The thief and the lizard killer get irons and go into the dungeon until this is sorted out."

"They will stay with me."

"You're expected, Queen. They are not. I follow orders from the Eternal Empress of Papyria, not the witch queen of Almira."

Bershad gave Ashlyn a little shrug at that news, as if to say they should have expected that. She didn't look happy, but he could tell that she knew better than to fight it.

"They are not to be harmed, Captain," she warned.

"'Course not," Po said, watching as Bershad and Felgor were shackled, then led onto his ship.

Just as Felgor was walking past Po, his shackles dropped to the deck with a wooden thump. Felgor held his wrists up and gazed at them in wonder. "Always did have slippery wrists."

"Very amusing," Po said. Then he backhanded Felgor in the face with an armored glove, sending him to the deck.

Bershad was about to jerk forward, but the large number of crossbows aimed in his direction stopped him. He relaxed.

"Captain," Ashlyn called from her spot on the ship. "I warned you."

"Harm's one thing," Po said. "Roughing up an asshole a little is another."

He smiled at Felgor.

"Welcome to Papyria."

9

ASHLYN

Papyria, Port City of Nulsine

"Your widow will remain on the ship," Captain Po said when they docked. The city beyond was sparse and plain, only a few dozen buildings made from cedar huts and slate roofs.

"No," Hayden said simply. "I will not."

For the first time since they'd met him, Po seemed uncertain.

"But you may hold my weapons if I make you so nervous," Hayden offered, pulling her short sword and slings off her body and handing them over.

Po eyed them as if they might be snakes, but eventually took them. He handed them off to another soldier, grunted, and waved for them to follow him into the city. They headed for a medium-sized hut that smelled of chaff and had obviously been cleared of people just several minutes earlier. The signs of interrupted work were everywhere. Bundles of wheat and packets of peat lay half wrapped and packaged.

"Please wait here, Queen," Po said, giving the room a once-over.

"For what?"

Po didn't respond. He was gone again without a word.

For a long time, Ashlyn and Hayden sat in silence.

"I never thank you for the things that you do," Ashlyn said eventually.

"My queen?"

"You've spent more than half your life in service to me," Ashlyn said. "Helping me chase dragons. Standing in corners while I spent hours stooped over an alchemical station. Attending the endless bureaucratic meetings. And then after my father died . . . fighting in all of those battles. You've saved my life so many times, and I've never thanked you."

"You don't have to. I'm a widow. Protecting you is my job."

"Not for much longer."

Hayden frowned. "I don't understand. Have I disappointed you?"

"The opposite. You have been the best bodyguard . . . the best friend that I could have wished for. But whatever I do next, I won't do it as a queen. I don't deserve your help anymore."

"Being queen never brought my help. It was your blood. As long as it is warm in your veins, I am yours to command."

"No, Hayden. I won't. I can't. Against all odds, you've returned safely to your homeland after a lifetime of dangerous service. Now, I want you to enjoy a life of your own."

Hayden seemed to think that over. "I appreciate what you're offering, Ashlyn. I do. But while you can release me from your service, I will always be a widow. And the widows without a charge have their own work to do for the empire."

"Like Shoshone?"

"Yes."

Ashlyn shook her head. "No. Not you. My blood has to earn me some kind of sway over Okinu. And I will use it to grant you the life of peace that you deserve."

Hayden opened her mouth so respond, but stopped short. Looked around. "She's here."

"How do you know?"

"Because we're surrounded."

A score of widows melted out of the shadows without a sound. The door to the hut opened, and the Eternal Empress Okinu came through the other side.

She wore a dress made from a layered series of black and red silks that blossomed around her small frame. Her face was coated with white powder. Eyebrows and lips defined by precisely drawn black makeup. Her black hair wound around her forehead like a serpent, then poured down her back. A widow stood to her left and right.

"Empress," Ashlyn said, bowing low. Hayden did the same.

Okinu stared at Ashlyn in silence for a full minute. With the makeup on, it was difficult to read her age, although Ashlyn knew that the empress had seen seventy-three summers.

"Black skies. I bet one of my widows two gold pieces you were a charlatan." Her voice reminded Ashlyn of old paper rubbed against rough river stones. "But you have your mother's nose. Your father's eyes. And from what Captain Po tells me, a singular knowledge of cures for the bloody runs. It seems I have accrued a debt today, my niece."

Ashlyn dipped her head again. "Thank you for providing me with shelter, Empress. I bring urgent news. Something happened on our voyage that is—"

"Is it true that your old lover assassinated Mercer Domitian in Balaria?"

"He did as I ordered."

Okinu's face darkened.

"You should have consulted with me before taking such drastic action."

Ashlyn swallowed. She knew what Okinu was doing. Putting Ashlyn on her back foot quickly so she would have the upper hand in whatever negotiations needed to occur before she granted them sanctuary in Papyria. She refused to be pushed around.

"I did what was necessary. Mercer Domitian would have up-ended the world."

"Mercer Domitian was predictable. That is no longer true of Balarian leadership. Actus Thorn. Your younger sister. And most of all, Osyrus Ward."

Ashlyn frowned. "You know Osyrus Ward? How?"

Okinu ignored the question.

"Along with your lover's stint of murder in the Clockwork City, there are also quite a few stories about you, my dear niece, and the alleged demoncraft you unleashed before leaving Flood-haven." She motioned to Ashlyn's wrist. "Show it to me."

Ashlyn hesitated. She'd hoped to bring up the dragon thread after a deal was made, but if the empress already knew, there was no way to avoid it. Ashlyn rolled up her black sleeve so that Empress Okinu could see the charred cord wrapped around her wrist.

"What is it?"

"Spinal tissue from a Ghost Moth dragon," Ashlyn said.

"So," Okinu said softly. "You found one, too."

That was not the response that Ashlyn expected.

Okinu read the surprise on Ashlyn's face and smiled. "Did you think you were the only one who was aware of the secrets hidden inside the dragons of Terra?"

Ashlyn licked her lips. "How do you know about them?"

"We'll get to that. First, I want to see you use it."

The widow to Okinu's left cleared her throat.

"Spare me the passive-aggressive throat noises, Chiya." She motioned to Ashlyn. "Well? Do you need to murmur an incantation or something? Get on with it."

"The stories you heard about what I did at Floodhaven are true. But we were attacked several times during our voyage north, and I was forced to use the thread, which is what I was trying to tell you," Ashlyn said. "It was damaged."

"Define damaged."

"You seem to know what these threads can do. Call it a biological phenomenon augmented by alchemical properties. Call it demoncraft. Call it what you like. But I overloaded the thread's capacity and changed its reactive properties. It no longer activates from the catalysts I have available."

"What does it react to?"

"I'm not sure. Maybe nothing."

"Well, that's a shame."

"That is not the only problem we have. I damaged the thread while destroying a flying ship made from dragon bones and steel."

"Hm. One less to worry about, at least."

Ashlyn frowned. She expected more of a reaction to the mention of the ship. There was only one explanation for Okinu's lack of surprise.

"You already knew about the ships."

"Of course. They tend to attract attention, and I have eyes and ears everywhere."

"Tell me what's happened."

"Here is the thing, Ashlyn. When your lover killed Mercer Domitian, all he did was replace one problem with a more brutal one. Balaria is now ruled by a general named Actus Thorn. Your sister and her husband are nothing more than figureheads—it's a military dictatorship, and one on the cusp of disaster due to famine. Mercer planned to solve the problem with trade agreements and a global monopoly on dragon oil. But Actus Thorn is a soldier to his core. Tell me, if you were Thorn, and your country had no food, but they did have a fleet of skyships, what would you do with them?"

Ashlyn thought about that. "Oh, no."

"Yes." Okinu pulled a series of rolled pigeon missives from a pocket. Squeezed them.

"These are reports from the widows who survived Floodhaven. There are not many of them left, but no eyes in the realm of Terra could be more reliable. And they all say the same thing. While you were sailing north along the Broken Peninsula, Linkon Pommol's entire fleet was turned to flotsam. After that, a flying ship made from steel and dragon bones appeared above every city in Almira with a decent-sized Clear Sky market. Balarian soldiers dropped from the ships and stole the harvests. Then the skyships fire-bombed the cities and disappeared. Almiran casualties were very high."

"Why just take the food and leave? If they have that many ships, they can conquer the whole of Almira with them."

"No. They can conquer the whole of Terra," Okinu corrected. "But Lysteria is in full revolt, so for the time being, Actus Thorn and his armies are occupied. But that will not last forever. When Thorn has dealt with the pale-skinned barbarians, what do you think he will do next?"

Ashlyn knew Actus Thorn by reputation. He was a brutal man who had committed terrible atrocities in every province of the Balarian Empire that he had ruled. Now that he had the skyships, she had to assume he would use them to spread his cruelty to the entire realm of Terra.

"I need to go back to Almira."

"With a charred, useless thread on your arm and an emperor-killing exile at your side? No, I think not." Okinu grimaced. "You need to look at the bigger picture. Actus Thorn is certainly a concern. But he is not the root of the problem."

"Who is?"

"The man who built his armada. Osyrus Ward."

Ashlyn frowned. "How do you know that Osyrus built it?"

"Because fifty years ago, that is what I hired him to do. Although I didn't ask him to make them fly."

Ashlyn was unable to hide her surprise. "That is going to require an explanation."

"Yes." Okinu waved at the table in the middle of the dusty room. "I am old. My ankles are swollen and sore. We'll sit."

They moved to the table. Okinu took a moment to gather herself back into a stiff, regal posture. "I heard that you once contracted an alchemist for a full decade to go up to some hill in the jungle and study bees. Is that true?"

Ashlyn shrugged. The alchemist was named Frula. And as far as she knew, he was still up on that hill.

"Aunt. In the last moon's turn, I have sailed hundreds of leagues and I have ended thousands of lives. Just tell me what passed between you and Osyrus Ward."

Okinu smiled. "That's what I like about you, Ashlyn. You cut through the dragonshit. But I am not obfuscating my actions. I asked, because hiring crotchety old scholars is certainly one way to make use of the gray-robes. But when I was a young empress— younger than you are now, in fact—I elected to obtain something more practical out of them."

"Define practical."

"I wanted ships and soldiers armored in dragon bones. My logic being that the only thing better than the largest navy in the world was an indestructible one. And while historically, there have never been many preserved dragon bones in Terra, the ones that do exist are impossible to damage. If some of these things existed, it stood to reason there was a method for mass production. I wanted to find it."

Ashlyn narrowed her eyes. Okinu was speaking plainly, but there was a lot of obscure knowledge wrapped into those words. "How did you come by the information to make these leaps of logic?"

"I stole it from the Alchemist Order's archives in Pargos."

"You what?"

"Imagine for a moment that when you took the Almiran throne, instead of inheriting a mud pit devoid of functioning roads and full of backstabbing, drunken warlords, you'd acquired two thousand highly trained bodyguards, assassins, and infiltrators. What would you have done with them?"

That was a fair point.

"So, your widows stole the method for preserving dragon bones?"

"Not exactly. Despite the layers of secrecy that shroud the Alchemists, most of the documents contained nothing more than theories and speculation. The only actionable intelligence was a location where the mystery could be solved." She paused. "Ghost Moth Island."

"You're joking."

Ghost Moth Island was a myth. A children's story. Some hidden place full of dragons and demons and treasure.

"Oh, I thought it was ridiculous, too. But I assure you the island is quite real. It's located far to the north, deep in the Big Empty. The gray-robes have known its exact location for three hundred years. They've just kept it a secret, buried deep in their vault of records."

"Why?"

"Because they think it holds the secret to immortality." She snorted. "Such a childish venture. But they have been pursuing it for centuries. The reports that I acquired detailed a number of research stations on the island. The last alchemist they'd sent up there was a botanist named Kasamir. Apparently there was some unique mushroom growing there that he had ideas about. Fucking alchemists. They were sitting on a treasure trove of docile dragons, and instead of attempting to make use of them, they decided to play with mushrooms."

"Docile dragons. What do you mean?"

"Kasamir reported an uncommon number of Ghost Moth dragons that began roosting on the northern rim of the island several years into his project. That caught my attention. Given their notoriously meek behavior, I thought this the perfect place to send my own agent, task in hand. I couldn't hire an alchemist, seeing as I was using stolen information, so I did the next best thing: hired someone who had been expelled from their order."

"Osyrus Ward."

"Yes."

"Why did they expel him?"

"He told me it was because of a violent curiosity. That struck me as an oversimplification, but I didn't care."

"Why?"

"Because he was the perfect mixture of young, ambitious, intelligent, and completely devoid of moral blockades. He was not unlike you, Ashlyn. Minus that last part, of course. Osyrus will push every limit that he encounters—collateral damage does not even register. These were all valuable attributes given my objective.

But they came with a rather large cost down the line. It is costing me still."

Ashlyn remembered what Bershad had told her about his time as Ward's prisoner. The amputations. And the clinical way in which he carried them out. Imagining that man having influence over Balaria's skyships made her stomach burn.

"What did he do on Ghost Moth Island?"

Okinu pushed a sheaf of documents across the table.

"Best you read it firsthand. When Osyrus Ward departed, we agreed that I would send a supply ship every six months to keep an open line of communication. This was the message he sent back on the ship that delivered him."

13 Noctar—210

To the Eternal Empress Okinu,

I have found the island. Currently, I write to you on the outskirts of a thick and untamed wilderness unlike anything I have previously studied in the realm of Terra. As your intelligence promised, Draconis wisp somniums are as common as rabbits and as docile as newborn deer. In addition to their inexplicable population density, there are countless novel species of flora and fauna. A remarkable type of Cordata mushroom grows from the ground in great sizes—some are taller than aspen trees. From a single day of exploration, I have also identified fifteen new beetle species, three mantises of incredible color, and the tracks of an ursine mammal that are so large, I can only assume they belong to an undocumented species as well. Certain areas of the island—when explored—throw my compass and instruments into a flurry of confusion. It stands to reason there is a powerful magnetism to portions of the bedrock, which can potentially be mined and crafted into lodestones.

Your instincts were correct in sending me here. The alchemists have left all manner of tools and research stations around the island over the years. I am positive that I will be able to discover a preservation process and use it to build Papyria an armada that will make the nations of Terra quiver. The only uncertainty is time. I can make no predictions without setting baselines, which will take one year.

Incidentally, I have made contact with the lone alchemist on the island. The botanist. Kasamir. He has discovered some interesting properties of the Cordata mushrooms during his search for eternal life.

But he has no sense of scope. I will still keep him around for a time.
His work might lead to more practical applications in the future.
   Do not worry about him. Your orders were clear.

                                                   —Osyrus Ward

"What orders is he referring to?" Ashlyn asked.

"Ward's work was to be kept secret. From Terra, and more importantly, from the Alchemist Order."

"I see."

Ashlyn turned to the next report, which was scribbled in a hasty, angry hand. There was no address, date, or signature.

Stop sending your peons into the island's interior. They disrupt my work. When I have something to report, I will leave it for them on the beach.
   But if you require an update so badly, here:

— *Ninety-seven* Draconis wisp somniums *(Ghost Moths) dissected.*
— *Anomalous nerve tissue found on the spines of four specimens. Tissue is preserved without treatment, but electrostatic charge is lost. Further study required.*
— *Skin preservation method successful. A tanning tonic derived from Specimen 01 can be diluted and produced at scale.*
— *Bone preservation requires a higher concentration of fluid. Designing the apparatus now.*

   I will give you more information when I have it. Make sure the supply deliveries are on time and leave me to my work. I require a decade. Maybe two.

"Crotchety man," Okinu muttered to herself as Ashlyn read.

"What is this Specimen 01?" Ashlyn asked.

"Those notes are the closest you'll get to answers. Keep reading."

Ashlyn moved to the next report. The last.

                                             29 Lomas—221

To the Eternal Empress Okinu,
   I have perfected the bone preservation process. The details would require thousands of pages of explanation, so I will skip them. There

is nothing stopping me from constructing your dragon-bone fleet. The raw materials are already refined. I have also designed a prototype set of armor, but I am unhappy with the limitations and long-term side effects of use.

However, after my time on the island, I have realized that we are aiming far too low with our objective. The refinement process of the Ghost Moths has uncovered far more compelling possibilities.

I have been so focused on preserving animals that are prone to rot that I have ignored my ability to create something new which never decays.

You sent me to this island to build ships and armor, so that you might defend yourself against the chaos and rage of this world. But I can do better. I can end the chaos. Replace it with order. I can forge perfection.

The path will be long. Messy. But this island has opened the door to a world in which weapons and armor are no longer necessary because the animal-grasp for resources and power that afflicts Terra like a plague will be over.

My creations will replace the undignified meat sacks with which we are held prisoner. And you will be their goddess. A truly eternal ruler of Terra. Aeternita will shudder with jealousy to behold you.

I have already begun the process, but to proceed with human trials, I require two hundred souls sent to me on the next supply ship. They should be healthy, strong laborers. No dungeon scraps. No diseases. But they should also be people who will not be missed. The trials will claim many lives.

In return, all that I ask for is a place by your side, ruling the perfect world I shall forge for you.

—Osyrus Ward

Ashlyn put the paper down. Gave Okinu a look.

"When I read that fifty years ago, I assumed that the decade of isolation had bent Ward's mind to madness. An easy conclusion, seeing as the man was always a little unhinged to begin with. When I first met him, he walked around with a glass jar on his hip filled with flesh-eating beetles devouring a fox's head. And this talk of meat sacks and goddesses . . . it's insane."

"Insane or not, the details of what he was proposing are not clear." That information about preserved spinal tissue was compelling— perhaps this island was the place where she could forge another thread. The rest of it was concerning. "Ward sent no other information?"

"None."

"Did you send him the people he requested?"

Okinu licked her lips. "No. I sent soldiers to bring back the dragon bones that *I* requested in the first place."

"What happened?"

"That is what you are going to figure out."

Ashlyn frowned. "You don't know?"

"My soldiers never returned. I sent more, of course. Again, nothing. Eventually I sent a widow who was so lethal she makes Shoshone Kalara Sun look like a declawed house cat. She never returned. Papyria is a wealthy country, but there is a limit to the number of frigates and highly trained warriors that I will dispatch into the Big Empty to no effect. Time passed. My sister married your father. The Great War started, and the powerful fleet I *did* possess was required to end it. I moved on, assuming that Osyrus Ward had perished, along with a vast sum of my resources. I abandoned my ambitions of commanding a dragon-bone fleet. But it appears my dreams were—as he said—aiming too low."

She paused.

"I need you to travel to Ghost Moth Island and uncover what Osyrus Ward did there. Bring me back a way to stop him and the Balarians."

Ashlyn kept her face blank. Waiting to see if Okinu would reveal more information.

"Of course, you are under no obligation," Okinu said after a long silence. "You've had a long journey, and this would require that you embark on another one immediately. Any sane person would—"

"I'll go."

Okinu smiled. "Such conviction. Why?"

"Because I started something in Almira, but I didn't finish it. And the answers I need are on that island."

"Good. I was confident you'd do the right thing."

Ashlyn narrowed her eyes. "You speak as if this is entirely my mess to clean up, but *you* created this problem when you financed Osyrus Ward fifty years ago."

"Let's skip the part where we blame each other for causing this goatfuck. Osyrus wouldn't be nearly as big of a problem if you hadn't assassinated Mercer Domitian."

"Why not?"

"Because Mercer kept that insane greaseball busy with the production of clocks and copper curiosities, and ultimately he held Ward's leash and maintained at least a modicum of respect for other nations. Now that he's dead, there is no way to predict what Ward will do next, but mark my words, before the spring thaw he will outsmart Actus Thorn and use that fleet to destroy Papyria, and any other nation that is in his way."

"On what are you basing such certainty?"

Okinu paused. "Before he disappeared, Osyrus sent one, final message to me. I've kept it close for all these years as a reminder."

She pulled a piece of paper from an inner pocket of her robe. Held it out for Ashlyn to take and read.

To the eternal Papyrian dog,

You will never see me again. But when your horizon is filled with calamity, know that it was me who filled it. Me who killed you and turned your country to chemical burns and ash.

You corrupt rulers. This corrupt world. I will take it from you all. Then I will fix it. Make it clean. Make it perfect.

—Osyrus Ward

Ashlyn gave the paper back. The ravings of a madman were one thing. But a madman with access to an armada of skyships needed to be stopped.

"If I'm going to do this, I need to know everything that you know about this island. Starting with the exact location."

Okinu smiled again. "Chiya. Map."

10

BERSHAD

Papyria, Port City of Nulsine

"This isn't bad, so far as dungeons go," Felgor said, looking around their cell. "Nice little window there—probably gets sunlight for twenty or thirty minutes a day. Only seen three rats so far."

"Five," Bershad corrected.

"Still pretty good. And they even laid out hay for us to sleep on!" Felgor flopped down on the wet and moldy bedding. Inhaled as if he was smelling lavender perfume instead of putrid dungeon rot. "Not too bad at all."

Felgor produced a nail from between his toes and begun rubbing it against a stone on the floor.

"What's that?"

"Lockpick."

"Good," Bershad said. Being confined to such a tight, dark space made him itchy and anxious.

"I think I swallowed my tooth," Felgor complained, tonguing the gap in his mouth. "Might be it flew into the water, but I don't think so."

"Your teeth are small. Shouldn't hurt too much crapping it out."

"Hey, I can't regrow pieces of my body like you. A lost tooth is a big deal."

"Uh-huh."

They were both quiet for a few minutes.

"You know," Felgor said. "Since we've met, I've spent a lot more time in chains than I'd prefer."

"You were in chains when I met you."

Felgor squinted. "Was I?"

"The boat to Argel. Vera had plucked you from the Floodhaven dungeon."

"Oh right. I got caught robbing that highborn brothel during their weird orgy. Good times, my friend."

"How many brothels have you robbed in your life?"

Felgor weighed that. "Ninety-four. So being caught a handful of times isn't bad, in terms of a percentage. Raw numbers are unfair when you deal in the volumes of Felgor." He scratched his chin. "Although your dragon-killing volumes are similar, now that I think about it. Hm. Well, we can't all be flawless like you, can we?"

Bershad shifted around a little. He didn't like thinking about his reputation, and all the black deeds behind it. "How'd you get the name Brothel Burner?" he asked.

"That? Oh, that was a total misunderstanding that got blown way out of proportion. You see, I was up in the attic with a particularly lovely maiden, and she was using a big candle to drip wax on my—"

"Never mind," Bershad said. "How's that coming?"

Felgor looked down at his work.

"Got some bad news for you there."

"Which is?" Bershad shifted a little so he could glare directly at Felgor.

Felgor motioned to the cell door, which was made from black iron bars. "I can make a pick for pretty much any lock that ain't a Balarian seal, and even those have some weak spots I'm curious to explore. But I can't reach that lock from in here. See those long struts running out of sight to the left?" He pointed with his half-carved pick. "The keys are inserted into a lock on the far end o' them. Impossible to open from the inside. Papyrians know how to build a dungeon, I'll give them that."

"Felgor," Bershad growled. "If you couldn't reach the lock, why carve a pick?"

Felgor shrugged. "Something to do. And it improved your mood considerably. From the look on your face, I see that lovely period of time is now ending."

"There has to be a way out."

"There is," Felgor said, going back to his carving. "Wait for a jailer to open the door and let us go."

"That's not a plan. That's just waiting around."

"We have a queen on our side. Sometimes waiting around is all you can do. Don't tell me I've got more faith in your lover than you do?"

Bershad gave him a look.

"What?" Felgor asked. "We all know the details of your gross little love saga over the years. *And* we know what you two were doing in that private cabin each night while we sailed north. It was a small ship, and you weren't very quiet."

Bershad didn't say anything.

"Anyways, the two of you make a good couple," Felgor continued. "The Lizard Killer and the Witch Queen. Play practically writes itself."

"I got enough fucking plays about me already."

"And there isn't a single one about me yet, just inaccurate nicknames," Felgor muttered. "A brutal injustice."

They were quiet for a while. Bershad picked at the scab on his palms. Felgor continued to carve the useless lockpick.

A while later, the sound of an iron door opening farther down the hall echoed through their chamber. Bershad straightened up. Felgor disappeared the lockpick between his toes. Gave Bershad a confident nod and a smile.

Captain Po came to their cell. He had a grim look on his face, and was followed by ten more soldiers.

"Think you brought enough assholes with you?" Bershad asked.

Po ignored the comment. "By the orders of Her Eternal Majesty, you and the Brothel Burner are to be released into the care of Queen Ashlyn Malgrave at once." He delivered the news in a flat, monotone voice. "She is waiting for you in town."

Felgor sprang up and cracked his knuckles. Smiled at Bershad.

"Told you."

———————

Po marched Bershad and Felgor to a small hut on the edge of town. The place smelled of cheap wheat and good peat moss—earthy and thick. Ashlyn was sitting at a half-broken table, sipping from a ceramic cup while sifting through a pile of maps and papers.

She looked up when they came in.

"The empress and I have come to an arrangement," she said. "You're both free to go."

"She ordered them free from the dungeon," Po said, grabbing Felgor by the back of his neck. "But this slippery bastard's not spending another second in Papyria. I'm sailing you past the jetty and dumping you in the sea."

"You will do no such thing, Captain Po," Ashlyn said, putting her cup down. Po frowned at her, but didn't move.

"You will take Felgor to the closest dining hall in this town and give him as much food and ale as he can fit inside his body. Then you'll take him to the most expensive brothel, where he will be treated as an honored guest. Any expenses he accrues between now and midnight will be taken from your salary, Captain Po."

Po's face turned red with rage.

"But that could be my entire fucking—"

"I told you not to harm them, Captain Po. You disobeyed me. A month or two's salary is a small price to pay for loosening the teeth of a queen's friend." Ashlyn turned to Felgor. "Thank you for what you've done for me and Silas. I trust you'll enjoy yourself."

Felgor beamed at that news, his remaining teeth on happy display.

"Felgor," Bershad said, grabbing the thief by the shoulder. "Have your fun, but do not steal anything, clear?"

"Nothing? Or nothing people'll miss?"

"Felgor."

"Fine, fine." He put his hands up in mock surrender. "To the Squatting Loon we go!"

"I'm not taking you to the Loon," Po said. "Their companions cost three silvers an hour."

"And they're worth every shaving."

Felgor put his arm around Po and started walking out of the room as if they were old friends.

"And how many hours are left in the day?" Felgor continued as they walked. "Eight? Nine? Don't worry, I'm not one of those one-and-done-type men. I generally got three or four good ones in me each day, and I've been a bit clogged up from the voyage, if you know what I mean. The widows on the ship were not flirtatious."

"I'm going to kill you, thief."

"Sounds good," Felgor said happily. Bershad noticed that Felgor lifted something from the captain's belt just as they were moving out of sight.

"Thanks for that," Bershad said to her.

"I did it for you, too."

"An open tab at a brothel?"

"A chance to say good-bye." Ashlyn motioned to the maps. "You and I have a very long and dangerous journey ahead of us."

Bershad frowned. "Where is Hayden?"

"I sent her back to Himeja with the empress." She paused. "You and I need to do this alone."

Bershad sat down across from Ashlyn. "Tell me."

When Ashlyn was done explaining everything, Bershad reached for the pitcher and refilled Ashlyn's cup, then poured one for himself. It was warm tea that smelled of jade and cinnamon. Bershad took a sip. Wished that is was rice wine.

"The empress will get us a ship?"

"We leave tomorrow."

Bershad sipped the tea.

"Surprised that you managed to convince Hayden to leave."

"She wasn't happy, but widows are obligated to follow direct orders from their empress. And Okinu understood. I won't let Hayden die for me. Not when she's finally home and safe. I won't do it." She looked at him. "I've said my good-byes. Go say yours."

Bershad bowed his head. He could tell that Ashlyn wanted to be alone.

He headed for the door.

"Silas?" Ashlyn called, stopping him. "If you get into the whores while you're out there, I'll smell it on you when you return. And you'll pay for it."

That smallest of smiles spread across her lips.

"Wouldn't dream of it, Queen. Wouldn't dream of it."

Bershad found Felgor in the common room of the Squatting Loon. There were three low fires and several long tables. He counted five other patrons and fourteen companions—seven men and seven women. All of them were wearing thin black skirts and nothing else. They were all beautiful.

Felgor was naked except for a silk breechcloth. He was drinking from a half-gallon jug of rice wine.

"Silas!" he called when he saw Bershad walk in. "Silas, you old bastard! Come drink with me."

Bershad took a seat and then a long gulp from the jug. It was chilled and smooth.

"This place is pretty nice for some harbor city brothel," Bershad said, looking around.

"Now you're revealing your ignorance, Silas. Harbor cities always have premium brothels. First stop for freshly paid sailors who've just spent the last few moons staring at the same grubby faces all day. Man'll part a hefty portion of his new coin for an unfamiliar and beautiful bed companion."

"So will a woman," one of the male companions murmured with a smile.

Bershad scanned the room a moment longer.

"Where's our friend, Captain Po?"

"Gone." Felgor smiled. "That asshole was on the verge of tears when I rounded the corner on my second jug of wine. Probably because these things cost half a silver each. But we have an open line of credit all night."

Bershad looked at the jug.

"Best order two more, then."

"Agreed."

Felgor whistled to the barkeep—a woman with swirling black tattoos running down both of her sinewy arms—to bring them more.

"So, already had your fill with the women?" Bershad asked.

"Please. This is just the first of many intermissions. Isn't that right, Kiko?" Felgor asked, raising his glass to a nearby companion with bolts through both nipples and her nose.

"You gonna talk the entire time again, Balarian?" Kiko responded.

"Probably," Felgor said. "My cock wears out long before my capacity for conversation."

Kiko shook her head, but she was smiling.

"How'd it go back there?" Felgor asked.

"I didn't get my head cut off and Ashlyn wasn't burned alive for being a witch. So, not bad, I guess."

"Not bad, he says. Fuck, man, lighten up, will you? Think of all the shit we survived. The Razorbacks. That nightmare in Taggarstan. And it wasn't that long ago you were bolted to a table in a dungeon getting your limbs cut off by that crazy old man. Things can't get much worse than that."

"Things can always get worse, Felgor."

He took another long gulp of wine. Grimaced.

"What's the problem, Si?" Felgor asked, watching him.

"Ashlyn and I have a long journey ahead of us. Out to a place called Ghost Moth Island."

"Never heard of it. Anything to steal out there?"

"It's a pirate hideout in a freezing wasteland to the north."

"Sounds terrible." Felgor cracked a smile. "Might be you wanna head upstairs and get a little professional comfort before you go back to sleeping in a fucking boat?"

"I'll pass."

"Aye," Felgor said. "Wouldn't want the witch queen hearing about that type of thing."

"Careful, Felgor. She doesn't like that name."

Felgor grabbed the jug, smiling. "You know how I can tell you love her?"

"How?"

"That little jab *actually* pissed you off, instead of you just pretending it did." He took a sip. "It's good to see."

Bershad grabbed the jug back. The rice wine helped cool the discomfort of being indoors and surrounded by people.

"What'll you do next?" he asked Felgor.

"You mean, what'll I do after I'm paid, right?"

"Sure."

Felgor pursed his lips. Thought it over. "Well, islands are shitty places for a thief to operate. Nowhere to run."

"Ashlyn's going to give you two hundred pieces of gold, Felgor. Even for you, that's enough to take an extended vacation, at least."

"I'm hurt, Silas. After all this time, you still don't understand me. I don't steal things for the money. Never did."

"Why, then?"

"Because it's fun. People put too much stock in gold and riches. I like watching their faces when I relieve them of their burdens." Felgor polished off the wine jug. His face got serious. "Gonna miss you, Silas. You're the best friend I've ever had."

"I'll miss you too," Bershad said. And he meant it.

Felgor gave Bershad a slap on the shoulder.

"But you need to be more careful without me around to protect you."

"Is that what you've been doing all this time?"

"You've got a shit memory, dragonslayer. I've saved your life more than you've saved mine."

Bershad frowned, thinking.

Felgor sighed, and started counting on his fingers. "You killed that Skojit in the Razorbacks right before he caved in my head, but I rescued you at the docks. The dungeon. *And* I found the moss after the battle of Floodhaven. Three to one. That's significant."

Bershad smiled. "Fair enough."

"I can't believe we've been together since you dropped down into the hull of that Papyrian dogger in the Floodhaven harbor. Last spring. Been almost a year."

Bershad narrowed his eyes. "You gonna get weepy on me?"

"Not drunk enough for that. Yet." Felgor raised a jug. "But when two bastards tear a swath of mischief and destruction across not one or two, but three different countries, and then part ways as friends, they got to get shit-hammered together on their last night. That is the law."

"Whose law?"

"Mine. Felgor's Law."

Bershad hesitated.

"C'mon, don't tell me Ashlyn has you whipped that bad already. Anyway, that asshole Po is buying. Remember?"

Bershad ran a hand through his beard. It was probably the last time they'd ever see each other.

"One more jug. That's it."

"Another jug, he says!" Felgor shouted, motioning to the barkeep.

———————

Eight jugs of rice wine later, everyone in the Squatting Loon was sweaty from dancing and red in the face from drinking. Bershad felt the warm buzz of wine in his belly and head. Felgor was crying on Kiko's shoulder.

"I just . . ." he muttered, sniffling a little. "I'm gonna miss him, that's all. Not afraid to say it. A real man doesn't cram his emotions down in his guts. That kind of stubborn repression leads to an early trip down the river."

"Poor Felgor," Kiko said, cooing at him and pressing his face into her tits. She gave Bershad an expectant look.

"I'll miss you, too, Felgor." He paused. "You're a true friend. And in this shit world, that's a rare thing."

Felgor turned to him. Eyes wet. "A true friend," he repeated in slurred words, nodding his head.

He was about to pass out. Bershad stood up.

"I'm shoving off," he said. "And I'm taking this with me. You've had enough." Bershad snatched the last, half-full jug of wine from the table. "Stay out of trouble until you get paid, yeah?"

"Sure," Felgor muttered, eyes closed. "Outta trouble."

Felgor started snoring with his head cradled in Kiko's arms.

"Poor thing," she said.

———

Bershad walked back to the rooming house Okinu had cleared for them. The streets were quiet, and Bershad took occasional pulls from the jug. Even though he'd put more than a gallon of expensive and strong wine into his belly, he was barely drunk. A year ago, he'd have blacked out from that kind of drinking. Woken up with splinters in his cheeks from the barroom table.

The Nomad was circling overhead. She'd mostly stayed above the clouds during their journey, but now that Bershad was in one place—and night had fallen—she was drifting lower.

The closer she got to him, the sharper his senses became. The odor of earthy pitch rising from every chimney filled his nostrils as it mixed with fresh lavender and lilac incense that rolled out of the rice-wine shops and public houses. The wheels of wooden carts rolling over a distant cobblestone street thundered in his ears. He passed an alley cat and could smell mouse blood on her paws.

"Best keep your distance," Bershad whispered to the Nomad. "Don't wanna set off the lizard alarm and cause the whole city to crap themselves. Or start firing arrows at you."

To Bershad's surprise, the dragon seemed to hear him. She caught a thermal and headed back above the clouds.

"Huh."

The innkeeper told him that Ashlyn was in the bathhouse attached to the main building. Bershad crunched along the small gravel path leading to the separate structure. He yanked his boots off and laid them by the door before entering. Steam and heat rushed out of the room when he opened the door.

"Sorry," he muttered, moving to close the door again.

"No," came Ashlyn's voice. "Leave it open for a second. It feels good."

Bershad stood for a moment between the heat of the room and the cool night air.

"Okay, that's enough. Get your tattooed ass in here."

Bershad had to take a few steps into the hazy steam before he could see Ashlyn. She was leaning back in a small cedar tub—breasts and arms rising out of the water. The sawtooth lines on her scars were ignited from the heat of the water, pulsing bright blue. She'd removed the bandage on her arm, leaving the charred thread visible. There was an empty glass of rice wine on a small table next to her.

"Brought more, if you're thirsty," Bershad said, lifting the jug.

"Just a little," Ashlyn said, holding her thumb and forefinger an inch apart.

Bershad came over and filled her glass to the brim.

"I said a little!"

"It's a small glass."

"And that's a huge jug of wine," Ashlyn said. "How do you drink so much without passing out?"

"Practice."

He took off his clothes. Ashlyn smiled as he struggled with the buttons of his shirt.

"You've slain sixty-six dragons, but still can't conquer a set of buttons. How is that possible?"

"Life's full of contradictions."

He stepped into the tub, which was just big enough for both of them to fit if they intertwined their legs. The water level rose to the lip of the tub, but didn't spill over.

"What have you been up to?" he asked.

"Trying to get more information about this island. Osyrus Ward was extremely opaque in his letters. The other alchemist—Kasamir—published dozens of reports, but they were all focused on the cultivation methods and medicinal applications of Cordata mushrooms. He had some interesting ideas for healing degenerative tissue, but that doesn't do me any good right now." She paused, lost in thought for a moment. "We need more current intelligence, but most of what I've found is focused on reasons to avoid that stretch of the Big Empty entirely."

"What kind of reasons?"

"Well, the whole area around the island is a hunting ground for Naga Soul Striders. So that's a natural deterrent. Most sailing charts and captain's logs that I dug up don't even mention the island, just the dragons that can tear a merchant carrack in half with a single tail swipe."

"And the ones that do mention the island?"

Ashlyn sighed. "They read like drunken tavern stories. A Ghala-marian admiral who allegedly shipwrecked on the island wrote an account. He said that it's a demon-infested wasteland with an open hole to the underworld in the middle, and claimed his entire crew was eaten by demons. He barely escaped with his life and braved the Big Empty on a raft made of flotsam."

"Colorful."

"Oh, that's just the beginning. In Taggarstan, it's apparently common knowledge that Ghost Moth Island is home to a band of murderous pirates who sold their souls to the demons in exchange for black magic. Dragon scales grow from their skin, wretched and blackened teeth sprout from their mouths. They eat everyone aboard the ships they raid and never leave survivors."

"If they kill everyone, then I guess they're splitting time between the island and telling stories about themselves in Taggarstan."

Ashlyn snorted. "You of all people should know how rumors go. There's a kernel of truth that gets inflated each time it passes from one drunken mouth to the next, until you have an enormous drag-onslayer with a foot-long cock pissing down the neck-stumps of decapitated dragons."

"Or witch queens shooting fireballs out of their nether regions."

"Who said that?"

"One of the companions at the Squatting Loon."

"Ugh. That's as crude as it is inaccurate."

"I know. And the rumors about you will probably only multiply while we're sailing to this remote island." He leaned forward and gave her a long kiss. "On the bright side, before we plunge into this demon's lair, we've got one night together on a bed that doesn't rock back and forth constantly."

Bershad was about to move in closer, but she pushed him away.

"Seriously, you smell like a distillery. And I bet Felgor is on the floor of the Squatting Loon if he tried to keep up with you." She studied him. "Has it always been like that?"

Bershad leaned back on his half of the tub with a sigh. He knew he wouldn't get anywhere until he satisfied Ashlyn's curiosity.

"No," he admitted. "My hangovers never last long, but I spent most of my exile stone drunk. Don't even remember some of the dragons I killed. But ever since Burz-al-dun and the dungeon . . ."

"Osyrus Ward changed you."

"Removing and regrowing my limbs was bound to have an impact."

"Sure. But sometimes I wonder if that part is a symptom of some other alteration. You said that there were jars and beakers in the workshop when you woke up."

"I did?"

"Yes. What was in them?"

"I don't even remember saying that."

"Try, Silas. Try to remember."

Bershad thought back. "When I woke up, they were empty."

"Osyrus might have injected the contents inside your body. Sparked the regrowth of your limbs in the near term, along with other changes. A higher tolerance to alcohol would mean increased liver function."

"What does it mean to have a dragon following me around?"

"I don't know, but it's all connected somehow. And it all leads somewhere."

"But you don't know where," Bershad finished.

"No."

Ashlyn looked away again. Started chewing on the thumbnail of her left hand, which gave Bershad a clear look at the thread wrapped around her wrist.

"Do you want to talk about the fact that those black lines running along your veins are growing?"

She flinched. Put her hand in the water. "Not particularly."

"Looks like they've spread about four finger's widths since the day it happened."

"I said I didn't want to talk about it."

"Sure. We can dissect the changes to my body that were brought on by brutal torture to your heart's content, but the dragon tissue that's bound and spreading through your body is obviously an off-limits subject. That's fair."

"I'll figure out what's happening to both of us," Ashlyn said, rubbing her wrist. "But the answers are on that island, not in this tub."

"True. But there are some interesting things in this tub that are less mysterious." Bershad lowered himself a little further into the water and started running his hand up her leg. "You can try to understand what's happening to us both all you want. But it won't change who we are. Comes a point, you just have to accept your fate and enjoy the time you have left."

"That's a terrible strategy."

"Strongly disagree," Bershad said, as his hand drifted above her knee, and then higher still.

"Careful, dragonslayer," Ashlyn warned.

"Always." Bershad slipped one finger inside of her. Ashlyn let out a slow breath. "But if you're not interested in the current moment, we can keep talking about liver function and dragon threads and—"

"Shut up," Ashlyn whispered, putting one hand on Bershad's submerged forearm and squeezing her nails into his tattooed skin. "And keep doing that." She pulled him a little deeper inside of her. "Right . . . there."

For a few minutes, there were no sounds except moving water and Ashlyn's rising breaths. Her cheeks and neck flushed, and she arched her back with pleasure.

"Mm," she said, opening her eyes again afterward. "Well, seeing as you can't get drunk anymore, there's no way you've had too much wine to give me a proper fuck before we go to this island, correct?"

Bershad smiled.

"Correct, my queen."

PART II

11

CASTOR

City of Taggarstan

Castor watched with disgusted fascination as Vallen Vergun ate his breakfast.

Vergun was eating the same dish he'd eaten the previous morning, and every morning since Castor had entered his service: a heavy slab of gray-pink meat, seasoned with pepper and turmeric. Both spices were ludicrously expensive. Imported from Juno, the land beyond Taggarstan. A little juice lingered on Vergun's pale lips, which were the same color as the rest of him: bone white.

The only part of Vallen Vergun that had color was his bloodred eyes.

The origin of his daily carnivorous breakfast was a source of wild rumor and conjecture in Taggarstan. Half the city was convinced that Vergun ate part of a human every morning. The other half believed it was just an odd cut of pork, although their conviction never stood on firm ground.

The meat came from a back-alley butcher named Lim, whose larynx had been removed with a spoon twelve years earlier over some kind of unpaid debt. The man sold meat to nobody else, and all attempts by curious criminals to gain clandestine access to Lim's ramshackle warehouse had failed. The only man who'd ever managed to creep through a back window never came out again, fueling the rumor that he'd become Vallen's breakfast the following morning.

Personally, Castor was constantly trading sides between the cannibal and swine camps. Today, the dish was markedly reminiscent of a plump woman's bottom. But yesterday's had been very lumpy and piglike.

Castor suspected that this waffling doubt was exactly what Vergun wanted his meals to achieve. Most people will be afraid of a man who might eat people for breakfast.

Vergun stabbed his meat with a fancy silver fork that only a baron or prince would use, but cut it with a massive knife made from a dragon's tooth. That blade generated almost as much attention as the meat Vergun cut with it. Far as Castor knew, it was one of a kind.

And so was the man he'd taken it from.

Castor hadn't been in Taggarstan for Vergun's duel against the Flawless Bershad—an issue with a crooked smuggling crew had taken him to Graziland on a flat barge. But according to the flood of rumors that surged through the city upon his return, Vergun had crippled Bershad, killed his donkey, and taken his priceless dagger before throwing him in a riverboat to die. Some of the alleged witnesses said that Vergun also ate Bershad's foot and made the poor bastard watch.

Castor didn't believe the foot thing, but the dagger aspect was undeniable. Vergun flaunted the evidence of it during every meal, despite the fact that the weapon was better suited for stabbing bears than slicing plated meat. When Castor had asked Vergun about his choice in cutlery, his boss had said that he enjoyed the dichotomy.

Castor knew what *dichotomy* meant—Horellian guards were trained to operate in the Burz-al-dun palace without sounding like simple thugs—but he couldn't puzzle out why it was enjoyable in this instance.

"Tell me again," Vergun said, putting a fresh slice of juicy meat into his mouth before finishing his sentence. "How exactly did Tumbler Tom manage to lose my Papyrian asset and put the Dice Den belly-up in a single night?"

Castor fidgeted. "Well, I wasn't there personally, so—"

"But you are here now, giving me the information. So, give it."

Tumbler Tom was the proprietor of Tumbler's Dice Den—a high-end gambling establishment that was bankrolled and silently owned by Vallen Vergun. The fact that Tom had gone bankrupt last night meant that Vergun had lost a decent amount of his own money, too. So things were tense.

"As I understand it, boss, the incident didn't occur in a single night, but rather a single dice game that lasted for two and a half days."

Vergun swallowed his food. "That's very precise, Castor. Thank you. That's why I always jump at the chance to hire disgraced members of the Horellian Guard—you've lost your moral bastion, but retained your eye for detail. What's the saying about Horellians? Twice the size of a widow, and almost half as dangerous?"

The mention of Castor's past made him cringe. "I don't like comparing the two, boss."

"Why not?"

Castor shrugged. "Never had much use for generalizations is all. I'll leave the clever adages to the tavern dwellers who piss themselves at the sight of widows and Horellians both."

"Mm." Vergun smiled. He tapped the side of his temple with the dagger. "Continue."

"There was a stranger who arrived earlier this week. Method and vessel unknown. There are reports that he spoke with a Balarian accent, but others say it was Ghalamarian. And others still insist it was Lysterian. The physical descriptions of the man are oddly varied as well—some say he was tall, others short. There are reports of a mole on his face that seems to travel from his chin to his forehead with alarming alacrity for a skin condition."

"Skin condition," Vergun repeated, as if the words were the key to some locked door in his mind. "What next?"

"Well, the rest is pretty simple, actually. The man was gambling with Balarian bank credits. He lost seven thousand gold to various patrons whilst playing dice over the course of many hours. At that point, he declared himself bankrupt and asked Tom for a loan that was twice the value of the coin he'd lost. The stranger even volunteered to eat a twenty-percent interest rate on repayment, should it become necessary. Tom was all too happy to agree to these terms, despite the fact that this put him in a position where his entire vault was leveraged."

Vergun sucked on his teeth. "And I assume there was a winning streak in this stranger's near future."

"An unbroken one." Castor took a breath. "And with dice, that only means one thing."

"He was cheating."

"Yes, boss."

Vergun tapped his index finger against the massive knife. "Why didn't someone kill him?"

"Things happened very quickly after the streak. It seems the man had a beast of burden ready to relieve Tom of his stores in such short order that nobody thought to murder the man before he was in and out of the vault."

"And where is this man now?"

Castor cleared his throat. "He disappeared."

Vergun continued tapping his knife for a few more seconds—staring at his meat.

"And the Papyrian?"

Castor shifted. That had been the crap icing on shit cake. A goatfuck within a goatfuck.

"He hanged himself in the vault sometime during the confusion."

"How does a man who is fully restrained and in possession of less than half of his fingers procure and tie a noose, then strangle himself with it?"

The Papyrian man who'd been imprisoned within Tumbler Tom's vault was an interesting piece of business. Apparently, he was some well-informed minister in the Papyrian government with a head full of state secrets and military intelligence. Vergun had bought him from a crew of corsairs with plans to torture him for information, then sell that intelligence to the highest bidder at an extreme markup. It was a complicated and indirect method of generating coin, but an extremely effective one. One of the reasons that Horellian guards and widows existed was to prevent this kind of thing from happening. But there were always occasional foul-ups.

"Dunno, boss. Tom was managing the situation."

"Yes. Where is Tumbler Tom?" Vergun asked, voice soft with suppressed rage.

"Just outside. Figured you'd want a word."

"No," Vergun said. "Just cut his throat on your way out and dump him overboard."

"Over fourteen thousand gold?"

"I don't give a shit about the gold that Tom lost in his rat-infested establishment. But that Papyrian's secrets were worth hundreds of thousands, and he lynched himself before turning over a single shred of a valuable information." Vergun cursed. "Tom's stupidity has spoiled a major investment, so I do not want to see Tom ever again. Kill him and get rid of his body."

Castor's stomach tightened. He'd learned the hard way that there was nothing to be gained from questioning Vallen Vergun once he'd decided to end a life. And voicing doubt over the decision's wisdom was an easy way to lose one of your own fingers, ears, or even tongue.

"Understood, boss."

He waited to be dismissed, but Vergun failed to give the perfunctory hand wave that meant he was finished. Instead, he looked out the small aft window, red eyes distant and unreadable.

"I am sick of this nonsense," Vergun muttered.

"What nonsense?"

"Making investments. Idiots allowing those investments to hang themselves. The endless smuggling of opium into Burz-al-dun in exchange for the dregs of dragon oil. It's . . . uninteresting."

Vergun was one of the most powerful and wealthy men in Taggarstan, and he was bored? Castor didn't know what to say to that, so he kept his trap shut.

"What about Silas Bershad?" Vergun asked. "Any information?"

Vergun always asked him about the legendary dragonslayer. Castor required every last drop of his soldier's discipline to avoid glancing to his right, where the heads of Liofa and Devan sat in pickled jars. Castor *had* been in Taggarstan when Borgon—the drunk riverboat captain who'd taken the crippled Bershad into Balaria—had returned with the severed heads of Vergun's lieutenants.

Apparently, Bershad hadn't been quite so crippled as previously thought. He murdered Devan and Liofa, along with a large number of their smuggling contacts in Burz-al-dun. Then Bershad sent Borgon back with the heads and a message that he was coming for Vergun. No specifics on when that'd happen, though.

Vergun had been so angry that he set one of his own ships on fire while a large number of his crew were still inside. Most got out, but not everyone. Vergun had vowed to keep the heads while he waited for Bershad. Saying he would make him eat their pickled brains before killing him.

"Actually, yes."

Vergun's red eyes snapped back to Castor. "Why didn't you start with that?"

"Word came in late last night. And with Tumbler Tom's whole situation—"

"Forget it. Tell me."

Castor blew out a breath. "The Madman sent word down the canal. Said that he had an . . . interaction with Bershad while he was in Balaria, and knows where he'll turn up next."

"Where?"

"Osyrus says that information has a price."

"I see. And what does the royal engineer of Balaria want in exchange?"

"The three best killers you have sent up to Burz-al-dun for a wet job. Said that if it works out, he'll come down and give you the information personally."

Vergun was quiet for a moment.

"Send him Gyle and those Lysterian twins."

"Rike and Wun."

"Whatever." Vergun smiled at Castor. "You're my best, Castor, but you stay with me. Those three will suffice for whatever mischief the Madman has in mind."

Castor agreed that those three weren't as good as him. Nobody in Taggarstan was. But they were about as vicious and competent as Vergun had among his ranks of criminals and enforcers, which were growing by the day. Last Castor checked, Vergun had nine hundred and seven men on his payroll. Almost a proper legion. There were whispers that he was rebuilding Wormwrot, his old mercenary outfit. Just hadn't said it out loud yet. Given his complaints of boredom, the rumors just might be true.

"I'm on it," Castor said.

Vergun nodded. Finally dismissed him with a wave.

Castor drew his sword and went to see about Tumbler Tom.

12

VERA

Balaria, Burz-al-dun, Imperial Palace

Vera had been attending the feasts and celebrations of royalty ever since she first came to Almira as an eighteen-year-old widow. She'd become accustomed to standing guard while enough food to feed an entire village of peasants for a week was served to a few scores of highborns. They'd eat their fill, then cast aside the ample leftovers so they could continue drinking and dancing and—in Almira, depending on the crowd and the moon phase—engage in a sweaty orgy.

But the galas that Ganon Domitian threw nearly every night in the name of Aeternita, the Balarian time god, put even the most opulent Almiran feast to shame.

There were three statues of Aeternita in the room, each one made from a different metal—gold, silver, copper. Each statue was packed with so many synchronized clocks that passing by them felt like listening to a metallic heartbeat. Where Almirans favored dark rooms and earthy smells, everything in this room was brightly lit by freshly polished dragon-oil lanterns. Strange contraptions shaped like massive beehives filled the corners of the room and wafted aromatic steam in different flavors. Pine. Lavender. Peach.

While the metal decorations were unfamiliar, the food was not. Vera recognized the pineapple, rice, and salted pork from the fields and harvests and slaughterhouses of Almira. So did Kira.

"It's a disgrace," she muttered.

"Empress?" Vera asked.

"They've taken it all for themselves," Kira continued. "Every ship that came back from Almira brought their plunder directly to the palace, where it's been stockpiled. No rations made it to the slums or the working districts, and half of what's here won't even be touched tonight."

"This is what you expected, though. Correct?"

"I didn't think there would be *enough* for all districts, but I did think they would at least attempt to feed the hungry. But to take it all for themselves. It's unforgivable."

"I agree."

To their right, Ganon was pointing and laughing at a clockwork automaton spider that Osyrus had brought to the gala. Its metal limbs creaked and whined as it walked. Steam sprayed from a vent tube in the center of its body.

"A metal pest!" Ganon shouted, cheeks red and eyes full of drunken excitement. He motioned for a nearby Horellian guard to hand over his automatic crossbow. "And like all pests, it must be squished."

Ganon squeezed the trigger. Held it down. Four bolts tore into the spider in rapid succession. One bounced off the automaton's armor and skittered into the crowd, forcing a skinny minister who was wearing seven bracelets to duck for cover—his jewelry spraying across the floor. The other three bolts punctured the metal core. The spider limped and stumbled in a disturbingly natural series of death throes, then crashed onto the floor with a steel shudder.

The repeating crossbow was another one of Osyrus Ward's inventions. Actus Thorn complained that they jammed too frequently to be used in combat, but apparently Osyrus had recently designed a new model that was far more reliable.

"The pest is slain!" Ganon shouted. People around him smiled and cheered. Applauded. "What do you think, my muddy wife? Shall I get a spider tattooed to my arm?"

"If you wish, my dearest husband."

Kira kept a smile plastered on her face until Ganon's attention was snatched away by a servant arriving with pork buns and another bottle of bubbled wine.

"I am married to a child," Kira muttered in Almiran, low enough so that only Vera could hear. "A beautiful, fully grown infant. Gods."

She glared out at the gala for a few moments in brooding silence. Then stood.

"Well, if my husband is going to drink and shoot automatons all night, then I will have to do the real work myself."

"Which is?" Vera asked, standing as well.

Kira just smiled, then strode into the thick of the gala.

"Minister Ato," she said, switching to Balarian and greeting the pudgy man with a warm smile. "How is your wife recovering from her illness?"

The minister bowed. "Quite well, Empress. I must thank you for the alchemist that you sent to us. But I am curious, how did you—"

"I spoke at great length with one of Lady Ato's dear friends at a gala earlier this week, and she informed me of her ailment. I could not sit idly by and do nothing! I am so glad to hear that she is doing better."

"Yes. Much better."

Kira leaned in close. "Although, now that she's recovered, I fear that your hobby may suffer."

"My hobby?" Ato asked. "Whatever do you mean?"

"I'm referring to the orgies you secretly attend in the basement of Lochmoran Hall, Minister Ato. I believe you visited fifteen times last month. Certainly that level of attendance qualifies as a hobby."

"I-I don't know what you're talking about," Ato stammered.

Neither did Vera. She couldn't watch Kira every hour of every day, but she was quite certain that the empress had not been to an orgy since she'd arrived in Balaria. She had certainly not been to fifteen of them in the last month.

"Oh, yes. I forget such things are taboo in Burz-al-dun. In my country, it's the people who forgo such delights that become pariahs. Isn't it strange how different two cultures can become just from the separation of a tiny little sea?"

Kira taunted Ato with a wriggling index finger. Ato looked like he was about to shit himself.

"Of course, from what I hear, there's nothing tiny about you, Minister Ato." Kira nibbled the tip of her finger. "I heard a rave review from Mistress Brazar."

Vera wasn't as good with Balarian socialites as Kira, but she knew Mistress Brazar because she was—according to the rumors—expected to be engaged to Actus Thorn within the month.

"Mistress Brazar? But I never—"

"She was the one in the red fox mask, last time. Tell me, do you always do that thing with your tongue, or is it only on special occasions? Don't you get tired after a while having it all twisted up inside—"

"Empress! Please. Please stop talking." Ato shook his head, jowls wriggling. "I beg you. I had no idea that was Mistress Brazar in the mask."

"Relax, Ato. Relax. It'll be our little secret."

She put a hand on his chest, which caused Ato to jerk backward so fast he nearly fell over. Kira closed the distance again like a cat.

"But shared secrets are precious commodities. I would be foolish to keep such a big one for free."

Ato's face hardened. He was a minister, so he recognized Kira's prelude to extortion. "Anything. Name it."

"Velesar Nun is going to approach you tomorrow and ask for a seal permit for Fort Edgemar, with administrative access to all areas. You are going to give it to him."

"Edgemar? On the Lysterian front? That is highly unusual—regulations do not permit that level of access to anyone except for Echelon One officials. Nun is Echelon Three. They'll never approve—"

"They approve it, or Actus Thorn finds out where your tongue has been traveling."

Ato's left temple was pulsing. His cheeks were purple. "I'll figure something out," he croaked.

"I am confident that you will. Velesar will come to you first thing tomorrow, so you best leave and start the figuring-out right now."

After Ato stumbled away, Vera grabbed Kira by the arm and pulled her close.

"Ki, how did you know all of that?"

"Oh. I found a chambermaid who shares a likeness with Mistress Brazar and paid her to attend their sad excuse for a proper orgy in a red fox mask. Apparently, she had a wonderful time, which surprised me. I've been screwing highborns my whole life, and I've never met one who wasn't selfish in bed."

"I wouldn't know."

"Not sure I believe you, Vera. But that's a conversation for another night. Velesar Nun is right over there, and turning the corner on his third drink. The perfect time to strike."

Before Vera had time to ask more questions or restrain her very young, bold charge, Kira had crossed the room and attracted Nun's attention with a light touch to his forearm.

"Minister Nun, good evening. Are you enjoying yourself tonight?"

"Insomuch as one can enjoy a useless event," the minister replied, keeping form with the military's outlook on Ganon's numerous and lavish celebrations.

"I know. My husband's a fucking moron."

Nun's eyes widened. Suddenly, she had his attention.

"Are you surprised by my candor, Nun?"

"I suppose I shouldn't be," Nun replied, suppressing his momentary vulnerability. "Your people have a reputation for barbaric manners."

"We do," Kira agreed. "But having now spent time on both sides of the Soul Sea, I can say that surface-level manners are the only real difference. In your hearts, you Balarians are just as wild and devious as Almirans. You just cloak yourselves in false, polite skin."

"Cloak ourselves," Nun repeated. "What does that mean, exactly?"

"Where to start? You call us a country of muddy warlords, but a third of your empire is currently rebelling against you and forcing a bloody, vicious conflict. You say we live in the wilds and subsist like animals, and yet Balarians had to steal my homeland's harvest last month in order to keep the so-called civilized lords fed. Meanwhile, the slum districts go hungry and more rebellion foments." Kira paused. Lowered her voice. "And on a personal level, your spouse plays the part of pious, dutiful wife to you. But I know for a fact that she has been screwing Grakus Flay every Monday for the last three years."

Nun's jaw tightened. "Liar."

"Monday at eleven thirty? Is she typically in your presence at that time?"

More jaw clenching.

"My wife has a standing appointment with her sister for tea on Mondays."

"She has an appointment for something, but tea is not involved. Nor is her sister, to my knowledge. But who knows?"

"I don't believe you."

Kira shrugged. "That is your prerogative. But consider this: General Kun shipped off to Fort Edgemar three weeks ago to lead the Lysterian offensive. The first time he has left Burz-al-dun in three years, since he returned from the Ghalamarian campaigns. Did his departure date perchance coincide with a sudden and consistent cancellation of your wife's tea appointments?"

Nun said nothing for a long time. Ganon laughed drunkenly in the background. He was still holding the crossbow, but one of his Horellian guards had the good sense to unload it.

"I am going to kill that bastard," Nun concluded.

"I completely understand that desire," Kira said. "But it will be difficult, given his location. Edgemar is quite restricted with the war."

"I'll find a way."

"I can help, if you wish."

Nun glared at her. "Why?"

"Because even barbarians know what it's like to be betrayed. We don't enjoy it, either."

Nun said nothing, but he didn't walk away, either.

"Go see Minister Ato in the morning," Kira continued. "He will give you everything that you need to exact your revenge."

Nun's eyes narrowed. "I suppose you'll want some favor down the road for this."

Kira smiled. "Let's worry about that after you've shoved Grakus's cock down his own throat, shall we?"

Nun nodded. "Deal, Empress."

Vera kept an eye on Nun as he stormed his way through the crowd, leaving the gala.

"Do you see it yet, Vera?"

"I see you filling this gala to the brim with everyone's shit."

"They filled their own pots. I'm just stirring things up."

"To what end?"

"You'll see."

Ato and Nun were the only people that Kira manipulated with such graphic fervor, but she flirted and gossiped with ministers for hours. Despite having been the empress of Balaria for only a few months, Kira had managed to perform some small kindness or minor favor to almost every minister in the room. When she hadn't specifically helped them, a flirtatious touch of a shoulder and glimpse down her low-cut gown was often enough to get a minister talking—and sharing more information than they should. Who was having an affair? Who was addicted to opium? Who worshipped the wrong gods? Who was greedy? Who was loyal? The politicians of Balaria were more than happy to fill Kira's rumor quiver with ample secrets and leverage. Vera had to admit that Kira's ability to effortlessly siphon sensitive information from people was impressive.

Up on the dais, Ganon was attempting to reload his crossbow with a dinner fork. One of his Horellian guards—a man named Pij—was trying to get him to stop while the second—Thrash—scanned the crowd with careful, relentless eyes.

There were thirty-three Horellian guards at the gala, but those two typically stayed closest to Ganon, so Vera had learned as much as possible about them. Unlike the widows, who were trained from birth, Horellian guards were hand-plucked from the standard military ranks after proving themselves in battle. Pij and Thrash had both earned their positions by killing Ghalamarians in large quantities during their rebellion ten years ago.

Kira continued mingling. She joked and laughed and built small alliances, one secret at a time. Eventually, she circulated toward the outskirts of the gala and snatched a glass of bubbled wine from a servant.

"This place is more of a rat's nest than Floodhaven court—everyone vying for the smallest advantage over their peers. No priorities beyond their own self-interest." Kira took a sip of the wine and surveyed the thinning crowd. "It's thrilling to make them dance."

"*Thrilling* is not the word that I would use."

"Oh, come on, Vera. Don't pretend you don't sometimes feel the same way. Perhaps not from political subterfuge, but I've heard stories about the thrill of battle. The bloodlust. Did you not feel that up in the Razorback Mountains, cutting your way through the Skojit to reach me?"

"Bloodlust makes people sloppy. It is a weakness, not an advantage."

"This is why people joke about widows having ice water in their veins," Kira said, smiling. "Does my work seem sloppy to you, Vera?"

"It seems risky," she responded. "If Nun composes himself between now and tomorrow, he might start to wonder why Ato is providing him such special access. They could talk, and your extortion would be revealed."

"Maybe. But Nun is a very long way from wrapping a rope around his composure."

"All the same, you are making the job of protecting you extremely difficult."

"If you're so worried about it, go talk to Osyrus Ward about that name you brought him. He should have run down the details by now, and the full moon is not far off."

Vera glanced at Osyrus Ward. She wasn't eager for whatever the next part of his dragon-oil caper involved, but Kira was forcing her hand.

"I'll talk to him," Vera said.

"Good." Kira emptied the last half of her bubbled wine in a single gulp and set it aside. "While you're doing that, I'm going to have a little chat with the chief minister of city levies. He looks just drunk enough to be talked into relaxing the taxes on our municipal fisheries."

"By the way, Empress, you should adjust the top of your gown," Vera said, pointing to the place where the top of her areola was showing. "You're revealing a lot of skin."

"Oh, Vera. The key to all of this is giving people a glimpse at something they want, but shouldn't have. You tease it, so they can imagine the rest of it, hiding just out of sight. Then you let them salivate until they'll do anything to get the complete picture, regardless of whether it makes sense or is in their own best interest or actively against it. That minister is going to relax those taxes, and he'll do it for nothing more than a long look at the top of my left nipple."

"And why do the fisheries deserve a tax break?"

Kira smiled. Glanced at the enormous clock set in the middle of the room. "This gala will be over soon. You need to get an update from Osyrus Ward, and I need to torment that minister. After we're both done, let's go back to my chambers and spar."

"I've told you many times before that training after drinking isn't a good idea."

"I used to watch the wardens of Almira practically drown themselves in ale before riding off to a skirmish."

"The wardens of Almira are savages."

"Ha! I knew you felt that way, I've just been waiting for you to admit it. But savages or not, a little training after a gala burns my hangovers away and helps me relax. Thirty minutes?"

Vera sighed. Truth was, sparring with Kira was her favorite part of the day, regardless of the time and circumstance.

"Thirty minutes."

Vera broke off to speak with Osyrus Ward, who had pulled his mechanical spider into a corner and was unscrewing the shield plate with a long, crooked tool. He stopped fiddling with the machine when he saw her approach.

"It took me two months to build Bartholomew," he said. "Our emperor destroyed him in a few drunken seconds. Pity."

"You name those things?" Vera asked.

"Of course. They are my creations. And everything needs a name."

Osyrus ran his hand over the puncture marks on the spider in an oddly tender way—as if it was a favorite dog who'd been ravaged by wolves. Vera found the gesture unsettling.

"Maybe you shouldn't build expensive toys for drunken emperors."

"I did not build Bartholomew for Ganon. I built him for me. But the emperor visited my workshop for a hangover cure and saw him. Took an interest. He is nothing if not keen on ways to make these gatherings more . . . exciting. And here we are." Osyrus sighed. "You have not been serving the rulers of this world for as long as I have. Mark my words, they will always disappoint you, Vera. Some with careless cruelty, like Ganon. Others, with a narrow-minded hunger for power that precludes true vision, like Actus Thorn."

"Kira is a ruler of this world. Does she disappoint you?"

"Not so far. Perhaps she will be the anomaly that I have been waiting for. The ruler with true vision."

Vera took a long look at the spider. "What vision compels you to build mechanical insects for fun?"

Ward tucked the tool he'd been using into his dragonskin jacket. Looked at Vera. "We humans are made of such flaws. I seek to build creatures who are unburdened by defects."

"Something cannot be beautiful without flaws."

"Is that a Papyrian outlook?"

"It is my outlook."

"Interesting. But I respectfully disagree. True beauty lies in perfection."

"Actus Thorn did not make it sound like there was a lot of perfection occurring in your laboratory below the castle."

Ward smiled. "Yes, he mentioned his disapproval for my work in the council meeting, didn't he? You need not be concerned. My work is not sinister. Just messy. The path to perfection always is."

Vera didn't trust the word of Thorn or Ward, so she'd checked the sublevels of the palace in an attempt to learn the truth for herself, but the laboratory had been completely cleaned out by Thorn's men. The only thing that remained in the sublevels was charred bricks and rat shit. That was unfortunate, but so was the fact that Vera's list of assets and allies was desperately short. The reality was that if Osyrus was willing to help her build contingency plans to ensure Kira's safety, she didn't really care what he'd been doing in that basement.

"Have you learned where Clyde Farus is smuggling his dragon oil?" she asked.

"You were hesitant at the start of this. Why so eager now?"

"I just want the job done."

"Well, my informants are making progress," Osyrus Ward said. "I hope to have the location for you within a few days."

"Hope? Before, you made it sound like it would take you no time at all."

"Farus is a cautious man—using a large web of intermediaries and shell registries to conduct his business with the Malakar crime family in Taggarstan. He runs all their black-market dragon oil out of the city—a job you do not keep long if you are stupid. To be honest, I am curious how you managed to suss out his name so quickly."

"I had to kill four men."

"Is that a lot for you?"

"It is a lot for anyone."

"Hm, well, they were criminals. Violent deaths are an occupational hazard. Once I determine where Farus will be stockpiling his next shipment of dragon oil, I will need you to go fetch it for me."

Vera narrowed her eyes. "I cannot steal a shipment of dragon oil by myself."

"No, no of course not. Knowing that Farus is a creature of the Malakars, I have already seen fit to drum up some qualified assistance."

"What assistance?"

"Three mercenaries from out of Taggarstan working for a competitor outfit. They're competent. And untraceable back to you or the empress."

"Taggarstan? You're joking."

Vera had been to Taggarstan. It was a nest of criminals and murderers and thieves.

"Trust me, Vera. This is the best way to get what we need. The only way."

"You must earn my trust, Ward. You haven't done that yet."

He bowed his head. "I look forward to the challenge."

———

Vera blocked Kira's jab with her forearm, then slapped the empress of Balaria on the side of the head with an open palm.

"Ow!"

"You're dropping your hands," Vera said. "You do it when you're sober, too. But the bubbled wine makes it far worse."

They'd retired to Kira's bedchamber and cleared the sofas off the carpet in the middle of the room. Vera had removed her armor and Kira had changed into a black tunic and simple pants that allowed for kicks and lunges.

"Again," Vera said. "Try an *iga* counterattack this time."

Vera advanced and threw a powerful but obvious kick directly at Kira's chest. The empress sidestepped, batted Vera's leg away with a strong push, then went for Vera's throat, belly, and groin. Vera blocked and dodged the *iga* sequence, but the attacks were done well.

"Good. Again, but this time use an *oroku* sequence."

They met in a flurry of blows and blocks and grunts.

"Decent. But keep a firmer wrist. Remember, your hand is the blade."

"My hand is the blade," Kira repeated, looking down at her arm.

"Free-form this time. Be unpredictable. Focus on improvising. Go until your lungs give out."

They started again, shifting and grappling and wrenching each other's bodies. Vera let Kira stay on the offensive, dodging each strike and launching a quick counterattack. At the twenty-nine-minute mark, Kira collapsed—gasping for air in big, heaving breaths.

With most disciples, you had to force them to find their limit. But Kira always pushed herself to the breaking point on her own. In a widow, that was the sign of a dedicated warrior. But in an empress, Vera was not sure what the trait portended.

"Quiz me," Kira said, still gasping.

Vera shook her head. Suppressed a smile.

"Weakest points on an armored man with a gorget. In order."

"Armpit, thigh vein, elbow joint."

"Missed one."

Kira chewed her lip. "Eyes. Eyes after armpit, depending on the man's height."

"Correct." Vera paused. "Why did you go through so much effort to send Nun to Lysteria in a fit of jealous rage?"

Kira smiled. "Ah. The topic shifts from battle to politics."

"That wasn't politics. That was extortion and manipulation."

"Like I said, politics."

"Answer my question. What's special about Nun?"

"He's not special at all. But his rage is potentially useful. With administrative access to Edgemar Fortress, there is a very good chance that he will successfully kill General Grakus when he arrives. That will leave a hole at the top of the military command that can only be filled by one person."

Vera thought about that. "Actus Thorn."

Kira smiled. "Correct. Grakus served under Thorn for decades— so he was the logical choice to run the campaign. Corsaca Mun would have been another good candidate, but Thorn sent him to the western coast of Almira to captain the *Time's Daughter*. If Grakus dies, Thorn will be deprived of trustworthy subordinates to manage the armada's first real campaign. So he'll do it himself. And while everyone agrees the Lysterian revolt will be short-lived, Actus Thorn will still be gone from Burz-al-dun for at least a few weeks. And that is all I need to remove him from power."

"You're going to arrange a political coup in a few weeks?"

"There's no need. The Balarians wrote their laws much differently than Almirans. As emperor, Ganon is certainly within his rights to appoint a prime magnate to rule in his stead, but the ministers can override the appointment with a seventy-percent majority vote."

Vera dropped her hands. "Kira . . ."

"Of course, this would have been much easier if Ganon had simply dissolved Thorn's position when I asked him for the fiftieth time. But he is uniquely stubborn when it comes to shirking his duties as emperor. So we'll do it the long way. The first step was getting Actus Thorn out of the city for a while—the ministers would never call a vote while he looms over them. But once he is gone? There are plenty of powerful politicians in Burz-al-dun that harbor no love for Actus Thorn. And plenty of ways to change the minds of those who do."

"I see."

Beneath all the gossip and lies and complex manipulation, there was a certain simplicity to her plan.

"Just watch. Actus Thorn will return from Lysteria to find his job legally dissolved. No coups. No bloodshed. Just politics. Of course, Ganon will become overwhelmed by the position within hours, but this time, I will be there to help. And before long, I will be in control of this empire."

Vera wasn't sure things would be quite that simple. But the general plan was sound.

"And that last thing with the fishery taxes, how does that fit in?"

"That's separate. The minister of fisheries is named Freemon Pence. He's an unimportant bureaucrat, but those fisheries are one of the few places within the city limits that produce food. Relaxing his taxes might open the door for me to compel Pence to send an allotment of fish to the slum districts."

"Where is the political advantage in that?" Vera asked.

"No advantage. It's just the right thing to do."

Vera gave her a measured look.

"Okay, okay. Pence is also one of Ganon's closest drinking companions. I will compel him to keep my husband occupied while—as Ganon would put it—I fuck about. But there is no reason that I can't do some good for the people while I oust their militaristic overlord."

Vera smiled. "Caught your breath?"

Kira nodded. "I'm ready."

"Good. *Ichikaro* feign this time. Make me believe the lie. You're going to need the practice."

13

BERSHAD

The Big Empty

As promised, Empress Okinu provided Bershad and Ashlyn with a fully stocked ship to sail north, beyond the Soul Sea and into the vast ocean they called the Big Empty.

There were several sets of armor in the ship's hold. Steel plate. Lamellar. A decent chain-mail hauberk. Problem was, nothing fit. Bershad tried three breastplates, all of which felt more like torture devices than protective garb. There were several well-made pairs of steel-shinned boots, but he couldn't cram his feet into any of them. Nothing worse than ill-fitting shoes on a long walk, even if he could heal the blisters each night.

"Seems that Papyria isn't used to accommodating warriors of your stature," Ashlyn said, making a quick inventory of the charts, food, and alchemy supplies while Bershad sorted out his armor. Okinu had also stocked the ship with almost every type of alchemy ingredient there was, including ten ounces of Gods Moss.

"I'm not that big."

"Above average for an Almiran. Makes you a giant in Papyria."

Bershad tried a set of molded black leathers that looked a little larger than the other options. The breastplate had heavy buckles along the ribs that he was able to loosen enough so he could breathe. The gauntlets and boots were snug, but workable. There was no skirt to cover his thighs and groin. No pauldrons. No gorget. It was far lighter protection than Bershad was used to, but at least it came close to fitting. And seeing as they were headed out to sea, he didn't hate the idea of wearing something that wouldn't turn him into a human anchor.

For weapons, Okinu had provided the pick of the armory. Three short swords, two perfectly balanced and honed Papyrian blades, and an array of spears. Bershad tried each, but didn't like their feel. The swords were meant for a much shorter man. And after fourteen years of Almiran ash spears and Rowan's custom points, the Papyrian lances felt like waterlogged sticks. He put them back and turned his attention to a massive sword that was hung against the stern wall. From tip to pommel, it was almost as tall as he was.

He took the sword off the wall. In addition to the length, the blade was two hands wide, even at the tip. Not only did its size make most Papyrian swords look like daggers, but it put Almiran greatswords to shame, too.

"Never seen a blade like this," he muttered.

"It's called a Curdachi," Ashlyn said, looking up from her work. "Means 'giant's iron.' But I'm pretty sure that's an antique that came with the boat, not one of Okinu's gifts. Is that really the one you want to use?"

"If we're going into the territory of cannibal pirates and demons, I'll need something with heft." He examined the blade, which was made of good steel, but dull and rusted. "And cleaning it up will give me something to do on the way."

The journey to Ghost Moth Island took them northeast along the foggy and cedar-clad Papyrian islands until they left the Soul Sea and entered the open ocean beyond. Bershad had never seen the Big Empty before, but now he understood how it had earned its name. The massive, swelling waves heaved and churned across an endless expanse that made the familiar waters of the Soul Sea feel like a subdued and sheltered lake in comparison.

For two days, Bershad and Ashlyn sailed across the open ocean without seeing a single speck of land. Just waves and high clouds and the Nomad, circling overhead. The smell of salty brine dominated everything.

But on the third day, Felgor emerged from the ship's hold, rubbing a hand through his greasy hair.

"By Aeternita, I think I'm still hungover from that brothel," he said.

Bershad blinked. "Felgor, what the fuck are you doing here?"

"Oh, after you left the Squatting Loon, I had a long, long chat with Kiko. And it was decided that you're not ready to strike out on your own just yet. I'll come along and watch your back." He smiled. "Plus, I heard a rumor that the pirate hideout on that island has a king's fortune of loot tucked away in their vaults. I wouldn't be a respectable thief if I didn't risk a little peek." Felgor examined the ship's rigging. "And judging from the state of all this, you two could use a capable captain. This here is all wrong. Damn travesty of seamanship is what it is."

"Where were you hiding?" Ashlyn asked. "I've been in and out of that hold constantly."

"And I should have been able to smell you," Bershad muttered.

Felgor smiled. "Secrets of the trade, my friend. Secrets of the trade. You can't smell everything, Silas."

Bershad looked at Ashlyn. She shrugged.

"He's your friend, so it's your choice," she said. "But it's too late to turn around, so he comes along or goes overboard."

Which was no doubt why Felgor had hidden for so long in the hold. The Balarian gave Bershad a shrug. "What'll it be, Silas?"

"You can join us. But I better not hear any complaints if things get rough."

"Do I ever complain?"

"Constantly."

"Huh." He scanned the horizon. "Well, I'm gonna go below and look for something to drink. You never sail sober if you can avoid it—that's another one of Felgor's Laws."

"*Oh, the Red Skull stalks in the mountains high while the empress sleeps and softly sighs!*" Felgor bellowed. Paused for a drink. "*And the red moon rises in the darkened sky while Aeternita watches with her copper eye!*"

"Felgor," Ashlyn said, not looking up from the map she was scrutinizing. "Please be quiet."

"You don't like the song? It's a Balarian classic."

"I liked it the first five times. But we're well past the fiftieth performance. It's distracting."

"I know plenty of others, that one is just my favorite. I could sing—"

"Please. No." Ashlyn raised her sextant and made a few calculations. "We need to adjust course, anyway. Three degrees north-northeast."

Felgor got up from his spot and moved over the wheel. "Aye, aye, Royal Navigator. Three degrees north-northeast. Coming right up."

Bershad was the worst sailor among the three of them, so he

spent most of his time sharpening the Curdachi. After a few days of careful attention he got the blade gleaming and sharp enough to split a hair.

On the morning of their tenth day on the ocean, Bershad clambered on deck an hour or so after dawn, carrying a bowl of rice and pickles in one hand and a heavy ermine cloak in the other. Every morning was colder than the one before it.

"Here," he said, offering the cloak to Ashlyn, who was sitting near the wheel and poring over more documents that she'd brought with her. Information about the island that Okinu had given her.

"I don't need it," Ashlyn said, breath puffing in the frigid air.

"Really?"

To keep warm, Bershad was wearing the thickest wool shirt he could find, plus a heavy oilskin cloak. Felgor was bundled up in so many furs and wool and his own oilskin that he looked like a swaddled baby. But all Ashlyn wore was black riding leathers and heavy boots, plus a dark blue and lightly armored vest from the hold, which she wore overtop a white shirt with long sleeves that obscured her wrist.

"Only you could get so absorbed in a book you don't realize how cold it is out here," he said.

"It's not that. I'm just not cold."

"I'll take hers," Felgor said, shivering under his layers. "'Cause I feel like I got a rod of ice jammed up my ass."

"All yours, I guess," Bershad said, handing it over. Felgor added it to his layers with rushed desperation.

Bershad watched the water. There was a pod of orcas skimming the surface—dark fins slicing in and out of the surf.

"Find anything useful in those?" Bershad motioned to her papers.

"By most accounts from the last decade, the island is a nest for flesh-eating demons that maraud the Soul Sea with impunity, arriving on a strange fog and leaving the same way."

"Sounds like more tavern stories," Bershad said.

"The details, yes. All this business of demons with scaled skin and dragon jaws attacking ships from a blanket of mist is nonsense. But I also have insurance records from four different outfits that specifically void policies to merchant vessels that go anywhere near the place we're sailing."

"So?"

"If the stories were just stories, these companies wouldn't bother with a clause like this."

"Dunno," Felgor said. "In my experience, insurance companies will take pretty much every chance they can get to properly fuck you over."

"You have a lot of experience with insurance policies?"

"Lot of experience compelling rich folk to test the strength of 'em." He smiled. "I like to check in after a score, see how they fared. It's often very problematic for them."

"Anyway, this is good news," Ashlyn said.

"Heading into an uncharted island, known for demoncraft or piracy or both . . . how is that good?"

"Because if there is anything consistent about the world of Terra, it is that technological advances are frequently confused with demoncraft. If there are people on this island—and if they are marauding ships and collecting a reputation as demons—then there's a good chance they're using something that Osyrus Ward left behind. Remnants of his research. His machines." She looked at her wrist. "If we're lucky, he might have also left behind enough dragon threads to destroy the Balarian skyships."

"Pretty sure I used up all my luck killing dragons for fourteen years," Bershad said.

He glanced up at the Nomad.

"Can you feel any others?" Ashlyn asked, following his gaze.

"No. Just her." Bershad watched her a while longer. "How much further, do you think?"

"Another day. Maybe two. Due north."

Ashlyn pointed without looking up from her map, and when Bershad followed her finger, his heart sank.

"Shit."

The northern horizon was blanketed by looming, black clouds. Even from leagues away, he could see massive ocean swells and whitecaps. Lightning pulsed in the clouds.

Ashlyn looked up. Saw it, too.

"Black skies."

"In the literal sense," Felgor said. "Don't worry, I am a master sailor, and I will get us through this debacle unscathed."

Felgor crashed their ship into a shoal a league from the island.

They were forced to swim to shore with the few possessions they could grab before the boat sank into the churning, wild ocean.

Ashlyn grabbed an oilskin satchel from deep in the hold. Bershad bundled his sword and armor together with a tight line of rope, tied that whole thing to his ankle, and hoped that he had the strength to tug it along, rather than the other way around.

Felgor grabbed a pair of boots and a pipe and was first in the water.

Bershad lost track of them both during the swim. Waves crashing into his face. Tether around his ankle squeezing and threatening to pull him to the bottom of the sea. He was just about ready to give up and drown when his feet found sand. He hauled his armor and sword through the waist-deep water, cursing under his breath the entire time.

Ashlyn and Felgor were waiting for him on the shore. Both of them still gasping for air.

"I couldn't get much," Ashlyn said, motioning to the satchel. "Most of the Gods Moss is at the bottom of the ocean."

Bershad turned to Felgor. "Master sailor, is it?"

Felgor shrugged. "Not much that can be done about sneaky shoals in unknown waters."

The rain had let up sometime between the shipwreck and their arrival on the coast, but the air was still frigid.

"Need a fire," Bershad said. He was already starting to shiver from the damp cold.

Ashlyn produced a tinderbox. Flint and some dried strips of bark. It wasn't much, but when she combined it with some driftwood, it was enough to get a decent flame going.

They all huddled around the fire until they had some semblance of warmth. Then Bershad put his armor on and motioned to the edge of the beach, which gave way to a thick, cedar forest. The sky was hazy and gray, but there were still hours of daylight left.

"Might as well get started."

Bershad led Ashlyn and Felgor into the forest. The ground was covered with rain-dampened ferns and soft moss. There were hundreds of spiderwebs stretched across the trees above their heads, all of them dappled with rain. In the middle of each web, a lone spider the size of Bershad's head stood sentinel. They had long black limbs wreathed in bright yellow stripes.

The gnarled and twisted trees created a dense maze that was difficult to navigate. Once they'd moved a few leagues inland, there was so much undergrowth that it became impossible to walk in the same direction for more than a minute or two. After getting blocked by three impassable walls of foliage, then wasting an hour walking a river only to find it ended in a waterfall and a sheer granite cliff, Bershad called a halt.

He sat down on a rock, sucking cold air into his lungs fast enough to make them burn.

"This isn't working," he said to Ashlyn. "We need a better way. Some kind of path."

"I'm all for a little finesse, but we're not likely to come across a road," Ashlyn said. "This place is a wilderness."

Above, the Nomad circled. She was high up—coasting above the rain clouds that still dominated the sky—but her presence brought a few new scents and smells to his nose. He focused on a specific one that was a mixture of musty stink and fresh clover.

Bershad knew that smell. Bear.

The beast was a few leagues north of them, and moving farther in that direction with each passing second, but its trail from a few hours earlier wasn't far from where they were currently resting.

"Might be we can get help from one of the locals."

Bershad found a way up the back of a steep cliff, then led them through an aspen grove. There were half a dozen other game trails in the forest that belonged to mountain goats and deer, but they'd be too erratic for them to follow easily—cutting up sheer cliffs and leaping over hedges full of thorns. So Bershad kept pushing through the tangles of ferns and vines and shrubs until they intersected with the bear's trail.

Bershad had never seen bears native to Ghost Moth Island, but judging from the sign, they were far larger than their mainland counterparts. The paw print alone was as wide as his chest, and this one had torn a trail of snapped aspens and crushed foliage straight through the wilderness, into another heavy forest of cedars.

"We'll follow these tracks inland."

Felgor scratched his head. "You're the expert and all, but the size of that paw print is concerning. Is it wise to use such a large predator as our guide?"

"We'll be fine. He's far off."

———

It started raining again. Just a cold drizzle, but steady. The sky darkened and a brutal wind beat the tops of the cedar trees in wild directions. They pressed on, but the Nomad had veered westward, taking her sharpened senses with her. Bershad lost track of the bear's location after about an hour of following the trail.

Eventually, he hacked through a thick wall of ferns and stumbled into a clearing. There was a small lake ahead of them, surface rippling and busy from the falling rain. But that wasn't what caught Bershad's attention. It was the three men who were backed up against a stone cliff, pointing weapons at a bear the size of a juvenile Blackjack.

"Gah!" one of them screamed—a barrel-chested and pale-skinned man clutching a double-headed axe with white knuckles. He swung at the bear, but missed. Sparked his blade against the rocky ground.

"They don't look like cannibal pirates," Ashlyn said.

"You expected a necklace made from ears or something?" Bershad asked.

"Whoever they are, they're fucked," Felgor said.

"Yeah." Bershad looked closer. Two were grown men, and both had a blue bar tattooed on each cheek. Dragonslayers. The third was just a boy. Bershad didn't have much sympathy for morons who'd gotten themselves ambushed by a bear—even if they were fellow exiles—but he wasn't in a hurry to watch the kid get mauled.

He pulled the Curdachi off his back.

"Wait here."

The other adult—a black-haired and wiry man—attacked the bear with his sword, but he might as well have been using a rotten log for all the damage it did. The hide was far too thick. Same problem as a dragon's scales. You needed momentum to punch through.

Bershad skirted to the left and worked his way up the gentle-sloping shoulder of the cliff that the men were cornered against. As he moved, the bear made an angry swipe at the pale man, which caught him in the shoulder. He went to the ground howling.

"Behind me, boy!" the dark-haired pirate shouted, corralling the kid.

Bershad scaled the cliff with a few more quick hops and scrambled across the ridge until he was directly above the bear. It was about a fifty-stride drop, which was going to hurt. No choice.

He stepped to the cliff's edge. Hefted his sword.

Jumped.

There was a rush of wind on his face. A whir in his stomach. Then his blade connected with the bear's neck, just behind the skull. The head separated and flopped against the ground. Hot blood sprayed across Bershad's face as his legs slammed into the rocky ground. He felt an unsettling number of bones in his feet crack from the impact.

The bear's body slumped over. Its head was a stride away, eyes open. Snout frozen into a snarl.

Bershad's sword was halfway buried in the churned earth. He stood, wincing at the pain in his feet, then yanked the blade free. Turned to the men. They were still clutching their weapons and breathing hard. All of them clearly trying to process what had just happened, but failing.

"Evening. I'm Silas Bershad."

None of them said anything.

"You the assholes that eat people and such?" he asked, bracing for a fight if it came to that.

They all glanced at each other. Passed some unspoken understanding between them. The big pale man stepped forward and spoke in a Lysterian accent.

"We don't eat people, Almiran. But seeing as you saved our hides just now, we'd be more than happy to split some o' that bear with you."

14

VERA

Balaria, Burz-al-dun, District Five

Vera met the three mercenaries that Ward had hired in a vacant basement three blocks away from Clyde Farus's warehouse. Clyde was planning to transport the dragon oil out of Balaria the following night, which meant it would all be in one location tonight.

She removed the seal from behind her breastplate when she reached the door to the basement. Slipped it into the lock. There was a series of clicks, then it opened. The men were already inside and warming their hands around a small furnace that was designed to burn dragon oil, but was currently stuffed with dirty rags and the remnants of a broken chair. Shortages, and all.

Two of them were enormous Lysterian twins who wore red, scaled armor and had tattoos of open eyes on their eyelids. They reminded Vera of Devan—the man who'd killed Rowan on their way into Balaria.

She pushed the memory of his death away.

The third was Almiran. She could tell from his long, dark hair that was festooned with silver rings. He wasn't as tall as Bershad, but they shared similar features. The man wore charcoal gray armor, and had both his hands clasped around the top lip of his breastplate in a relaxed posture.

They were all armed with a wealth of knives and short swords. Ideal for close-quarters combat. Each also had a Balarian crossbow on his back.

"Vera?" the Almiran asked.

She nodded. Kept her distance and her balance.

"Your names."

"I'm Gyle," said the Almiran.

He thumbed to the Lysterian on his left.

"This one's Rike."

He thumbed to his right.

"That's Wun."

Vera nodded. Those were the names Osyrus had given her.

"You know what we're after?" Vera asked.

"Shitload o' dragon oil," growled Rike in a thick Lysterian accent.

"Yes." Vera unrolled a blueprint of the warehouse and placed it on the ground by the furnace. One hand moved to her dagger as she did it, ready to slash a throat if any of the men made a move. None did.

She'd already scouted the warehouse from the rooftop of the building across the street. It was a single building protected by a wall that was fifteen strides tall. There were ten sentries patrolling outside, but only one was up on the wall. The rest were spread out around the compound and mostly standing still, which made things simpler. She'd marked their locations.

The mercenaries all looked down at the blueprint with the familiar concentration of men who had raided plenty of fortified positions.

"We'll approach from the eastern alley," Vera said, pointing with her boot. "I'll kill the one on the wall with my sling and then the three of you go over in the gap that creates."

"Narrow alley," said Wun. "Long shot. Sure you got the muscle for it?"

"Stow that dragonshit," Gyle hissed. "She's a fucking widow, you moron."

Wun frowned, but said nothing.

"Rush the two men here and here," Vera continued. "If either of the sentries along the north or south wall wander over, I'll have an angle on them. When they're down, I'll meet you here. We'll clear the perimeter, then split up. Gyle and I go in from the north door. Rike and Wun from the south. Push anyone inside toward the middle."

"Simple enough," Gyle said.

"The key is silence and speed. We need to kill at least half of them before they realize we're attacking, otherwise—"

"All due respect for the fact you're a coldhearted mistress of planning and murder, but this isn't our first infiltration and annihilation of a fortified position." Gyle smiled. "We'll get it done nice and clean."

Vera gave each of them a long look.

"Fine. Let's go."

———————

Vera came up behind a sentry and slit his throat just as Rike was cutting another one's head off. The two dead men fell to the ground in an eerie unison. You kill enough people, strange moments of synchronicity like that happen.

Vera surveyed the warehouse grounds. Ten corpses were spread out across the compound. Three had crossbow bolts in their faces. One had his head caved in from Vera's sling. The other six had open throats or missing heads.

All of them had died surprised.

Gyle walked over to Vera. Gave a nod. Rike and Wun reloaded their crossbows, then headed for the south door to the warehouse without a word.

Vera let Gyle walk ahead of her on the way to the north entrance. She wanted to keep the Almiran mercenary where she could see him. Gyle had a sword in his right hand and tested the door with his left. He gave Vera a happy nod when it came back unlocked.

They rushed inside. The room was illuminated by half a dozen dragon-oil lanterns hanging from the ceiling. The perimeter was dominated by bundles of cotton stacked on high shelves, but as soon as they slipped past the first row, the space opened up. There was a high stack of metal barrels in the middle. Twenty or thirty, at least. A plump merchant in a blue silk robe was standing in front of them, consulting a ledger. Clyde Farus.

He was flanked by another ten armed sentries.

"Black skies," Vera hissed to herself, already starting to swing her sling.

Rike and Wun came into view on the far side of the warehouse just as Vera reached enough momentum with the sling to release. They raised their crossbows and fired just as Vera released her shot. Call it luck, or call it killers' instinct, but all of them found a different target—Vera hit the sentry closest to Clyde. His brain matter splashed all over the merchant's face. Farus dropped to the ground with a panicked squeal.

Vera drew Bershad's sword from her back and rushed forward. Gyle did the same.

The remaining sentries reacted fast—drawing swords, angling up. Vera headed for a tall man in full plate armor and a round shield. He saw her coming and coiled into a defensive posture. Vera sprinted forward and feigned a high attack, causing the armored man to raise his shield. When he did that, Vera dropped to the ground and allowed her momentum to carry her beneath the lip of the man's shield and between his legs. She sprang up behind him—drawing *Owaru* at the same time with her off hand—and buried the blade into the back of the man's neck.

She heard a snarl to her left and brought her sword up on instinct—parried a vicious swipe that would have cut her in half at the waist. The shock of impact shot up both her arms and made her teeth hurt. The man beat at her again and again with a two-handed broadsword. He was strong, but his footwork was sloppy. Vera allowed the man to push her backward and think he was winning.

She waited until he was lurching forward, then kicked his rising boot, sending him into a stumbling fall and faceplant. Vera put all her momentum into the downward stab through his back-plate and into his heart.

She left the sword. Drew *Kaisha*. Looked around. But everyone was dead except for Clyde, who was still crouched down on his knees, covering his face and trembling. He'd pissed himself.

Vera stepped closer—figuring he might have some useful information—but Rike stalked over and cut him in half at the waist, then hacked off the back of his skull for good measure, as if it might have been possible for the merchant to survive being divided.

"Why did you do that?" she demanded.

Rike looked up, frowning. A worm of gray brain matter was sliding down the edge of his blade. "Orders."

Vera glanced at Gyle, who just shrugged. "We were told to secure the oil and kill everyone." He motioned to the tower of barrels. "Job well done, seems like."

"Those were not the orders I gave."

"No," came a new voice. "But I did."

Vera turned to find Osyrus Ward in the room. She frowned. How had he snuck up behind her?

"I wasn't finished with him."

Osyrus ignored her, looking up at the barrels of dragon oil with greedy eyes. "Yes. Yes, this will serve our purposes well."

"So these are Malakar's men, huh?" Gyle asked, surveying the corpses.

"Correct."

"Good. Commander Vergun's always looking to screw with their operation."

Vera's blood went cold.

"What did you just say?" she hissed.

"Oh, just that the Malakars are competition. The three families have a truce of sorts, but this'll give 'em a nice big black eye to suffer without anything coming back on us directly."

"No. Your commander. Who is he?"

"The vampire. Sorry, Commander—"

"That'll be all, Gyle," Osyrus cut in, voice firm. "Please wait outside."

Gyle appraised the spindly man. "Aye. Sure. Whatever."

He motioned to Rike and Wun. The three of them filed out. Rike hadn't wiped his sword off, so he left a trail of blood and brain as he made his exit.

"You hired Vallen Vergun's men for this?" Vera hissed when they were alone.

"Is that a problem?"

"That pale asshole killed—" She stopped herself when she saw Osyrus's curious expression. Eyes wide and ready to absorb whatever she had to say. There was no value in telling him what had happened, or revealing how she felt about it. Any information she offered could be used against her in the future. So Vera swallowed her rage. "He is dangerous."

"He is also hundreds of leagues away in Taggarstan. Meanwhile, we are here with more than enough dragon oil to power Kira's ship once it is complete."

"When will that be?"

"The construction of the hull is ahead of schedule."

"And the engine?" Vera asked.

"Oh, progress is consistent and promising."

"Define promising."

Osyrus studied the crates. "If the finished product adheres to my projections, the Kor engine will only require five or six of these barrels to keep Kira's ship in the sky for months. We have stumbled into quite a surplus."

There was a noise outside. The clank of the warehouse gate opening. Vera raised her daggers on instinct.

"Not to worry, Vera *the widow*. I had porters waiting nearby. They will arrange a clandestine transport of the oil to the skyship bay where I am building Kira's ship."

"If you had men to transport it, why did you need me?"

"Clandestine transportation and clandestine murder are two vastly different skill sets, wouldn't you say?"

Vera glared at him. "Do you require *my* skill set for anything else tonight?"

"No. You may return to the palace and give Kira the happy news, if you'd like."

15

BERSHAD

Ghost Moth Island, Southern Coast

The bear meat smelled like sweet clovers as it cooked over the fire.

"I want to see your tattoos," said the Lysterian, who'd lost a chunk of shoulder in the bear attack. The dark-haired man was stitching the wound for him. He wasn't doing clean work, but the Lysterian had been drinking heavily from a gallon jug of surprisingly expensive-smelling rum, and didn't seem to feel any pain from his wound. "Reveal your arm and I'll accept that you're truly the Flawless Bershad."

"Quiet about the fucking tattoo," muttered the dark-haired man. "And stay still."

They were the first words he'd spoken.

"You're Almiran," Bershad said.

And from the Dainwood, judging from his accent.

"Used to be."

"Way things go, pretty much everyone on Ghost Moth is from somewhere else," the Lysterian said.

"Not me!" the boy piped. "I'm a trueborn son of Naga Rock and the best tracker on the island."

He beamed with pride.

"Don't boast," said the Almiran. "It's not our way."

Definitely from the Dainwood.

"Sorry, Dad." The boy hung his head a little.

Bershad studied the men. Given the calm, practiced way they were dealing with the Lysterian's injury, they were clearly warriors—used to injuries and the bloody cleanup that followed. But they didn't seem like murderous cannibals. Either the stories about Ghost Moth Island's pirates were grossly exaggerated, or this was a different bunch.

"What are your names?" Bershad said. He'd introduced Ashlyn and Felgor, but they'd fixated on his identity and the introductions had stopped there.

There was a pause. The dark-haired man didn't seem eager to answer Bershad, and the kid followed his father's lead of silence.

"I'm Goll," said the Lysterian, softening first. He jerked his chin to the dark-haired man. "That sour bastard is Vash. And the kid's Wendell."

Goll took another big swig of rum with his uninjured arm.

"Good to meet you," Bershad said.

"Right, right. So that's us. Short names with no titles or dynastic surnames attached. But you are allegedly the Flawless Fucking Bershad, shipwrecked on our island with Ashlyn Malgrave, the queen of Almira, and a Balarian. Sounds like the start of some stupid southerner joke." Goll burped. "I believe none of this without proof. Do you know how many blue-barred assholes claim to be the Flawless Bershad if they're tall enough to pull it off?"

Felgor cracked a smile. "Man has a point."

"Ha! Your Balarian agrees with me. Reveal your arm."

Bershad sighed. "Fine."

He took off his gauntlet and unstrapped enough of his armor so that he could roll up his sleeve and show them the sixty-six tattoos running up his forearm and biceps.

Goll blinked. "Fuck me. It's really you."

"Of course it's him," Wendell said. "He cut that bear's head off with a single chop. A *flawless* chop."

"The fall did most of the work," Bershad said.

"Do not undercut your accomplishment," Goll said. "I have great respect for you, Flawless. Me and Vash only have four tattoos between us. And he is carrying the majority of the ink."

Goll lifted his sleeve, revealing a single lizard tattooed just above his glyph. Looked like a Lysterian Round Belly. They were a small but vicious breed. Killing one couldn't have been easy.

Bershad turned to Vash. "Three, huh?"

"You aren't the only one who can kill a lizard," he said, but didn't elaborate.

"They were all Blackjacks," his son added to the awkward silence. "One was fully grown."

Wendell glanced at his father. The look on Vash's face halted the story in its tracks.

Goll offered his jug of liquor to Bershad. "Never mind the lizards we've killed, I owe you a blood debt for beheading that bear. One that I will repay in turn. For now, it would be my honor to share my personal rum stores with the Flawless Bershad."

"I'm all right."

"You sure? It's decent stuff." He wiggled the jug a little, but when Bershad shook his head again, he pulled it back under his arm. "Suit yourself."

The fire crackled.

"I'm pretty thirsty," Felgor said, inching a little closer to Goll.

"Flawless saved my life. You did nothing, little Balarian."

"I did nothing today. But I've personally saved Silas's life on three occasions."

"Is this true?" Goll asked, raising his eyebrows and looking at Bershad.

"Yeah, actually."

"See! The Law of Indirect Proxy says that since I saved his life, and he saved your life, *I've* saved your life, and thus deserve some of the rum."

"I have not heard of this law before," Goll said, frowning at Felgor. "The proxy does not include the blood debt, correct? Owing even one of these is a significant burden."

"Hmm. In this particular case, I'll consider my portion of the heroics settled with rum alone."

"I accept your terms," Goll said, nodding gravely, then passing the jug.

Felgor drank enough for Goll's eyes to darken. Smacked his lips when he was done. "Decent stuff? By Aeternita, this is top shelf! What's a salt outlaw doing with such a good vintage out here in the middle of nowhere?"

Goll shrugged. "That is average at best. Back in Naga Rock I have a sixty-year-old, oak-aged brandy that warms a man's very soul. We confiscated it from a Pargossian senator last spring."

Ashlyn cleared her throat. "That's the second time you've mentioned Naga Rock. Is that your camp?"

"Camp? *A camp* does not begin to properly describe the Rock. It's a whole city burrowed deep in the limestone cliffs. Got about a thousand citizens, more or less."

"You couldn't count to a thousand if you had a week to do it," Vash said.

"Doesn't change the figure. You know how Kerrigan is with her logs."

"Is everyone in Naga Rock an exile?" Bershad asked.

Running into another dragonslayer anywhere in the world was uncommon, given their short lifespans. But finding two in the wilderness of the most remote island in Terra couldn't just be a coincidence.

"Not everyone," Goll said. Paused. His brow furrowed in thought. "'Bout half I'd say. Rest are hired craftsmen, traders, and entertainers. Or people who just got sick o' the laws that come with living in Terra."

"Five hundred dragonslayers in a subterranean city on an island in the middle of the Big Empty. How'd that happen?"

"Oh, Kerrigan made plucking unfortunate exiles out of their plight a special project of hers way back. She rescued the first few scores herself, then put up a permanent reward with no expiration date or limit for anyone who brought another blue-barred face to Naga Rock. Five hundred gold, even if they don't pass the interview. Whole thing snowballed from there." He motioned to Vash. "That grumpy bastard's the one who found me trudging around in Treindhorn harbor with a writ for a Silver Scale in my pocket. Mean fuckers, those. I did not take much convincing to piss on the writ and relocate."

"What's the interview they have to pass?" Bershad asked.

"Some people deserve the bars on their cheeks," Goll explained.

"So, Kerrigan interviews each exile that's brought to Naga Rock. Decides for herself who gets to stay. She reads their glyph, looks into their souls, and clears out the rapers and the murderers and the other particularly unsavory types. You pass muster with her, you're invited to join Naga Rock as a citizen."

"And if you don't?"

Goll shifted. "Let's just say you get a different set of choices."

He coughed. Looked uncomfortable.

"But she's typically real lenient," he continued. "Says it's more about character than specific actions performed in the past. Take Cormo, for example. He was a field surgeon in the Balarian army who got himself exiled for drunkenly amputating the wrong leg o' some general. I mean, that's a big fuckup, seeing as the poor bastard still had to lose the bad leg, but in Kerrigan's eyes it don't quite warrant getting yourself turned into dragonshit. He's been the Naga Rock surgeon for four years."

"What carved such a soft spot for lizard killers into Kerrigan's heart?" Bershad asked.

Goll smiled. "You ever meet her, you'll understand. But *a soft spot* is accurate. She's turned Naga Rock into the friendliest place a blue-barred face is likely to encounter. Makes for a perfect hideout to lay your head between reavings, too."

"Reavings," Ashlyn repeated. "So, you are pirates?"

"No," Goll said quickly. "Corsairs."

Ashlyn frowned. "Pardon my ignorance, but what's the difference?"

Goll smiled. "See, now I believe you're the queen of Almira from that question alone. Proof's in the proper grammar and a polite tone. Both are in desperately short supply out here."

Felgor laughed. "A Lysterian wouldn't know proper manners if they bit him on the cock."

"You reveal your ignorance, little man," Goll growled. "Lysterians hold skill in etiquette, battle prowess, and lovemaking in equally high regard."

"Always thought you were a bunch of savages."

Goll spat. "That is the lie you clock fuckers tell yourselves to justify the massacre of our people."

"Oh, clock fuckers, is it? Where are those highly regarded manners now?"

Goll crossed his arms. "They are reserved for people of honor who ask things politely. Balarians ravaged my homeland. Turned our bountiful valleys into blackened mud pits. My entire family was killed on the ends of Balarian blades."

"Well, I didn't kill them," Felgor protested. "I've never killed anyone."

"Really?" Bershad asked. "That can't be right. All the shit we've been through."

"It's true."

Bershad thought about that. "Huh. Weird."

"Returning to my politely asked question," Ashlyn pressed.

Goll turned to Ashlyn, face still twisted into a frothy rage. He swallowed. Calmed down. "Apologies, Queen. What question?"

"What's the difference between a pirate and a corsair?"

"Well, you hear the word *pirate,* you think rape, pillage, murder. General nastiness. Corsairs are more professional. Now, we'll deprive a loaded merchant ship of their cargo, have no doubt on that. And if that deprivation requires a bit o' drawn steel and thumped heads, we'll oblige. But in general, we get our business done without bloodshed. Just the looming threat of it, you know?" He grinned. "Shit, half the time, the ship's cargo's insured to hell and back so they don't even put up a fight. You just have to toss the crew a little gold and the whole thing becomes a business transaction that's pure profit for both parties."

"Kerrigan always says that mutually beneficial relationships last the longest," Wendell added.

Vash didn't say anything. But he gave his son an approving nod.

"I'm surprised by all of this," Ashlyn said. "The inhabitants of this island do not have a reputation for tempered behavior, or scruples of any kind, for that matter. It might be your company works clean, but the stories about this place have to come from somewhere."

Goll's grin disappeared. "Aye. There's another outfit up north. But we have nothing to do with those bastards. They're banished from Naga Rock for consorting with demons."

"Demons?" Ashlyn asked. "What do you mean?"

"We don't speak of it," Vash growled.

Everyone was quiet for a while. Bear fat crackled and hissed as it dropped into the fire.

"All right," Felgor said eventually. "So if Naga Rock is some comfy paradise, and the nasty outfit lives amongst the bears and the demons and the freezing rain, what the fuck are you three doing out here?"

"Foraging," Wendell said, when it became clear nobody else was going to respond. "We're to gather as much meat as possible before winter. Kerrigan's orders."

"Which makes no sense to me," Goll said. "Last time I was in the cold room there was meat stacked to my chin."

"There's plenty now," Wendell said. "But it'll be a different story come the middle of winter if we don't stockpile. And there's no time to go reaving again before the autumn storms."

Goll squinted at the boy. "Yeah, well. Bear meat tastes like shit."

"Regardless of the taste, we need it," Vash said, looking at the carcass, which Goll and Wendell had stripped of meat and washed in the nearby lake to cool it off. "In fact, you should start salting, Wendell."

"Yeah, Dad," Wendell said, moving to one of their traveling packs, which was filled to the brim with salt. Wendell started scooping out handfuls and rubbing it along the slabs of extra meat.

"Surprised you're able to throw that around with such abandon," Bershad said.

Salt wasn't as rare or valuable as Gods Moss or dragon oil, but it wasn't cheap, either. In Almira, a lot of wardens still got paid their monthly wages with a modest pouch of it.

"We took a whole carrack of the stuff last spring," Wendell explained. "But Kerrigan says we should try to conserve."

"Yeah, yeah, yeah," Goll said. "So our business here is pretty straightforward. Just some corsairs collecting our nuts before winter. Hunting and harvesting and salting shitty meat for the long winter." He took a large gulp from his jug. "But I am thinking whatever brought you three to Ghost Moth Island is a lot more interesting."

"Yeah," Felgor said. "We're here to save the world."

Goll raised his eyebrows. Turned to Ashlyn. "This is true?"

"That's a bit of an oversimplification," Ashlyn said, then took a breath. "A new kind of war is coming to Terra. One that isn't fought from the land or the sea, but from the sky. We came to this island because, many years ago, this is where the technology for these new wars was created. So this is where we can find a way to fight it."

"*Technology*," Goll repeated slowly. "Define this word. I don't know it."

Ashlyn tilted her head. "It can mean a lot of things. Machinery. Tools. Weapons." She hesitated. "But we're primarily looking for preserved dragon parts. Hide. Bones." She tugged on the sleeve covering her wrist. "Anything like that."

"Doesn't sound familiar," Vash said quickly.

"But Dad, what about Simeon's armor?" Wendell asked.

"Quiet, boy. We do *not* speak of him."

"Fuck the tight grip you keep on your tongue," Bershad cut in. "You and your kid would be bear shit if it wasn't for me. Least you can do is let us hear what Wendell's got to say."

Vash glared at Bershad. The fire crackled between them. Eventually, he gave his son a single, curt nod.

"It happened before I was born, but I know the story," Wendell said. "Kerrigan and Simeon founded the Naga Killer Corsair Company together. They discovered the island, then hired the crews and brought them out to start building the city and rescuing exiles. But they weren't the only ones here. The demons live in the middle, behind the wall of bones. They came out of their hole that leads to the underworld, and made Simeon and Kerrigan an offer."

Bershad waited for Vash or Goll to correct the kid. Neither did.

"Demons. You're joking, right?"

Goll shook his head. "They're real. I've seen one."

Bershad decided to let the argument over whether demons were real or not sit.

"What was the offer?" he asked.

"The demons crave human flesh," Wendell said, voice dipping to a whisper. "It's their favorite thing to eat. So they told Kerrigan and Simeon that they would be rewarded if they brought people back to the island and gave them to the demons." He swallowed. Glanced at his dad. "Kerrigan refused. But Simeon agreed."

"Evil bastard," Goll muttered to himself.

"What did he get in return?" Ashlyn asked.

"The demons gave him a set of armor that they built in the under-world. It's made from dragon scales, and even the best castle-forged steel snaps against it. Arrows crumple like stalks of wheat. He wears it when he raids ships. That's why nobody can beat him. I heard he captured the crew of a Ghalamarian war frigate and took them back to the demons last year."

"Alone?" Bershad asked.

Wendell shook his head. "There were others who made the pact. The demons gave them gifts, too. Crossbows that can fire twenty bolts in a row without being rewound."

Bershad glanced at Ashlyn, who was frowning. Deep in thought. "When was this pact made?" she asked.

Wendell looked up at his dad, unsure.

"Kerrigan and Simeon founded Naga Rock fifteen years ago," Vash said. "The demons offered their pact around then."

"Then it wasn't Osyrus," she said. "He was in Balaria by then."

"Osyrus?" Goll asked. "Is that a type of demon?"

"No." Ashlyn sucked on her teeth, thinking. "Where is this bone wall?"

"Crossing the bones is forbidden," Vash said. "Kerrigan's orders."

"She doesn't have too many rules, but she's real firm about that one," Goll added. "No citizens of Naga Rock go beyond the bones."

"Good thing we're not citizens of Naga Rock, then." Bershad cracked his knuckles. "Where is it?"

"Twenty-two leagues north-northwest," Wendell replied.

Vash glared at his son. "Why do you know that?"

Wendell shrugged. "I go look at it sometimes."

"How many times have I told you to avoid the middle of the island?"

"I don't go up close or anything."

"It's still dangerous. You—" Vash cut himself off. Blew out a frustrated breath. "We'll speak of this later."

Vash turned to Bershad.

"You heard the boy. Twenty-two leagues that way." He waved into the darkness. "You want to get yourselves killed, be my guest. Take as much bear meat with you as you want."

Wendell scrunched up his face, thinking.

"Problem is, there's no direct path from here. Your best bet's probably going around the lake and following the river on the far side till it gets you into a thick cedar forest, but that turns into ten leagues of nasty swamp that'll bog you down."

"That swamp's a bastard," Goll said. "Uncas chased a boar in there last year and didn't come out for three weeks. Had the most disgusting rash on his face I've ever seen when he finally returned. Was also crapping brown water for a month."

"We can't afford to get lost in some swamp," Bershad said. "Time's a factor."

"Why?" Vash asked.

"It just is."

"I can lead you through the swamp," Wendell said. "I crossed it in two days last time. I know the way."

"No," Vash said.

"But—"

"Out of the question."

Wendell stared at his feet.

"If I don't get what I need from this island and return to Papyria before the end of winter, people will die," Ashlyn said.

"How many people?" Goll asked. "Because a handful here and there isn't such a big deal to us, being honest."

"Tens of thousands," Ashlyn said. "Every country in Terra will suffer. Lysteria. Papyria. Almira."

Vash spat. "Balaria tried to invade Almira once before. Didn't turn out so well for them."

"True. But thirty years ago, Balaria didn't have an armada of flying ships made from dragon bones. They do now. And they've already used them to reduce half the cities in Almira to cinders. Glenlock and Umbrik's Glade were both destroyed."

"The baron of Umbrik was a fucking prick," Vash said.

"Agreed," Bershad said. "But the people of the Dainwood living in his city weren't."

Vash crossed his arms, as if that would protect him from the validity of that comment. "If Balaria is tearing up Almira with dragon-bone ships, what good can the three of you do all the way up here?"

"As I said, this is where Osyrus Ward invented the skyships," Ashlyn said. "Which makes it the same place I can learn how to destroy them."

Vash weighed that. "No. You're spewing dragonshit. Ain't no such thing as flying ships."

"You're the ones telling us stories about demons tinkering on armor in the underworld," Felgor pointed out. "If that's true, what's so far-fetched about a flying ship? After all, if a ten-ton Red Skull can fly, so can a ship."

He winked at Ashlyn.

"I believe the queen," Goll announced. "And if helping you will hurt those clock-toting dogs, then I will do it." Goll glanced at Vash. "But I don't know the way across the swamp," he added.

Wendell turned to his father, too. But Vash appeared resolute. "It's too dangerous."

"Aren't you always the one who's saying there's a way of doing things?" Wendell asked. "They need our help."

Vash glared at his son—somehow managing to look annoyed and impressed at the same time. Then he glared at the fire. And lastly, he glared at Bershad and Ashlyn.

"We'll take you to the wall," he said eventually. "No further."

Wendell's face broke into a huge grin.

"Will you tell some stories about dragonslaying along the way?" he asked.

Bershad eyed the boy. "Maybe."

Vash tied off the last stitch of Goll's arm. The Lysterian gave his injury a once-over, then took a long gulp of rum. Smacked his stomach happily. "Perhaps an opportunity will arise for me to pay my blood debt to Flawless along the way. I do not like carrying extra weight upon my honor."

Vash turned to the meat. Poked it with a callused finger. Grunted.

"This is ready."

"About time," Felgor said. "I'm starving."

Goll snatched Felgor's wrist before he could reach the meat.

"I paid my debt to you with the rum. You eat last, Balarian."

"Well, that hardly seems fair."

"It's Goll's Law." He glared at Felgor. "And it will be respected. Clear?"

"Clear," Felgor said unhappily, leaning back as the others took their fill.

But Bershad noticed the Balarian thief chewing on something long before Goll finally gave him a turn to eat.

Everyone woke up with the sun. Goll groaned about his arm. Felgor groaned about his hangover. They all gathered their gear and weapons. Then Goll press-ganged Felgor into helping him bury the salted bear meat.

"No arguments, little man," he said, when Felgor tried to squeeze out of the work. "You will pay for the liquor in your belly with labor."

"We covered this, that was for the Law of Proxy."

"The amount that you drank was excessive. Come with me."

They disappeared behind a bend in the lake to find a place where they could stash the surplus meat that was too heavy to take with them. The plan was for them to pick it up on their way back to Naga Rock.

"So, what do you think of it all?" Bershad asked Ashlyn when they were alone.

"Judging from their stories, we've come to the right place," Ashlyn replied. "But I can't suss out what all the talk of demons is about."

"Guess we'll find out soon enough, once we get past this wall of bones."

"Yeah." Ashlyn yawned, then secured her sleeve, hiding the dragon thread from sight. "I'm going to forage around a little."

"There'll be plenty of bear meat."

"Twenty-two leagues through forest and swamp is going to take a while. I'm not eating bear meat for every meal."

"I liked it."

"Well, I like a little variety." She smiled. "There's a field of wild onions over there. Some mushrooms, too. I'll be done before they are."

"You want me to go with you?"

"Has your patience for foraging increased in the fourteen years you spent killing dragons?"

"Not really."

"Then you can skip it."

She headed into the meadow. Bershad ambled over to the lake. Found Wendell making some final stitches on the bear's hide, which he'd cut it into two matching cloaks.

"You did all that in one night?" Bershad asked.

Wendell shrugged. "It's not that hard. And you and the queen will need them." He looked up at Bershad. "I didn't have enough for Felgor."

Bershad glanced around the lake. Everything was covered in hoarfrost, and while they'd passed the night without dying, Bershad had woken up shivering on three separate occasions and had to fuel the fire before getting to sleep again.

"I'm grateful. Not used to places that get this cold."

"Dad doesn't like the cold either. He grew up in the Dainwood where it's always warm."

"So did I."

"Really?" The boy stopped sewing. "Have you ever seen a jaguar?"

"Lots of them." Bershad squinted. Paused. "Your father didn't talk about me?"

"He never talks about Almira."

"Can't blame him on that front."

Wendell spent a few minutes focusing on his sewing.

"Is killing a bear easier than killing a dragon?" he asked eventually.

"Depends on the dragon."

Vash appeared from around a rocky boulder, tying up his pants as he walked.

"You finished with those?" he asked his son.

"Just about."

Vash inspected each cloak. Nodded once, but didn't say anything.

Bershad pulled the larger one over his shoulders. It still smelled of blood, but it staved off the morning chill.

"Why don't you take Ashe's to her?" Bershad said to Wendell.

"Really? Okay!"

Wendell collected the bearskin, then trotted off to Ashlyn, who had already accrued a handful of onions from the meadow, but was picking more.

"Thank you," Bershad said to Vash. "For agreeing to help us last night."

"Didn't do it for you," he said. "Boy needs to learn how things are done. You kept us all from taking the long swim, so we'll help you out. Simple as that."

Bershad nodded. "How did you get your bars?" he asked.

Vash looked at him. Dark eyes hard to read.

"Same way you did."

"You were at Glenlock."

"I was."

Bershad had heard that Elden Grealor tattooed a good chunk of the Dainwood wardens who'd helped him massacre Wormwrot Company. It was one of the many reasons he'd spent the first few years of his exile blind drunk.

"I'm sorry."

Vash shrugged. "Not like you didn't suffer the consequences, too. But you should know I'm the only Dainwood man who was picked up by Kerrigan. Everyone else died ugly."

Bershad opened his mouth to say more, but Vash stopped him with an open hand. "We'll take you to the gate, and that'll be the end of it."

"Yeah, all right."

Wendell picked his way back through the field, bear cloak still in hand.

"She said she didn't need it," he explained. "But that Felgor could have it."

Bershad glanced at Ashlyn. She wore less clothing than anyone, but seemed the most comfortable in the morning chill. That dragon thread might not produce lightning anymore, but it still had power, and it was flowing through her body.

"Well, she's half Papyrian," Bershad said. "They're better with the cold."

Felgor and Goll came back around the bend, hands dirty with dark soil from the business of burying the salted bear meat. They were passing another jug of rum back and forth. Bershad had no idea where it had come from.

"The meat'll be safe!" Felgor called, already seeming to have burned off his hangover with more alcohol. "Old Felgor knows how to bury a bear better than anyone."

Goll just shook his head. "We'll reach the gate in, what, four days?"

"Six," Wendell corrected.

"Huh." Goll considered his jug. "Gonna have to start rationing this a little more carefully."

Then he took another massive gulp.

Wendell led the way across the island, picking along rocky cliffs, dipping into drainages, and following pathways through thick forests. He moved naturally between game trails and rivers, adjusting to whatever obstacle they encountered with natural ease.

"Is it true that you cut off a Red Skull's head and shat down the neck hole?" Wendell asked.

"No."

"Did you throw a spear from the top of Mount Kuldish and hit a Blackjack twenty leagues away?"

"No."

"Well, you did kill two dragons in the same day, though, right? One in Levenwood, and then one in Vermonth?"

Bershad hesitated. "Yeah. That one's true."

"I knew it! Gods, I wish I was a hero like you."

"No you don't, kid."

Wendell ignored him. "What about the Needle-Throated Verdun outside of Otter Rock? I heard that you threw a spear through its skull and then pissed in the hole."

"Where did you hear that story?" Vash asked, frowning at his son.

"From Goll."

Goll gave a shrug. "It true?"

"I don't shit or piss inside the dragons that I kill," Bershad said. "Why would anyone do that?"

"Dunno. But if it ain't true, why are there so many stories about it?"

"Because tavern drunks are morons," Bershad said.

They kept walking. Bershad probably could have gotten them north without the boy, but it would have taken forever. The landscape was a wild mess of impassable forest, valleys choked with thornbushes, and thick swamp. But Wendell seemed to know the land like a farmer knows his fields—able to find a workable path no matter how dense the undergrowth.

"How'd you learn the island so well?" Bershad asked the boy.

"Dad won't let me go on reavings. So, I'm stuck on the island all year."

"You're too young for reavings," Vash said.

Wendell shrugged. "Anyway, Naga Rock gets boring, so I explore."

"Kid, you are the only person I know who could get bored in Naga Rock," Goll said. "The theater troupes and companion caves alone are enough to keep a man busy for weeks."

"I've seen all the plays a hundred times. And Dad won't let me go into the companion caves, either."

"You're—"

"Too young," Wendell finished. "Yeah, yeah."

"Your father is wise to make you wait," Goll said. "The Naga companions are very . . . advanced. Not a good choice early on in your life."

"Advanced? I like the sound of that," Felgor said. "Maybe we can visit when we're done saving the world?"

"What's the matter, didn't get your fill back at the Squatting Loon?" Bershad asked.

"That was ages ago," Felgor said.

By the time the sun had reached its highest point in the sky, Felgor and Goll had emptied another jug of rum. Goll immediately produced a fresh one from his pack, but Bershad stopped him from opening it.

"How about you two give that a rest until sundown?"

"But I am still thirsty," Goll protested.

"Drink some water, then." Vash slapped a canteen against the Lysterian's chest. "I agree with Bershad. We do not know what's out here."

"The Almirans are ruining our party," Felgor said. "Well, if the liquid entertainment is canceled, I want to hear a story about these demons. They the kind that sneak into the bedchambers of bad children, or what?"

Goll's face turned serious. "You jest, Balarian. But they are real. I've seen one."

"What did he look like?" Felgor asked.

"Well, the Almiran stories always have them with red eyes and ashen skin. But it's the opposite. This one had green, glowing eyes and waxy skin that was all swollen and puffy around the cheeks and throat. Kind of like a maggot's flesh."

"You're talking out your ass," Bershad said.

"I am not."

"What did he do?" Felgor asked.

"Why are you humoring him?" Ashlyn whispered.

"I like scary stories," he whispered back, then turned back to Goll. "Well?"

"First off, it was a woman."

"A demon woman? Oh, now this story is getting good. Was she pretty?"

Goll frowned. "I just finished telling you about the eyes and weird skin."

"Still."

"No. She was not pretty." He sipped his water. "Her clothes were all rotten. And there was this smell. Like a root cellar that's flooded—damp and foul. She stared at me from across a clearing for a long time, just looking at me. Then she muttered strange words."

"A curse?" Felgor offered.

"Possibly. I didn't understand her, but I remember the words. *Oska. Katlan.*"

"Definitely sounds like a curse to me."

"That's not a curse," Ashlyn said. "That's Grazilandish. It means 'bone' and 'flesh.'"

"Hm, interesting," Felgor said. He took a drink from the canteen, thinking. "So, it was a demon from Graziland who wanted dinner."

"That's a pretty strange way to ask for food," Bershad said.

"Well, it's not like Graziland demons are going to have good table manners." Felgor motioned to Goll. "Well? What happened next?"

"She rushed me. Moved faster than a fox chasing a rabbit, too. But I had my axe with me."

"You killed her?" Bershad asked.

"You can't kill demons," Felgor said. "That's obvious."

"Why not?" Wendell asked.

"Because they're not real," Bershad muttered.

"No," Felgor said. "Because their souls are locked in a metal box that Aeternita keeps in a rucksack underneath her bed."

"Couldn't say if you can kill 'em either way," Goll continued. "I gave her a tap with the axe, but it was a glance shot off the shoulder. She hissed, and disappeared into the woods. I picked around the clearing for a long time, looking for her. But I couldn't even find footprints."

"That's it?" Felgor asked.

"Yes."

"That's a pretty disappointing climax," Felgor said. "Usually with these stories there's a hex . . . or someone from her past abused her and got away with it. A local lord or an uncle, generally. Then you have to avenge her, and in return Aeternita comes down and returns her soul so she can rest peacefully."

"What are you talking about, Balarian?"

"I'm explaining how to tell a decent ghost story."

"This is not a ghost story. It is just what happened."

"Well, beef it up a little next time. That was mediocre at best."

They had bear jerky for dinner. Despite not eating much during the day, Bershad lost his hunger for the tough meat after a few bites. Ashlyn turned her portion down, and instead dug around inside Goll's pack until she found a cast-iron pan, which she coated with bear-fat grease then filled with onions and mushrooms.

She put it over the fire and within a few minutes the fragrance of frying onions filled the campsite. Bershad liked having a better sense of smell—but a side effect was that it made her cooked vegetables infuriatingly enticing.

"All right, all right, you were right about the vegetables," he said to Ashlyn when she bit into a mushroom while giving him a self-satisfied look. "I want some."

"Wouldn't mind a bite or two myself," Felgor muttered.

"There's enough for everyone," Ashlyn said. "Throw the bear meat into the pan."

They ate in a happy, ravenous silence. When Goll had finished his portion, he licked his fingers and looked around at everyone with a huge grin on his face.

"What're you so happy about?" Vash asked him.

"Never in my whole life did I think a queen of Terra would make me dinner."

"That wasn't a dinner," Ashlyn said. "That was a pile of vegetables."

"An exciting experience all the same."

"Don't get too excited. This is the only thing she knows how to cook," Bershad said.

"Careful, dragonslayer," Ashlyn teased.

"Always, Queen."

"So, what's the deal with you two?" Goll asked. "You married or something?"

Bershad looked at Ashlyn, who raised an eyebrow.

"Came close once," he said. "But things went a little sideways."

"Sideways," Goll repeated. "How's that?"

"Oh, Silas got exiled and spent fourteen years killing dragons," Ashlyn said. "I married a drunk Gorgon Valley lord who got himself drowned on a pleasure barge. Then I inherited a kingdom that I lost last summer trying to save dragons from extinction."

"Sideways," Vash repeated. "That's one way to put it."

"In Lysteria, we would call that a proper goatfuck," Goll said.

"Almira, too," Vash agreed.

"Did you save them?" Wendell asked Bershad.

"Huh?"

"The dragons. Did you save them?"

Bershad looked at Ashlyn. "Yeah. We did."

"How'd that go, exactly?" Goll asked. "Because I heard a crazy story out of Taggarstan that the Flawless Bershad got the shit beat out of him by the vampire, but nobody believed it 'cause there's another story floating around you killed the emperor of Balaria and set the palace on fire, which must be dragonshit, too."

"No, no," Felgor said. "You're missing the most important part, where I saved Silas from certain and painful death. Then, we burned the palace down together!"

"Aye, right. Your proxy law again, is it?" Goll asked.

"Exactly."

"The craziest story I heard doesn't belong to the Flawless Bershad," Vash said, speaking up. "It belongs to her. Word is she toasted Cedar Wallace's entire army with fireballs from her eyes. Turned 'em all to smoking meat by herself."

Bershad turned to Ashlyn. Shrugged. "Hey, at least this version of the story has the fireballs coming out of your eyes."

"It wasn't fireballs," Ashlyn said, annoyed. "It was lightning. Well, a form of controlled current, anyway."

"Sounds like demoncraft."

"If you want."

Wendell tucked his knees to his chest. Looked scared. "You're a witch?"

Ashlyn smiled at the kid. "There's no such thing as witches."

Felgor quickly launched into a Balarian story about witches. Something about covens and spells that involved baby goats and a big cauldron filled with brandy. It sounded like he was making it up on the spot.

The pull of the dragon was nagging at Bershad. He stood up.

"I won't go far," he whispered to Ashlyn before heading into the thick of the forest.

The Nomad followed.

He came to a small lake with glass-calm water that was so clear, he could see the mossy bottom despite the fact that it was thirty strides deep. Dozens of tiny blue fish darted around the shallows. There was a small, rocky island in the middle. Bershad stripped naked—propelled by an itchy, primal sensation that made his clothes feel foreign and rough—and dove into the water.

Swam toward the island.

The cold water shocked his body. But it felt good to wash off the layers of sweat and grime and grease—like carving the dirty rind off a ripe fruit. He felt alert. Awake.

He pulled himself onto the island and found a shelf of flat rocks that still radiated heat from a day in the sun. Sat down and closed his eyes. Listened to the forest. Focused on his connection to the dragon above him, which felt like a pit in his stomach that was tied to a string running up to the sky.

Back in Nulsine, he'd shooed the Nomad off when she'd wandered closer to him. But there was no reason to do that now, and he was curious what would happen. Maybe Ashlyn was rubbing off on him.

"I know you're tired, girl," he whispered. "You can rest. It's safe."

The Nomad kept her spot in the sky for a few minutes, then slowly started to descend.

Bershad's senses sharped as the dragon got closer to him. The swarming crackle of fish heartbeats came alive against the bottoms of his feet. The lethargic, thumping pulses of painted turtles that were hiding in the mucky shallows throbbed along his ribs. The rustle and scrape of rodent claws on leaves filled his ears and prickled the skin on his neck. A fox was hiding from a wild boar that had mud and raccoon shit caked down his back. A crow was tucked against the trunk of a pine tree, trying to sleep.

And beyond all of that, he could feel five human heartbeats sitting around a fire. Smell the rum on their breath.

"Gods," Bershad muttered, lost in the swarm of smells and sounds and feelings that radiated across his naked skin.

There was a crash of snapping wood. Bershad opened his eyes to see the Nomad had dived into the trees and snapped up the wild boar in her jaws. She killed it with a quick bite to the back of the skull. Ate the boar in three quick mouthfuls. Bershad could taste the dirty hide and tough meat in his own mouth.

When she was done eating, the Nomad licked her maw clean, then gazed at Bershad from across the water with curious, glowing eyes. It was strange to see such vulnerability in a dragon. For years, all he'd gotten from the great lizards was a predator's stare.

The Nomad opened her wings, preparing to leap back into the air.

"No need to rush off so soon. Ain't going anywhere tonight."

The Nomad hesitated. Cocked her head as if she expected a trick, but didn't depart. He studied her body. There was a large metal barb hooked into her shoulder—the remnant of someone's attempt to spear her. Broken arrows peppered her flank. Dozens of other scars were cut into her snout and throat.

"Guess you've had some experience with dragonslayers. Makes you cautious. But I'm done with all that. Promise."

The dragon took a little more time making up her mind, but eventually she spread her wings and flapped across the water like a hawk switching hunting perches. She landed on the little island. Curled up against the warm rock slab like a dog beside a fire on a winter's night.

Fell asleep.

Bershad stayed on the island for hours, letting his connection to the dragon grow stronger. He could feel her steadily drawn breaths in his chest. Sense her blood warm from the rocks. Her energy and strength returned, and so did Bershad's. He knew he should go back to the others. Ashlyn would understand, but Felgor would get drunk and start worrying. Still, in that moment, he couldn't bear to leave the dragon's side. Something about the proximity felt natural and right. Like going home.

So he stayed.

16

VERA

Balaria, Burz-al-dun, Skyship Construction Hangar

"Isn't it beautiful?" Kira asked Freemon Pence, the chief minister of fisheries and ponds.

"Quite," Pence responded, looking up at the skyship.

Above them, Kira's royal skyship was raised onto several large platforms. The hull was made from a complicated interweaving of dragon bones and steel, but it was only halfway complete, allowing Vera to see into the lower holds, which were filled with a complicated mess of machinery, gears, pistons, and pipes of a thousand different sizes.

The wings were both a hundred strides long. There were black sails made from dragon leather pinned underneath them, no doubt ready to be dropped and opened by one of the confounding mechanisms inside the bowels of the ship. The hull was built from bleached-white dragon bone, which Kira had requested be painted blue.

"I heard a rumor that the royal engineer preserves the dragon bones in the Heart of the Soul Sea," Pence said. "That he has some factory hidden among those dragon-infested islands. Is there any truth to that?"

"I don't know," Kira said lightly. "The details of the construction process don't interest me. Just the outcome."

There was a score of men at work on the ship. Some worked from the wood scaffolding that had been erected around the skyship. Others were clipped into leather harnesses and hanging from the gunwale—laboring with wrenches and dragon-oil torches. All of them wore heavy leather aprons fit for blacksmiths. Their thickly muscled forearms were covered in grease, their faces obscured by strange gray masks made of leather. Instead of eyeholes, there were twin black orbs over their eyes. Vera didn't understand how any of them could see what they were doing.

Unlike the empress, Vera was *very* interested in the construction process of the skyships, particularly the strange men that Osyrus was using for the work. She had no idea who they were or where they had come from, which made them a potential threat to Kira's safety.

"Does your ship have a name?" Pence asked.

"Not yet," Kira responded. "In Almira, it's bad luck to name a ship before her maiden voyage."

"And when will that be?"

"Not soon. As I am sure you know, all spare dragon oil must be used for the war effort. The royal engineer is not even building an engine for my ship. For now, I simply want to give the people of Burz-al-dun something to look forward to in these bleak times."

"An excellent idea, Empress Domitian. These are indeed bleak times. You heard of the trouble at Edgemar Fortress?"

"Terrible," Kira agreed.

General Grakus had indeed been murdered by a furious Velesar Nun, who accessed Edgemar Fortress with the administrative seal Kira had arranged for him. Velesar Nun was swiftly executed, and the entire incident had been mostly swept under the rug, but the rumor mill around the palace spun. As Kira had predicted, Actus Thorn departed yesterday to take command of the war effort.

"But I wouldn't worry," Kira continued. "With Actus Thorn in command, the Lysterian revolt will be smashed to pieces in a matter of weeks. We just need the weather to clear so the skyships can do their work."

"Yes, of course."

"But while he is gone, there is plenty to keep us busy. I believe your offices have received word about the relaxation of your pond taxes, with my compliments."

"We have, Empress. I must admit, I am curious how you made the levy ministry budge. In my experience, those ministers would rather murder their own firstborn than lower taxes."

"Everybody wants something, Minister Pence. Sometimes, all you have to do is ask nicely."

She looked at him expectantly.

"I see. And I am, of course, more than willing to repay your goodwill in any way I can." He hesitated. "Perhaps a portion of the surplus in revenue . . ."

"Not necessary. In fact, you have my word that you may skim

the entirety of the extra pond profits for yourself, and nobody in the government will hassle you or go looking for the missing coin."

"That is very generous . . ." Pence said, waiting for the true cost.

"All that I ask in return is a small favor. Well . . . *two* small favors."

————

After Kira was done with Freemon Pence, they went to see Osyrus Ward in his workshop. Despite the fact that Actus Thorn had refused his request for more specimens—whatever that meant—Ward had filled the room with dozens of glass tanks that held different kinds of insects, mice, and rodents.

Kira strode in and surveyed the long line of tanks. Bent at the waist to examine one that was placed in the middle of the room.

"What's this one all about?" Kira asked, tapping the glass. Ward glanced up from his table, which was strewn with gears and wire. He was fiddling with a stone orb the size of a baby's heart—stringing a translucent thread around it in a careful and tight pattern.

"That is a mapping experiment," he said absently, then turned back to the orb.

"Mapping? All I see are a few butterflies. And the, uh, the things they make. Cocoons."

"A chrysalis."

"Chrysalis. Right. Do the butterflies have names?"

"Specimen 879 and Specimen 880."

"Those are boring."

"Everything needs a name," Osyrus replied without looking up. "But in time, you learn to forgo colorful choices with high volume experiments. They are a sentimental distraction. Nothing more."

Kira looked closer. "Why do you have those wires attached to them?"

"As I said, it's a mapping experiment. The caterpillar's entire body is reduced to a soup of nutrients and biological information, which then forms into a completely different creature. The butterfly. The process is incredible, but also mysterious. Each transformation that I monitor peels back a bit of the enigma."

Vera studied the tank. The wires that Ward attached to the chrysalis ran down the side of the glass case, then funneled into a small hole in the floor, mixing in with all the other machinery and piping that ran through the palace and was powered by the Kor Cog.

"Why do you care how butterflies work?" Kira asked.

"I don't care about butterflies in particular. But these creatures reduce themselves to a formless soup, then grow themselves anew in a completely different form. That ability has a wide array of potential applications. A very wide array."

Kira turned away from the glass tank. Gave Osyrus a look. "You're an odd person, Osyrus."

"I take that as a compliment."

"How is my engine coming along?" Kira asked, motioning to the orb. Long ago, Kira had learned to switch topics frequently and without warning to maintain the advantage in a conversation, but the tactic seemed to have little impact on Osyrus Ward.

"Progress is being made," Osyrus said, halting his work. "I placed the alpha build in the *Time's Daughter* before the skyship began its overwatch mission on the western coast of Almira. Initial diagnostics are positive, although the mechanism is less efficient than I'd like. Yours will be far superior—a true explorer's ship, bound by nothing except the constitution of the captain."

"Mm. I like the sound of that. But *when*?"

"Soon. Soon."

"You said that last time."

"I was occupied with Actus Thorn's request for the cold-weather uniforms so his rebellion quashing can begin in earnest. My poor hands." He rubbed them. Seemed to feel genuine pain. "But the new design is complete." He motioned to the corner of the workshop, where a uniform made from dark leather hung. There was a heavy clock apparatus over the chest, with wiring that streamed down both arms. "It's truly a remarkable achievement—along with the added insulation, each device is synchronized to the central Kor, allowing different skyships to communicate with each other across leagues of mountain, ocean, and forest. Almost as powerful an advantage as the skyships themselves. I have ensured that every deployed skyship crew will be outfitted with them. Thorn even approved my request for a skyship to resupply the *Time's Daughter* while she performs her precious overwatch of Almira's western coast. Even from so far away, she will be connected to the fleet."

"Impressive," Kira said absently.

"Of course, Actus Thorn offered little in the way of thanks. And he has refused yet another request of mine for fresh specimens. I had to collect those caterpillars myself from a public garden in District Three. These city creatures are not ideal for study at all. Too many degradations and impurities." He sighed. "Anyway, my acolytes are handling the mass production and distribution of the uniforms, so my work on the engine can continue. I am close."

Vera's attention perked up at the mention of Ward's acolytes. Those were the strange, masked men who had been working on Kira's ship.

"Where did those acolytes come from?" she asked. Vera had checked empire immigration records—as well as palace entry logs—but found no mention of them, which was strange. Even Gyle, Rike, and Wun had come through customs on false documentation and the pretense of being Ghalamarian wheat traders.

"That is an interesting question," Osyrus Ward replied. "In one sense, they are from far away. But in another, they were born in Burz-al-dun."

Vera was about to press Ward for a straight answer, but Kira was already moving toward the door.

"You're making excellent progress, Osyrus. I'm happy. And do not worry, when I am in control of Balaria, I will make sure you get all the bug specimens that you want. Come on, Vera. We have another gala tonight, and I need to get ready."

17

BERSHAD

Ghost Moth Island, Central Wilderness

They made the long trek north without incident, following a river, then traversing a forest, and finally crossing leagues of decrepit swamp dominated by massive black mushrooms the size of trees. The mushrooms were pocked with specks of green and orange and red pustules. The farther inland they moved, the more putrid the landscape became.

"How much further?" Ashlyn asked after it took them twenty minutes to navigate around a sludge pit.

"We're close," Wendell said, then pointed ahead at a big wall of rotting, weeping mushrooms. "This is the last bit of nastiness, then the wall."

"Wish I still had my mask," Bershad muttered, drawing his Curdachi and preparing to start cutting through the mess.

"I usually squeeze through real careful," Wendell said when he saw what Bershad was about to do. "So as not to disturb anything, you know?"

Bershad kept walking. Hefted his sword and hammered it through the first swollen, corrupted vine. It sprayed apart in a shower of gore that smelled like a popped pustule on a dying man's asshole. Felgor retched. Goll turned away with a Lysterian curse.

Bershad reared his sword up again.

After a few minutes of brutal hacking, his blade got caught in a disgusting vine covered in black slime. He tried to wrench it out. Failed. Then dropped his shoulder and shoved his weight against the mass until it strained, tore, and gave way. He stumbled into a clearing. Struggled to regain his balance. Looked ahead.

About three hundred strides past an expanse of flat, dead grass, there was a massive palisade built from sun-bleached dragon bones. No other animal was large enough to account for the size. The wall was four times taller than Bershad. The entire upper third was wreathed with red-tipped thorns the length of daggers. The bones had been carefully arranged so that there were no gaps in the barrier, but the pattern was complex and ornate—ribs placed perfectly next to femurs and wing bones and fingers.

Behind him, the others picked their way out of the mess. Stared at the wall, too.

"Well, that is extremely unsettling," Felgor said. "And I've seen the Line of Lorbush back in the Razors."

"Line of Lornar," Bershad corrected.

"Whatever."

Ashlyn took a few steps toward the wall. Eyes narrowed.

"Who built this?" she asked.

Goll scratched his armpit. "The demons. Obviously."

"No," Ashlyn said. "Not demons."

"Why not?" Goll asked.

"Because you have to actually exist in order to build something," Bershad said.

Goll gave Bershad a look. Spat. Then crossed his arms and raised his chin in silent defiance.

Bershad studied the wall. "Osyrus could have done it, right? The bones don't seem that different from the hull of the skyship you shot down."

"I don't think so," Ashlyn responded. "The skyship's design was strictly functional. No frills. No style. No wasted elements. But look at that." She pointed at the twisting bones—which cascaded and locked together in a complicated pattern. "There was no practical reason to make it so elaborate. And it must have taken years. Whoever built this had a deep sense of aesthetics. Of beauty."

"That does not sound like Osyrus Ward."

"No," Ashlyn agreed. "But regardless of who built the wall, the answers I need are behind it."

They all took a moment to look for a way across.

"Those thorns near the top do not look friendly," Felgor said, pointing to the festooned rim.

"It's Snake Grass," Wendell said. "The barbs are full of poison that bring visions."

"I stand corrected. That does sound fun," Felgor said.

"Not good visions," Wendell said. "The last man who got stuck with one wound up popping his own eyes out because he thought a dragon had laid eggs behind them."

"Oh."

Bershad scanned the wall. "There has to be some kind of gate," he muttered.

"Why, there some rulebook that comes along with building dragon-bone fences?" Vash asked.

"Let's get a closer look," Bershad said, ignoring him.

"No," Vash said. "We agreed to take you here. We took you. Whatever you do from this point, we'll have no part in it."

"But Dad, I want to see if they can open it!" Wendell protested.

"And I want your mother to still be alive," Vash snapped. "We're leaving."

"Do what you want," Bershad said, picking his way down to the wall. Ashlyn came with him.

He didn't turn around to check on Vash's decision, but he didn't hear any of them walking away just yet, either. When they reached the wall, Bershad pulled off a gauntlet and pressed his bare palm against one of the bones. The surface was unnaturally warm, and his hand came away with a wet, sticky film that felt like the interior of a freshly cracked eggshell. Ashlyn examined one of the long seams between the bones.

"They're perfectly aligned," she said. "But they haven't been honed or carved. Incredible."

"How do we get it to open?"

"I'm not sure yet."

"Well, I got one thing to try. Stand back."

"Wait," Ashlyn protested when she saw Bershad heft his sword. "Just wait a minute before you start—"

Bershad stabbed the blade into one of the seams with enough force to drive it through a warden's armored chest. The tip of the blade got lodged between the two bones and stuck there. Bershad shoved all his weight into the side of the sword, trying to pry the bones apart.

"Silas, that isn't going to work. The whole framework is tied together."

"Uh-huh."

Bershad shoved harder—feet sliding in the mud, fingers and palms aching as he pressed more of his weight into the hilt.

The tip of the blade snapped off.

"Fuck," Bershad hissed. Shaking the pain out of his hands.

"Told you," Ashlyn said.

"It was worth a try."

"No, it wasn't. Brute force won't work here. We need a little more finesse." Ashlyn frowned. Looked around. Her eyes settled on the pack of supplies Bershad had dropped back near the others. "Come on, there's something I can try."

They headed back across the field.

"Looked like you bashed your finger pretty good," Felgor said when they were back within earshot.

"I'm fine."

"Uh-huh. Well, how're we planning to get through, then? Don't see any locks to pick, and I am very much opposed to exposing myself to the possibility of plucking my own eyeballs out."

Ashlyn ignored him. Started rummaging through the pack of alchemy supplies that she'd rescued from their ship. But before she'd done more than remove a few vials, all the birds in the trees around them went quiet in unison.

"Something's wrong," Bershad said, turning around to study the wall.

A section of bones shuddered, then opened along jagged seams like the grisly maw of a massive creature. A foul stench hit Bershad's nose—a mixture of fetid rot and decaying meat. It was overpowering.

There were two men standing on the far side. One was average height, but so thin he looked skeletal. A white leather cloak covered his right arm. The second man was so massive he could have passed for a giant out of a children's story, but his size wasn't natural. His forearms and stomach were lumpy and deformed. Joints swollen. Mushrooms sprouted wild and erratic from his heavily muscled shoulders, and worms wriggled from holes in his bloated ankles. He wore a thick iron collar around his neck and he was holding an enormous club that had been carved from a Ghost Moth's finger bone. His eyes were rimmed with infected, putrid green liquid.

"Fuck me with a clock gear," Felgor muttered. "They really are demons."

18

ASHLYN

Ghost Moth Island, Central Wilderness

Bershad looked at Ashlyn. Shrugged. "You wanted the gate open. It's open."

Ashlyn studied the men for a moment. Their anatomy was clearly human, but both had been altered in significant ways. Ashlyn could guess who was responsible for that, but she needed details.

"I will go talk to them."

"They are demons," Goll said. "You cannot just . . . go talk to them."

"Yes, I can."

Ashlyn crossed the field again, taking the satchel with her. The thin man moved forward, too, keeping his visible hand completely still. The giant mirrored his motions half a heartbeat later, and they all met in the middle of the field, stopping about twenty strides away from each other.

"Outlanders," the thin man said in a raspy voice. He spoke Balarian with a Pargossian accent. "You approach our domain un-invited. Why?"

"We come seeking knowledge," Ashlyn responded in Balarian.

The thin man studied her. "I have none to offer."

"That is not the deal you made with Simeon."

"Simeon craved weapons. Armor. Is that what you desire?"

"No. I want to understand how the weapons and armor were created. How they work."

The thin man seemed to consider that.

"You speak with an Almiran tongue, but your hide stinks like one of Okinu's dogs," he said. "It has been many years, but we remember the scent."

"Okinu told me where the island is," Ashlyn admitted. "But I am not her dog."

"Yes, you are." He grimaced. "The last hound in a dismal pack. All of you sniffing around Osyrus Ward's footprints."

Ashlyn narrowed her eyes at that comment. Studied the thin man a little closer. His right arm was covered, but there were tat-ters of gray fabric burned into the skin and wrist of his left arm. Alchemist's robes. When Osyrus arrived, he'd written that there was only one alchemist on the island—the botanist who was searching for immortality in the mushrooms.

"Kasamir?" she asked.

The thin man's right eye twitched. All the muscles in the giant's right arm rippled in an involuntary tremor.

"That is an old name. Do not use it."

So, it was him. Still alive, after all these years.

"As you wish." Ashlyn paused. Swallowed. She needed to change tactics—get some kind of leverage. "You mentioned Osyrus Ward. Did you know that he is still alive?"

"That does not surprise me."

"He has continued the work that he began here. I've come to learn more about it, so that I can stop him."

"That is foolish. Osyrus is nothing more than a deranged creator of stunted nightmares. He twisted and tore the Ghost Moths. Tried to break them like horses."

"You can't break a dragon. Same way you can't scream at the rising tide and scare it off."

Kasamir laughed. "If you said that to Osyrus Ward, he would have built a screaming canal with automatic drainage just to prove you wrong. He might not have broken the Ghost Moths, but he still used them for his vile purposes."

"Maybe. But he never unlocked their true potential," Ashlyn said. "I did."

Kasamir laughed—a wet and mocking rasp from damp lungs.

"Boastful words are nothing but hot breath. I do not believe them."

"I'll prove it."

Slowly, she rolled up her sleeve and unwound the black bandage, revealing the charred dragon thread. Ashlyn had kept it covered since they'd reached the island, but she'd felt its reach expanding across her arm with each passing day. Sinking deeper into her bones. She saw now that every vein in her forearm had turned black.

"I have incinerated armies with this thread. Struck dragons from the sky."

Kasamir cocked his head, curious. A moment later, the giant's had cocked, too. Interesting. The two shared some kind of connection, and Kasamir seemed to be the one in charge of it.

"A clean application, but primitive." Kasamir sniffed a few times, then sneered. "You have no governor. That is why you broke it."

"Governor," Ashlyn repeated. "What do you mean?"

He shook his head. "You say that you seek knowledge and understanding. But you lie. I know what you want." He pointed at her wrist. "More of those."

"That's right," Ashlyn said. "I need a thread that Osyrus Ward never manipulated."

"Ward manipulated everything on this island. *Everything.* Stay long enough, and the remnants of his work will manipulate you, too."

"I am willing to accept that," Ashlyn said.

"You will regret that outlook in time. I certainly did." He paused. "Do you plan to kill Osyrus Ward?"

"If necessary."

Kasamir's eyelid twitched while he considered this information.

"Then I will help you. But you must pay for your passage."

"I have valuable alchemical ingredients," Ashlyn offered. "Gods Moss."

"No. I trade in bone and flesh. Nothing else."

Kasamir turned to Wendell. The giant's gaze followed.

"The child is strong," he said, studying Wendell with hungry eyes. "Born with the mother's spores tucked gentle and quiet in his lungs. The crop will grow strong in his belly. Perhaps it is enough to finally repair what Osyrus Ward broke. After all these years."

Ashlyn saw where this was going, and she didn't like the direction.

"There must be another way. Kasamir—"

"Do not use that name!" he snarled, eyes flashing wide with anger.

The giant roared, guttural and wild. Muscles twitching with a potent and barely contained rage.

Ashlyn took a small step back. Kasamir returned his cold gaze to Wendell.

"You will give us the boy. In return, we will take you beyond the bones and let you walk amidst the nightmares that Osyrus has sown."

Vash stepped in front of his son. Drew his sword. "The fuck you will."

Ashlyn motioned for him to calm down. "The boy has no part in this. There must be another way."

"Our offer is made. It will not be changed. What is your answer?"

"We will not give you the child," Ashlyn said.

Kasamir's face darkened. "If you will not trade the boy willingly, then we will take him by force."

Ashlyn's mind raced. Searching for some other way besides violence.

"Take the kid and run," Bershad growled to Vash.

Vash didn't hesitate. He picked Wendell up by the waist and sprinted for the mushrooms they'd cut through to reach the wall.

"You, too, Felgor!" Bershad said, then rushed toward Ashlyn. Felgor ran, but chose to hide behind a nearby rock rather than cross the long, open field.

"Bring me the child," Kasamir hissed. The giant hefted his enormous club and lumbered forward. His muscles twitched and heaved. Ashlyn noticed that there was machinery beneath the layer of fungus on his shoulders. Metal pipes that sank into his rotten flesh.

"I'll deal with this," Bershad said, reaching into Ashlyn's satchel and coming up with a pinch of Gods Moss that he promptly ate.

Then he raised his sword and charged the giant.

When he was five strides away, the giant swiped at him with the bone club. Bershad leapt into the air, kicked off the top of the club as it came tearing toward him, and jettisoned himself forward. He jammed his sword hilt-deep into the giant's neck. Twisted. Ashlyn saw flesh and tendons and blood vessels tear away from the wound.

But instead of falling or screaming or registering the injury at all, the giant smiled. His teeth were festooned with orange tendrils of fungus.

Bershad dug his sword deeper into the giant's neck and twisted even further, churning up a mess of fungal tubes and swollen, infected flesh, but causing no discernible pain in the giant.

"Oh shit."

The giant clamped an enormous hand around Bershad's thigh and squeezed. Ashlyn heard the bone pop from ten strides away. He cast Bershad across the field with the lazy indifference of a farmer scattering seeds. Silas hit the ground with a thump and tumbled to a muddy, battered stop.

Despite the broken leg, Silas was on his feet moments later, but the giant ripped the sword from his own throat—green bile spraying from the wound—and threw it at him. The sword whipped end-over-end, caught Bershad in the stomach, rammed him back to the ground, and pinned him there like a trapped insect. Bershad tried to pull himself free, but couldn't. Half the blade was buried in the ground.

The giant kept moving. Ashlyn went down on one knee, grabbed a paring knife from the satchel, and sliced her palm open.

She ripped her hand across the charred thread, desperately trying to produce a charge. Nothing happened.

The giant reached her. Raised his club. But before he could slam it down on her, Goll's war axe sliced into the side of the giant's skull, knocking him off balance just enough for the club to smash cold mud instead of Ashlyn's body.

Goll sprinted toward the giant, yelling something in Lysterian. The giant yanked the axe out of his skull, revealing a gash that was bursting with severed tendrils and tubers, and tossed the weapon aside. If it hurt the giant to pull an axe out of his own head, the creature didn't show it. He took a vicious hack at the charging Lysterian with his club, but Goll slid beneath the killing stroke, grabbed Ashlyn by the waist, and kept running, putting a good thirty strides between them and the giant.

"Do not worry, Queen, I will get you to safe—"

Kasamir darted across the field with surprising speed and cracked Goll in the temple with a bony hand, knocking him unconscious.

Kasamir turned to the giant. "Get. The. Boy."

As the giant lumbered after Vash—who had almost made it back to the mushroom swamp—Kasamir grabbed Ashlyn by the wrist and lifted her up, bringing the thread closer to his face.

"Osyrus would have envied the strength you coaxed from this. But he also would have mocked you for your inability to harness it. That is his true genius. Controlling the chaos of this world."

"Get back!" Vash shouted from across the field. He'd squared off against the giant once he saw that he'd never outrun the hulking creature.

Kasamir's cloaked arm jerked and moved. The giant backhanded Vash with a lazy swing, which sent him flying into the black mushrooms.

Kasamir was controlling that creature with his hidden arm. On impulse, Ashlyn pulled his cloak away.

The sight beneath was horrifying.

His hidden arm had no skin—just exposed muscle. There were dozens of thin dragon threads wrapped around his fingers that cascaded up his arm and around his back where they were connected to open nerve endings along his spine. The threads were coated with Kasamir's blood, which was a bile-infected yellow instead of healthy red. In his hand, he had a palmful of black stones the size of acorns, each one connected to a thread.

"What is this?" Ashlyn whispered.

Kasamir dropped her on the ground. Put a foot on her neck.

"Prying eyes," he hissed. "You do not deserve to behold my work."

"Dad!" Wendell screamed. He'd gone over to his unconscious father and was shaking him.

Kasamir's fingers started working again beneath his cloak. The giant scooped the boy up and turned around, carrying Wendell back toward the wall under one arm like a sack of wheat.

Kasamir took his foot off Ashlyn's throat and followed the giant toward the gate.

"We are not thieves," Kasamir called over his shoulder. "You have paid for your lives with the child. Keep them, but leave this place. You do not belong here."

The dragon-bone fence spread open for the two men when they approached—bones once again yawning open like a beast's mouth, edges rimmed with packed fungus. It closed behind them, seams reconnecting to form an impassable barrier.

The field was silent. Ashlyn's pulse hammered. Goll stirred from his spot on the earth, rubbing his head. Vash was struggling to his feet, too. Felgor was peeking out from around the side of the boulder he'd taken cover behind once the fighting started.

"Hey, Ashe," came Bershad's voice. He was still pinned to the ground by his sword. "Need some help here."

19

BERSHAD

Ghost Moth Island, Central Wilderness

"Do you believe in demons now?" Goll asked.

They were all huddled around a small fire that Ashlyn had started. Bershad could still feel a few final strands of his ruined guts pulling themselves back together. The healing burned up the last scrap of Gods Moss in his system. Vash had spent half an hour banging his sword against the dragon-bone wall, sweating and grunting and cursing with each powerful blow. All he'd managed to do was chip his blade in a few places.

"Those weren't demons," Ashlyn said.

"No?" Goll asked. "Flawless and I both laid killing blows upon that giant, yet he did not die. If that is not demonic behavior, what is it?"

"Those were men who have had their body chemistry altered by teleomorph-stage Cordata fungus."

"I speak your language," Goll said. "But understood very little of what you just said."

"Osyrus was sent here to perfect a method for preserving dragon bones, which he obviously succeeded in doing." She motioned to the wall. "But when he was done, he veered into some wild tangent of experimentation. He spoke of ending decay, freeing people from their meat sacks."

"Doesn't look like he was as successful on that front," Bershad said. "That giant was just one massive decaying meat sack."

"Osyrus said the process would be messy. That many would die." Ashlyn chewed her lip. "He might have begun using the Cordata mushrooms to alter people's biology. Turn them into . . . I don't know what, exactly."

"How could a mushroom do that?"

"Cordatas all follow the same behavior—they invade their host, and replace its tissue with their own. Eventually the fungus can even impact the host's actions in simple ways. Send an infected mantis into an ant's nest. Or bring an ant to the top of a grass shoot or small bush. But all known species of Cordata function at the insect level—they attach to ants, grasshoppers, mantis. They're actually quite common in the Dainwood, and—"

"Ashe," said Bershad. "Simple answers for us simple folk, yeah?"

"Sorry," Ashlyn said. She paused. Started again. "Judging from that giant's body, either Kasamir or Osyrus found a way to bind Cordata fungus with human flesh. That's why the giant didn't die from the wounds you incurred—you were just hacking at fungal growth, not organs. I'm not sure the giant has any organs left. But Kasamir was also controlling him with his right hand. The one he kept hidden."

"What, like a puppet?" Felgor asked.

Ashlyn shrugged. "Sort of. I only caught a glimpse of the mechanism—there were a few dozen dragon threads fused to his muscle and nerves. His biology is definitely bound to the mushrooms, too, but in a different way. He's using them, not the other way around. And he had these stones, too. Small black stones. I think they were powering or controlling the mechanism . . . but how would that work?"

Ashlyn trailed off. Lost in thought.

"Well, regardless of the particulars, these mushroom demons hit very hard," Goll said. The entire right side of his face was swollen and purple from the blow he'd taken from Kasamir.

"You're still here," Vash said. "Don't complain."

Vash poked the fire with his sword, sending coals flying.

"I'll get your son back," Bershad said to him.

"He never would have been taken if it weren't for you," Vash said, without looking up from the fire.

"I know. That's why I'm going to make it right." Bershad thought of all the innocent people he'd gotten killed at Glenlock Canyon. Then he thought of Rowan and Alfonso. There were so many mistakes he could never take back. But this wasn't one of them. Yet. "I promise."

"Hollow words." Vash spat into the fire. "He might already be down the river."

"I don't think so," Ashlyn said, stopping her work. She had been mixing some kind of dragon-oil concoction ever since she got the fire started. "They clearly wanted Wendell alive for some reason."

"So they can fucking *eat* him," Vash hissed.

"No," Ashlyn said. "It sounded like Kasamir wants to use him as a host."

"That's worse."

"It's slower," Ashlyn pressed. "A lot slower. We have time to stop them."

Vash glared at Ashlyn for a moment, but said nothing.

Goll peered at Bershad's stomach wound, which was almost gone. "You are not dead yet. Why is that?"

"That's nothing," Felgor said. "I watched him regrow both his legs before."

Goll frowned at Bershad. "Really? Do you also have these mushrooms inside of you?"

"No," Bershad said. "I have something else."

"What?"

"It doesn't matter right now," Bershad said.

"Nothing matters except finding a way through there." Vash motioned to the wall.

"I'm working on that, but this mixture has to be precise if it's going to explode with the proper force," Ashlyn said.

She had a flask of dragon oil in front of her, and had been carefully measuring different ingredients and placing them in a stone mold. The last thing she added was a finger of Gods Moss before putting it into the fire. Everyone crowded around to watch.

"The last time I did this, I had a queen's fortune of equipment and a room with no wind and zero humidity," she said. Then looked up at everyone. "The least you all can give me is a bit of space."

They all leaned back.

"How is such a small mixture going to destroy the massive wall?" Goll asked, puzzled.

Ashlyn didn't respond. Only twisted the stone mold in the fire so it heated evenly.

Goll sighed. "The giant threw your own sword straight through your belly," he said. "And I threw my axe directly into that giant's skull. Yet both of you are still alive and potentially taking orders from mushrooms. Now she intends to destroy dragon bones with a pint of lantern oil." He seemed to weigh these facts. "The rules of the world seem to have gone for a very long fucking walk."

"The rules haven't gone anywhere," Ashlyn said, taking the mold out of the fire and carefully pouring the contents into the flask of dragon oil. The orange goo of the melted concoction mixed with the oil in a strange way—almost like two living things intertwining. "There are just more rules than you realized."

She looked up at everyone.

"You should all step back."

With that, Ashlyn stood up, taking a stick from the fire, and walked toward the wall. She used her boot to kick a depression into the dirt directly in front of where the bones met the earth, then placed the flask inside of it and covered it with dirt again. When that was done, she put the glowing stick on top of the disrupted earth and returned to the others.

They all stared at the stick for a few moments. Bershad cleared his throat.

"You sure the stick'll light it through the—"

The explosion sounded like the roar of a thousand Red Skulls ready to massacre a city. A heap of earth blasted into the sky, and then rained down a shower of dirt and grass and splintered bones. When the detonation had cleared, there was a gaping hole in the wall wide enough to ride a dragon through.

"I'm sure," Ashlyn said.

20

BERSHAD

Ghost Moth Island, Beyond the Bone Wall

The land beyond the bone wall wasn't a swamp, exactly. Bershad didn't know what to call it. The air was thick with a foul moisture. There were more of the massive, crooked mushrooms, but these grew from dirty puddles of green sludge. It was a rotten place.

Bershad found the giant's tracks easily enough. Nothing else was cutting such large footprints through the corrupted country. They followed.

Their boots clumped and sucked down into the mud, slowing their progress. After just a few minutes of walking, everyone's skin was coated in a film comprised of thousands of tiny yellow spores.

"This is not right," Goll said, doubling over after they crossed a particularly foul cesspit that was brimming with bright yellow maggots. He coughed and wheezed. "I once ran twenty leagues in a single morning without so much as a droplet of sweat. Now I feel like a thirty-year-old chicken with a pus-filled heart."

"There's no way you weren't sweating at all," Felgor said. "Everyone sweats after twenty leagues."

"Lysterians are infamous for their conditioning. My story is true. But this place . . . it weakens me."

"We're not staying any longer than we need to," Bershad said. "Let's just keep moving."

Overhead, the Nomad was circling, but from a great height. Bershad tried to coax her down as he'd done by the lake, but she refused. Rose even higher. As she moved further away, Bershad's senses turned soft and dull.

"Can't blame you," Bershad muttered. "I wouldn't want to spend time in this shit if I could fly, either."

They cleared the corrupted swamp around midday. At least, Bershad thought it was midday. With the constant, cloudy haze, it was difficult to tell. The ground turned hard and sharp beneath their feet. They scrambled across a massive slab of gray rock that was covered with jagged fractures that splayed out in erratic directions. The edge of the slab overlooked a valley below. There was a river flowing with rusty red water. Islands of black, broken rock interrupted the current.

And on the largest island, an enormous Ghost Moth was sprawled out on the ground. White hide contrasting with the black rocks like a flash of lightning through a dark sky.

Felgor squinted down at the dragon. "Is it sleeping?"

"No," Bershad said. "It's dead."

"You sure? I think it's sleeping."

"Look closer, Felgor."

From where they were standing, all they could see was the dragon's back, but there were seven iron rods sprouting from its body, almost like support beams. At the top of each rod, there were three blades spinning lazily in the fetid, thick air.

"Huh," Felgor said. "Kind of reminds me of a windmill. Just . . . more disgusting."

"Windmill," Goll repeated. "Are the demons baking some kind of infernal bread?"

Ashlyn scoffed, then started picking her way down the cliff. "Only one way to find out."

They worked their way into the valley, then splashed across the shallow river to get a better look at the dragon. Up close, the dirty water smelled like sulfur and left rusty specks on their boots after they'd crossed to the far shore. Bershad wiped a finger along the muck and rubbed it against his thumb. Came back with broken bits of metal and earth.

"It's from a mine," Ashlyn said, glancing at him. "Somewhere upstream, there must be a tunnel into the earth that's—"

She stopped in midsentence. Stunned into silence by the sight of the dragon's belly.

It was carved out—no organs or bones, except the spine. The dragon's shape was maintained by a web of copper wires that sprawled along the spine and through the carcass, then wrapped around the thicker support beams that were speared through the hide. The windmills at the top of the beams creaked as they turned.

"There's something strung up in there," Bershad said, pointing to the middle of the dragon's belly, where the wires converged about ten strides off the ground. There was so much machinery that it took a moment for the shape to resolve in his mind. "A person."

They all moved closer. The person had been dead for a long time—yellowed skin hanging from an exposed cheekbone. His limbs were bare, but his chest was covered in a black leather cuirass.

"Papyrian armor," Bershad muttered, tapping his own breastplate, which shared the same design.

"It must be one of the soldiers that Okinu sent to collect Ward's research," Ashlyn said.

"So, is this how he preserved the dragons?"

"No," Ashlyn said. "This is something else."

"How can you tell?"

"Because by the time Okinu sent soldiers, he'd moved on from dragon-bone preservation. He said that he wanted to build creatures without flaws."

"That looks pretty fucking flawed to me," Goll said.

"Yeah," Bershad agreed, continuing to study the soldier.

He was hanging from one arm, which was wrapped in a bundle of slimy yellow wires that connected to the underside of the dragon's rotten spine. The soldier's other arm hung limp at his side, and had been stripped of flesh.

"Wait," Bershad said, taking a closer look at the yellow wires. "Are those what I think they are?"

"Dragon threads," Ashlyn confirmed. "Ward exposed the spinal column and entwined the threads with all of this machinery. And with the soldier."

"Why?"

Ashlyn didn't respond. Just stepped into the yawning opening of the dragon's belly and started poking around the bottom. Her boots squelched against the dragon's hide, which was coated with a thick mixture of sprouting mushrooms, rotten paper, and black water.

Along with the thick bundle of threads around the soldier's arm, there were also a few strands that protruded from holes in his feet and connected to a small metal box with five black stones embedded in the surface.

"I've seen these before," Ashlyn muttered, squatting near the box. "Kasamir had a similar setup—dragon threads wrapped around lodestones."

"What's a lodestone?" Goll asked.

"A magnetized mineral with either a positive or negative charge, which can compel a repulsion or attraction depending on the alignment."

Goll scratched his balls. "I regret asking."

"They're incredibly rare in Terra," Ashlyn continued. "And most of them carry such a weak charge that they're little more than idle curiosities used in children's toys. But Osyrus mentioned that the very bedrock of the island was magnetized. He must have mined these stones out, then refined them. These markings . . ." She squinted. "He's got them organized into some kind of system."

She touched one of the black stones with her fingertip.

The soldier's left arm jolted. Ashlyn jerked backward. Surprised.

Goll raised his axe. "The demon lives."

"The soldier has been dead for thirty years," Ashlyn said, regaining her composure. "That was just an electrical impulse."

The big Lysterian didn't move.

"Lower the axe, Goll."

Slowly, Goll obeyed. But he continued staring at the dead soldier with focused concern.

Ashlyn frowned down at the lodestone. Turned to Bershad.

"Put your hand on it."

Bershad hesitated.

"Don't worry. If I'm right, nothing will happen."

Sure enough, when Bershad placed his hand on the lodestone, the soldier's arm remained still.

"So, it's my dragon thread that powered the apparatus," Ashlyn said.

"Thought yours was broken?" Bershad said.

"It's changed. Bound to my body instead of reactive to it. But the thread *does* still react to lodestones."

"Okay. If that's true, why wasn't that corpse twitching when we got here? He's connected to a thread that's fifty times longer than yours."

"Because Osyrus Ward never figured out how to unlock the thread's full potential. Look. Those threads are yellowed and sickly and covered in blisters. He must have used chemicals and acids to make the threads reactive again, but when you do that, they aren't able to generate much power on their own. That's what those windmills are for—enhancing the charge."

She paused. Looked around.

"This wouldn't have satisfied him. The size, the waste. It's too inefficient. But he obviously kept going."

"How is any of this obvious?" Goll asked.

"Because Kasamir was controlling his giant automaton with a similar mechanism. But the design was far more efficient and compact. Able to operate across open distances. I'm not sure how he powered that, though."

"Demonic energy," Goll said. "From the souls they suck into their hell pit."

"It could be the Cordata mushrooms," Ashlyn said to herself. "Or that machinery I saw beneath his skin . . ."

"What does any of this matter?" Vash cut in. He'd been pacing in the rear while they'd been talking, but had apparently lost his patience. "We're wasting time. We need to catch up with the demons and get my son back."

"Kasamir and his giant could have killed us as easily as a dragon kills a cow sleeping in an open field. If we want a chance at beating them, something needs to change."

"How does this strung-up corpse change anything?"

"The giant is being run on the same system as that soldier," Ashlyn said. "And that system is vulnerable."

Ashlyn bent down and touched the lodestone again. But this time, instead of lightly placing a finger on the orb, she grabbed it with her fist and flexed her forearm so hard that Bershad could see every muscle and tendon between elbow and wrist.

The soldier's arm jerked, spasmed, then exploded into a mist of dried bone and desiccated skin. Ashlyn stood up and gave Vash a look.

"If you can do that, what are we waiting for?" Vash asked.

"It's not that simple. These are closed systems. To manipulate one side, I need access to the other."

"Fine," Vash said, impatient. "How do we get that?"

Ashlyn paused. Chewed her lip for a few moments before speaking again.

"We'll all have a part to play," she said, turning to Bershad. "Yours is going to be the most painful."

Then she looked at Felgor. "And yours is the most important."

21

CASTOR

City of Taggarstan

The greasy old man who had come to dine with Vallen Vergun made Castor's asshole clench.

Osyrus Ward had arrived from nowhere on a plain canoe with no supplies—not even a water canteen. He carried no weapons, but there was a confident malice in his eyes that put Castor on his guard. "The men you sent knew their business," Osyrus said, showing no interest in the food or wine that was placed in front of him.

"You asked for my best." Vergun cut a fresh slice of meat with his dragontooth dagger.

Castor tried not to stare at the alleged pork loin that Vallen was eating. Failed. He always failed.

"Indeed." Osyrus glanced at Castor. A smile touching the corners of his greasy beard. "You served in the Balarian military, yes?"

"Horellian guard," Castor said.

"Yes, of course. I can always tell a Horellian by the tightness in their shoulders. It never leaves them, even if they leave the order. Tell me, did the empire take issue with your service?"

"I took issue with the empire."

"Hm. And what—"

"Ward. I didn't offer my hospitality to you so that you could interview Castor about his past. Let's have it."

"You want to hear about Silas Bershad."

"When that asshole left Taggarstan last summer, I had broken every meaningful bone in his body. I want to know how he managed to haul himself out of that boat—murder seven of my men—and continue on to supposedly assassinate an emperor."

"Oh, there is no supposition about it. Silas Bershad killed Mercer Domitian, along with a roomful of Castor's old comrades."

Osyrus Ward glanced at Castor, who kept his face blank. He wouldn't have cared if someone had killed every Horellian guard in existence.

"How?" Vergun pressed.

"The short version? He has a rare blood condition that allows him to recover from wounds with great alacrity."

"Blood condition? Dragonshit."

"The principle itself is quite common, despite his specific condition being rare. Take your skin, for example. The albino gene lies dormant in generations of men, only to crop up in unexpected and unpredictable intervals. Of course, your anomaly comes with more drawbacks than advantages."

"Keep talking about my drawbacks. See what happens."

Osyrus shrugged. "Your skin condition is far less of a disadvantage than your propensity for sadism, which allowed Bershad to survive. If you had simply lopped off his head when you had the chance, it would be soaking up vinegar in one of those jars right now." Osyrus waved at the heads of Devan and Liofa. "But I must express my thanks. It allowed me to compel him into my custody and examine him personally."

Vergun narrowed his eyes. "You still have him?"

"Afraid not." Osyrus's left eye twitched. "We were making excellent initial progress. Several breakthroughs with the new cultivation formulas. But Silas Bershad has some very irritating and resourceful friends. He escaped from my laboratory before I was able to begin the crux of my trials. He also incinerated a large amount of very important research before disappearing. Overall, a catastrophic loss from which I am only now beginning to recover. Still . . . he will carry the remnants of my work in his blood forever. A small but interesting consolation."

"Not to me. You said that you knew where Silas Bershad was."

"No, I said that I knew where he *would* be."

"And that is?"

"I expect him to rotate back through his homeland within the next several moons."

"Almira."

"Yes."

"Where does this expectation come from?"

"Predicting the future is not hard, Vergun. Humans are all caught in an endless loop of the same simple mistakes. Bershad will return to Almira. And you will help me prepare for him."

"Presumptuous."

"Not really. It's no secret that you have quietly rebuilt Wormwrot Company. Your ranks have expanded to nine hundred and ninety-four, yes?"

One thousand and three, Castor corrected internally. Nine Lysterians had filtered down from the north that morning—stowaways on a merchant carrack, escaping the ruination that Balaria was dropping on their heads. They'd fit right in.

"Surely you did not swell those numbers with plans to keep them all cooped up in Taggarstan collecting debts and ineffectually guarding gambling dens," Osyrus continued.

Vergun sucked a piece of meat from between his front teeth. "Are you proposing another engagement?"

"Yes. I would like to hire twenty men. They must all speak fluent Balarian, and they cannot get seasick. That's important."

"How does this get me to Bershad?"

"It's a process, Vallen. A long process. But everything is already in motion."

"My men will not work for more promises of intelligence and rumors," Vergun said. "Especially when the information you've brought lacks the desired detail."

"Details are delicate. Easy to break when exposed to extra eyes.

But I can arrange for five barrels of dragon oil to be delivered to you at my earliest convenience."

Vergun kept his face blank while he considered the offer, which was worth about twenty times more than the going rate for a score of mercenaries.

"And, of course, if the operation goes smoothly, there will be more work. I will require a full engagement from Wormwrot Company in Almira. You'll return to the world's stage, Vergun. Your company restored at long last to their old glory. Wouldn't that be such sweet justice, to send Bershad down the river with the knowledge that all his work at Glenlock Canyon was undone. Everything he loved taken and tarnished and ruined."

Again, Vergun's face was blank. But that didn't mean he wasn't moved by the notion. Castor had learned a long time ago that the only emotion Vergun couldn't suppress with monklike discipline was rage.

"You'll have your men," he said eventually, then picked up the knife. "But if this turns into a goatfuck, I will cut your heart from your chest, and the last thing *you'll* see before going for the long swim is me eating it."

Osyrus bowed his head, as if Vergun had just offered a formal pleasantry instead of a cannibalistic death threat.

"Since they're already in Burz-al-dun, the three you sent me before are logical choices. I'll need names and physical descriptions of the other seventeen for their seals, and I'll run operations through Gyle."

"Fine," Vergun said, dismissing the details and Osyrus with the same wave of his hand.

Osyrus rose. Eyes shifting to the dragontooth dagger as he stood.

"I couldn't help but notice your rather unusual cutting knife," Osyrus said. "It belonged to Silas Bershad, I assume?"

Vergun thumbed the blade. "Yes."

"That looks like a Gray-Winged Nomad's tooth."

"What does it matter?"

"It doesn't, I suppose. Just interesting."

Osyrus bowed. Left.

When he was gone, Vergun went back to eating.

"Whatever you want to say, spit it out," he said to Castor, who realized he'd been frowning and staring at his boss.

"Sorry, it's just . . ."

"Castor, do not make me pry your opinion out of you with force."

"I don't understand why we're making more deals with that greasy bastard, is all." Castor crossed his arms. "I heard plenty of stories about the Madman back in Burz-al-dun. They say he buys corpses off people so he can fuck them. It's unsavory."

Castor realized that he was describing Osyrus as unsavory to a man who was potentially eating a person in a tent that was definitely made from human skins, but still. There was a line, and it lay somewhere between making tents out of dead people and sticking your dick in them.

"I don't care what he does with dead men, or live ones." Vergun took another bite of meat. "That greasy bastard might be withholding details, but he *does* have a way to bring Silas Bershad to me. And that's what I want, Castor."

Castor didn't say anything. Vergun laughed—a rare and odd noise.

"You don't see it, do you?"

"See what?"

"He's got what *you* want tucked up that lizard-hide coat, too."

"That right?" Castor asked. He didn't recall keeping Osyrus apprised of his personal desires.

Vergun pointed his knife at the door that Osyrus Ward had just used to leave and spoke with a full mouth of meat. "Mark my words, whatever that man is planning, it will involve a paradigm shift within the Balarian Empire. Those who hold power now will lose it. Violently, I expect."

"Seems like heavy work for such an old man."

"Oh, I expect he's got someone doing the heavy lifting for him back in Clockwork City. Same way he'll have Wormwrot doing the lifting later. That's how slimy creatures like him operate. But I couldn't give a fuck so long as it ends with Bershad's heart in my hand and his corpse at my feet."

Castor grunted. He didn't fully believe Vergun, but if there was a chance that his boss was right, he'd go along for the ride. One way or another, Castor was going to fill the rest of his days with black work. Might as well do the work that could make things hard on the top brass of Balaria.

The clock fuckers deserved it.

22

VERA

Balaria, Burz-al-dun, Imperial Palace

"Will you stop with that?" Kira said. "We're late."

It had taken many galas—and many favors—but Kira had finally formed the majority of ministers she needed to remove Actus Thorn from power. They were all waiting for her in an audience chamber to carry out the vote.

"Thirty more seconds," Vera said, continuing to run *Owaru* across the sharpening stone.

"If the first hour of honing didn't get the blade sharp enough, what's an extra thirty seconds going to do?"

"Help me relax."

"Are you nervous, Vera?"

Vera gave her a look. "Of course I am. Every man in that room is supporting you for a different reason, and if they start talking about the source of their manipulation, this deception will topple over."

"Hm. Well, do not worry. I will be the anchor of composure for us both. Now can we please go?"

Vera sheathed *Owaru,* then began checking the straps of her armor.

"You know, the longer we leave the ministers in that room, the higher the chance one of them *will* say something they shouldn't."

Vera stopped fiddling with her gear. That was good point.

"You remember your part?" Kira asked as they moved around the familiar ring of the palace.

"Look angry and intimidate anyone who seems like they are getting cold feet?"

"Exactly."

They reached the door. Kira stopped so that Vera could put her hand on the large metal handle.

"Ready, Empress?"

Kira took a breath.

"Do it."

Vera opened the door to the ministry chamber. But instead of a crowded roomful of greedy, cowed ministers, there were only three men. Two of whom were fully armed and armored Horellian guards. Pij and Thrash—Ganon's two favorite bodyguards.

The third was Emperor Ganon Domitian, smiling joylessly. There was a covered platter next to him.

"You've been fucking about, my muddy-haired wife."

"Ganon? What a pleasant surprise. I had called the ministers here to—"

"Remove Actus Thorn from power," Ganon finished. "Freemon informed me."

Ganon removed the cover of the platter. Freemon's head was on the plate beneath.

"It was that business with the surplus of fish that caught my attention. Freemon was never the generous type. A little extra juniper liquor and a few extra questions was all it took to learn that my savage of a wife has been playing all of my friends against me— concocting a scheme that would have gotten them all executed when Thorn came back. I forgave the others, but Freemon was my favorite drinking companion. Such a personal betrayal couldn't be overlooked. To turn against me for some fucking tax breaks," Ganon continued. "Terrible."

"You've spoiled everything," Kira whispered.

Ganon replaced the platter's cover. Looked at Kira.

"I took you as a wife for two simple reasons. You've got the best tits in Terra, and because Almirans are famously dirty in bed. I put Actus Thorn in power for a simple reason, too. This empire is falling apart. My brother spent decades holding it together with his infrastructure and administration. He might even have saved it, but all that went to shit when Silas Bershad rammed a sword through his body. There is nothing to be done now but enjoy the final dregs of the great Balarian Empire before it disappears down a dirty gutter. Thorn will make sure we get our share."

"Our share?" Kira repeated. "Actus isn't preserving your fucking share, he's stealing this country out from underneath you!"

"You were doing the same thing!"

"No, I was trying to take it back for both of us," Kira seethed. "You might have married me for my tits and the way I suck your cock, but I married you so that I would stop eating *shit* day in and day out. I married you so that I would finally have a say in the way my life went. And all that I've gotten is a drunken moron who isn't even smart enough to stay out of my way!"

Ganon shot up from his seat and backhanded Kira so hard that the crack of leather on flesh echoed across the large chamber. The empress fell to the ground, holding a hand on her red cheek.

Vera drew her daggers in the blink of an eye. The Horellians were half a heartbeat behind her with their own blades.

"Give it a try, widow," Pij growled. "After I slit your throat, I'll use that armor of yours to wipe my ass."

"Gah!" Ganon cried.

They all looked over to see that Kira had gotten up from the floor, drawn Ganon's ornamental dagger from his belt, and rammed it through his eye.

The eye without a dagger in it was wide open. Ganon's gray iris had disappeared due to the panicked dilation of his pupil. The two rulers of Balaria stood there for a moment—locked in what could have almost been a lover's embrace, minus the blade through Ganon's brain—before Kira dropped him.

She looked at Vera, face full of bitter rage, but quickly shifting to abject panic.

Vera threw *Owaru* and *Kaisha* at the same time. *Owaru* caught Pij in the throat and put him on his back, gurgling and grasping for the blade. He'd bleed out in twenty seconds. But *Kaisha* glanced off the collar of Thrash's breastplate.

He grunted. Dropped his guard for a spit second. That was all Vera needed.

She drew her sword and dashed across the room before Thrash recovered. Cut his head off.

Kira was staring at Ganon's corpse. Her eye was starting to swell shut.

"I've killed us both."

"No, you haven't," Vera said, checking the room. Empty. There hadn't been any guards outside the doors, either. Good. That was good.

"But the ministers will know he was going to confront me. There's no way to explain what happened in this room."

"We're not going to explain anything." Vera used a scrap of cloth to wipe the blood off Kira's face. "Come on, Empress. We need to find Osyrus Ward, and hope he finished that engine."

23

JOLAN

Almira, Dainwood Province

"You're lifting your heels," Oromir said.

"What?" Jolan asked. He'd been running potential Gods Moss concoctions through his head for hours, and was barely paying attention to the road.

"Your heels," Oromir said patiently. "They should point at the ground."

"Oh, okay." Jolan adjusted his posture. The wardens were all expert riders—and of them, Oromir was the best—but Jolan hadn't spent more than a few hours atop a horse in his life.

"Better. You should pay more attention to your surroundings, too," Oromir said.

"I pay attention," Jolan responded.

"To the plants and mushrooms and animals in the trees, maybe. You should be looking for soldiers in the woods. We're safe enough on this side of the Gorgon, but that'll change soon. The gods only know what we'll run into as we get closer to Black Rock. If they left that skyship above the city, the whole province might be crawling with Balarians."

"I'm not sure I'd know what to look for."

"Flashes of metal reflected from the sun. Shifting shadows between trees. Twitching ferns. But those are all from sloppy soldiers. We run across a decent crew, first warning you'll get is the sound of a crossbow clicking as it locks. If you're setting an ambush and waiting around for hours, you generally leave that to the last moment, otherwise all the tension drops out and the bolt won't punch through a thick napkin, let alone armor."

Jolan swallowed. "Got it."

Oromir saw that he'd scared Jolan. "Don't worry, I'll keep an eye out for you. If we run into trouble, just stay close to me."

"I will."

The Devil's Confluence was the place where three branches of the Upper Gorgon River met in a surge of current. The middle branch was the widest, and flowing with silt-packed, brown water from the lowland mudflats. The other two came down from the mountains, clear and pure. But those two mixed with the lowland waters and within a few hundred strides the whole thing was a brown, churning torrent.

"On me," Cumberland called to their line of horses. "We'll ford the river branches in chapters."

The first river was easy—their horses didn't even get their bellies wet. But the muddy middle was far wider and deeper. And warmer, which wasn't good. Lurkers liked the warm water.

"Armor off," Cumberland said, already working on the straps of his breastplate. His crew followed suit. Cumberland gave Shoshone a look when he saw that the widows weren't following suit.

"What, you widows can breathe underwater or something?" Willem asked.

"Not quite," Iko answered. She had hazel eyes that reminded Jolan of a cat's eyes. "But our armor does not double as an anchor, like yours."

"Can it stop an axe to the chest, though?" Willem smiled, tapping the hatchet on his belt.

To Jolan's surprise, the widow smiled back. "Depends on the axe. And the strength of the arm swinging it."

Once the wardens had their armor tightly bundled onto the backs of their horses, Cumberland spurred his mount forward.

"Follow my line exactly," he called.

Jolan's heart was thundering as he looked at the opaque current, scanning for the black hump of a Lurker cutting through the surface. But he didn't see anything.

Before long, Cumberland's horse was chest deep in the water, then swimming—keeping his head high and snorting hard from the effort. Willem and Sten entered the water after him without any hesitation from their mounts. But when Jolan got his horse far enough into the water to get his boots wet, his nag stopped. Jolan froze. He was afraid to push her too hard and spook her.

"It's all right, girl," Oromir cooed, coming up alongside and patting the horse's neck. He gently took the reins from Jolan and started leading them across. "Just follow me now. It's all right."

Oromir looked back at Jolan and smiled. "Nice and easy, yeah?"

To Jolan's immense relief, his horse obeyed and after a few heart-pounding minutes, they reached the opposite bank.

Shoshone forded next. Everyone gathered up near Cumberland while they waited for Iko—the last in their line—to finish crossing. Jolan could feel everyone relax a little, start planning the last crossing, which looked shallow and straightforward.

Then Iko disappeared.

It happened in the blink of an eye. One moment she was there, astride her black horse, then something sucked both widow and beast beneath the surface.

"River Lurker!" Jolan called, pointing.

Everyone turned. Saw the expanding ripples where the widow used to be.

"Iko!" Shoshone called, spurring her horse back toward the river. "Iko!"

A plume of blood blossomed out of the water close to where she'd gone under, but nothing else came to the surface.

"Iko!" Shoshone shouted again. Nothing.

There was a blur of movement to Jolan's left, followed by a splash. Jolan flinched, thinking the Lurker was surfacing. But nothing had come out of the water.

Willem had gone in.

"Are you fucking thick?" Cumberland hollered. "Get out of the water!"

Willem ignored him. Kept paddling toward the blood plume. Oromir leapt off his horse and moved to follow him.

"Don't even think about it, boy," Cumberland growled, stopping him with a strong hand on the back of his neck. He turned to the water. "Willem! Get back here. That is a fucking—"

Willem dove beneath the surface. His feet kicked once and then he was gone.

For a long stretch, nobody moved or said anything. Just scanned the riverbank, eyes darting to different areas, waiting for movement. It went on until Jolan couldn't imagine anyone being able to hold air in their lungs for that long.

"They're gone," Shoshone said eventually. "Nothing to do except—"

Willem burst to the surface with a gasp and a sputter. He had one arm wrapped around a black figure.

"I got her!" he shouted, starting to kick back to shore. "I got her!"

Oromir waded out to meet them, despite Cumberland growling for him to stay put. They met in waist-deep water and hauled Iko out together. Oromir put his ear to her chest.

"She's not breathing!"

Jolan was off his horse an instant later and digging through his pack.

"I can help her!" he shouted. "She needs a Sailor's Cough."

Gods Moss, wicker root, and salt fumes, he thought, remembering the tonic recipe from an obscure tome in Morgan's apothecary. *Two grams per stone.*

He glanced at the widow, approximated her weight, and mixed the concoction as fast as possible. While he worked, the others crowded around with worried, helpless expressions. Sten was on his knees, pinching a totem together from river mud.

"Fuck, Jolan, hurry!" Willem shouted.

Jolan finished, corked the vial, and shook it rapidly as he rushed over. That would produce vapors that—when inhaled—caused a strong series of muscle spasms that could expel water from a person's lungs.

"Get her on her side!" he said as he uncorked the vial, careful to hold it away from his own face.

He held the vapors just beneath the widow's nostrils. A moment later, her entire body twitched and thrashed and then she retched up what seemed like two complete lungfuls of brown water. She sucked in a huge, ragged breath.

Jolan stumbled back on his ass, breathing almost as hard as Iko.

"Black skies," Iko rasped. "I thought I was going down the river."

"You were," Willem said, looking at her. "Literally."

Cumberland grabbed Willem by the collar and lifted him off his feet.

"You ever disobey my orders again, and I will drown you my-self," Cumberland said. Then he dropped Willem, spun, and went to his horse in a huff. Started unstrapping his armor from the beast's back.

"Some thanks," Willem muttered. "Fuck."

"Thank you, Willem," Iko rasped. Then she turned to Jolan. "And you."

Jolan nodded. He decided it wasn't worth mentioning how lucky Iko was that he was carrying Gods Moss, or how expensive that tonic was. "The spasms might have broken a few of your ribs."

Iko smiled. "I can handle broken ribs, kid. Drowning is a different story."

———

After the river crossing, they moved fast and hard through the backcountry, only stopping to rest their horses and nap in short shifts. Jolan had no idea that his ass and back and thighs could endure so much pain.

But the brutal pace paid dividends. Two weeks later, they reached the outskirts of Black Rock—Cedar Wallace's old city. They stopped just shy of the tree line so as not to be noticed by anyone who might be on one of the nearby farms, but they still had a good view of the valley.

The Black Rock fortress was built on a wide hill that over-looked acres of fertile farmland. Its walls were obsidian black, and stood out from the green, ripe fields like a circle of advanced gan-grene on otherwise healthy flesh. Jolan remembered reading a book of histories several times that Morgan kept. Black Rock's fortress was one of the oldest in Almira, but for generations, the Wallace high lords had poured an enormous portion of their tax revenue into maintenance and improvements. They also built roads in the Balarian fashion going to and from the fields, which allowed them to quickly move provisions behind the fortress walls in the event of an attack. By many accounts, it was the only truly impregnable fortress in the country. From the land, anyway.

Thing was, there was an enormous skyship filling the sky above it.

This one was at least three times the size of the skyship that had attacked Umbrik's Glade. The bloated sack that hung above the actual ship and seemed to keep the whole thing in the air was large enough to fit all of Otter Rock inside of it. Jolan was pretty sure the sack was made from Blackjack leather. The hull of the ship was armored in gray steel and had long wings made from dragon bones stretching out from both sides. There were black sails tucked underneath.

"Well, we got you here," Willem said, looking up at the ship. "How in the name of all the forest gods' assholes are you going to pluck that thing from the sky?"

"I am not sure yet," Shoshone said. "Iko and I will go find out."

She nodded to Iko. Without a word, they dismounted and started unbuckling their armor. There was a shallow ravine just behind the tree line, where they stacked their sharkskin in neat piles, then pulled off the linen shirts and pants underneath without a moment of hesitation or modesty.

They undressed so quickly that Jolan was still looking at them when their flesh was revealed. Iko had three noticeable and severe scars on her body. Shoshone had dozens of them.

Jolan decided it would be a good time to take another, longer examination of the skyship.

The widows weren't naked for very long. They pulled Almiran garments out of their saddlebags and threw them over their bodies. A few minutes later, they looked like a pair of local farmhands instead of two highly trained, foreign killers.

"Quite the transformation," Cumberland said.

"One of the many advantages women have over men during clandestine operations." Shoshone gave Cumberland a long look. "You couldn't hide your killer's body underneath a whale's skin. But us?" She motioned to her plain tunic. "All it takes is some cheap fabric and a subservient look in our eyes. We'll fit right in."

She glanced at Iko, made sure she was ready, too.

"We will return before dawn with a better sense of the situation," Shoshone said.

"Meaning a sense of whether you need our help or not to steal that thing?" Willem asked.

"Correct."

"You're not taking horses or nothing?" Willem asked.

"Do you know a lot of peasant women who ride horses back to town after a day in the fields?"

"Um. No."

"There you go."

"What about your weapons?" Sten asked, motioning to the blades they'd left near their armor.

"We do not need them." Shoshone paused. Focused on Cumberland. "I suppose it would be unnecessary to remind you and your men not to start a fire while we are gone?"

"We're Almirans," Cumberland said. "Not morons."

Shoshone gave a wry smile, then headed toward the city on foot. Somehow, both she and Iko had changed their gait to seem labor-weary and stiff rather than aggressive and intimidating.

"I think Shoshone kinda likes you, boss," Sten said when they were gone.

Cumberland spat. "Not sure that woman likes anyone."

"Oh, I dunno," Willem said. "All that talk of killers' bodies and whale skins. She even smiled at you." Willem blew a line of snot out of his left nostril. "You guys think I got a shot with Iko?"

"No," Sten said, already digging into his saddlebag for some trout jerky.

"But I saved her life. That means something, even if you're a widow."

"Wouldn't be so certain about that, my friend," Sten said. "Those women are colder than the northern waters of the Soul Sea that they call home."

"But you said that Shoshone liked Cumberland!"

"I did." Sten studied the darkening sky for a moment. "But that's different."

"How?"

"Just is." Sten lay back on his saddle, which he'd propped up against the incline of the ravine to use as a pillow. "I'm taking the first nap. Wake me when it's my turn for the watch."

He was snoring less than a minute later.

Jolan helped Oromir tend to the horses. Partly because he'd grown fond of his horse during their journey—he'd named him Rain, after rain ale—but Jolan also wanted an excuse to talk to Oromir alone. There hadn't been much privacy during the journey.

"What will we do with the horses if we have to go inside the city?" Jolan asked.

Oromir rubbed his horse's muzzle. "Set them loose. But don't worry. Mustard here's a free spirit. He'll make sure they get on in the wilds."

Jolan faked a smile, since he knew that Oromir was trying to cheer him up.

"None of the others named their horses," he said. "Just you and me."

"Most wardens avoid getting attached," Oromir admitted. "This lifestyle doesn't lend itself to long-term relationships with animals."

"But you don't. Avoid it, I mean."

"No. But I'm still young and foolish. That's what Cumberland would say, at least."

"I don't think it's foolish to get attached to things."

Oromir smiled. "Good."

They finished with the animals and settled down together in the ravine, away from the others. Oromir took out his brandy flask for them to share.

"What made you want to become a warden?" Jolan asked after his third sip.

"I guess you could call it an inherited desire. Five generations of jaguar blood flows through my veins. My dad was a great warrior. The best swordsman in the Dainwood, if you believe Cumberland and Sten. Although I think they blow smoke up my ass about it since he died before I could remember him."

"How did he die?" Jolan asked.

Oromir swallowed. "He was at Glenlock Canyon. One of Bershad's men. Not everyone who fought that day got a pair of bars, but my father did. He was a proud man. Refused to hide from the king in the gloom."

"Oh," Jolan said.

"He killed two dragons before the end," Oromir said. "A Blackjack and a Cinnamon Wex. But then he drew a writ for a Red Skull, and, well . . ."

"I'm sorry, Oro."

"That's okay. I was just a little kid. And Cumberland looked after me. Brought me up right. He's the only father I've ever truly known. And the only one I need."

"I never knew my father," Jolan said. "But I guess Master Morgan filled the role, more or less. He got killed by a dragon, too."

Oromir gave a sad laugh. "In Almira, the brotherhood of boys whose fathers have been sent down the river by a great lizard is a big one."

"Yeah."

They passed the brandy back and forth for a while in silence.

"Are you scared about stealing the skyship?" Jolan asked.

"Willem told me once that it was a waste of energy to be scared of something before you're sure it's going to happen."

"If that's true, I'm wasting an awful lot of energy right now."

Oromir rolled onto one side so he was facing Jolan instead of the stars. "What are you scared of, Jolan?"

"Getting killed by Balarians." He paused. "And if that doesn't happen, I guess I'm pretty terrified of riding back to the Dainwood and never seeing you again. I've never met anyone like you."

"I'm just a warden. Nothing special about a killer in a mask."

"I've known killers. They carry a . . . coldness in them."

"You mean the widows."

"Them. And a man I traveled with for a while. But it's in Cumberland and Willem and Sten, too. They're good people, but they're closed off. They never laugh all the way. They never relax their shoulders. You're different. The way you drink that brandy. The way you smile." Jolan paused. Summoned his courage. "The way you look at me, most of all. I'm terrified of getting separated from you, and never being looked at like that again."

Oromir put a hand on Jolan's wrist. "But are you sure that's going to happen?"

"I guess not."

He smiled. "Then there's no reason to worry."

Jolan smiled. Took another nip of brandy. But he couldn't help thinking to himself that most of the time, you weren't sure something was going to happen until it was already done.

True to their word, Shoshone and Iko came back to the ravine before dawn. They were driving a heavy wagon pulled by an old ox with milky eyes. The wagon was covered with a brown oilskin tarp.

"Any trouble?" Cumberland asked as they rolled the cart past the tree line.

"No," Shoshone said. "We have information. And a way in."

"Okay," Cumberland said. "Let's hear it."

"The Balarians sacked the city when they arrived in that massive skyship, but there wasn't much to sack. One of Cedar Wallace's old lieutenants who survived Floodhaven had styled himself the new lord of Black Rock, but he only had a few scores of wardens sworn to him. They died easy."

"How'd you hear all this so fast?" Willem asked.

"Men will tell you all sorts of things if they think they'll get to fuck you after," Iko said, smiling at him.

"Anyway," Shoshone said, "with the wardens gone, the Balarians took hold of the city without much trouble. The whole operation is run by a general called Corsaca Mun. He's Actus Thorn's second-in-command."

"Those names mean nothing to me."

"Thorn rules Balaria now. And Mun is heading the Almiran occupation."

"Got it." Cumberland scratched his beard. "If all the other ships left, why'd this one stay? And why here?"

"It is as we suspected. They are waiting to see if a Papyrian navy shows up on the horizon. If it does, they'll destroy it just like they did Linkon Pommol's fleet."

"Hm."

"There's only one way to reach the skyship," Shoshone continued. "They have a cable running from a fortress turret to the bottom of the hull. At night, the ship itself is lightly guarded when the crews come down for rest and meals, which is good."

"But you have to infiltrate a fortress to get there," Willem finished. "Which is bad."

"That depends," Iko said. "Were you hoping to part ways with us, or do you want to stay until the job is done?"

Willem smiled. "Oh, I'll stay."

Iko smiled back.

"Willem's personal conviction, if that's the word we want to use, isn't a factor here," Cumberland said, turning to Shoshone. "I need a sense of the logistics."

"The job's very doable," Shoshone said. "The Balarians are stretched thin—they're only patrolling the city's choke points. And we have these."

Shoshone pulled away the tarp from the back of the oxcart. There were a few sacks of lumpy potatoes, and five sets of Balarian armor bundled on the back.

"Where did you get those?" Sten asked.

"From men who did not need them anymore."

"There's a lot of blood on this one," Sten said, picking up a breastplate.

"Yes."

Cumberland studied the armor. "It could work. If they're on a skeleton crew and we move quick, plenty of confidence. It could work. But there's a problem."

"What is it?"

"None of us can speak Balarian."

There was a silence.

"I can," Jolan said.

They looked at him.

"Although Master Morgan always said my accent was a little funny," he added.

Cumberland gave him a long look. "You sure?"

"I've come this far." He glanced at Oromir. "I want to finish it."

Cumberland turned to Sten. "I won't force this upon anyone."

Sten spat. "Day comes when a boy alchemist has bigger walnuts than me is the day I'll drown my own self in the nearest puddle. I'll go. Need to pay them Balarian fuckers back for killing half my family anyway."

"Oro?" Cumberland asked.

"Insulted you even asked."

"Okay, then." Cumberland bent down. Put a hand on Jolan's shoulder. "Guess we'll make a soldier of you yet, boy."

24

VERA

Balaria, Burz-al-dun, Workshop of the Royal Engineer

Osyrus Ward was in his workshop. Since the last time they'd visited, the butterflies had hatched from their chrysalises.

Ward had killed them. Put them into jars filled with amber fluid.

"Empress." Osyrus stood when Kira and Vera entered the room. "What a pleasant surprise."

"Quiet," Vera hissed, pulling Kira into the room and closing the door. They'd managed to traverse the palace without attracting attention; she didn't want to screw that up now.

Vera guided Kira toward the far wall of the workshop and squeezed her shoulders—a silent reminder to stay put. Then she turned to Osyrus, who was watching Vera with a calm curiosity.

"We need to leave Burz-al-dun tonight," Vera said. "Is it possible?"

Osyrus frowned, although he did not seem upset. "Did something happen?"

"Is. It. Possible."

Osyrus pursed his lips, then unlocked the metal clasps on a heavy metal box that was set on his desk. Vera prepared to throw *Owaru* at his head if he produced a weapon. But instead he came up with the orb he'd been working on earlier. The translucent strands were now pulsing with a clean, white glow.

"Yes. The engine Kor is ready."

Ward pushed a button on his desk, and a section of wall behind Kira opened, revealing a spiral staircase leading down.

"If you'll follow me."

————

They entered the skyship dry dock through a trapdoor in the floor that opened into a long gutter. The lights were dim. Empty crates and piles of copper pipes were everywhere.

Vera came out before Kira and scanned the area. Seven of Osyrus's acolytes were working in the far corner of the room. They wore their strange masks and black aprons, and were struggling to work the lever on a small crane. Nobody else was around.

"Follow me, Empress."

The royal skyship was now suspended from the ceiling. Vera gazed up at the fusion of metal and dragon bone. The last time they'd visited, the ship's innards had been on disorganized display, like the entrails of a whale that had been torn apart by orcas. But everything was neatly forged together now—the hull smooth and sleek and painted a pale blue that reminded Vera of the sky on cold, clear morning. The levitation sack was deflated and laid out above the deck on metal support struts.

"You finished her," Kira whispered.

"Yes," Osyrus said. "Four days ahead of schedule. We'll need a crew to fly it, of course." Osyrus consulted his watch. "But as fate would have it, we need only wait a few moments, and one should present itself. The longbowmen have been performing dawn dry drills every day for the last month."

Forty-nine seconds later, the far door to the hangar opened and twenty soldiers carrying longbows walked through it.

"Black skies," Vera hissed. "Empress, back down the trapdoor. Quickly now, there—"

"Don't panic, Vera. If you will allow me just a few words with these men, they are exactly the people that we need to leave Balaria safely."

"They have no reason to help us. They're soldiers."

"They're humans. Which means they'll react to the situation that is presented to them. Wait here a moment, and I will get us on our way."

Osyrus popped up from the gutter and walked toward the men. Vera kept a hand clamped on Kira's shoulder, and got ready to yank her back down the hatch if Osyrus Ward's persuasion skills turned out to be lacking. She'd memorized the path they took through the secret passageway to get here and reversed them in her head. Four rights, six lefts, straight through three intersections, then two rights.

Of course, there was nothing for them back that way besides a swift execution.

"Seventh platoon of the illustrious longbowmen!" Osyrus shouted, opening his arms. "I see that you are punctual as always. Arrived for another morning of dry training?"

He motioned to a wooden apparatus on the far side of the hangar that was built to mimic a skyship's deck.

"You know that we are," said one of the men. "It's by your orders."

Vera squinted at him—she knew that face. It took her a moment to realize from where.

Decimar. The soldier from Aeternita's Grace.

"You are unhappy with the assignment?" Osyrus asked.

"We should be in Lysteria with the rest of our company, not playing pretend on a dry dock."

"I would have thought a reprieve from the bitter Lysterian chill would be welcome."

Decimar spat. "What are you doing here, Ward?"

"There has been a slight change of plans. Rather than the usual rigmarole today, the empress has personally requested a live demonstration of her new royal skyship's capability."

Decimar blinked. "What kind of demonstration?"

"Kira Domitian would like to fly today," Osyrus said.

A few of the men cracked smiles. Thumped each other on their breastplates. But Decimar wasn't convinced so easily.

"I'll need to check with my captain. Might be you requested us for the training detail, but he's my commander. Not you."

"Certainly," Osyrus said. "However, I must warn you that Empress Kira is not a particularly patient person. Nor does she have much time—there is a diplomatic envoy from Pargos arriving in several hours that she must greet, and then her schedule will be quite tight for the next several weeks. If she were to miss her chance to fly her newly completed ship, I believe she might hold a grudge against the soldiers who caused the delay. The officer, in particular."

Decimar seemed to chew on that, and arrived at the conclusion that angering his captain was a lesser evil than pissing off an empress.

"All right, Ward. The empress'll have it her way. Being honest, we've all been eager to see how this new one flies." He frowned, as the logistics began dawning on him. "There's dragon oil for the ship? I thought it was all sent to Lysteria?"

"A small amount was left behind, and marked for discretionary use by Kira Domitian. Those crates over there."

"They're marked as gears and copper pipes."

"Clerical error. But do not worry about the fuel, my acolytes will handle that. Onto the ship, please. Time is wasting and the empress has insisted that we view the sunrise from the sky!"

Decimar and his men clambered up the rope ladders on the side of the ship's hull. Osyrus waved at the masked men—who had stopped their struggle with the crane and seemed to be waiting for instruction.

Osyrus rattled off a series of orders in a language that Vera had never heard before. The acolytes twitched into action, pulling ceramic jugs of dragon oil from the crates and loading them into the hull of the skyship.

"What language was that?" Vera asked, coming over to Osyrus as he surveyed his men's progress.

"Hmm?" Osyrus said pleasantly.

"The one you used to address the workers."

"Oh, it is a rather obscure dialect from the eastern reaches of Graziland. But do not worry, you can speak to them in Balarian once they're aboard the ship and they will understand."

"They're coming, too?"

"Of course."

"Is that necessary?" Vera didn't want extra bodies on the sky-ship. That just meant more threats.

"Absolutely. The ship can take off without them, but it will plummet from the sky within minutes if my acolytes are not in the engine room to keep everything . . . pristine."

"You don't have your acolytes in the other skyships."

"Different engine, different needs."

Vera gave Osyrus a long, measured look. She couldn't tell if he was lying. And given the fact that Ganon Domitian was lying dead in the palace, she had no choice but to trust him.

"Fine. But keep them belowdecks at all times. I don't want them near the empress."

"As you wish." Osyrus Ward pulled the engine Kor from his pocket. "If you'll excuse me, I need to install this."

Osyrus headed for the bowels of the skyship. Two acolytes followed him.

———

Thirty minutes later, the skyship was fueled and they were stand-ing on the deck. Overall, the layout was similar to a Balarian plea-sure yacht, although the deck was twice as wide and the hull far deeper.

At the stern, there was a lavish, two-level cabin that Osyrus had designed specifically for Kira. Toward the bow of the ship, there was a small cockpit set into the deck. One of the longbowmen was seated inside of it—the lower half of his body obscured by the in-ner workings of the controls. The other longbowmen hustled around the deck, adjusting various levers and cranks.

Vera had been checking the entrance to the hangar constantly, waiting for scores of Horellian guards to swarm through it and put a stop to their escape. But none arrived. It was possible that no-body had found Ganon's body yet.

The crew finished their preparations. The pilot lifted a gloved hand and gave a signal to Osyrus, who nodded.

"Everything is ready, Empress," he said to Kira, who was sitting on a plush sofa bolted to the middle of the deck. "Shall we depart?"

Kira's face was flush, but determined. "Yes."

Osyrus moved to the gunwale and yanked on a long chain that was attached to the ceiling. A deep, metallic rumble echoed through the hangar as thousands of gears tumbled and clicked and worked. The ceiling of the hangar split apart. Each half retracted. Vera looked up at the pale gray sky. Felt a wave of cold air rush across her face, cooling the sweat behind her armor. Sunrise was seven minutes away.

"If you'd like to give the order . . ." Osyrus said.

Kira smiled. "To the sky!"

The pilot gave another sign of affirmation. Two men hustled to opposite sides of the ship and began spinning circular wheels at-tached to large pipes that ran from the levitation sack to the lower holds. The smell of dragon oil filled Vera's nose. Overhead, the levitation sack began to expand.

"Filling and maintaining pressure levels in the levitation sack is what requires the dragon oil," Osyrus Ward explained as the sack rose off its metal struts. "But once we are in the air, the Kor's power and the sails will propel us forward."

Once the sack was fully inflated, men rushed to the gunwales and began unpinning the metal cords that had been holding the skyship in place.

They started to rise.

It was slow at first, as if they were underwater and allowing themselves to float to the surface. The men bustled about the dock, tightening down ropes and turning cranks.

"Levels?" Decimar called from his place near the center of the ship, voice rising above the churning at their feet.

"Steady as your bow draw, sir," replied the pilot.

"All right. Begin full-powered ascent."

The pilot flipped a few more switches, which caused the hull to hum with energy. They rose faster.

Kira whooped, grabbing Vera's hand and squeezing. Vera counted the seconds. Clung to them in her mind, just to have something familiar in such a surreal moment.

Eighty-three seconds later, Burz-al-dun looked like a coin below them, instead of the largest city in the realm of Terra. They leveled off just as an orange slice of light started cutting across the horizon. Sunrise.

Dawn was different when you were looking down on it. Vera watched the squat trees and dying grasslands of eastern Balaria ignite with color. A flock of white gulls flew underneath the ship—winging into the west.

Underneath.

Vera's stomach lurched. She closed her eyes. Steadied herself with one hand on the edge of the sofa. Took ten breaths. Opened her eyes. Looked down to see if Kira was all right.

But the empress wasn't there. She'd moved to the gunwale, and was looking out over the side.

"Kira!" Vera yelled, rushing toward her. "Kira get back from there!"

She took Kira by the shoulder tried to pull her backward, but the empress shrugged it off.

"It's all right, Vera. I'm not going to fall." Kira took a deep breath in—although hers was clearly not to avoid emptying her stomach. She had a look of pure glee on her face. "Wonderful, isn't it?"

Now that Vera had taken a few moments to calm her body, she had to admit that there was a certain appeal to the feeling of flight. A freedom. "Yes," she whispered.

"Empress," Osyrus said, coming over as well. "Would you like to see how the controls work?"

"Definitely."

Osyrus led Kira over to the cockpit. Vera followed—abandoning her usual distance of two strides back, one to the left, and instead keeping a hand on the empress's shoulder at all times.

"The larger frigates require a team of three men to properly control—two navigators and a highly trained pilot. However, I designed your skyship so that a single person can manage everything, and with far less training."

Osyrus crouched next to the pilot. Pointed deeper into the

cockpit, by the pilot's feet. "See down there? Those pedals dictate height and speed," Osyrus said, motioning to a set of pedals that were attached to a larger apparatus of gears and pipes that funneled into the bowels of the ship. "Turning the wheel left or right will lilt the ship in the corresponding direction."

"That's it?" Kira asked.

"Takeoffs and landings are a bit more complex, but those are the basics."

"It seems simple enough," Kira said.

"Bad weather and wind complicate things in a hurry," the pilot said. "But Aeternita was kind to us on our first flight."

Vera's stomach tightened again. "This is your first flight?" she asked.

"Of course. All the frigate pilots are in Lysteria, 'cept for the *Time's Daughter* and her crew that's covering the western coast of Almira."

Osyrus stood up. "I think that's enough of a demonstration for now, Entras. Thank you."

"So, should I head out over the bay?" Entras asked. "Maybe do a quick loop and then head back?"

There was a silence. Vera had been so preoccupied with getting Kira out of Burz-al-dun safely, she hadn't had a chance to think much beyond that.

"No. Head south, I think," Osyrus said.

"For how long?"

"Until I tell you to stop," Osyrus said.

Decimar—who'd been moving from man to man, surveying their work—came over when he heard that. "What about the Pargossian envoys?" he asked.

"That? Oh, that might have actually been tomorrow. No need to rush home!" Osyrus turned away before Decimar could protest. "Empress. Vera. Perhaps you would like to retire to the royal cabin for refreshment?"

The royal cabin was plain compared to the palace, but comfortable. There was a large globe in the middle of the room and there were several more sofas. Up a small flight of stairs there was a sleeping chamber with a feather bed.

Osyrus dug around in the cabinets and produced a bottle of

bubbled wine and three glasses. Popped the cork with a yellow, thickened thumbnail.

"It's not chilled, I'm afraid. But it will suffice."

Kira ignored the offered glass and drank directly from the bottle. Her cheeks were flushed.

"I can't believe we just did that," she said.

Vera's mind raced. They might have escaped safely, but they were thousands of strides up in the air and surrounded by trained soldiers who had sworn eternal loyalty to the emperor Kira had just killed. They were still in a huge amount of danger.

"We can never return to Balaria," Vera said.

"Agreed. However, with the skyship at our disposal, a return is unnecessary." Osyrus moved to the globe and gave it a spin with one of his knobby fingers. "Shall we select a destination?"

Vera looked at the globe. "We should go to Papyria. Empress Okinu will give shelter to anyone who shares her royal blood, and I can protect you there."

Kira took another long drink before responding.

"No," she said, voice firm. "I won't do that."

"You'll be safe in Papyria."

"But what will I be besides safe? I'm not Okinu's heir. I am not anything up there, which means that I will be shoved into another colorful and comfortable drawer. It will be the same dragonshit all over again. I won't do it."

Vera waited a beat for Kira to calm down before she pressed harder. But before she could try another angle, Osyrus Ward cleared his throat. "If I may point something out, Kira will not actually *be* safe in Papyria. None of us will."

"Why not?"

"This skyship is smaller than the frigates, but it is large enough to be noticed wherever we take it. Word will get out, and Actus Thorn will send the armada after us. There is no place in Terra where we can hide from those ships."

"Then we leave Terra," said Vera. "Go south to the jungle nations. Beyond that, even."

"Anywhere we go, the armada will eventually follow," Ward pressed. "But there is another option." He smiled. Took a sip of warm bubbled wine from his glass. "We take control of the armada ourselves."

Vera frowned. "We have one unarmed ship and a score of long-bowmen who think we're on a joyride. How are we possibly going to take control of the entire armada? By flying to Lysteria and shooting arrows at them?"

"No. We'll fly to Almira. Floodhaven, to be precise."

"What's in Floodhaven?"

"An opportunity. The unrest in Almira made it easy for me to inject a substantial number of spies into Floodhaven over the last few months. They brought me Ashlyn's research, which has proved immensely useful. But they also brought me reports of a large surplus of dragon oil in the sublevels of Castle Malgrave—far more than we ever would have been able to access in Balaria. Linkon Pommol accrued it with plans of opening new trade lines."

"Dragon oil won't save us from skyships," Vera said.

"No. But if the reported volume is accurate, there will be enough oil to power an experimental apparatus that I built to work in conjunction with this ship's Kor engine. As luck would have it, the apparatus is currently aboard the ship. Right underneath our feet, actually. If successful, the machine will nullify the armada's strength."

"*Nullify*. Explain that."

"The process is extremely complicated. But rest assured, the ships will be under our control when it is complete."

"If you have a machine like that, why are you just telling us about it now?"

"There was no reason to mention a machine for which there was no available power source. It will likely burn through the entirety of Linkon's oil surplus in a single use—an expenditure that could topple entire economies. But that is a worthwhile sacrifice."

Vera frowned. "You said it was experimental."

"A prototype. Yes."

"What if it doesn't work?"

Osyrus shrugged. "Then I would imagine the three of us will be swiftly executed by a very smug Actus Thorn."

"That is no different than the position we are in right now," Kira said. "And the potential reward is worth the risk. A fleet of my own, which I can use to *help* Terra instead of conquering it."

"You're both forgetting the fact that Linkon Pommol rules Floodhaven," Vera pointed out.

"Pommol is weak," Osyrus said, dismissing the obstacle with a wave of his bony hand. "His strongest asset was his navy, which is nothing but flotsam now. The Malgrave and Wallace armies are destroyed. The soldiers that Linkon does control are embroiled in a civil war with the wardens of the Dainwood that will not end soon. The jaguars are nothing if not stubborn when it comes to defending their precious forest." He pursed his lips. "I would say that Floodhaven is more vulnerable today than it has been in a thousand years."

"Just because Floodhaven is vulnerable doesn't mean Linkon Pommol will simply give us his dragon oil," Vera said. "And I cannot sneak into Floodhaven and kill everyone who guards it like I did in Burz-al-dun."

"Don't worry about Linkon Pommol," Kira said. "I know how to deal with him."

Vera was extremely worried. But Kira was beaming. "It's decided. We are going back home, and I am taking the throne of Almira for myself. No husband. No prime magnate." She looked at Vera. "Just you and me."

Vera let that sink in. She didn't want to admit it, but Ward was right. Actus Thorn would never let them live in peace. Never let Kira's crime go unanswered. Despite the risks, this was their best chance at long-term safety.

"I'm willing to try," Vera said. "But we also need to convince Lieutenant Decimar and his men. They still believe they are taking the empress on a joyride."

"That won't be a problem," Kira said. "I will tell them we have embarked on a secret mission to avenge my fallen sister and conquer Almira for the good of the empire." She shrugged. "They'll be heroes. More famous than the Flawless Bershad."

She seemed sad, despite her confidence. That was how Vera knew she could do it.

"There is just one more thing, then," said Vera.

"What?" Kira asked, impatient.

"Now that your ship has begun her maiden voyage, she needs a name."

Kira smiled. "The *Blue Sparrow*."

25

BERSHAD

Ghost Moth Island, Beyond the Bone Wall

Once Ashlyn had explained everyone's part in rescuing Wendell, they continued into the heart of the island, trekking across corrupted forest and meadow and marsh. The farther they traveled, the more machinery they encountered that was intertwined and implanted into the landscape. The air reeked of chemicals.

They passed fetid pools of thick slime that were fed by copper pipes sprouting from the broken ground. Enormous mushrooms that had been festooned with wires and attached to arcane machinery, which had turned their caps black and shiny. The few animals they did see were mostly deformed rodents or lizards—ridges of fungus ran along their skulls and sprouted from their ears and mouths and noses. The animals scurried into the shadows as they passed. Watched them with weeping, corrupted eyes.

Eventually, they reached more Ghost Moth carcasses. Scores of them.

They'd all been killed the same way—a ballista bolt through the forehead. Their bellies had been cut open and their bodies excavated, then propped up with iron rods. But these hadn't been completely hollowed out like the first one. They passed a juvenile with an intact heart and liver, both of which were connected to wide ceramic pipes that ran along the ground, disappearing into the murky gloom ahead. Another one nearby had the bones of its hind legs preserved and attached to the same type of ceramic pipe.

"So this is how Osyrus did it," Ashlyn said, tapping the place where the pipe was fused to the bone. "He ran some kind of preservation fluid through the bone marrow." She followed the pipe with her eyes. "The rest of the apparatus must be up ahead."

"So is Kasamir and his giant," Bershad said, motioning to the tracks, which followed alongside the pipe, too. They were fresh. He turned to Felgor. His part in Ashlyn's plan was the most important, but it was also the most dangerous. "You sure you're up for this?"

"Don't worry about old Felgor—these fingers haven't failed me yet." He wiggled his right hand.

Bershad crossed his arms. He was worried, even if Felgor wasn't. "This doesn't work if you don't take him by surprise," he said.

"I have some significant sneak to me."

"You do. But this is Kasamir's territory. He said he could smell us. I'm thinking that all the time he's been on this island, anything fresh—anything that doesn't belong—stands out to him."

Bershad looked around. Eyes settling on the Ghost Moth carcass with the preserved heart and liver.

"But he won't notice a dragon's scent," Ashlyn finished.

"Right."

Ashlyn stepped closer to the dragon, examining the liver, which was the size of a baroness's bed. "Goll, hand me your knife. The liver enzymes will make the perfect mask for Felgor's scent."

"What? Enzymes? Mask? What are you talking about?"

Goll laughed. "They're gonna coat you in dragon juice, Balarian. That's obvious."

"But . . . but that's . . . there's got to be another way."

"Goll. The knife."

———

Ten minutes later, Felgor was completely coated in wet strips of liver, and completely miserable.

"I expect to be amply compensated for this," Felgor said.

"Two thousand gold do it?" Bershad asked.

"No. I'm gonna need some property. Two, three brothels at least. Good ones."

"No problem," Ashlyn said. "Just don't get yourself killed before, yeah?"

"Yeah."

He snuck off into the gloom without a word—strafing around to the east like they'd discussed. Bershad waited for a few minutes so Felgor had time to get into position.

Everyone else was quiet while they waited. Vash paced nervously. Ashlyn continued examining the Ghost Moth. Goll drank from his canteen, which he swore was water but was clearly rum.

"It's time," Bershad said eventually. "Keep back a ways, like you're trying to stay out of sight. And don't make your move until—"

"We all know our parts, Flawless," Goll interrupted. "You focus on yours." He winced. "It is not a pleasant one."

"Yeah. All right."

Bershad drew his sword and headed forward, following the ceramic pipe's line.

He passed scores of Ghost Moth carcasses as he moved forward. Some were hatchlings, no larger than a white-tailed deer. Others were hulking matriarchs—their bodies rising out of the gloom like ragged hills.

All of them had pipes running out of their carcasses.

The landscape began to change again, but not in the way Bershad expected. Everything had been getting more infected the farther inland they went. But instead of more fetid puddles, corrupted creatures, and blackened mushrooms, Bershad started seeing clear pools of water full of blue-shelled snails. Brightly capped mushrooms began poking through the muck and pocking the ceramic pipes. Their colors reminded Bershad of Dainwood songbirds—yellow, pink, orange, green, blue.

The mushrooms became more and more frequent, until eventually Bershad couldn't see the pipe at all, just a channel of fungal color. Their scent was so potent it almost felt thick in his nostrils, like honey. But the spiraling pattern of cap colors was too orderly and geometric to be natural. Someone had planted these individually. Cared for them.

The channel led him to a sheer wall of vibrant mushrooms that sprawled toward the sky, growing along a skeleton of metal beams and copper mesh. There was a circular hole in the barrier that Bershad stepped through. He bent down near the edge of the interior. Looked around. Ahead, the channel of mushrooms expanded into a spiraling garden, with hundreds of different types and sizes and colors. Looking up, Bershad caught his first glimpse of a clear blue sky since they crossed the bone wall. No fungal haze. Just a wisp of a cloud.

And then a flash of gray hide.

The Nomad.

When she passed overhead, a burst of sensation poured across Bershad's skin. Sparked his senses. The rotten smell of the giant filled his nose. The sound of his lumpy, fungus-ridden heartbeat squelched in his ears. He could sense Wendell's pulse, too, which was clear and strong but also hammering with panicked fear. And Kasamir's, which was consistent and calm.

The Nomad began to circle the tunnel to the sky, giving Bershad the chance to focus his hearing on Kasamir. The sounds of his hands working rough dirt filled his ears like a mudslide. Beneath the sounds of moving earth, Bershad could hear Kasamir whispering under his breath.

"The boy will make a good crop," he muttered. "Next to the Pargossian sailors, perhaps? No. No. Too acidic for his young flesh. The aged batch of Ghalamarian soldiers? Yes . . . yes, that is the spot. The Ionitian tendrils will treat him well." He turned to the giant. "Clear off the top soil of plot seven."

Bershad could just barely see the hulking, mushroom-festooned shoulders of the giant thrusting up and down through the undergrowth. The sound of dirt flying.

"Gently. Gently. We want to expose the tendrils, not sever them."

The giant paused. Groaned. Resumed digging.

"That's it. Much better."

Bershad listened a while longer. Along with the digging and the whispers, he could hear the steady scrape of a sharpening stone against rough steel.

The Nomad dipped lower in the sky without warning. The proximity released a cascade of new sensations. Those three weren't the only living creatures in this grove—suddenly Bershad could also feel hundreds more, all of them buried beneath the ground at various levels. For a moment, he assumed they were burrowing animals. Groundhogs and rodents and such. But their heartbeats all matched the same calm cadence of Kasamir's. And they all had the familiar weight of a specific creature. Humans.

Bershad tried to pull the Nomad a little closer, but as a response she veered away, taking the burst of sensation with her.

"You might as well come out in the open, lizard killer," Kasamir called. "There is no reason for the two of us to play games."

"Fair enough."

Bershad stood up. Dusted the loamy soil off his knees, and walked down a garden row. The mushroom caps in this row were blue and yellow—glowing with the iridescent and clean pallor of an oyster's shell. He noticed that when his boots fell near a mushroom, the fungus recoiled from his foot the same way a startled rodent will scurry into the undergrowth when you surprise it.

Bershad stopped when he was about twenty strides from Kasamir and the giant. Wendell was hog-tied at their feet, drool leaking around his gag. Eyes wide with terror. Bershad could smell the boy's urine drying against his pant leg.

There was a freshly dug pit in front of them that was about a stride deep. A tangle of purple roots sprouted from the open hole. They were wreathed in green fungus that smelled strongly of valerian root.

"So, you managed to cross my barrier," Kasamir said. "I give you credit for perseverance, but you have made a very foolish choice. I built the wall to keep the corruption contained."

"Uh-huh." Bershad motioned to the boy and the pit. "And what're we up to here?"

"Restoring the balance that Osyrus Ward tore asunder."

"How's that working out? 'Cause things still looked pretty chewed up on my walk in here."

Kasamir's pale lips curled. "Sarcasm. A blunt tool, clutched tight by morons. You know nothing of my accomplishments. My years of careful carving and craft. This garden used to be a pit of chemicals and acid and degradation, now look at it." He raised his hands, and with them, every mushroom cap swelled and stretched. "The sky is clear once again. The ground clean."

"Pretty sure the ground is full of people that you buried alive. Wouldn't call that clean."

"Ah. Of course. Your lizard came through here with her hunter's senses. A Gray-Winged Nomad, yes? Interesting breed. Interesting implications."

"Fuck your implications. I came for the boy."

"But you did not come alone. Your three friends cannot hide from me. Tell them to enter my garden." Kasamir gestured behind Bershad, where Ashlyn, Goll, and Vash had set up on the fringes, pretending to hide.

"They're good where they are," Bershad said, glad to hear Kasamir's incorrect count. "Give me the boy and I'll leave you to tend your fucked-up garden in peace."

"The boy will join me in the yoke of equilibrium. There is nothing you can do to stop his journey."

"Let's test the truth of that notion."

Bershad reared back and heaved his sword at Kasamir's chest.

It was truly a beautiful throw. Moving with enough force to slice a plate-armored warden in half or puncture deep into a dragon's heart. Problem was, the giant's arm blurred with motion, and he caught the sword by the cross guard like a chameleon snatching flies from the surface of a bog. He glared at the blade as if a bird had just taken a shit on his palm. Tried to shake it off. But the edge had cut deep into the meat of his hand and gotten stuck there.

Kasamir hadn't flinched. Hadn't broken eye contact with Bershad.

"You keep getting separated from your sword, lizard killer. I'm not a warrior, but that specific tactic does not seem wise."

Bershad shrugged. "Never been accused of wisdom with much regularity."

"Well. Wise men and stupid men die in a similar fashion."

Kasamir's cloak twitched. The giant lumbered forward, gaining momentum and speed with each step. He raised the club over his head.

Bershad popped the rest of the Gods Moss into his mouth, which was a nugget about the size of a crow's egg. Swallowed it with effort. Stood his ground as the moss's strength coursed through his veins.

"This better work," he muttered. Then closed his eyes.

The giant's club caught him on the left side of his chest. As Bershad was lifted off the ground, he felt his rib cage and pelvis shatter. When he landed, a bunch of his ruined ribs speared into his lungs and liver. He stayed facedown, letting the Gods Moss work. When most of the damage was healed, he looked up from the soft, loamy dirt.

The giant was about fifty strides away. He'd already turned around, showing Bershad his back, which was covered with angry red mushrooms.

"That far enough?" Bershad groaned to Ashlyn. He'd landed about ten strides away from her.

"Not quite."

"Figured."

With an effort, Bershad got to his knees, then to his feet.

"Hey. Asshole."

The giant stopped. Turned.

"Yeah. You. Asshole. Gonna take more than a tap to kill me."

The giant's jaw opened slightly, releasing a long, frustrated breath. Kasamir stepped forward. "So, you've learned what the moss does," he said. "That explains how you survived a sword through your spine."

"Naw, you missed my spine. Mostly caught stomach, which isn't a big deal. I've regrown the old food bag dozens of times."

"You don't understand our curse, lizard killer. Ending your life is a kindness."

Bershad shrugged. Ignored the implications of that statement. He couldn't afford to get distracted.

"Get on with it, then. I like it when people do me favors."

Kasamir smiled. "Very well. Let's see if you can regrow your brain after we pound it to mush."

The giant's body twitched with irritation, then he twisted on his heels and rushed back to Bershad. Club raised.

This time, Bershad kept his eyes wide open.

The giant tried the same attack as before—a powerful uppercut. Kasamir was right—he wasn't a warrior. A true killer stays unpredictable.

Bershad shifted to the right so the club whooshed past him in a rush of air. The giant brought the club down in a backswing as soon as Kasamir realized he'd missed, but there was a delay between realization and action. Not much—the skinny bastard could have been a master puppeteer in another life—but it was all that Bershad needed. The shadow of the club flickered, and Bershad ducked to the left. A spray of mushroom shrapnel splashed across his face.

"Little too slow there, Kasamir," Bershad said, backpedaling. "C'mon. You wanna do me that kindness, you gotta move faster."

The giant unleashed a havoc of club swipes—each one faster than the next. Low. High. Low. Low. High. Bershad dodged and wove, guiding the giant farther away from both Kasamir and Ashlyn. He heard the giant's shoulder muscles tearing from the wild rage of his blows. Kasamir was running the show, not the limitations of this hulking bastard's limbs.

But it turned out that Bershad's reflexes ran out of luck right before the giant's muscles ran out of strength.

Bershad skipped left of a killing blow, but the giant tore the club through the earth, dislocating his own shoulder and catching Bershad in the right temple. He went down. Dazed.

Before he could push himself up, the club slammed down on his back.

Again.

And again.

As the third strike pancaked his spine, Bershad had one final, lucid thought before the pain made him black out.

Don't fuck this up, Felgor.

26

ASHLYN

Ghost Moth Island, Beyond the Bone Wall

It took every ounce of Ashlyn's willpower to remain still while the giant beat Bershad deeper and deeper into the ground with his club.

"Where is the Balarian?" Goll muttered as he fidgeted with impatience. "Flawless is getting obliterated."

"Just wait," Ashlyn whispered, eyes darting between the giant and Kasamir. "He'll move when the time is right."

Or Silas will die in the next ten seconds.

Vash remained motionless. Didn't say anything. But he was grinding his teeth hard enough to make Ashlyn cringe.

"Come on, come on, come on," Goll muttered.

A clump of ferns behind Kasamir twitched. Felgor shot out of them—body still coated slick with dragon liver juice. He brushed up against the right side of Kasamir's body and then darted away again, sprinting toward Ashlyn, who leapt from her spot and rushed to meet him.

Kasamir was so surprised that he did nothing but frown at the departing Felgor—not understanding what the blur of a man had done.

"I got it!" Felgor called, rushing toward Ashlyn, holding up the black lodestone. "I got it!"

Ashlyn glanced at the giant. He was still looming over Bershad's broken body, but he'd dropped the club. His left arm hung slack and lifeless by his side. The lodestone controlling that limb must have been the one that Felgor stole from Kasamir.

"Balarian rodent," Kasamir hissed, coming to the same realization. His hand started twitching beneath his cloak and the giant spun away from Bershad. Charged Felgor. His dead arm flailed wild and erratic, but the other was raised, palm tightening around Bershad's sword, which was still stuck in the meat of his hand.

Ashlyn and Felgor met a moment later. He pressed the stone into her fist.

"You grabbed the wrong stone," Ashlyn muttered. She'd wanted the one controlling the giant's spine.

"There wasn't time to peruse the selection," Felgor huffed.

The giant was twenty strides away.

She squeezed down on the lodestone. Felt a charge ripple down her forearm and into the magnet.

Nothing happened to the giant. He just kept charging.

"Uh. Ashlyn?" Felgor asked.

She squeezed harder, which strengthened the buzzing resonance in her palm enough to make her teeth hurt, but still didn't do anything to the giant.

"Are we fucked?" Felgor's voice was high-pitched with panic.

"No," Ashlyn said. Jaw clenched. Heart hammering. "We're out of range."

She hoped.

"What does that—"

When the giant was ten strides away from them, his left arm burst apart in an explosion of rotten flesh and mushroom gore. The force of the blast was strong enough to tear through his chest and limbs. When the fungal dust settled, there was nothing left except two big feet standing in a puddle of putrid goop and black, rotten bones.

Felgor puked.

Ashlyn stood up and looked around. She didn't see Kasamir, but she could hear him laughing. The sound was unnerving. Throaty and maniacal. It was coming from a clump of heavy ferns.

Vash jumped from his place and ran over to his son. Pulled the gag out of his mouth and started talking to him in low tones.

Ashlyn got to her feet and started moving toward the laughter. To her left, Silas was up on his knees but seemed to be having trouble rousing himself further. The right side of his body was a mess—armor battered and broken and smashed inward in dozens of places.

"You all right?" she called.

"That's a stupid question," he replied, struggling for breath.

"Going to die?"

"Not right this moment, no. But it'd be nice if someone could help get this armor off me before I heal into the shape of a rotten fucking pear."

"Goll," Ashlyn called.

The Lysterian headed toward Silas at a trot. Drew a knife and started cutting the armor off his wounded body. "I'll sort you out, Flawless."

Kasamir was still laughing when Ashlyn reached him, which was odd because he'd been sliced in half at the waist. His entrails were spilled across the ground and his right arm was sheared off at the elbow. She looked for his hand but didn't see it.

"How'd that happen?" Felgor asked, coming up behind her.

Ashlyn pointed to Silas's sword, which was stuck point-first into the earth behind Kasamir. Still smoking.

"It must have been blown over here when the giant exploded," Ashlyn said.

"Huh," Felgor grunted. "Can't tell if that's a good or bad thing."

"Bad for you," Kasamir said. "Irrelevant to me."

"Looks pretty relevant from where I'm standing," Felgor said. "Don't even see your legs . . ."

"Where did Osyrus Ward take the other dragon threads?" Ashlyn asked Kasamir.

She'd examined scores of the preserved Ghost Moths on their way into the garden, looking for threads that Osyrus hadn't ruined with chemicals. Aside from the carcass with the Papyrian soldier hung inside of it, every spinal column was empty, but showed evidence of surgery and extraction.

"Even if you found them, it wouldn't matter. Like I said, Osyrus touched everything on this island. There's nothing for you here."

"All the same. Where did he take them?"

"To the Proving Ground. That is where he took everything, once he was done with me."

"Where is that?"

"North. But you'll die before you get there."

Ashlyn ignored the vague threat. Kasamir wouldn't survive much longer. He couldn't. She needed to scrape as much information from him as possible.

"What did Osyrus do to you?" she asked.

Kasamir smiled. His teeth were coated in bile. "You're the one who figured out the secret to the dragon threads. You can't figure out me? It should be obvious."

Ashlyn looked around. She hadn't absorbed much of her surroundings because of the fight. But now that she could look around, she saw that all the ceramic pipes Osyrus had connected to the dragons converged around a metal pallet not far from where Kasamir had planned to bury Wendell.

The pallet was designed to restrain a human, and there were twelve rubber tubes—six on each side of the pallet. They all had frayed ends that funneled into the ceramic pipes.

Ashlyn looked back at Kasamir. Saw six metal sockets running down each side of his rib cage. The sockets on the left side had been sealed over with pink scar tissue, but the ones on the right side still had severed lengths of rubber tube connected to them. The ends were leaking a yellow bile onto the ground.

"Osyrus used you to preserve the dragon bones?"

"My blood."

Ashlyn's skin prickled.

"You're a Seed."

"I am Specimen 01. The first anomaly. The dried-up, putrid well."

Ashlyn looked back at the pallet. There were teeth marks around the frayed ends. Kasamir had chewed his way free.

"How long were you attached to that?"

Kasamir sniffed. Narrowed his eyes. "Longer than you have been alive, half-breed."

"And when you broke free . . . what did you do?"

Kasamir coughed up some blood.

"Osyrus never understood the mushrooms. Same as he never

understood the dragons. By the time I escaped from Osyrus Ward's torment, he'd left. His failed experiments were roaming this island like demons. I was the one who got them under control. Used them to build the bone barrier. Stop the spread of Osyrus Ward's corruption. Then I put them to sleep, except for one of his final creations."

"The giant."

"Yes. Osyrus called him Specimen 9009. He also thought him a failure. Left him in the deep pit. *I* saw 9009's potential for construction. And protection."

"Which you needed, because you made a pact with the pirates," Ashlyn said.

"There was no other way to get it back."

"Get what back?"

"Don't you understand? I *found* what the alchemists have been searching for all these long years. I found everlasting life. But it came with a sacrifice—to bind with the Cordata mushrooms for eternity. I lived here in perfect balance for two hundred years before Osyrus Ward arrived. He surveyed my achievement, then corrupted it beyond measure. Said I had no sense of *scope*. He stayed for decades. He poisoned the soil. Killed the dragons. Pulled his precious lodestones from the ground and planted them beneath my flesh. When Okinu's dogs came after him, he imprisoned them, too. The things that he did to them were far worse. Everything I did was to fix what he broke. To get it back. I *had* to get it back."

Ashlyn glanced behind her. Goll had gotten all of Silas's armor off, and was helping him limp in her direction. His gait got stronger with every step. She turned back. For everything Kasamir had done wrong, there was value in keeping him alive. She still had a thousand unanswered questions. Why had the Ghost Moths come to the island? How had he manipulated the mushrooms?

"You don't have to die here," Ashlyn said. "I can help you."

"He's been cut in half," Felgor muttered.

"You're a Seed," Ashlyn pressed. "We have Gods Moss."

"That won't save me. They're going to wake up now. And there will be nothing to govern their behavior besides the fungus. Its orders are simple." He smiled. "Bring me bone. Bring me flesh."

Kasamir started seizing. His eyes rolled back into his head.

Hands jolting. Intestines wriggling. After a few seconds, he went still.

"Dead?" Bershad said, coming up alongside her.

"Yes," Ashlyn said.

A massive clod of dirt blasted into the air to her left. Another to her right. Then all around the garden. Scores of them.

"Uh, what is happening?" Felgor asked.

Nobody answered. But Bershad was staring up through the tunnel of vines and plants, where the Nomad had returned, and was spinning in low, tight circles.

"We need to leave," he said.

"No, I need to study Kasamir and the apparatus he was attached to. There's more to learn about what Osyrus did here."

"Ashe, trust me. This is not the time to set up a research station."

He turned to Vash, who was inspecting his son's bruised and bloody ankles. "Can he run?"

"Not fast."

"Then I'm gonna carry him." Bershad scooped the boy up. "We need to get as far away from here as possible, as fast as possible."

"No, I need more information," Ashlyn said, bending down and spreading Kasamir's entrails apart with her gloved fingers. "Give me ten minutes."

"We don't have ten minutes," Bershad said, moving past her and yanking his sword from the ground. "We don't have one minute."

Ashlyn kept digging around. There were dozens of lodestones implanted inside Kasamir's body. Some were the size of peas, tucked between skin and muscle. Others were as big as apples and wedged between major organs. They were all connected by a tangled system of chemical-burned dragon threads that were fused with tendrils of pulsing blue fungus. Unlike the giant's flesh, which had gone to rot around the fungus, Kasamir's body was healthy and perfectly preserved.

"Gods," she whispered. "What did you do to yourself?"

Bershad grabbed her wrist. Hauled her up.

"Wait, I'm not finished!"

"Yes, you are."

He spun Ashlyn around so she was forced to look back at the garden.

To Goll's left, a mushroom-laced arm burst from the ground, followed by a swollen head with fungus pouring out of one ruined eye socket. The intact eye was swampy green and angry. Goll clubbed the head with his axe. A chunk of skullcap chipped off, revealing gray matter beneath. But the creature kept crawling out of the earth.

"Fucking mushroom demons!" Goll shouted, hacking at the head and arm until they were reduced to pieces. Even then, the torso kept on thrashing around like an angry, injured snake.

Behind him, there were scores of figures sprouting from the earth. Their torsos and limbs radiated with fungal growth. Once they emerged, they began sniffing and scanning the area.

Looking for bone. Looking for flesh.

"They're blocking our way back," Vash said.

"Then we go deeper in," Bershad said.

———

They cut their way out of the garden and ran north, twisting between the hulking dragon corpses Osyrus Ward had left behind. After half an hour of running, they'd put a decent stretch of distance between themselves and Kasamir's buried creatures, which thankfully didn't move very fast.

The situation seemed under control until they reached the river.

The water had the same rusty red color as the first river they'd seen. But instead of ankle-deep water and a gentle current, this river was deep and rushing fast. The current was filled with horrific debris—colorful shreds of fungus and mushrooms, bloated rats covered in green blisters. The whole thing reeked of sulfur and decay.

Ashlyn had to hold back the urge to vomit. Felgor didn't even bother. He took one whiff and doubled over, puking.

"Again?" Bershad asked.

"I have a sensitive stomach."

"What now?" Vash huffed. His face was flushed. Hair soaked with sweat. Everyone was heaving air and sweating hard except for Silas, despite the fact that he'd carried Wendell this whole way.

That meant the Gods Moss was still coursing through his body. Giving him strength.

"We need to cross," he said.

"No way," Felgor said, still doubled over. He spat a little. "I am not getting in that water."

"It's that, or stick around to fight a hundred of those things."

"We need a boat," Goll said.

"Little short on time to build a boat," Vash said.

"But I don't swim."

Everybody looked at him.

"You're a pirate," Bershad said. "What do you mean you don't swim?"

"I'm a corsair," Goll corrected, then shrugged. "And it was never a problem before."

"Well, it's a big problem now." Bershad looked around. "Lysterian pirate who can't swim. Gods."

"*Corsair,*" Goll said again.

"Whatever."

"I have an idea," Ashlyn said, pointing to an enormous mushroom with a stalk as thick as a cedar tree and a cap the size of a cabin's roof.

"Will that even float?" Vash asked.

"Only one way to find out." Bershad walked over to the mushroom and hacked through it with a brutal slice. "Goll, help me turn it over."

The two of them struggled to get the mushroom upside down, but managed it with a few minutes of grunting effort. Underneath, the gills of the mushroom were thick and colorful, comprising a thousand different hues of blue and purple.

"They're kind of pretty when they're not all rotten and jammed into body cavities," Felgor said, looking at it.

"Yeah," said Silas. "Help me scrape it out."

They all got to work hollowing out the mushroom. Even Wendell helped. Ten minutes later, the meat of the mushroom had been cored out and piled next to the river, and there was enough space for ten men to stand comfortably in the space they'd created.

"Get it in that eddy," Ashlyn said, pointing.

The giant fungus bobbed easily in the crimson current once they got it in. Goll stepped onto it experimentally, hopping up and down a few times.

"It seems to be a seaworthy vessel."

"Good," Ashlyn said. "Everybody on."

Vash didn't hesitate to corral his son onto the mushroom. "Crouch down here, near the middle," he said. "You can hold on to the stem to brace yourself."

"Look at that!" Felgor said, pointing at a dead possum floating down the current. "That's disgusting."

Silas poked him in the ribs. "Just get on the mushroom, Felgor."

"Yeah, yeah."

Ashlyn and Silas followed him. Vash had lashed their scabbards to Goll's axe to create a makeshift paddle. As soon as everyone was aboard, he used it to push the boat away from shore. He straightened their path down the river with a few controlled strokes.

Behind them, the shoreline filled with mushroom-infected bodies—green eyes glowing. Staring. Thankfully, none of them seemed eager to enter the water. Ashlyn watched them until their mushroom boat disappeared around a bend in the river, leaving the monsters behind.

The river was moving fast, but there were no rocks or rapids ahead. Ashlyn sat down on the mushroom, leaning against its stem. She picked at the charred cord on her wrist and chewed her lip.

"What's on your mind?" Bershad asked her.

"More than one thing."

"Look, Ashe. We had to get out of there."

"I know. That isn't it."

"What, then?"

"That was where Osyrus started his work. I need to see where he finished it. And after all that we've been through on this island, we're no closer to finding what we came for."

"I wouldn't say that. Your trick with the lodestones is something."

"But that's all it is. A trick. There's a big difference between overloading one side of a simple system and bringing down an armada of skyships. The range. The thresholds of force. What I can do with this thread right now . . . it's not enough. It's not even close."

Silas didn't say anything. Just went back to scanning the shoreline.

"You saved my son," Vash said quietly. "That's something."

"Like you said, we're the ones who got him in trouble to begin with," Ashlyn said.

"All the same. I'm in your debt." He looked between Bershad and Ashlyn. "Both of you."

"What about me?" Felgor asked.

Vash nodded. "You, too, Balarian."

Felgor smiled. Leaned back and put his hands behind his head. "Don't mention it. I'm here to help."

———

They floated down the river in silence for a while. Each person collecting their composure in their own way. Felgor cleaned each of his fingernails with a focused concentration. Vash poked and prodded every inch of his son's body, looking for injuries but not finding anything beyond bruises and scrapes. Goll and Bershad watched opposite sides of the shoreline.

Ashlyn picked at the fringes of her dragon thread, which sent a dull pain through every tendril of the fiber, letting her map its reach. She could feel it stretching past her elbow, woven deep into the nerves and muscles. The scars on her arm from the battle at Floodhaven—which had once been a cold pale blue—were black all the way to her shoulder.

The thread was a part of her now. And it was spreading. She had no idea whether it would stop, or what it would do to her as it expanded.

They rounded a bend. Ahead, the river forked. One branch narrowed and turned into a torrent of rapids and cataracts. The other widened, becoming easy and calm.

"Which way?" Vash asked, picking up his makeshift oar again.

Bershad sniffed the air in each direction. Glanced up at the sky.

He pointed to the branch of rough water. "That way leads to the sea. I can smell the salt. Just barely, but it's there."

"And the other?" Ashlyn asked.

He motioned to the woods, which were sickly and overgrown with fungus. "More of this crap."

"If we make it to the sea, we can get back to Naga Rock," Vash said. "To safety."

Ashlyn and Bershad exchanged a look. "Your call, Ashe."

She and Silas had to keep going. That was obvious. But Ashlyn wasn't in a rush to force the rest of the journey on the others, even though she knew that they'd be willing. In fact, she would probably need to convince Felgor and Goll to split ways. But that was doable.

"We'll stop at the fork," Ashlyn said. "Decide there."

Vash guided them toward the split, where there was a good eddy and a rocky bank. Scrub brush and wild grass led into the murky foliage of the forest. They were about five strides from the bank when the Gray-Winged Nomad swooped low over their heads—disrupting the fungal gloom with her powerful wings, and giving them a moment of sunlight on their faces.

Bershad's posture stiffened.

"Push back!" Bershad barked. "Get away from the shoreline."

Vash put two strong paddle strokes into the water, stopping their forward motion. But a crossbow bolt plunked into the meat of the mushroom stem before he could return them to the current. The back of the bolt had a long metal wire attached to it that streamed into the dark woods.

A metal crank started spinning, and they were reeled to the shore with surprising alacrity. The mushroom was dragged up the bank, then lurched to a sudden stop.

The woods were quiet for a few heartbeats. And then a deep voice started singing from the undergrowth.

"Oh, the Skojit went fishing, down by his river. Caught himself some people, stuffed in a mushroom. Sliced 'em to pieces and cooked 'em for dinner."

"Shit," Vash muttered. "We've just got no fucking luck at all."

A tall man separated from the shadows. Stepped forward and studied them. He was a Skojit, and stood a head taller than Bershad. His red hair was ragged and long, hanging down over both shoulders. But his armor was what grabbed Ashlyn's attention. The breastplate was built from a complicated weave of white Ghost Moth scales and chemical-burned dragon threads. It covered his entire body from the neck down. Perfectly molded to his limbs.

This was Simeon. The pirate who made a pact with Kasamir in exchange for Osyrus Ward's technology.

"Mushroom," Simeon said. "Hmm . . . what rhymes with that? Doom. Soon. Eh, who cares? Dumb song, anyway."

He surveyed them.

"So, how'd you lot wind up in this situation? Seems like a good story here."

"Simeon." Vash stood up. "We're corsairs out of Naga Rock. Under Kerrigan's command. We don't want trouble. Just trying to get home."

"Not wanting trouble and causing it are separate issues. The rules are real clear. Kerrigan's sheep stay safe, so long as they stay in their Naga Rock pen." He ran a hand through his dirty red hair. "But you idiots have wandered real deep into the wrong side of the bone wall. Means I'm within my rights to truss you up and turn you over to the demons. That'd save me the trouble of going reaving this month to make my quota, which is an attractive notion given the autumn storms are already sweeping through and we just came by a big vat of Lysterian potato liquor that needs some sustained attention."

Bershad got out of the mushroom. Rested his sword on one shoulder. "That isn't happening."

Simeon shifted his gaze. "Lizard killer. One of Kerrigan's recent recruits? She does love collecting exiles."

Bershad didn't say anything. Simeon eyed his bare arm.

"Lot o' tattoos. You pretending to be the Flawless Bershad or something?"

"I *am* the Flawless Bershad. And I'm gonna murder you if you don't let us pass."

"Bold talk. But you're a little light on armor to be making threats with that kind of certainty." He looked at Goll and Vash. "Might be you think with these two behind you that you've got the numbers on me. You don't."

"Your thirteen friends who are hiding in the bushes don't change the situation."

Simeon cocked his head. Surprised. He whistled, and thirteen men melted out of the underbrush behind him. All of them had blue bars on their cheeks. Most of them were carrying heavy crossbows with far more machinery and gears than a standard model. One of them had a shield made from the disk of a Ghost Moth's spine. He was carrying an odd-looking spear. It took Ashlyn a moment to realize that it was made from the preserved tip of a Naga Soul Strider's tail.

More of Osyrus Ward's work.

"You sure my boys don't change anything?" Simeon asked. "'Cause if I whistle again, they'll fill the lot of you with bolts.

Corpses don't shine for the demons as much as healthy prisoners, but they take 'em. The contribution's usually good for a little tweak to our gear."

"There's no such thing as demons," Wendell said. "Just bad people with—"

Ashlyn stopped him with a hand on his shoulder and a quick squeeze. The less Simeon knew about what they'd done to Kasamir, the better. She stepped off the mushroom and stood next to Bershad. One way or another, she needed to see the place where Simeon had gotten that armor. Because that was where Osyrus Ward had finished his work on the island.

"I'm worth a lot more to you outside the custody of demons."

Simeon grunted. "Who the fuck are you?"

"Ashlyn Malgrave."

"The witch queen of Almira? You wanna impersonate royalty, best to pick someone who isn't dead."

One of the other pirates—a man with blond hair and no ears—squinted hard at Ashlyn, then sidled up to Simeon. "Boss, I think that's really her."

"How the fuck would you know, Cabbage?"

"I got a tapestry of her back at the Proving Ground."

Simeon looked at him. "You and your fucking tapestries. Is that the one you're always jerking off to?"

"Naw," said the one with the dragon-bone shield, smiling to reveal a mouthful of gold teeth. "That's his other Malgrave one. The younger sister."

"Fuck off, Howell." Cabbage spat. Looked embarrassed. "My point is, that woman's either the spitting image of Ashlyn Malgrave, or we just lucked into the biggest ransom of our lives. You know she's Okinu's niece, right? And Papyrians always put a premium on the safe return of royal blood."

Simeon sucked on his teeth. "Aye. Papyrian ransoms are good money."

"Easy money, too," added Cabbage.

"Well?" Ashlyn asked.

"Don't rush me, woman. I'm thinking."

He scanned the others again. His eyes stopped on Felgor, who was huddled behind the stem of the mushroom.

"Show me your face, little man."

Felgor stayed put. Pretended he hadn't heard.

"Show it to me, or Cabbage will put a bolt through the top o' your skull. He's ugly as sin, but he's a good shot."

Felgor sighed. Looked up. "Hey, Simeon. Been a while."

"It's been five years and two months, Felgor. A man remembers when his favorite ship gets burned to cinders in Taggarstan."

"The *Esmerelda* was your favorite ship? She wasn't that nice as I recall." Felgor scratched his ear. "Don't think I lifted more than a week's worth of loot. Only worthwhile part was burning the thing down, to be honest. And that was just for a smile."

Simeon's face darkened.

"What?" Felgor asked. "You're not still raw about that whole thing, are you?"

"Yeah, Felgor. It turns out I am a bit raw." He tapped an armored finger against a scale on his thigh a few times. Wiped a strand of greasy red hair away from his face. "I'll take the alleged queen for the ransom, and Felgor for the tormenting. You Naga Rock boys are going into the chattel cages up in the Proving Ground until I decide how forgiving I wanna be about broken pacts."

His gaze settled on Bershad. "You, though. You got a bad look in your eyes, lizard killer. And I got no use for taking that back to the Proving Ground. But you're free to see if that scrap of fungus can navigate the rest of the Bloody Sludge. You get lucky, it'll wash you clear out to the Big Empty."

"I go where they go," Silas said.

"Nope. Either you go down the river in a literal fashion, or your soul takes the figurative journey. Your choice."

Bershad darted forward. Crossed the rocky beach in the space of a few heartbeats. His sword came down on Simeon's head in a blur.

Simeon caught the attack with a grunt. The impact of the blade rippled up Simeon's arm, making the Ghost Moth scales twitch. Ashlyn could hear gears straining from the impact.

"You hit hard, lizard killer," Simeon said, then squeezed the blade so hard it cracked. "But not hard enough."

Simeon slammed an armored fist into Bershad's chest. Sent him flying backward into the shallows of the red river. He slumped over in the water and went still.

Silas's sword was wedged between two of the scales that protected

Simeon's palm. He pried the blade loose, gave it a once-over, then threw it into the water. The scales on his left arm kept twitching. Gears hissing. He rotated his shoulder and muttered a curse under his breath.

"Take 'em," Simeon muttered.

Before anyone else could react, Simeon's men were hauling them out of the mushroom boat. Binding their hands and pulling black hoods from their belts.

"Simeon."

Everyone turned to see Bershad back on his feet. There was a massive and still-swelling contusion over his heart where Simeon had punched him.

"We're not done."

Simeon smiled again, wide and terrible. "I'll give you points for perseverance, lizard killer. Maybe you are the Flawless Bershad. But I *am* done with you." He whistled to his men. "Porcupine him. Then let's get moving."

Simeon's men raised their weapons. Aimed.

The steel release of the crossbows rattled through the blighted forest. The volley of bolts spun Silas around and put him on his knees in the water. The pirates' crossbows whirred, clicked, and reloaded themselves. They fired another volley into his back.

Silas was thrown into the current, which grabbed him and pulled him down the river.

Simeon spat. "Reckon that'll do it, boys."

Wendell tried to run into the water, but Vash grabbed him. Held him back. "Nothing you can do for him, boy."

"But he came after me!" Wendell cried, tears streaming down his cheeks.

"I know. I know."

Everyone watched as Silas disappeared around another bend in the river. Then Simeon moved up to the shore and kicked the mushroom into the current.

"Such emotion outta you lot over one dead exile," he said. "You're a bunch o' soft-shelled crabs."

He motioned to his men.

"Get the hoods on 'em. Then let's get back to the Proving Ground. I'm hungry."

PART III

27

VERA

The Soul Sea, Aboard the Blue Sparrow

Vera checked and rechecked her daggers, *Owaru* and *Kaisha*. Then made sure her sword was secure on her back. She still needed to give Bershad's old blade a name.

It was ten minutes after dawn. Vera had wanted to go in at night, but Decimar and Entras had both insisted that they needed at least some light to guide them, or they'd risk crashing into Floodhaven instead of flying over it.

"Increase thrust by ten percent!" Osyrus shouted to Entras, who pushed down on a lever. The *Blue Sparrow* jolted with acceleration.

"Good. Good. Now deflate the levitation sack and adjust the wing sails to a ten-percent gradient against the horizon."

"You sure?" Decimar said. "That's against standard procedure."

"There is nothing standard about this ship, Lieutenant. Trust me, that is all we need to stay airborne. Deflate the sack."

Entras followed his orders—there was a hissing release of air over their heads while the sack deflated and was then pulled down into the bowels of the ship by a series of ratcheting gears and cranks.

They approached Floodhaven from the east, flying low and using the freshly risen sun to mask their arrival. With the glare—and the deflated levitation sack—it would be easy to mistake them for a Soul Strider going for an early-morning hunt.

"More speed! Fifty-percent increase. Nobody will mistake us for a dragon unless we move like one."

The ship jolted forward again. The wind rushed around Vera's ears. Kira cackled with delight.

Vera looked down at Floodhaven. The city was built at the crest of a peninsula that speared up from the earth between the Atlas and Gorgon rivers. The walls and towers paled in comparison to the heights of Burz-al-dun, but when it came to natural fortifications, Floodhaven was among the best in the realm.

The harbor was empty, but the city and castle walls were manned with wardens, their armor glinting in the sun. They still hadn't noticed the skyship.

"Remember, we'll come back around in exactly ten minutes to pick you up," Kira said.

"I remember."

"He should be in his chambers at the top of the King's Tower. You *must* take him alive for the rest of this to work."

"I understand."

Vera picked up the rope and wound it around her wrist. Rolled her shoulders in a few quick circles to loosen them up.

"Thirty seconds out!" Entras shouted above the roaring engine and rushing wind.

"Perfect," Osyrus said. "Cut power to the Kor on my mark."

Vera stepped onto the gunwale, lowering herself into a squat to balance against the unsteady lilt of the ship.

"Mark!"

The engine went silent. The ship glided forward on the power of wind alone. After so many hours of dull engine roar, the quiet seemed strange.

Vera looked down—they were passing over the harbor, and approaching the seaward wall of Castle Malgrave. There were two wardens on the rampart, both of them squinting up at the rapidly approaching object. Vera took a breath. Waited for the angle to be perfect.

Then she jumped.

There were two seconds of free fall. Then the rope ran out of slack and whipped her forward. Vera was ready for the jerk, positioning herself so the pressure on her shoulder was dispersed through her body. She swung through the air in a long arc, headed directly toward one of the wardens on the wall.

Vera coiled into a ball to get the most speed possible. At the last moment, she shot her legs out and slammed into the warden's breastplate. He crashed into the far side of the rampart, cracking a crenellation and crumpling to the ground. Vera released the hemp rope and hit the stones at a crouch, sliding behind the second warden, who was still looking at the sky, trying to figure out what had just flown over the castle.

She grabbed him by the straps of his pauldrons and threw him into the sea.

Vera glanced back at the ship, which was rising fast. There was a loud boom as they relit the engine, but from that height and distance, it was easy to mistake it for a dragon's roar. A few moments later, the *Blue Sparrow* was hidden among the clouds.

The other wardens on the walls were focused on the strange object that had just flown through the sky. None of them had noticed the Papyrian widow who had dropped behind their fortifications and now had a clear path inside the castle.

Vera checked her watch.

"Ten minutes," she muttered, then went inside.

———

Vera knew the way to the king's chambers well. She'd escorted Kira up there anytime her father wanted to see her. She moved through the familiar halls and stairwells of Castle Malgrave with a purpose, passing servants and stewards in the halls. She didn't see any wardens.

"Was that a Papyrian widow?" one woman carrying an armful of laundry asked a bookish steward when Vera shoved past them.

"Gods, no. That was one of the actresses for tonight's play."

"She was carrying a lot of weapons for an actress—"

Vera passed out of earshot, then sprinted up several flights of stairs to put some distance between herself and the servants. She hustled down another long hallway with tall windows. Two more servants were in the hallway, but they were staring out the windows, pointing to the west and muttering to each other.

"A Soul Strider, maybe?"

"They don't go inland, though. Could have been a Red Skull?"

"Wrong color."

"Whatever it is, we best make totems."

"Agreed."

Vera reached the end of the hallway, went up two more flights, then jumped out the window. She landed on the top of a covered bridge that connected to the King's Tower. She sprinted across, then without breaking stride jumped onto the wall and began climbing.

She reached a large circular window—grabbed the top sill—then kicked her way through. Landed on the soft carpet in a spray of broken glass. Her eyes darted around the lavish room.

No king. Just a serving boy who was about fifteen years old. He was pouring a pot of coffee into a ceramic cup.

Vera crossed the room, which sent the boy stumbling backward. He spilled the coffee all over the front of his shirt.

"Where is Linkon Pommol?"

"I don't . . . I don't know. I just bring the coffee, whether he's here or not."

Vera thumped her sheathed sword onto his shoulder. "Tell me where the king is, and this sword doesn't get drawn."

The boy quivered. Eyes glassy with tears.

"What's your name, kid?"

"Dennys."

She nodded. "It's all right, Dennys. You can tell me. I'm here to help him."

A wave of relief washed over the kid's face. Vera was always amazed by the things that terrified people will believe if you look them in the eye and speak with confidence.

"I think he was going to eat breakfast with Lord Brock this morning. Brock usually takes it in a ninth-floor dining hall since they're closest to the main kitchen. Get can get his seconds hot."

"Good."

Vera turned to leave.

"Is it a dragon?" the boy asked. "I heard people shouting about something in the sky."

"Yeah, Dennys. It's a dragon."

––––––––

Eight flights of stairs and seven hundred paces later, Vera reached the ninth-floor dining halls. The smell of smoked pork and burning bread filled the air. Smoke wafted from the door to the kitchen, which was built into the center of the tower and had corridors leading to the four dining halls on this level. Vera checked the first hall, but found it empty, so she cut through the kitchen to reach the next.

A cook with white dough flecks all over her forearms was frantically pulling burned loaves of bread out of the oven.

"Fools," she muttered, to herself. "Ran off to look at the dragon and damn near burned the castle down."

Vera considered slitting the cook's throat. Witnesses were problems. But they could be useful, too. She dropped her voice into the best Almiran accent she could muster, and hoped the distracted cook stayed that way.

"Urgent message for King Pommol," she said. "He's needed elsewhere. Which dining hall?"

The cook extended her dough-dusted arm and pointed to a door on the far side of the kitchen. "Eagle's Roost."

"Is Lord Brock inside as well?"

"Just the king," the baker said. "Lord Brock went to use the privy before eating his second course."

"Thank you."

By the time the cook had turned around, Vera had already shouldered her way through the door and disappeared. She found the proper room and barged inside.

Linkon Pommol was seated at the far end of a very long table. Three wardens with turtle masks stood behind him. Everyone turned to her.

"You are not Lord Brock," Linkon said, frowning.

Vera threw *Owaru* into the closest warrior's throat, drew her sword, then rushed forward and stabbed the second through the heart. The third came at her hard, but got tripped up on a chair and only managed a clumsy side swipe. Vera parried and took his head off with a counter-riposte.

"Oh gods," Linkon muttered. "Oh gods, no."

"Quiet," Vera hissed, crossing the room and shoving Linkon onto his stomach. She used one of her slings to bind his wrists.

"Stay there."

Vera grabbed one of the dead wardens and threw him out the window in a crash of stained glass. Watched to make sure that he landed in the sea below. Satisfied, she threw the other two as well. With nothing but blood and glass as evidence, it would look like a dragon attack.

"You're next." Vera grabbed Linkon by the collar.

"No, no. Please! Please don't—"

Vera threw the king of Almira out the window.

But instead of dropping a thousand strides to the sea, he only fell ten. Landed on another bridge that connected two of the castle's towers. Vera jumped down after him. Hauled Linkon to the halfway point between the two towers, then looked up at the sky. Searching.

The *Blue Sparrow* was coming around from the west, banking hard over the forest of Almira. She watched as the ship leveled out. Headed directly at her.

"Good," she muttered to herself. "They see me."

A single black rope dropped from the hull of the ship. Vera tightened her grip on Linkon's wrist bindings, then held out her other hand.

Two hundred strides.

Osyrus Ward had assured her that given enough slack, her shoulder wouldn't be damaged in the pickup process, and that they could reel her in within a few seconds. All she had to do was hold on.

One hundred strides.

The vision of her arm detaching and her falling off the bridge in an arc of blood filled her mind.

Fifty strides.

A heartbeat later the rope connected with her open hand. She tightened her grip and was vaulted through the sky, taking the king of Almira with her.

28

JOLAN

Almira, City of Black Rock

"This isn't going to work," Jolan said, stomach churning with panic and fear.

He was having trouble controlling his breathing, and he was sweating profusely from everywhere a person could sweat from. They were a hundred strides from the gate to Black Rock, and he was driving the wagon. He counted ten Balarian soldiers ahead.

"Not if you keep on speaking Almiran," Oromir responded calmly. Jolan had spent four hours teaching the wardens common Balarian phrases, and Oromir had the best accent, so he sat up front. Jolan was glad to have him close by. "Keep a grip on your composure. This will work."

Jolan's armor didn't fit him. It was loose around his hips and heavy on his shoulders. He'd been forced to leave his backpack of ingredients in the woods back at their campsite, but Oromir had helped him bury the pack and promised they'd come back for it. Jolan had stuffed the most valuable ingredients—Gods Moss and a few other rare items from the warren—into a small satchel and wadded that up behind his breastplate. It was already starting to chafe.

Jolan pulled up on the reins as they reached the gate. Two of the Balarian sentries came over with hands on their swords. A third and fourth kept their distance, but watched them closely. Jolan heard the click of their crossbows locking.

They'd waited until dusk to approach so their faces would be harder to see. Nightfall would have been better, but the gates would be closed then. It had taken the wardens almost half an hour to get their ring-laden hair stuffed into the helmets. The widows had offered their blades during several points of the process and been refused each time.

"What's all this?" the first soldier called to Jolan. He had a gold sergeant's insignia above the clock on his breastplate. "You two take up farming in your free time?"

The best lies are based in truth, Jolan said to himself, remembering Garret's words when they snuck into Deepdale last spring.

"You didn't hear?" Jolan asked, doing his best to keep his voice even and natural. "Couple of local women stole this cart last night and fled the city. We went after 'em. Whole thing's a mess—lost three men."

"That right?" The smile on the sergeant's face disappeared. "I didn't hear anything."

They'd circled Black Rock on the hope that there'd be a believable lapse in communication. So far, it seemed to have worked.

"Lieutenant Lornus said something about a few missing soldiers," said the second Balarian. He narrowed his eyes. "But he didn't say anything about anyone chasing a cart. Just men who abandoned their posts without orders."

"There wasn't time to get orders. Damn mud pinchers hit me over the head with a brick and took off." Jolan gestured to his forehead, where Shoshone had painted a surprisingly realistic-looking gash. She'd also rubbed dirt and grime on his face to hide the fact that he was a sixteen-year-old Almiran. Jolan motioned to the skyship above. "Figured there was no need for General Mun to get word about this, you know?"

"Since when is it your job to figure anything? And how did some local cunts get the drop on you, soldier?"

Jolan shrugged. "The stories about Almirans are true. Even the women fight like cornered jackals." Jolan prayed he'd said the idiom correctly. "We brought back the men they killed, but the women disappeared into the forest."

The sergeant peeked into the back of the wagon, where Cumberland, Sten, and Willem were laid up over the tarp in full armor and covered in plenty of blood.

"My plan was to head back to Sergeant Lornus and tell him what happened," Jolan said. "But seems to me someone should get after those women before they get lost in the wilderness."

The first soldier surveyed the situation in the back of the cart for another moment, then glared at Jolan. At this point, they were surrounded by all ten of the Balarian soldiers. Nobody was aiming their crossbow at them, but they were inching in that direction.

"What is your name, soldier?" the man asked Jolan.

"Private Tam, sir."

"And yours?" he asked, turning to Oromir.

"Private Marus, sir," Oromir said without hesitation.

Shoshone had provided them both with their names. He didn't know how she'd obtained them, but suspected her cleaver had been involved.

"And what do you have to say about all this, Private Marus?"

Oromir looked at him. "I fucking hate Almirans."

His accent was almost perfect.

The sergeant looked at them both for another moment, then spat on the ground.

"Three casualties. No hostile bodies, and no fucking orders for any of it. None of this smells right. And I do not like things with bad smells coming through my gate." He turned to his men. "Consal. Remus. Keska. Ride with these two to the far side of the city—march them directly to Lieutenant Lornus and see what's to be done with them."

"Sir."

"Once they're through, seal this gate. We'll go looking for these Almiran women who have caused so much trouble."

There was a flurry of activity as soldiers hopped onto their cart and the gate opened. Two minutes later they were inside the city and rolling down one of the main avenues. Jolan couldn't believe it.

But they weren't done yet. Not even close.

———

The three Balarian soldiers rode in the back, sitting on the sides of the wagon, their boots uncomfortably close to Cumberland and Sten. Two carried crossbows that were aimed at Jolan and Oromir, respectively. The third had his sword drawn. None of them spoke.

Jolan guided the ox down a few more streets until he spotted a dark alley. He turned down it.

"What are you doing, Private?" one of the soldiers asked him.

"I know a shortcut."

The soldier jabbed him with the crossbow. Even with his armor on, the bolt's point dug into his back.

"No shortcuts, asshole. Turn this thing around and keep on down the main—"

Cumberland shot up, pushed the crossbow to the left, and jammed his dagger up through the bottom of the Balarian's chin. When the blade entered his brain, his fingers tightened and the crossbow fired a bolt into the brick wall of the alley.

"Hey!" shouted the other man with a crossbow. But before he could fire, Sten kicked the bottom of the weapon so he fired his bolt into the sky instead of through Oromir's face. Willem was on him a moment later, dragging him down into the cart and covering his mouth as he sawed a dagger across this throat.

The third soldier hopped off the cart and started sprinting down the alley. But Shoshone darted out from beneath the tarp, already swinging her sling in three quick arcs. She released her shot, and the man's helmet shattered. Brains spilled all over the cobblestone alley.

"Pretty clean," Willem said, leaning back against the cart. His entire forearm was covered in blood.

Jolan wasn't sure how anyone could call an event that involved so much blood and brain clean. But he didn't say anything.

"Sten, Willem. Get those bodies underneath the tarp," Shoshone said, already walking toward the man she'd killed. "Cumberland, help me with this one."

"Who put her in charge?" Willem muttered.

"Shut up and help me," Sten responded, grabbing a dead Balarian by the wrists.

When it was done, they snuck back to the entrance of the alley and looked around. The orange torchlight of patrolling sentries put a glow on the city avenue.

"What now?" Cumberland asked.

"We need to move fast, before they recover from the confusion we caused," Shoshone said. She turned to Jolan. Smiled. "You are about to deliver some Papyrian widows to the fortress as your prisoners, Jolan."

Jolan swallowed. "No. Not again. It won't work twice."

"You'd be surprised. Come on, the fortress is this way. Leave the cart here."

29

VERA

Almira, Aboard the Blue Sparrow

"Hello, Linkon."

The king of Almira looked up, squinting so see in the dim hold of the *Blue Sparrow*.

His hands were still bound behind his back. His scalp and lip were bleeding and there were shards of glass in this hair left over from when Vera had thrown him out the window.

"Who are you people?" he asked. "What did you do to me?"

"Come now, Linkon. It hasn't been that long. Surely you remember me."

Kira stepped forward so the dragon-oil lanterns lit her face.

"Kira?" Linkon asked. "What are you doing in Almira? What's happened?"

"Quite a lot," she answered. "I ran away from Floodhaven, and while I was gone my father died and you killed my sister."

"I didn't kill her."

Kira clucked her tongue disapprovingly.

"Linkon, Linkon, Linkon. None of that now. This room is a place of honesty." She gestured around the walls of the dim hold. "A place where kings and empresses may talk plainly with each other. Speaking for myself, I never liked Ashlyn very much. She was always so serious and gloomy. Droning on about dragons and wasps and plant goop. Gods, what a bore."

Linkon didn't say anything.

"You are going to admit the truth," Kira continued. "We can do this the easy way, which ends with you getting a stiff drink of juniper liquor and someone to help you clean that glass out of your hair. Or we can do it the hard way, which ends with you shitting yourself while Vera force-feeds your own toes to you. Either way, I will get what I want. The path we take to get there is up to you."

Linkon glanced between Vera and Kira a few times. A single tear dripped down his cheek.

"After you left Almira, I saw an opportunity. With Hertzog on his deathbed and you gone, the Malgraves were vulnerable. I hired an . . . operative . . . to weaken Ashlyn's position further, and then I manipulated Cedar Wallace into a rebellion. And when he and Ashlyn were at each other's throats, I convinced the other high lords to stand with me against her. But I didn't kill her."

"Your men. Your orders."

"No. You don't understand. We never found her. After the battle of Floodhaven, she disappeared. I said that she was dead to consolidate power, that's all."

"And how has that worked out for you?" Kira asked, smiling.

Linkon glared at her. "I didn't kill your sister, but I wish that I had. She really is a demon-fucking witch. And you, with this flying monstrosity. You Malgraves . . . you're all abominations."

"I know," Kira nodded. "Run-of-the-mill treachery pales in comparison, doesn't it? But let's move on from the past. I always found history to be tedious. I am far more interested in the present. For example, how many Almiran lords are currently in Flood-haven?"

"Twenty-three."

"And how many wardens in their service behind these walls?"

"I'm not sure."

"Guess."

Linkon grimaced. "Maybe a hundred."

"So few. Why?"

"The fucking jaguars are tearing the backcountry apart. The first army of wardens that I sent south never returned from the Dainwood. So, I sent more. And kept sending them. All that's left in Floodhaven are scraps."

"He's lying," Vera said. "Actus Thorn said the first wave of skyships scouted thousands of wardens in the city. Too large a force for them to conquer."

"That's what they saw," Linkon said. "It wasn't the truth. I took the armor and masks that your sister didn't turn to ashes and forced women and children to wear them. Man the walls and run patrols."

"Clever," Kira said. "Most of the lords of Almira are morons, but a lack of intelligence was never your problem. Do you know what your problem is?"

He looked at her. "What?"

"When you go to stir shit up, you don't use a big enough spoon."

"I don't know what that means."

"I know you don't. That's why you're the one on your knees and I'm the one standing over you, giving commands. But don't worry—you're going to make out just fine. You and I are going to get married, Linkon, and fast. First, we'll need to introduce the idea to your loyal lords and wardens. Are they all in Floodhaven currently?"

Linkon wiped the tear away from his eye, nodded.

"You're sure? All of them?"

"Yes, yes. With the war on—and all my men down south—I had to corral them all here. Make sure they didn't rebel."

"A shrewd choice." Kira turned to Osyrus Ward. "Give it to him."

Osyrus Ward stepped forward and produced a black pill the size of a man's thumb from his robes. In a practiced motion that made Vera think he'd done it many times before, Osyrus jammed the pill into Linkon's mouth, then held his knobby hand over the king's mouth and nose until he swallowed.

Linkon started coughing as soon as Osyrus released him. "What the fuck was that?"

"Insurance," Kira said. "I want to trust you, Linkon—and I think we'll be very happily married one day soon. But seeing as you betrayed my sister less than a year ago, I need to make sure you'll behave in the short term, before we have a chance to fall in love and all that dragonshit."

"What was it?" he repeated, voice cracking.

Kira turned to Osyrus. Nodded.

"A fatal dose of Yellow-Spined Greezel venom that I coated with a layer of pine resin," Osyrus said. "It's currently quite harmless, but your stomach is already starting to digest the resin. Once it is dissolved, your stomach will fill with the Greezel venom. You will begin vomiting and defecating blood, and you will not stop until you are dead."

Linkon's eyes turned wide with panic.

"Relax, Linkon. There's an antidote." Kira leaned closer to Linkon. "And I'll give it to you. But first, we're going to drop you off back at the castle, and you are going to do me a favor."

Linkon swallowed. "What favor?"

Kira smiled. "You will summon every loyal lord and warden in Floodhaven to Castle Malgrave tonight, where they will be crammed into Alior Hall for a feast. At this feast, you will announce that you have successfully brokered a marriage with me, and that I am now their queen. You will do this as soon as we return you to the ground." Her smile disappeared. "If you are late, or if you try to deceive me, you don't get the antidote and it'll be bloody shits and a bloody death. Clear?"

Linkon Pommol did as he was told. It was amazing how fast the threat of death could motivate a man into drastic action.

His staff had assumed that he'd been eaten by the dragon, but Linkon had explained that he'd left the dining hall just a few minutes before the attack to visit a secret lover, and had been with her all day. The plan was to reveal the lover as Kira that night.

It was a weak lie. But kings can get away with weak lies, along with so many other things.

Linkon had ordered the feast, and then smuggled everyone from the *Blue Sparrow* into the castle while arrangements were made.

His loyal lords and wardens filled Alior Hall. Vera watched them from a darkened upper gallery, alongside Decimar. The grunts and laughs and farts of the drunken wardens boomed through the chamber. The crowd was loud enough that they could talk in muttered voices without fear of being overheard.

"This is the nobility of Almira?" Decimar asked. "They behave like animals."

"Kira would say that they simply wear their true colors out in the open, unlike Balarians," Vera said.

"What do you say?"

She looked at him. "That this needs to be done."

"Aye. Guess I should have expected a little wet work on our secret mission to overthrow a whole government in one night. We ready?"

"Yes."

Decimar signaled to his men, who were positioned around the top gallery so they all had clean shots on the lords and wardens below. They were outnumbered five to one, but the feasters were unarmed, the doors were locked, and Decimar's longbowmen could each release five arrows a minute.

They nocked their bows and set them at half draws. Waited for their lieutenant's signal.

Decimar drew his bow back to his cheek. "Anyone specific you want gone first?"

"Just leave Linkon alive. And only Linkon. Kira's orders."

"Right."

Decimar released his arrow into the chest of a lord with rodent-like features. At that range, the arrow hit him with such strength that it went through the back of his chair and ricocheted off the floor with a metallic ping. Decimar's men released a heartbeat later. The laughs and belches of the lords were replaced with groans, cries, and the sounds of their dead faces slamming into their plates.

The longbowmen worked fast. Vera did not see any of them miss a target. She counted the pulses on her wrist bracer as they massacred the unarmed, helpless men below.

Eighty-nine seconds later, everyone in the room was dead, except for Linkon, who was frozen with a cut of pork halfway between his mouth and his plate.

"Keep this entire level sealed," Vera said to Decimar. "No servants in or out."

———————

Two minutes later, when Vera brought Kira into the hall, Linkon still hadn't moved from his chair. Just put down his fork. His eyes were wet. "Those were . . . the loyal nobility of Almira."

"They were loyal to you. That doesn't do me any good."

"You tricked me," he said to Kira as she moved into the room, stepping over a few corpses.

"Just as you tricked my sister."

"She was a witch."

"And you are a sniveling, dishonest prick. A month ago, I'd have tried to do all of this peacefully. Without bloodshed. But my time in Balaria taught me that peaceful approaches are not always effective."

"I did as you asked," Linkon said. He swallowed. "Please. May I have the antidote?"

"Oh, that?" Kira smiled. "I made it up."

"That pill wasn't poisoned?"

"No, the poison part was true. But the existence of an antidote was a lie." Kira held up Vera's wrist and checked the time. "And it should end your life in about three minutes."

"Gods . . . no . . ."

"You should not have betrayed my sister, Linkon." She rummaged around in one of her pockets and came back with a red seashell. Tossed it to him. "Here you go. Have a nice swim."

Kira headed for the exit. Linkon sank off his chair, curled into a ball, and started wailing.

Osyrus and Decimar were waiting for them outside. Decimar closed the door behind them to dampen the sounds of Linkon beginning to die. Kira took a breath.

"Well, that part's done. The castle is secured?" she asked Decimar.

"Yes. With all the lords and wardens gone, my men were able to seal the gates without incident. We're safe for the time being, but we're also trapped."

"Not for very long. Osyrus?"

"My acolytes have already checked the storerooms. The oil is there—just enough for the apparatus to operate. I will begin the preparations for activation."

"Apparatus?" Decimar asked. "Activation? What's all this about? I assumed we would be heading back to Balaria, now that the mission is complete."

"The mission is just beginning," Kira said.

"What do you mean?"

Kira glanced at Vera. They'd decided beforehand that Vera should be the one to handle this next part. One soldier to another.

"You should get some rest, Empress," Vera said. Then she put a hand on Decimar's shoulder. "And we should get some food. Meet me in the kitchen in twenty minutes."

––––––––

Vera made sure that Kira was safe, then headed to the kitchen. She found Decimar sitting alone. A half-drunk cup of coffee and an untouched roll were on the table in front of him. He was staring out the window, but smiled when he saw Vera come in.

"You Almirans are savages when it comes to toilets and table manners, but this drink isn't bad."

"I'm not Almiran," Vera said, sitting down across from him. She'd taken off her armor for what felt like the first time in months and put on a clean black tunic.

"Right."

Decimar looked down at his coffee.

"How are you feeling?" Vera asked him.

He cocked his head at her. "In all my years as a soldier, I'm not sure that anyone has ever asked me that question. Never thought a widow'd be the first to inquire about my feelings."

"It's been a hard few days," Vera said. "And that business with the lords. It's not exactly what I promised you when you agreed to help Kira."

"The blood doesn't bother me. But I agreed to help because Kira told me that we were conquering Almira on behalf of the Balarian Empire. Why aren't we getting ready to depart?"

"Almira isn't conquered yet. Just the one castle."

"Don't treat me like I'm stupid."

Vera picked a scrap of crust off the roll and ate it.

"We're not going back to Balaria. Ever."

"What did you and Empress Kira do?"

"I've devoted my entire life to protecting Papyria's royal lineage. Everyone in my order has. That's the reason it is the only line in the realm of Terra that has remained unbroken for almost a thousand years."

"Answer my question," Decimar said.

"Ganon tried to kill her. I intervened."

"You killed the emperor of Balaria?"

"I did what was necessary to keep Kira alive."

"Why are you so willing to die for that girl? Killing an emperor. That insanity you pulled kidnapping Linkon Pommol with the skyship."

"It's my job. My *only* job."

"But it is not mine. And I won't desert my country because of some Papyrian widow's sense of obligation."

Vera ate another piece of the roll. "What would you abandon Balaria for?"

Decimar hesitated.

"Gold?" Vera asked.

"No."

"Land."

"Not that either."

"To save my life?"

Decimar frowned.

"I will never abandon Kira. And she will not run from Almira again. The only way we survive here for more than a few days is with your longbowmen on the walls of this castle. Or you can go back to Burz-al-dun and rejoin Actus Thorn's army. Help him conquer and raid and spread ruin across this realm. And I'll be dead in a week."

"I like you, Vera. But you're not some innocent civilian. You just helped Kira kill a roomful of unarmed men."

"They were traitors."

"Everyone's a traitor to something. How is one ruler any better than the other? We're just grunts following orders."

"It's not that simple."

"Complicate it for me."

Vera pushed the roll aside. "You were on one of the skyships that destroyed Linkon's navy, right?"

"You know that I was."

"How many men did you kill that day between dropping Osyrus Ward's bombs and raining down your explosive arrows from the sky?"

Decimar thumbed the mug of coffee. "Hundreds. Thousands, maybe."

"Thousands," Vera repeated. "In one day. And while you and I are talking in this room, Actus Thorn is doing the same thing to thousands of Lysterians. With impunity."

"What's your point?"

"That is all Actus Thorn is ever going to use those ships for. I know that to a certainty. Kira will do more. She wants to use them for exploration. Trade. To help the starving and the needy. And if helping her achieve that goal means I need to murder some greedy lords while they're eating dinner, I will do it. And I will not have trouble sleeping tonight."

Vera said the last words with as much conviction as she could muster, even though they weren't true. Vera had not had a good night's sleep since she was eighteen years old.

"I'm asking you to give her a chance," Vera continued, lowering her voice to a whisper. "That's all I'm asking."

Decimar took a sip of his coffee.

"I can do that, I guess. Not like it really matters. Because you're right: Actus Thorn isn't going to change. That means he's going to come after Kira. After us. And he's not gonna discriminate the wrath he drops on this castle just because I'm still wearing my uniform and waving my hands in the air like an idiot."

"Osyrus Ward says he can deal with the armada. He has some kind of machine."

"What's it gonna do, turn this castle invisible when the armada comes looking for their missing empress?"

Vera took the coffee and drank the balance of it. "We'll find out together."

30

JOLAN

Almira, City of Black Rock

Jolan led them through the city. The streets were quiet, and it was easy to steer clear of the occasional Balarian sentry patrolling by torchlight.

Shoshone was right behind Jolan. For some reason, she'd attached her scary-looking meat cleaver to the back of his belt. It was far heavier than Jolan had thought, and he kept having to tug at his pants—which were already several sizes too big—to keep them up.

"Where is everyone?" Jolan asked.

"Occupied cities are always quiet at night," Cumberland explained. "Not surprised that one with a flying sack of dragon bones overhead produces a bit of a cryptlike atmosphere."

Jolan looked up at the ship. It hung imposing in the sky—a black mark on an already dark sky. Each gust of wind made it bob a little—rising only to be tugged down again by the long cord running from the fortress to the ship.

"I wonder what that cord's made from," Jolan said. "Must be strong to avoid breaking under all the pressure from the ship. Some kind of woven, metallic fiber, maybe."

"You're funny," said Oromir.

"What do you mean?"

"Ten minutes ago you were pissing scared in that alley. Now you're talking to yourself about woven fibers."

"I wasn't talking to myself. Just thinking out loud. And I wasn't piss scared."

Oromir gave him a look.

"I wasn't!" Jolan said. Then he thought about it a moment. "Just regular scared."

"Will you two focus?" Shoshone hissed. "We're almost there."

The fortress came into sight. Its high walls were aggressively angled forward to make it more difficult to scale them in the event of an attack. Unlike Deepdale Castle, which had been adorned with scores of jaguar statues and festooned with plants and vines and living things, this fortress was nothing but cold, sharp rock.

"There," Shoshone said, jerking her head toward a postern gate.

"It's closed," Jolan said.

"And you are going to knock until someone opens it."

"Won't that attract attention?"

"You just need them to give you an inch of leeway. I will take care of the rest."

"Be rude," Iko said. "Like you're in a hurry and don't have time to stand outside a gate explaining yourself. Rude and confident."

"Those your words of wisdom for getting through life?" Willem asked her.

"No. Just for getting past locked doors."

The postern door was made from heavy oak and reinforced with thick iron bands. There was a snarling wolf carved into a circular plate in the middle of the door. Jolan banged on it with his armored gauntlet, surprised by how loud it was.

Nothing.

"Again," Shoshone whispered.

He banged harder this time. Five heavy pounds.

When he was about to go in for a sixth, the wolf plate snapped backward on a hinge and a set of gray Balarian eyes appeared.

"What the fuck?" the sentry asked in Balarian.

"Took some prisoners. Need to get into the dungeon."

"Prisoners? If some local caused trouble, just kill them. We don't need any captives."

"These aren't locals," Jolan said, matching the guard's accent. "We found two Papyrian widows."

"Widows?" The man peered past Jolan, eyes widening when he saw Shoshone's face and armor. "What were they doing here?"

"If I knew that, I'd know how to sneak into Aeternita's bed, too," Jolan said, trying to make the Balarian goddess's name sound as natural as possible, but failing. But the sentry didn't notice the hitch in Jolan's pronouncement. He was still staring at Shoshone.

"They got the shark armor and everything," he muttered.

"The sooner they get to the dungeon the better," Jolan pressed. "The officers will want to interview them."

"Aye. All right. Come on in."

The sentry opened the door. Backed up to let them through.

The passage on the other side was dark and narrow. Jolan moved forward. The postern door slammed shut behind them. Metal groaned as it was locked.

"Just keep moving," Shoshone whispered. At the end of the passage, there was another door. Jolan went to open the handle, but nothing happened when he pulled it down.

"Hang on, hang on," the sentry muttered. Pushing past Cumberland and Willem. "Awfully eager to get rid of the scary Papyrians, eh?" He reached the door and pushed a key into the lock. "I get it. My cousin told me a story about some widow back in Burzal-dun who murdered a tavern full of people by herself because they poured her the wrong drink."

He turned the key. The lock opened.

Jolan felt Shoshone drawing the meat cleaver from the back of Jolan's belt.

When the sentry opened the door, light poured down the narrow passageway. The room on the far side was brilliantly lit by half a dozen dragon-oil lanterns. There were stairs going up and down. A large, metallic box was set up in the middle of the room. Tubes connected it to a barrel of dragon oil.

Five armed soldiers filled the room.

One of them was a lieutenant who was sitting next to the metal box, digging at his nails with a dagger and looking bored.

"We need to take these prisoners to the dungeon," Jolan announced.

"Seals," the lieutenant said without looking up.

Jolan hesitated. Was that some kind of password, or had he misunderstood? Why was this man asking about marine animals?

"Um. Seals?"

The man's dagger froze. His eyes shot up, scrutinizing Jolan, and then the Papyrian widows behind him. Back to Jolan.

"Private Drulls," he said, turning to the man who'd let them in. "Did the fact that you were letting a teenaged Almiran boy lead these widows into the fortress escape your notice?"

"Um."

"Arrest everyone in this room," the lieutenant barked. The four men behind him flashed their short swords free from sheaths.

Shoshone threw her meat cleaver into the exact center of the lieutenant's face.

"Down!" Oromir yelled as he drew his blade.

Jolan ducked. Someone kicked him over. He tucked into a ball, covering his head with his arms and closing his eyes. There was shouting and snarling. Steel ringing out against steel. A series of wet hacks. Then it was quiet. Nothing but a few desperate gurgles, followed by silence.

When Jolan opened his eyes, all of the Balarians were dead. Blood was everywhere: On the floor. The walls. And the faces of every warden and widow.

They all went quiet. Listening for an alarm. After a few moments, when they heard none, Shoshone relaxed.

"That way," she said, motioning to the stairs leading up. "We do not have much time."

"Going to be honest," Willem said, wiping his blade off with a sheaf of paper he'd taken from the desk. "If I knew the plan was to just slaughter everyone in our way and hope we reached the flying ship before anyone noticed, I'd have thought long and hard about joining this little adventure."

"Too late for second thoughts now," Iko said.

"I'm aware." He tossed the bloody paper on the floor.

The stairwell led to an upper rampart of the fortress. Whether it was by luck or design, there was a clear path to the turret where the skyship was anchored. They made their way to it as quickly as possible.

The cord was about as thick as an aspen trunk. One end was drilled deep into the granite stone of the turret; the other stretched upward into the darkness.

"Armor off," Cumberland said, already pulling at the straps on the side of his breastplate.

Oromir had to help Jolan get out of his armor. When that was done, Jolan took the wadded-up satchel from behind his breastplate and slung it over his shoulder.

"Are you sure there's a way inside once we reach the hull?" Willem asked, looking up at the ship. Iko was already pulling herself into the sky, using her arms and legs both in a practiced motion that reminded Jolan of a silkworm climbing its own thread.

"No," Shoshone said, then followed after Iko.

"Perfect," Willem muttered. He reached into a pocket and put a seashell into his mouth.

"What are you doing?" Sten asked.

"Not like I'm gonna have time to pop it in while falling to my death," Willem mumbled, talking around the shell.

"That's tempting fate."

"We're about to climb a fucking string that leads up to the sky. I think we're all tempting fate plenty as it is."

With that, Willem started climbing.

Oromir put a hand on Jolan's shoulder.

"Just don't look down," he whispered, before following Willem.

Jolan grabbed the cord with both hands. Blew out a breath, then started pulling himself into the sky, arm over arm.

At first it wasn't so bad, but within a few minutes, every muscle in his arms ached with fatigue, then started burning with pain. "I don't know if I can make it," he gasped, slipping.

"Use your feet more!" Oromir called. "Tighten them around the cord as support. See how I'm doing it?"

Jolan focused on Oromir's boots. Copied his posture.

"There you go," Oromir said. "Don't worry, we're almost halfway there."

"Halfway," Jolan repeated. "Gods."

For a long time after that, there was nothing except silent climbing. The wind grew stronger as they ascended. The air colder. Several times, a gust blew hard enough to make the cord swing them sideways, which rolled a swell of panic around in Jolan's stomach. But he held on. And then he kept climbing.

"Don't look down," he muttered to himself each time he put one hand over the other. "Don't look down."

He was sure that he was going to let go. But he forced himself to pull himself up one more time. One more time, then he'd let go and fall and try to get the seashell in his mouth before he splattered across the roof of Cedar Wallace's old fortress. Should have put a seashell in his mouth at the bottom like Willem. Stupid.

But when he pulled himself up for the agreed-upon final time before death, his head hit Oromir's boot. He'd stopped climbing.

Jolan looked up. The hatch was thirty strides above them, and Iko had her palm pressed against the metal hull.

The cord itself disappeared into the hull through a circular hole that was too small for anyone larger than an infant to fit.

"I don't see a way in," Iko said.

"Your plan better not be knocking and making Jolan talk his way inside again," Willem called up.

"Quiet," Shoshone said.

She worked her way up and around Iko, then felt around the hull until she found a seam in the polished metal and grafted bone. She followed the seam with her fingers until she reached a slight, grooved indentation. Keeping one hand on the rope, she twisted and pulled.

Something clicked, and the hatch slid sideways on a smooth, hydraulic release.

"Seems a little insecure for Balarians," Oromir said.

"You remember the part where we just murdered a score of soldiers and climbed five hundred strides into the air to get here?" Willem responded.

Shoshone pulled herself inside, then immediately turned around to help Iko through. The others followed quickly, with Oromir yanking Jolan into the cargo hold with a strong hand. Jolan just lay on his back for a few seconds, heart pounding in his chest. When his blood pressure felt somewhat close to normal, he risked a peek over the lip of the hatch.

From this height, the Black Rock fortress looked more like a large brick than an impregnable stronghold. He could see the entire city below, and the surrounding fields and forest they'd come from. The sight made his head spin. He turned away.

"What now?" Cumberland asked Shoshone.

"This ship might fly, but it is still a ship," she said. "That means it has a captain. We find him and persuade him to sail to the Dainwood."

"Simple enough. Which way?"

They all looked around. They were surrounded by hot copper pipes that radiated with pressure and heat. Gears the size of Jolan's chest were churning in a slow, almost restful rhythm.

"Whichever way we can fit."

Shoshone started crawling through the system of gears and pipes, moving deeper into the bowels of the ship. Everyone else followed. Some of the pipes were so hot to the touch they'd have burned Jolan's skin if it wasn't for the heavy Balarian gloves he was still wearing.

The air inside the ship was sticky and hot. It reminded Jolan of the warren in the middle of summer, except instead of the fragrant scent of wildflowers and honey, his nostrils were filled with the acrid, metallic fumes of heated chemicals and burning dragon oil.

Eventually, they found the engine room's exit. The next room was long and open. There were hammocks lined up against both walls—crude metal toilets and a small sink was placed between every third hammock.

"Balarians shit in those?" Willem asked.

"Smells like it," Sten agreed. He peered at the toilet. "Where does it go afterward?"

"Maybe that's how they keep the ship flying."

"No, it's powered by dragon oil," Jolan said. "That's why this whole place—"

"It was a joke, boy," Willem said. "You gotta learn how to keep a sense of humor in bad situations. Rule one of being a warden."

"But I'm not a warden."

"It applies to most vocations."

They moved down the chamber, toward the stern of the ship, where there was a ladder leading above deck.

"Gods," Sten said. "Not more climbing."

"This one'll be quick," Willem said. "And if you fall off and shit yourself, got plenty of places to take care of it."

They climbed up in the same order that they'd climbed the cord, with Iko opening the hatch and disappearing into the shadows. Shoshone was right behind her. Jolan's arms felt gooey and weak, but he managed to get up the ladder without much trouble.

The night air was cool on his skin. He took a long breath of fresh air, savoring the refreshment, before he noticed that the widows had already killed four Balarians. Jolan hadn't even heard them fall to the ground.

"Gods, but you two are gifted when it comes to quiet killing," Willem said, looking at the corpses, which Iko was dumping back down the hatch with perfunctory industry.

"Stop admiring and help me with this one," Iko said, motioning to a man's ankles.

When the bodies were hidden, Shoshone led them up a short

stair near the port side of the deck, which led to a raised cabin with
large windows. Probably the pilot's cabin. There was a metal door
with a complicated lock. Shoshone produced a round gray disk
from behind her breastplate, but hesitated before opening the
door. They could hear voices coming from inside. There were at
least two talking to each other.

"Navigator Septimus, explain to me again why you're not
wearing the proper uniform," came a gravelly and brusque voice.

"You say 'navigator' like you outrank me, Quinn. You don't.
And Mun ain't waking up anytime soon to ream me out for a non-
regulation uniform. I watched him add a spoon of liquid sticky to
his tea."

"You're dodging the question because you don't have a good
answer."

"Sure I do. The breastplate clocks on these new uniforms are
stupidly heavy and wearing it all day while I'm hunched over the
horizon orb is murder on my lower back."

"I have the same breastplate you do, and my back's fine."

"But I took that injury during training when we hit a nasty
pocket of turbulence while moving at full speed. It's in my service
record, and I've applied for a dispensation."

"And been denied three times."

"The fourth will be approved. And in the meantime, while
we're running a skeleton crew in the middle of the night and
General Mun asked me to draw up fresh air-current projections
for tomorrow's patrol, I am leaving the breastplate off. Why did
they even move the clocks to our breastplates? It's completely impractical. You can't see the bloody timepiece without a mirror, and
even then you have to work out the reversal of the hands."

"I don't know, Septimus. But I do know that a resupply skyship
flew all the way out here to give them to us and see them worn, so
they must be important. Orders are orders."

"Whatever. I am not following this one. Lower-back pain is the
recipe for an unhappy retirement. I won't risk it."

"Fine. But soon as I get promoted, I'm writing you up for a vio-
lation."

"That'll be the day."

Shoshone signaled to Iko that there were two men inside, then she slipped the gray disk into the mechanism. There was a hiss of steam, a series of clicks, and the door opened.

One man wore a red breastplate with a clock in the middle, the other simply a long red coat. Both were scrutinizing a set of charts on a table in the middle of the room.

"What is the meaning of this?" said Quinn, the man wearing his armor.

Shoshone was across the room a moment later. She tripped him and put a knife to his throat.

"Which one of you flies this thing?"

Quinn's eyes were wide with fear. "Neither. We're both navigators."

"Who, then?"

"General Mun. He's in his quarters." The man pointed to a door with a thin, shaking finger.

Iko and Sten restrained the navigators while Shoshone moved to the door and opened it. Dragon-oil lantern light poured from the room, but Shoshone froze at the doorway.

"Black skies."

Jolan peered into the room. General Mun was hanging from the ceiling by a noose.

Shoshone tightened her grip on the cleaver and went inside.

Jolan studied the hanging man. His face was contorted. Tongue swollen. There was a tapping noise that Jolan took a moment to identify. A trickle of piss was dripping off the captain's boot and forming a puddle on the floor.

He had seen that happen before. Back in Deepdale.

Shoshone had moved to the middle of the room, eyes darting from left to right. Jolan saw her focus on a circular, open window toward the back of the cabin.

"*Assassin,*" she whispered in Papyrian.

There was a blur of movement from the shadows. A man attacked her.

Jolan had never heard steel ring out in such quick succession. Four lightning-fast, stinging pings of metal on metal. The man skipped back, then lunged toward the window. But Shoshone intercepted him again with a flurry of her own attacks. The man parried them all and they parted, circling each other in the small room.

Before they could face off again, Oromir rushed up behind the man and kicked him in the back of the knee, dropping him.

Oromir raised his sword, preparing to cut the man's head off.

"Stop!" Jolan cried.

Oromir's stilled his sword. "You move, you die," he hissed at the man, then turned slightly to Jolan. "What is it?"

"Just hold on for a second," Jolan said, coming into the room so he could get a better look at the man.

Some of his features were unfamiliar. He had a chin shaped like a man's rear end and a massive mole on his forehead. But Jolan would have recognized those cold, gray eyes anywhere. Especially when they were staring at him.

"Hello, Jolan," said Garret. "Been a while."

31

ASHLYN

Ghost Moth Island, the Proving Ground

The hood prevented Ashlyn from getting a look at the Proving Ground when they were taken through it, but she smelled dragon oil and grease and mold. Some passages and rooms were furnace hot, others were blasted by powerful drafts of cold air that Ashlyn registered as frigid, despite the chill never biting beneath the surface of her skin.

Simeon and his men led them down a long series of narrow steps. They stopped frequently while metal doors were opened and then closed behind them. Ashlyn guessed that they'd descended at least four levels beneath the surface. Maybe five.

When they finally took her hood off, Goll, Vash, and Wendell were gone. It was just her and Felgor in a dark, domed room with stone floors and rusted iron walls. The space was dominated by cages of various sizes. Several hung from the sprawling system of copper pipes that ran along the ceiling like rafters—the same kind of cages they stuffed criminals in at crossroads. The biggest cage was placed in the middle of the room. It was a larger, vaulted design that was bolted to the floor. Ashlyn noticed the circular spot beneath the cage was made from metal, not stone. The metal was seamed with rivets and covered in black bloodstains.

"Give the queen the royal chambers," Simeon said, motioning to the big cage. "Felgor gets a chicken coop."

His men separated them and stuffed them into their respective cages. Locked them with Balarian seals.

Simeon propped a stool up in front of Ashlyn's cage and sat. The wooden legs strained from the weight, but held.

"Get us some light, Howell," he said, motioning to the pirate who carried the dragon-bone spear and shield.

"Aye, boss."

The man bent down in the dark and fiddled with some machinery, grunting out a few curses while he did it. There was a metallic click, then a spark. A flame spread around the perimeter of the room, illuminating the chamber with the orange glow of burning dragon oil. The piney scent filled Ashlyn's nose. She twisted in her cage, scanned the parts of the room that had been hidden in darkness.

Her pulse quickened.

There were rows and rows of stone pedestals. Each one held a different construct, but they all involved the fusion of dragon bones to metal. The first few were just fragmented fibulas and femurs with iron screws driven through in random, jagged angles. The next were more orderly—slabs of gray steel fused carefully along a framework of ribs to create a rounded, almost hull-like shape. There were also piles of spare parts. Wires, gears, pistons, and cranks. Rusted tools. Stacks of rotting paper with equations and notes scrawled in a hurried hand.

Set on a nearby pedestal, there was an unfinished helmet made from Ghost Moth parts that was clearly meant to complete Simeon's set of armor. She wondered for a moment why he wasn't wearing it, but the answer was obvious. The scales and bones had been cut and crafted, but all the wires hung loose and disconnected. Unfinished.

Ashlyn scanned the room again, more systematically, but didn't see any unrefined dragon threads.

Simeon spat on the floor. "Cabbage. Food."

The earless pirates scurried out of the room on hurried feet. Simeon focused his attention on Ashlyn.

"What are you doing on this island?" he asked.

"Looking for this room."

"Yeah? Guess your expedition's a wild success, then."

She shrugged. "Nothing's perfect."

"I'd think you'd be a bit more emotional, given your circumstances."

"What can I say? I'm a coldhearted bitch."

Simeon laughed. He motioned to the room of metal and bones. "What do you want with all this shit?"

"I need a way to destroy the Balarian Empire."

"Ha. Good luck with that."

She took a closer look at Simeon's armor. The general design was all Osyrus—a complicated fusion of dragon parts and clockwork machinery that activated and whirred with his movements. But the left rib guard had been modified. There was an intricate and complicated series of fused bones there, rather than scales. Ashlyn could see a line of blue fungus packed between the seams of the updated areas.

Ad hoc repairs. Kasamir's work.

"I can't imagine the empire's a friend of yours, and they're conquering the realm of Terra one country at a time," Ashlyn said. "If you were to help me—"

"Pass," Simeon interrupted. "Don't waste your breath trying to talk your way out of the cage. It ain't happening."

Cabbage returned with a wooden bucket that had blackened chicken inside of it. He handed it to Simeon, who grunted, then pulled a wing apart and took a massive bite.

He turned to Howell. "Who do we know with a reliable line into Himeja for a ransom?" he asked around the mouthful of meat. Grease dripped down his chin.

Howell tapped his gold teeth with a dirty finger. "Lionel's pretty tight with a palace sentry. He can probably get the thing sorted."

"Where's Lionel at present?"

"Reaving. But he's due back the day after tomorrow, assuming they dodge the storms."

"Good. Good." He turned back to Ashlyn. "So there it is, Queen. You'll spend a few days in that cage that you worked so hard to find, and then we'll get you shipped off. I expect you'll be safe and sound in Himeja within the moon's turn."

He turned to Felgor. "You, on the other hand, aren't gonna have such a pleasant stay."

Felgor was picking fungal remnants off his clothes. He pretended not to hear Simeon.

Simeon threw the chicken wing at him.

"Hey, thanks. I was hungry too." Felgor picked it up with a smile and started gnawing on the meaty remnants.

Simeon glared at him. Tore apart another piece of chicken and bit into it.

"Keep smiling while you can, Felgor. Got a feeling your sense of humor will depart in a hurry when the torture starts. Only question is the method. What do you think, Howell?"

"The fingernail thing?"

"Naw. We always do the fingernails first. It's become mundane."

"Mundane," Howell said. "That's a good thing?"

"No, Howell. It is not a good thing." He blew a snot rocket onto the floor. "Felgor is a special guest, let's give him special treatment. What's that one that Stump does? Some setup with a tub that he picked up out in Graziland?"

"Oh, yeah. That's a good one. You throw him in one o' them big vats, fill it with water up to his neck. Cover his face with honey so the flies get at him. Then you let him shit himself all day. Whole thing turns into a putrid mess of maggots before long. Truly awful stuff."

"Hm. Seems like a good option. But slow, yeah?"

"Few weeks at least to get a really good situation going."

"Pass."

Simeon glared at Felgor, who was no longer smiling.

"What to do?" Simeon pondered. "What to do?"

"How 'bout the rat box? We haven't done that in a while."

"With the steel bucket and the flame?"

"Yeah. The last rodent clawed straight into that Ghalamarian merchant's stomach and came out his mouth, remember?"

"Yeah. I liked that one. Do we have any rats?"

"Never a shortage of rats, boss. The boys could drum one up in no time."

"We need a good one, though. Your average rat'll just let himself heat up and die. Smells terrible and isn't any fun. That's why we don't do it much. And I don't wanna wait for them to find an industrious rodent." Simeon tapped his lips with two thick fingers. "No. I've got it. We'll do the saw."

"It's a mess to clean up," Cabbage said, frowning with the concern of a man who knew that job would land on his shoulders.

"But worth it." Simeon threw another bone at Felgor, who let it thump off his chest and sit in the bottom of the cage. "You know how the saw goes, Felgor? That's the one where I truss you upside down, then wait for all the blood to rush to your head. That's important, because if we do that, once I start sawing through your ass and balls, it'll hurt plenty, but you won't bleed out right away. Last time I got all the way through the guy's stomach before he finally gave out. Gods, but he screamed a lot."

"Exploded his own vocal cords, as I recall," Howell murmured.

Felgor had gone pale and sweaty. "Hang on now, Simeon, let's talk this through before you go splitting me in half. I'm a thief, you're a pirate. We're in the same general line of work! I can join your crew. Probably be a top earner."

"I got plenty o' good earners in my crew already. Don't need another one."

He threw another chicken bone at Felgor, but the scales of his left glove sputtered and twitched as he released. The bone missed the cage by a wide margin. He cursed.

Ashlyn studied the armor. In addition to the left glove being damaged, the wiring that connected everything was corroded from years of exposure to salty air and water. The armor was powerful, but it was falling apart.

"But you do need someone to fix that glove," Ashlyn said.

Simeon glared at her while he chewed. "The alchemist will fix it."

Ashlyn assumed that he was talking about Kasamir.

"That's not likely."

"The fuck do you know about my business with the alchemist?"

"Not much. But we killed him on our way in here."

He narrowed his eyes. "How'd that happen, exactly?"

"I blew up his giant and the explosion cut him in half."

Simeon's faced darkened. "If that's a true story, you've just brought a mountain of pain down on your head. Because this armor—and all the tinkering machines out of the Proving Ground—are more valuable than any queen's ransom. If you killed the only man who can fix them, might be I'm of a mind to put *you* in that previously discussed bathtub situation."

"I told you that I can fix the armor."

"Nobody can fix that shit besides the alchemist. Plenty o' my idiot crew have tried. At best, they lost thumbs. More than a few have gotten their whole fucking heads blasted off on crossbow backfires. These machines ain't gentle when they buck on you."

"I'll risk my thumbs, and my life. But not if you kill my friend."

"You're lying to save his hide."

"Maybe," Ashlyn said. "But what do you have to lose? Kill him now, I've got no reason to help you. Leave him alive, and I've got a strong incentive to succeed."

Simeon hesitated.

"You don't even need to let me out of the cage. Just throw the glove in. Give me some of those tools from over there." She pointed to the desk. "If I don't have the glove repaired by tomorrow, cut Felgor in half then."

There was another long moment of narrowed eyes and silent scrutiny. Eventually, Simeon looked down at his damaged gauntlet. Started twisting the clamps near his wrist. There was a hiss of pressure as the clamps released, and the dragon scales went slack around his hand. When he removed the glove, Ashlyn caught sight of a bone barb that punctured his flesh. The barb popped free from Simeon's wrist as he pulled the glove away, revealing a black mark that spread across his flesh like cracks in a mirror. So, the armor was connected to his body.

Simeon threw the gauntlet into the cage.

"Give her the tools," he said to Howell.

"You sure about this, boss?" Howell asked. "Glove don't seem that beat up to me."

"No, I'm lukewarm and figured I'd float the order and wait for your approval." He glared at Howell. "Do it."

The gold-toothed pirate grumbled, but passed a good mixture of dragon parts, lodestones, and work tools through the bars of the cage in a series of trips to and from the desk.

"I need those papers, too."

"Which ones?"

"All of them."

Simeon snorted. "Fine. Spend the night reading through that

pile of rot if you want. But come dawn tomorrow, if that glove ain't repaired, Felgor gets divided."

"I understand."

Simeon and his pirates left. Locked the massive, circular door behind them with a long series of rattles and clicks.

As soon as Simeon and Howell were gone, Felgor let out a long sigh of relief. Ashlyn started reading through the documents. There were hundreds of pages of diagrams and schematics. They varied from structural blueprints of the Proving Ground to lodestone charge orientations to a design for some kind of mechanical spider.

"Thanks for that," Felgor said. "'Bout damn crapped myself if I'm being honest."

"We're not in the clear yet," Ashlyn said, flipping through a dozen pages dedicated to the hydraulic system of mechanical spider legs.

"Right. I'll leave you to it." Felgor picked up one of the chicken bones he'd accrued, snapped it in half, and started using one half to whittle the other down. "You get to work on the glove, I'll see about getting myself out of this here cage." He stuck his tongue out as he worked.

Ashlyn looked up from the papers. "You can't pick a Balarian seal with chicken bones. They're unbreakable."

"First of all, nothing's unbreakable. Second, this design's rudimentary to say the least. No back-bite loops. Only four sequence layers. The ones from the Clock have fifteen, minimum."

"It's probably the first one that Osyrus Ward built. The prototype." She looked around. "Simeon's armor is a prototype, too. And these pages have the details."

The pages were yellowed with age and decay. They were definitely Osyrus Ward's notes—each written in a quick shorthand with a Pargossian date at the top.

---
19 Etchtar—217

- *Breakthrough. Blood of Specimen 01 key to preservation of the great lizards. Next challenge is volume.*

---
21 Lomas—218

- *Infinite and concentrated production loop achieved. Specimen 01 complains of constant and extreme pain from the apparatus, but there is no evidence the process will kill him. Scaled production of preserved dragon bones is underway.*

- *Okinu's second request is more complicated. Weight. Maneuverability. All obstacles for a viable exoskeleton. But I believe I can employ electrostatic power that taps into the wearer's biology. Despite the weak charge of the dragon tissue, the lodestones I have mined will amplify the apparatus enough for a prototype. Designs to follow.*

"Anything useful?" Felgor asked from his cage.

Ashlyn turned to the next page, where she found the schematic for Simeon's armor. Eighteen lodestones were mapped to various pressure points, including one against each wrist, which meant there was a lodestone in the gauntlet. Good. Two dragon threads ran down the spine. Scores of equations filled the margins, explaining how everything fit together.

"Very useful."

"So, you can fix it? Because I kinda got a lot riding on the state of that glove come morning."

"Pretty sure," Ashlyn said, examining the lodestones that Howell had put in the cage. They both held a strong attraction to each other, which was good. The orientation process that Osyrus used was confounding, but she didn't need to completely understand it so long as she had access to two charged opposites.

"Pretty sure?" Felgor asked. "The only thing standing between Simeon's saw and my balls is a 'pretty sure'?"

"There wasn't anything standing between them at all until I said something."

Felgor muttered something to himself. Went back to working on the lock with his chicken bones. After a few precious, quiet minutes, he paused. "Hey Ashe?"

"What?" she said, trying not to lose focus on the equation she was reading.

"You think Silas survived?"

Ashlyn hesitated. Looked up from the page.

"He still had a lot of Gods Moss in his bloodstream when he took those bolts."

"But he was facedown in the water. And he wasn't moving. I watched until the current took him."

"So did I."

Ashlyn dug one fingernail deep underneath the dragon thread. Winced at the pain.

"You should get some rest, Felgor."

———

It took Ashlyn two hours of reading to figure out the problem with the glove. And the rest of the night to fix it.

When she finished, it was an hour before dawn. Felgor was snoring in his cage and muttering something about a woman named Kiko. Ashlyn set the glove aside and went back to reading Osyrus's massive stack of research notes.

7 Crima—219

- *Prototype complete. The armor will bind to a subject's blood, just like the Ghost Moth spinal tissue. The apparatus provides nigh impenetrable armor to the wearer, should they be strong enough to operate it. The rulers of Terra would covet the design. But this application is crude. Dirty. Limited. Will use the gauntlet lodestone to experiment with hydraulic triggers, then shelve the prototype indefinitely. I am better than this.*

- *Yet, nothing is wasted. This design opens the door to a thousand new possibilities. The human body is so frail and flawed in its natural state. Simply wrapping the meat sack in armor is a messy, impermanent solution. But with the materials on this island, I can improve the human form beyond measure. Make it perfect. I must return to the basics. The building blocks. Beginning insect trials in the morning.*

Ashlyn sifted through several pages of insect diagrams. Spiders and mantises, mostly. They all had different artificial limbs implanted in their bodies. After that, Osyrus moved to larger animals and internal organs. Half a hundred pages were devoted to an acorn-sized heart fitted for a rat. When she'd skimmed through the diagrams, she found more notes. Unlike the previous entries, which were written in a careful and neat hand, these had turned messy and erratic.

26 Osra—219

- *Months of failure. Specimens continue to reject their implants and perish due to infection.*

- *None of the warren mosses seem to ward away the corruption, as they did for the preservation apparatus of Specimen 01. Frustrating. 01's survival of the procedures seems to be an anomaly on multiple levels. Must find a way to replicate its resilience on normative tissue, otherwise there is no way to scale.*

The next note was stuck to the page above it by a green film of rotted mushrooms. Ashlyn had to peel the pages apart as carefully as possible to avoid tearing them.

<u>11 Sorro—220</u>
- *Breakthrough. While imperfect, the Cordata mushroom can be manipulated to encase an implant and stave off infection. Remote triggers to the nervous system work nicely, especially in rodent specimens. But the process causes a number of undesirable side effects—fungus eventually consumes host, turns them to madness. But this can be improved in time. Like so many things, nature provides a flawed baseline from which to begin iterative improvements.*
- *I am ready for human trials. Will make contact with Okinu and update her on the new direction of the project. Whether she decides to support my work or not, she will deliver what I require to continue.*
- *The wait will be long. Must excavate a subterranean level and prepare it for the arrival of new specimens. Will install security measures, should they prove . . . disagreeable.*

Ashlyn remembered the missive Osyrus had sent to Okinu. The babble about undignified meat sacks and goddesses. This was what he was talking about. And she remembered that Okinu had sent soldiers and, eventually, a widow after him. Okinu had sent all the specimens that he needed, despite trying to do the opposite.

There was a final note in the stack, scrawled almost three years after the previous one.

<u>11 Etchtar—223</u>
- *Breakthrough. Human specimen 88 was the key. Moving all research to the lowest level of the workshop. I am near final stage.*

Ashlyn put the note down. Tried to think. Other than the bloodstain in her cage, there wasn't much evidence of human experimentation in this room—just tools, dragon bones, and metal. That meant this wasn't the lowest level of the workshop. There was more, beneath her.

And she needed to get there.

32

JOLAN

Almira, Aboard the Time's Daughter

Cumberland and Oromir hauled Garret into the main cabin and put him on his knees while Iko bound his hands with iron manacles.

"I need some detail here," Cumberland said, towering over Garret.

The assassin said nothing.

"Why'd you kill that man?" He motioned toward the captain's cabin.

Again, silence.

When he got nothing from Garret, he turned to Jolan. "How do you two know each other?"

"It's kind of a long story."

"We have time."

"Hate to be a stick-in-the-mud here, boss, but I'm not sure we do," Sten said, looking out the window. "It appears that our violent entrance is catching up to us."

Below, the entire fortress was aglow from torches. There was a big crowd of soldiers swarming around the turret that the skyship was anchored to.

Shoshone cursed. Then went over to Septimus—the navigator without his breastplate—who was cowering in the corner and weeping silently.

"If you lie to me, I will cut off your hand. And I will keep cutting things off until I'm convinced you're telling the truth. Understand?"

Septimus nodded.

"Can they get to the ship from down there?"

He nodded again. "The pulley operates from both sides. Captain Sidu just needs to input his seal, then they can ratchet her down in a matter of minutes."

"How do we disconnect the cord from our side?"

Shoshone raised her cleaver in expectation of a lie.

"From there," Septimus said quickly. He pointed to a group of levers near the helm. "But our levitation sack is filled to capacity for tomorrow's patrol. We're extremely buoyant."

"Meaning?"

"If we sever the anchor, we'll float away."

"That's the idea," Shoshone said.

"You don't understand, flying the *Time's Daughter* is incredibly complicated. General Mun was the only one on board who had the proper training."

He glanced toward the cabin, as if the dead man might spring to life and help them out of their current predicament.

"*Time's Daughter,* is it?" Willem said. "Even for Balarians that's a stupid name."

Septimus ignored Willem's gibe. "I am not lying to you. Flying the ship takes great skill. There are wind currents to read. Constant adjustments to make depending on the conditions."

"Can't one of you two do it?" Shoshone asked, looking between the two men.

"Us?" Septimus asked.

"By Aeternita, no!" Quinn finished. "We're the navigators. We make dozens of calculations a minute. The trigonometry alone is a full-time job, never mind the calculus and gas flows of the levitation sack, which require constant adjustment and care."

"There is no way that you flew this massive hunk of dragon bones across half the realm of Terra with only one man to fly it," Shoshone said.

"Of course not," said Quinn, who was far calmer than his panicked counterpart. "Captain Sidu and his second, Tritian, are fully trained pilots, but they had been in the air for nearly one hundred hours straight, and are both sleeping in the fort barracks. Well, they were sleeping, anyway."

Everyone was quiet for a few moments.

"Jolan can do it," Willem said.

"What?"

"Triga-whatever. Calculus. Those things sounded like alchemist stuff." He motioned to the helm, which was really more of a metallic pit filled with an astounding number of levers and gears. "You've been brewing potions and tonics all this time, it's the same general shit, right?"

"No," Jolan said. "It is not the same general shit. Just because I can brew a cock-rot tonic doesn't mean I can fly a skyship!"

"I must agree with the boy," Quinn said. "Pilot's training requires many months of careful—"

"Shut up!" Shoshone and Cumberland shouted at the same time.

They looked at each other, trying to think of a solution. Shoshone's jaw was so tense that the scar on her face turned white.

"We don't have a choice," Garret said. His first words. The sound of his voice sent a shiver down Jolan's spine. "You morons have destroyed my exit and muddied my work. If this ship stays in Black Rock, we are all dead. Jolan. Fly the ship."

For some reason, Garret's orders jolted him to action. Before he really knew what he was doing, Jolan was slipping into the cockpit. The wheel was made from carved and polished dragon bone that was fused to a complicated array of machinery that sank deep into the ship. There were levers everywhere, and two pedals at his feet.

"This is truly your plan?" Quinn asked. "To let some alchemist boy fly the *Time's Daughter* on a night mission?"

"Shut up and explain how it works," Shoshone said.

"That will takes days."

"You have one minute."

Quinn sighed. "The wheel controls our sky rudder, which in turn controls starboard and port movement. The pedals control the wing and sail orientation so you can tilt. Levers on the left are for the levitation sack's pressure. The large red lever on the right controls the engine thrusters. That's the one you'll need to use the most."

"What's this do?" Jolan asked, pointing to a button made from dragon bone that was pulsing with blue light.

"Never touch that!" Quinn shouted.

"Fine, fine," Jolan said. He put his hands around the wheel. Moved it a little in each direction.

"You ready?" Shoshone asked.

"Not really."

"Cut us loose."

Septimus cleared his throat. "Explaining the controls to a clever boy is all well and good. But I must stress that—"

Shoshone backhanded Septimus with the butt of her cleaver hard enough to spray at least three teeth into the far wall, and quite a bit of blood.

"Not another word. Do it."

While clutching his face, Septimus trudged over to the captain's cabin, opened the door, and removed a seal from General Mun's breast pocket. He returned to the controls and inserted the disk into a slot, which caused a series of clicks and whirs. Something unlocked. Septimus lifted the top of a control panel to reveal a series of red buttons. He moved to press one.

"A reminder, Balarian," Shoshone said, stepping closer. "You will be the first to die if we're taken back to the ground, or if anything happens besides the release of that anchor. The only way you survive this mess is by getting us out of it."

Septimus nodded and put his hand on a button. Jolan was fairly certain that it was a different one than he'd originally been reaching toward. As soon as he pressed it down, there was a heavy click in the floor beneath. The ship shuddered and all the wardens reached for something to steady themselves. Oromir swayed, then crouched down at the lip of the cockpit.

"Whoa, that feels weird," he whispered.

"Very weird," Jolan agreed, glad that he was in a seat.

"Anchor released," Quinn said, moving to his controls. Now that the ship was flying, the navigators seemed to compulsively slip back into their duties. Septimus pulled a silk cloth from his breast pocket, wadded it into the place where his teeth had been, and then hurried back to the instrument table that he'd been hunched over when they entered.

"Dropping sails," he muttered through the wad of cloth, then flipped a few switches.

"Lighting engines four and five with the Kor's spark," Quinn responded.

They went back and forth a few times, adjusting levers and levels and calling out numeric readings.

"Okay," Septimus said eventually. "Our gaseous mixture is at full potency. We're ready to begin a forward thrust. You remember the lever?"

"I remember." Jolan put his hand on the cold metal. His hand was slippery with sweat. "Here goes."

Jolan pulled the lever. The ship roared forward through the sky. Everyone reached for something to steady themselves.

As they careened forward, the ship started tilting to the right at an increasingly sharp angle. Jolan tried to correct it with wheel, but it didn't do anything.

"More port-side rotor depression!" Septimus shouted, voice distorted from the cloth in his mouth.

"What does that mean?" Jolan shouted back.

"Put pressure on the right pedal!"

"But isn't port on the left?"

"They're reversed."

"Why?"

"Do you want me to explain the mechanics of rotor depression or do you want to prevent this ship from crashing? Our horizon-line unbalance is approaching twenty degrees. At twenty-five, we capsize. Trust me, it is a much bigger deal on a skyship. Push down the right pedal, slow and steady."

Jolan gritted his teeth, then applied pressure.

"There you go, that's it. That's it." Septimus watched the orb as it tilted back into a level position. "Level off now. We're steady."

Dawn was breaking on the eastern horizon. Pink and orange hues colored the clouds, but the meadows and fields below were still shrouded in darkness.

"Keep level," Septimus reminded him.

"You're favoring the starboard pedal a bit," Quinn added.

"Right. Right." He made an adjustment and they leveled off. "There we go. Think I'm getting the hang of this."

For a few moments, everyone just looked out at the sunrise.

"We'll need a destination," Septimus said. "So that we can begin plotting a course through any adverse weather or topography."

"We're going back to the Dainwood," Cumberland said.

"I'll need you to be a little more specific."

Cumberland thought about that. "Can this thing float?"

"Of course," Septimus said. "All of the Balarian Empire's skyships were built as amphibious vessels. However, the machinery is quite delicate, so rough seas are—"

"Good." Cumberland moved to the map of Almira that the navigator had next to the table. Took a moment to orient himself, then pointed. "Right here. There's a lake."

"It's not on my chart," Quinn said, frowning. "All I have is forest."

"Trust me, it's there."

"By your orders." Septimus produced a steel compass divider and Quinn helped him plot a course—sounding off expected wind levels and a bunch of esoteric prattle about atmospheric conditions and humidity. When that was done, Septimus consulted his orb and gyro compass. Nodded. "Make a heading for nineteen degrees south-southeast."

Jolan did his best to adjust the ship based on those orders.

"How long will it take to get there?" Shoshone asked.

"There's a strong headwind that's throttling our speed." Quinn consulted his charts. "But we should arrive in ten hours and nineteen minutes."

33

VERA

Almira, Floodhaven, Castle Malgrave

Once Vera was satisfied with the castle security, she went down to the Floodhaven dock, where Osyrus Ward and four of his acolytes were unloading his machine from the cargo hold of the *Blue Sparrow*.

The machine was shaped like a massive and irregular seashell with three large conical openings. It was heavy enough that the four acolytes' arm muscles strained hard from the effort of moving it. Vera glanced into one of the openings, which contained the standard morass of pipes and gears and wires that she'd become accustomed to seeing tangled around Osyrus Ward's creations.

On one side of the machine, there was also a flat panel with scores of white buttons made from dragon bones. Each button had a small number scratched above it.

"This is our defense against the Balarian armada?"

"Indeed. And we are almost ready to turn it on. Just finishing the fueling process."

The machine was connected to a vat of dragon oil the size of a roadside inn. The acolytes had spent the last few hours carrying Linkon Pommol's entire cache of dragon-oil barrels to the vat and pouring them in.

"A pump apparatus would have been preferable, of course," said Ward. "But it was far too heavy to transport across the Soul Sea."

"How does the machine work?"

"The system uses a complicated network of synthetically oriented lodestones to activate machinery from long distances and override the navigation equipment of the skyship armada."

"What?"

"It is easier to show you. We are ready to begin."

Vera glanced up at the castle, where Kira was sleeping. She'd sent Decimar to guard her while the machine was turned on. If things went sideways, he had orders to sneak Kira out of Floodhaven and take her to a hidden grove a few leagues north of the city where Vera would meet them.

"All right," Vera said. "Go ahead."

Osyrus Ward barked a few orders to his acolytes, who moved to the vat of dragon oil. They turned a few circular wheels, which brought the machine pumping to life—all the internal gears churning. Pipes rattling. The piney smell of burning dragon oil quickly overpowered the salty scent of the sea. Vera watched as a fortune in dragon oil was burned in a matter of minutes.

Ward checked a few dials and gears on his machine's main panel, nodded to himself, and then yanked down on a large, copper lever.

A deep, booming vibration blasted from the openings of the machine. Vera's ears popped, and the waves around the harbor shimmered the way a puddle shakes from a heavy boot slamming into the ground next to it.

The machine went quiet.

"Did it break?" Vera asked. "Nothing is happening."

"Not here," Osyrus said. "But inside of every skyship that I built, I can assure you, things are getting lively."

34

JOLAN

Almira, Aboard the Time's Daughter

"I didn't touch anything!" Jolan shouted. They'd flown for hours without incident, but he'd suddenly lost control. "It changed course by itself."

"That isn't possible," Quinn said, studying his instruments. "You must have touched something. The skyships don't fly themselves."

"This one does!"

Jolan tried to jerk the wheel back in place, but even with a grunt and a curse and then Oromir's help, it refused to move. "It's locked in place. The pedals, too, no matter how hard I press. I don't understand."

"Which direction are we heading?" Shoshone asked Septimus. He studied his charts for a moment.

"Floodhaven," he said. "We're heading directly to Floodhaven."

"Why would the ship fly itself there?"

Septimus swallowed. "Oh, no. This is not good."

35

VERA

Almira, Floodhaven, Castle Malgrave

"Why would we want to bring every ship in the Balarian armada to Floodhaven?" Vera shouted after Osyrus Ward explained what was about to happen.

"Can't delay the inevitable," Osyrus said, checking a few more dials and gauges.

"I need to get to Kira," Vera said.

"That will not be necessary," Ward said.

"Why not?"

"Because the Balarian naval dress code requires that all crew members wear their military-issued uniform at all times while they are aboard a skyship, even while they are sleeping. A precaution, in case of a sudden attack."

"I don't understand."

Ward didn't respond. He turned around, gazing at the western horizon. "Ah, we have our first arrival. The *Time's Daughter,* which Actus Thorn ordered to guard the far coast. It will also have my other engine prototype, which will be most useful for future projects." Osyrus turned to one of his acolytes. "What number?"

"Frigate Seven," the man responded, voiced muffled by his mask.

"Seven," Osyrus repeated, moving back to the massive panel of buttons. "Seven, seven, seven."

He found the button he was looking for and pressed down with his knobby finger.

36

JOLAN

Almira, Aboard the Time's Daughter

There was a crushing noise—almost like glass shattering, but more metallic. Quinn grunted, then fell over.

Jolan turned, saw a huge amount of blood pooling underneath his body.

"Is he okay?" Oromir asked.

Jolan leaned out of his chair. Felt his pulse.

"No. He's dead."

"How?"

Jolan looked at the wall behind the place where the navigator had been standing. There was a splotch of gore pressed into the steel—a few bones from his spine and blue lung tissue.

"I think his clock exploded."

Willem started laughing.

"What's funny?" Cumberland growled.

"Oh, c'mon. It serves the clock-worshipping bastard right, getting killed by his own timepiece."

"Laugh it up while you can," said Sten. "Because we're still stuck on this skyship, and it is still heading for a city full of people who will kill us on sight."

The ship was speeding above the thick forest that surrounded Floodhaven. As they approached, the city outline became clearer.

"Is that another skyship?" Iko asked, pointing at the horizon. "It's so small."

"The empress's royal ship," Septimus said. "So, it's true. They really stole it. But that means . . ."

"Means what?"

By way of response, the navigator abandoned his controls and moved toward a big console in the center of the room. He used the captain's seal to unlock a panel, then pulled out a long metal tray that was connected to dozens of wires and tubes leading deeper into the ship. Septimus plucked a glowing orb out of the machinery, then ripped the wires free from their connections.

The engines went quiet beneath them. Overhead, there was a loud, pressured hiss.

"What did you just do?"

"Removed the Kor and dumped our levitation mixtures," Septimus replied.

They coasted forward for a few quiet moments. Then the sails lost their wind and the ship began to sink.

"Okay," Septimus said calmly. "We are now going to crash."

"By the fucking gods, this is getting ridiculous." Willem started digging around behind his breastplate for his seashell. "First we're climbing up the wire, then we're flying across Almira like a bunch of fucking geese, now we're crashing. Whole thing's some kind of cruel joke."

"There isn't a way to keep it flying?" Jolan asked. "I can feel pressure in the pedals again."

"Latent energy in the released coils, that's all. The ship is powerless now. But that means the Madman can't get to us."

"The Madman?"

"It doesn't matter. All hands to the captain's quarters!"

"Why?"

"He kept a lot of pillows in there. With some luck, a few of us might survive." Septimus rushed into the cabin, and everyone else followed. But Jolan struggled to get out of the cockpit.

"Jolan, get out of there!" Cumberland shouted.

"My pants are stuck on something," he said, kicking at the machinery. "Damn Balarian uniform is all baggy."

Oromir's strong hands were underneath his armpits a moment later, yanking him backward. The fabric on his uniform tore, but didn't give.

"It's no good. Get one of the scalpels from my bag. Over there."

"Which one?" Oromir asked, rooting through the sack.

"I don't care, just give me one."

Oromir snatched the first scalpel he found in the bag and rushed back. Gave it to Jolan, who sliced the caught fabric away using the same technique that Morgan had taught him for removing armor from an injured warden. His leg slipped free. Oromir hauled him out.

They rushed toward the captain's cabin—hands clasped together. But the ship crashed into the forest before they got there.

37

VERA

Almira, Floodhaven, Castle Malgrave

"Well, that was unexpected," Osyrus Ward said, still looking at the stretch of sky that had been occupied by a skyship a moment earlier. "By the way it crashed, it looked as if the Kor was disconnected from the primary combustion port. But by whom? Perhaps one of my clocks misfired?"

"A known risk," one of his acolytes rasped from behind him.

"Yes. Quite. I will investigate the logs at a later date. For now, there is nothing to be done but proceed."

Osyrus pressed all the remaining buttons on his massive machine. Dragon bones clicked. The apparatus whirred. "There we go."

"What did that do?" Vera asked.

"Overloaded the lodestone mechanisms of the clocks I built inside of the new breastplates, causing an acute and powerful release of energy," Ward said, distracted by a smudge of dirt on one of the buttons he'd just pushed.

"What does that mean?"

"That upon the arrival of the fleet, our largest problem will be cleaning up the mess inside of those airships."

38

ASHLYN

Ghost Moth Island, the Proving Ground

When Simeon returned, Ashlyn had his glove waiting for him just outside the bars of her cage. She sat cross-legged in the middle of her enclosure, waiting.

He came into the room without a word. His lackeys filed in behind them. All of them carrying those repeating crossbows. Ashlyn noticed that while some were in strong working order, many were rusted and bent and looked like they could barely fire one bolt, let alone multiples in quick succession.

"Doesn't look much different," Simeon said, eyeing the glove.

"The lodestone's orientation to the armor's centralized current was damaged. All that I needed to do was calibrate one of the spares and install it as a replacement."

The interconnected system of lodestones was an incredible invention. For the prototype armor, they were placed in close proximity to each other, but if Ashlyn's calculations were correct, the lodestones could retain their connection across massive distances if the orientation signal was boosted by enough power.

"Lot o' big words in those two sentences. How do I know you ain't making them up?"

"Put the glove on and test it," Ashlyn said.

Simeon smiled. "Boys."

His men fanned out and leveled their crossbows at her.

"Their orders are clear as a mountain lake," Simeon said to her. "If I put this on and feel even the slightest pinch of discomfort, they're gonna porcupine you like they did your lizard-killer lover. You still want me to put it on?"

"I want you to stop wasting time."

"Huh. For royalty, you got some salt. I will give you that."

Simeon picked up the glove and slipped it over his fingers. Snapped the clasps around his wrist. There was a shudder and hum from the armor. The Ghost Moth scales tightened to fit perfectly around his hand. He flexed and relaxed his fist. Wiggled his fingers.

"Better than before," he murmured, still looking at his hand. "More responsive."

"The old lodestone's charge was weakened from frequent use. The replacement was fresh."

Simeon turned to her. "Welp. I guess you've gone and saved Felgor's life for the time being. But you've fucked yourself over, because despite the fact Lionel turned up a day early, meaning your ride home is sitting in our harbor, I've got a burning urge to see what else my new tinkerer can spin up from all this shit. A queen's ransom doesn't shine nearly as bright as tools for easy killing."

"I would imagine that, to you, nothing does."

He grinned. "What's the matter, Queen? You find me distasteful?"

"I find you unimpressive and uninteresting. You're just a killer. And the world is full of them already. Men who are incapable of anything besides wanton destruction. Peel away the armor and muscles and the viciousness, and there's nothing left. You're empty."

"Won't argue with you." Simeon flexed his new glove a few more times. "Funny thing, though. I didn't start my life mired in the blackness and the murder. Back in the Razorbacks, I was a carpenter."

Ashlyn tried to hide her surprise. Failed.

"Aye. Learned it from my father. Who learned it from his. My pop was known for his rocking chairs—legendary comfort on those bastards. But I tended to focus on houses. Barns. I liked making big things. Something that would last through the harsh winters and heavy spring rains of the mountains. But when the

Ghalamarians came past the Line of Lornar hunting Skojit, all they saw was a savage village to burn down." He looked down at his hands. "I learned to build things from my father. But it was you flatlanders who taught me to break 'em."

"So it's not your fault that you became a vicious murderer?"

"Naw. Not saying that, exactly. Just saying that once that kind o' thing's been carved into your soul, there's no way to uncarve it. No way to start fresh."

Ashlyn didn't say anything. But she did think of the things she'd brought into this world, and could never take out.

"Guess some spoiled queen who's spent her whole life on a cushion would say that killing's against the natural order of things, but—"

"It's not," Ashlyn said.

Simeon raised an eyebrow. His turn to be surprised.

"The natural order depends upon killing. From pea-sized spiders to castle-sized dragons, everything in this world either kills to survive, or dies to keep something else alive. The peacefulness of nature is an illusion. A trick played on untrained eyes."

Simeon smiled. "I like you, Queen. You're full of surprises."

"If you like me, let me out of this cage."

"Eh. Don't like you that much."

"There's another room below this one," Ashlyn pressed. "I want to see it."

"And what do I get from satisfying this curiosity of yours?"

"More tools for easy killing." Ashlyn licked her lips. "You've become a legend of the sea with an incomplete set of armor and a few crossbows. If I'm right about what's down there, I could make a full suit of armor for everyone in your crew."

Howell glanced at his boss, clearly interested in that idea. But Simeon was already shaking his head. Smiling.

"The Skojit got a saying. *The more natural the boulder looks, the more likely it's a Stone Scale waiting to tear your guts out.*'" He spat. "Might be I'm a savage and a murderer, but I ain't stupid. And for a queen, you ain't so good at the whole lying and deceit portion of this business. Naw. We're gonna do this in real short chapters that *I* write. No big promises, no little tricks from clever queens."

He yanked the unfinished helmet off the pedestal and threw it into the cage, followed by a few more of the lodestones.

"Finish that. Same deal as before, except I'll give you a week. Felgor dies if that's not working when I get back. Clear?"

"As a mountain lake," Ashlyn said.

———

Once they were alone again, Felgor went back to picking the lock with his chicken bones.

"Well, that didn't go so good," he muttered.

Ashlyn stood up and went over to the helmet. The dragon scales and metal had all been tied together, but none of the lodestones were installed. That was why it didn't react to the rest of the armor. She saw three sockets, and recognized the orientation markings from Osyrus Ward's schematics. She could get this working. Even better, Simeon had thrown four lodestones into her cage. That meant she had one extra.

"There's more than one way out of this cage, Felgor."

Ashlyn dug through the stack of schematics until she found the designs that detailed how to link a lodestone to a thread that was fused to dragon bone. Her thread was fused to human bone, but the principle was the same. It was just really going to hurt.

She picked up a razor-sharp piece of dragon scale from the pile of materials. Placed the edge against the place where her dragon thread met flesh.

"Uh, what are you doing?"

Ashlyn didn't respond. Just pressed down on the scale and tried not to shake.

39

JOLAN

Almira, Wreckage of the Time's Daughter

Jolan woke up with a dead body on top of him. Everything smelled like mint.

The body was heavy, and pinning him to something cold and sharp. For a moment, he was afraid to give the corpse a close look. Afraid that it was Oromir. But once he worked up his courage, he quickly saw that the man had close-cropped, gray hair and a noose around his neck.

General Mun.

Jolan tried to push the corpse away, but all he could manage was jostling him a little before he slumped down on him again.

"Oro?" Jolan called.

Nothing.

He looked to his right. Frowned, not understanding what he was seeing. It was the trunk of a large tree, but the bark was stripped off in a bunch of places, revealing green and red and yellow strips of color. Rainbow eucalyptus. It must have crunched through the cabin when they crashed into the forest.

"Oromir!"

When Jolan didn't hear anything, he shoved the captain again. And again, he got nowhere.

"Stop struggling," came a harsh voice. Shoshone.

"Where's Oromir?"

"I don't know. Stop moving."

Shoshone's scarred face appeared above him. She was bleeding from her scalp, but seemed otherwise uninjured judging by how easily she grabbed the captain and hauled him off Jolan. He got up slowly, rubbing the small of his back. Jolan turned around and saw that he'd been jammed up against the big map of Almira that Septimus had used to plot their course. But that didn't make sense. His bearings were mixed up. It took him a moment to realize that the ship was on its side. He was standing on the wall, not the floor.

"Is anyone there?" came a quavering voice. "I am severely injured."

"Who is that?" Shoshone hissed.

"Septimus."

"Who?"

There was a silence.

"The navigator."

Shoshone muttered something under her breath in Papyrian, then grabbed Jolan by the shoulder. "Stay close. Do not stray until we get a sense of things."

The captain's quarters were a disaster. Pillows and broken glass everywhere. An entire wall was missing and beyond it there was nothing but a tangle of eucalyptus trees and rain-soaked ferns.

The navigator was crumpled up in the far corner of the cabin. Both of his legs were broken. Compound fractures.

By force of habit, Jolan started working out the treatment in his head. Numb with barbaroy root. Stop the bleeding. Set the bones. He'd need to be immobile for three months, using crutches for six. Walking again within the year, likely with a limp and chronic pain.

Shoshone went over and ran a form of triage of her own.

"Can you walk?"

"Well. No. Look at my legs! The left one is facing the complete wrong direction. Shouldn't it hurt by now? I can't feel anything in either one."

Shoshone frowned at his broken limbs for a moment. Then she looked back at Jolan.

"How long will he live like this?"

Septimus's eyes widened with panic.

"It's a complicated injury, I need to find some medical supplies and treat him."

"We have a medical bay!" Septimus squeaked.

"Quiet," Shoshone snapped. "How long if you do nothing?"

Jolan bent down. "His arteries are shredded. I need to at least stop the bleeding."

"Then stop it."

Jolan used two metal rods and some errant cloth to tourniquet both of Septimus's legs.

"I should make him something for the pain."

Once the shock wore off, it would be excruciating.

"No. Not yet." Shoshone drew her cleaver. "You'll get treatment after you answer my questions. Clear?"

Septimus nodded. Scared out of his mind.

"Why did you remove that orb?"

"To stop the ship, of course."

"The ship was flying itself. We'd lost control. Why would you want to stop that?"

He swallowed again. "There have been reports of unrest in Balaria."

"What reports?"

"They say that Empress Domitian killed her husband and fled the capital on a skyship. Osyrus Ward helped her escape."

Shoshone's face changed. "Osyrus Ward. You're sure."

"Well, no. But I'm sure that was the empress's stolen ship hovering over Floodhaven. And Osyrus Ward is the only person who could have overridden the navigation of the *Time's Daughter* like that. He built everything." Septimus lowered his voice. "They say that he experiments on *people.* Cuts them up while they're still alive. Those gray-skinned servants he keeps around with the strange masks—a lieutenant told me that they fuck the dead bodies and eat them after. I just . . . in the moment, crashing seemed better than being brought to him."

"Tell me more about the orb."

"That's the ship's Kor."

"Elaborate."

"It's classified. Highest level."

"I will cut your balls off and feed them to you if you don't answer my question."

"The other frigates run on dragon oil," Septimus said quickly. "And we do, too, but only to start the engines. The Kor fuels our propulsion, which is the most taxing aspect in terms of fuel. That's why we were left to guard the western shores. Even with the long coastal patrols we were running each day, we wouldn't have needed to refuel for weeks."

"There is only one Kor?" Shoshone said, tone changing. She sounded excited.

"That's right," he said slowly. "We were outfitted with it right before we departed Balaria. Actus Thorn wanted a field test somewhere away from the main fighting in Lysteria. General Mun always complained about Thorn's slow pace and desire to test everything. Called it a moronic compulsion. But I always thought it was quite sensible. You never know how weather conditions will impact a complicated machine."

"You did well, Septimus." She turned to Jolan. "You can brew him a pain tonic now."

"Where's the medical bay?"

"Go down the long hallway running against our port side," Septimus said, clearly relieved. "Last cabin on the left."

Jolan nodded. Stood up.

"I'm so glad we could work something out," Septimus said. "Once I'm on my feet again, perhaps I'll smuggle myself back into

Clockwork as a civilian. Find my wife and son. No, no, that's too difficult. But I'll get word to them through back channels to meet me in Dunfar. I've heard it's sunny almost every day there."

"Tilt your head down," Shoshone said to Septimus.

The navigator obeyed with the blind obedience that Jolan had seen in scores of desperate patients at the apothecary. They know they can't fix themselves, so they will do anything to make it easier for someone else to do it for them. But Shoshone didn't heal him.

She chopped her cleaver into the back of his neck. Septimus died instantly.

Jolan was so stunned he couldn't get words out—they dried up in his tightening throat. Shoshone wiped her cleaver on a pillow and sheathed it. Took the Kor from Septimus's dead hand and scrutinized it for a few moments.

"Why did you do that?" Jolan said. "I could have treated those wounds!"

"He was the enemy."

"But he helped us."

"Because I forced him to. He was a Balarian. Warm blood in his veins and breath in his lungs was a bad thing."

"It's not that simple."

"It is to me." Shoshone turned to him. "Have you forgotten Umbrik's Glade? Septimus was one of the men who guided these ships across the Soul Sea and into your homeland. Killed your countrymen and stole your harvest. Just because a man appears meek and frail and scared does not make him harmless."

"But he had a wife. A son. The way he looked at you . . ." Jolan said. "Looked at me. He needed help. He was so sure that we were going to give it to him."

She softened a little. "You're not cut out for this, kid. Cumberland was wrong to have brought you along."

A twig snapped in the forest.

"Jolan? Shoshone?"

"Oromir!" Jolan said, rushing through the broken wall of the ship and into the forest. His arm caught in a splinter of dragon bone on his way out, biting into his skin, but he didn't care. He ran into the darkness and embraced Oromir, who was picking his way through the undergrowth.

"I thought you were dead," Jolan whispered.

"I thought the same."

Oromir held him tight. Despite the young warden's calm exterior, Jolan could feel his heart thundering in his chest.

"Are the others alive?" Jolan asked.

"All accounted for except you and Shoshone. Have you seen her?"

Jolan nodded. "She's back that way." He swallowed. "Oromir, she—"

"Iko," Shoshone barked from the skyship. "Report."

The other widow had come out of the darkness behind Oromir. Willem was close behind.

"Minor injuries, mostly. But Sten has a broken ankle. Cumberland's helping him over."

"Where is the gray-eyed man?"

"Oh, we collected him as well," Willem said, then jerked on a length of rope. Garret came tumbling forward on the other end of it. His wrists were still bound in irons.

Garret looked up at everyone, eyes revealing nothing.

"Who hired you to kill that Balarian general?" Shoshone asked him.

"The same person who hired you to steal the ship."

"You're lying," Shoshone hissed.

"It bothers me, too. You hire the one, right person for a job. Multiple teams for a single job is messy. I guess Okinu didn't have much faith in her trusty widows." Garret shrugged. "Or in me."

Shoshone glared at Garret for a moment. Cumberland and Sten made their way up to the others. Sten had one arm slung over Cumberland's shoulder and he was hopping to avoid putting weight on one ankle.

"It doesn't matter," Shoshone said. "The job's done."

"So, what do we do now?" Cumberland asked.

"I'm going to Floodhaven," Shoshone said.

"The city with a skyship hanging over it?"

"There is someone there that I need to kill."

"Who?"

"When Okinu sent me out into the world as her assassin, she told me something before I left. If I ever learn the location of a man named Osyrus Ward, I am to find him and kill him, along with anyone who supports his work. An order that supersedes all others. The Balarian navigator said that Ward is in Floodhaven. So, I go."

"We can help," Cumberland offered.

"You would just get in my way."

"Haven't so far."

"True. But this is a different type of job. And you have wounded." Shoshone turned to Iko. "Help them. The last pigeon that knows the path to Papyria is at Frula's research station. Go there, send word to Okinu that the western coast is open."

"Yes, mistress."

Then she threw the Kor to Cumberland. "That's your responsibility now."

"What is it?" he asked.

"Ask the kid."

Before anyone could argue further, Shoshone was digging through supplies—grabbing a canteen and a small bag of rations. It only took her a few minutes.

She looked at them all one last time. "You fight well, tree cats."

Willem opened his mouth, but stopped when he saw her smiling.

"*Jaguars,*" she said. "My apologies."

And then she was gone.

Jolan explained what the Kor was and did as best he could. Cumberland, Sten, Iko, and Oromir focused on the implications with a careful intention, as did Garret. Willem picked his nose and looked around the forest.

"Might be we weren't able to turn up a whole skyship for Carlyle," said Cumberland after looking at the orb for a long time. "But we can take this to him, at least."

"And keep it away from the Balarians," Oromir added.

"Aye," Cumberland agreed, then held it out to Jolan. "You hold on to it for now."

"Why me?"

"You understand that kind of crap."

"I really don't."

"All the same."

Jolan sighed and took the orb. It fit nicely in his satchel.

Willem drew a deep breath. "Where are we? It smells like we

landed in some kind of herb forest. I've never seen these trees before."

"I enjoy the aroma," Iko said. "Reminds me of a dream."

Willem gave her a look. "You never would have said something like that with Shoshone around."

Iko smiled. "But I am saying it now."

There was a silence.

"It's eucalyptus," Jolan said, suddenly happy to have a simple question with a simple answer—unlike the morality behind murdering an unarmed, foreign soldier. "It only grows in this region. Well, they're actually native to a specific and remote valley in Dunfar, but Traitian Malgrave enjoyed them, so he had an entire cargo ship filled with saplings and brought back to Almira, where he—"

"Jolan," Sten interrupted. "Please stop the tree history lesson and do something to make my ankle stop feeling like a dragon's gnawing on it."

"Right. I'll get supplies from the ship's infirmary."

"The assassin is injured as well," Iko said. Then added, "Although I'm not sure it's worth wasting the supplies."

Jolan looked back at Garret. He hadn't noticed the wet bloodstain on his shirt at first. Sloppy. Morgan would have chastised him for the oversight.

"I'm sure the Balarians have plenty of inventory," Jolan said. "But I'll help Sten first."

Technically, a bleeding wound should be triaged first, but Jolan was willing to break protocol in this instance.

"We're stuck here for the night," Cumberland said. "Oromir and Willem, clear the perimeter and see about some food. I'm going to have a look around the ship."

"Right, boss." Oromir and Willem sprang into action. "We're on it."

———

Despite the ship being tipped on its side, it was surprisingly easy to traverse the hallways of the skyship by walking on the walls.

Jolan had expected the crash to cause more damage, but unlike the equipment in an alchemist's apothecary, which was primarily made from glass, everything in the skyship's infirmary was steel.

Whoever had stocked the infirmary had knowledge of the alchemist's trade, and an uncommon access to warren ingredients.

Jolan found a vial of Gods Moss. Three ounces each of Crimson Tower and Spartania moss. And behind that, dozens of vials of processed warren ingredients. Everything was in small quantities, but it was a bounty. He mentally calculated a few new experiments he could run with these, then remembered that his backpack—and most of his supplies—was buried outside Black Rock. He wasn't sure how he'd get back there now.

Jolan started packing supplies for a splint into his satchel, along with a few vials of moss.

When he got back to the others, they had a fire going near Sten.

"We found dragon eggs," Willem said, motioning to three massive eggs they'd placed near the fire to cook. "Want one?"

Jolan studied the eggs. They were from a giant Almiran cockatrice, not a dragon. But he wasn't in the mood to correct Willem.

"I'm not hungry."

While the others ate, Jolan splinted Sten's ankle and brewed him something for the pain. Gave him the usual instructions for dosage.

"Appreciate it, Jolan," said Sten. It was the first time he'd used Jolan's real name.

"I call the captain's quarters," Willem said, wiping some half-cooked egg from his beard. "The room's destroyed but that big feather bed in the back wasn't touched."

"The fuck you do," Sten said. "I'm the one with the broken ankle."

"Broken bones don't give you right of way when it comes to sleeping arrangements."

"Neither does calling it out first." Sten started rooting around in his pockets. "We dice for it, same as always."

"But I need the bed. Think I just about broke my ass during the crash."

"And I broke my ankle all the way. Look, there's a way of doing things, and you don't just claim a fancy bed like that when we were all in the damn crash."

Willem cursed. "Yeah, yeah, yeah. All right. I'll get the fucking dice." He looked around. "Should probably ask Iko if she wants in, too."

"You tried to call it without dice and now you're bringing her into the stakes?"

"Like you said, there's a way of doing things."

"You're just hoping to invite Iko into the bed if you win. Or vice versa."

"Fuck yourself."

Jolan cleared his throat. "Um, what happened to Garret?"

"Iko chained him to the stove in the galley."

"Okay. I'm going to go check on him."

———

Iko had secured Garret's irons to the base of a cast-iron stove and left him there. The front of his shirt was soaked in blood from belt to solar plexus.

"You got taller," Garret said.

"And your accent got better," Jolan said.

Garret grunted. He eyed Jolan's satchel.

"What happened to that big backpack of yours?"

"I had to leave it behind."

"Too bad."

"I have enough to help you," Jolan said, although he didn't enter the room. "But I'm wondering if I should. You're a murderer."

"There are a lot of murderers in this world," Garret said. "And judging from the company you keep, I'm not the only killer you've tended to."

Jolan chewed on the inside of his cheek. "Last spring you lynched Elden Grealor. But he ruined the Dainwood. Everyone said so. The Mudwall lord you killed before him wasn't much better. Tybolt. There were whispers that he sacrificed children every summer and winter solstice. And that skyship captain would have killed thousands of Almirans."

"So?"

"Do you only kill bad people? People who deserve it?"

Garret leaned back against the stove. "One way or another, everyone deserves it, Jolan."

"You speak as if there are no good people in this world at all."

"There aren't. Just people you haven't gotten to know very well yet."

"And you'll kill them all for a price. Is that it?"

Garret looked at him. "Making sense of my work is a fool's

errand. Help me, don't help me. It doesn't make a difference to anything except your ability to sleep at night."

Jolan started unpacking his supplies.

He told himself it was because an alchemist needed to help people if he could—forget the coin and forget the person. It was just the right thing to do. But the threat of a guilty conscience moved him more than he wanted to admit.

He took a scalpel from his pack and swiped it down the side of Garret's shirt, pressing just hard enough to slice fabric but not flesh. He checked the wound. There was a circular hole the size of a coin in his upper left abdomen.

Jolan put on Morgan's sealskin gloves and probed the wound with his finger, getting a sense of things. If it hurt Garret, the assassin didn't show it.

"You were fortunate," Jolan said. "The injury came within a finger's width of your aorta, liver, and kidney, but missed all three. All you have is a small hole in your intestine."

Garret didn't say anything.

Jolan started stitching. The hole wasn't large, but it was difficult to keep the intestine still, so the work went slow. Master Morgan had never struggled with that when Jolan had observed his surgeries, but there were a lot of secrets Morgan died without sharing. The secrets of the warrens. The powers of the Gods Moss. And whatever trick kept intestines still when you were stitching up a hole in them.

While he worked, Jolan noticed a fresh scar along Garret's ribs.

"Who repaired that one? The stitches are terrible."

"I did it myself."

"How did it happen?"

"There were some complications in Floodhaven."

"You fought in the battle?"

"Not in the sense that you mean," Garret said. "But I was there."

"Is it true that Ashlyn Malgrave killed Cedar Wallace with demoncraft?"

Jolan figured if anyone was going to provide a straight answer about what happened at Floodhaven, it would be Garret.

"She killed him with something."

"People are saying it was lightning. Or fire. What did you see? Was there a specific smell? Acrid? Sharp?"

Garret looked at Jolan. "I forgot how many questions you can ask in the space of a minute, once you get going."

Jolan shrugged.

"How did you wind up stealing a skyship with a crew of Dainwood wardens and Papyrian widows?" Garret asked. "Thought you were heading into the Daintree warrens to solve some great mystery. You've strayed."

"No." Jolan tightened his jaw. "I was in those warrens for months. I saw things that you wouldn't believe. A cat-sized lizard that could mimic the colors of its surroundings for camouflage. Talking birds with long, plumed tails. Orange eels that shocked the water with electric jolts to stun River Lurker babies, then eat them with razor-sharp teeth. Bone-white trees with iridescent red and blue leaves. And more exotic plants than most city-dwelling alchemists see in a lifetime. I collected hundreds of warren ingredients, just like I'd planned. Then I left the wilds to rent a workshop where I could conduct experiments and learn the secret of the Gods Moss. But I ran into Cumberland and his men before I reached Glenlock. They, uh, asked me to join them."

"Press-ganged. I've been there."

"Really?"

He gave Jolan a look. "How do you think I got started in this life?"

"I guess I . . . assumed you wanted it."

"No." Garret looked down at his boots. A moth was banging against the metal ceiling of the galley over and over—dust from its wings rubbing off on the gray steel. "When I was your age, I wanted to be in a theater troupe. Always liked costumes. It felt good to spend a little time wearing other people's skin, even before mine got so dirty."

"Why didn't you, then?"

Garret shrugged. "I was a shit singer."

"Oh."

"Don't go soft because of a little backstory, kid. Everybody's got one."

Jolan closed the exterior wound and applied a newly concocted

Gods Moss poultice. Depending on how long Cumberland kept Garret as prisoner, he could see how the mixture handled any infection that might develop in Garret's gut.

"This is done. You'll make a full recovery."

Garret looked at him. "Saving my life is a mistake, Jolan. Why do you keep on making it?"

Before Jolan worked up a response, Oromir's head popped into the galley.

"There you are," he said.

"Here I am."

"You all right being alone with him?" Oromir eyed Garret.

"Fine."

"I won the dice game for that feather bed."

"Willem must be pissed," Jolan said.

"Very." Oromir paused, then added, "There's room for two. In the bed."

"Oh." Jolan's belly churned with excitement and panic. "Um, I should check on Sten. Make sure his splint isn't too tight."

"Makes sense. But if you're coming, best do it soon. I'm so tired the backs of my eyes ache." Oromir yawned. Smiled. "But I'll wait up as long as I can."

When he was gone, Jolan went back to bandaging Garret's belly.

"How long are you going to drag your feet on that stupid bandage?" Garret asked after Jolan started making the seventh pass.

"It needs to be tight."

"It's fine. That boy wants you. And you want him. Get to it."

"What would a cold-blooded assassin know about it?"

"More than you, apparently."

Jolan kept wrapping the bandage.

"What's the holdup?" Garret pressed.

Jolan swallowed. "I'm afraid it won't go right. If it stays in my head, it's perfect. Always."

"You're a smart kid, Jolan. But that is one of the stupidest things I've ever heard."

Jolan bristled. But Garret kept talking.

"We almost died today. If that ship came down at a slightly different angle, you'd have been skewered by a tree branch. We're safe in this moment, but you don't know what tomorrow will bring. Might be none of us get out of this forest alive. Do you want to go down the river with a perfect dream trapped inside your head, or do you want something real?"

"I want it to be real," Jolan whispered.

"Then go."

Jolan sat there for another moment, clutching his roll of bandages as if they were the gunwale of a ship during a storm. Outside, the rain started. A soft whisper of water on leaves that grew into an ear-pounding deluge.

"I keep on helping you because it's the right thing to do," Jolan said eventually. "And I think you spared me in the Dainwood for the same reason. You aren't as cynical as you pretend to be. The good man inside of you is just buried beneath thick layers of dirty skin."

———————

Jolan checked on Sten, who was snoring loudly by his fire. Then he went out and stood in the rain for a few minutes, working up the courage to visit Oromir's cabin.

When he was on the verge of shivering, he went back inside and knocked on the door of the dead captain's quarters.

"Yes?" came Oromir's voice from inside.

"It's Jolan?"

He didn't mean to, but it came out more like a question than a statement.

The door opened a moment later. Oromir was shirtless—a dark smudge of grimy mineral oil ran from his nipple to the muscles along his lower ribs. Behind him, his sword was leaning against the wall. A goatskin rag next to it.

"You're soaking wet," he said. "How'd that happen?"

Jolan shrugged. "I went outside to listen to the rain. Sorry, I guess I should have come sooner."

"Now is perfect. Come on, I can make a little fire."

While Oromir made a fire from broken chairs, Jolan removed his soaking cloak and hung it up on a broken pipe near the door. Then, since all the other furniture was destroyed, he sat on the feather bed. The idea of sinking into the softness made his blood pressure spike, so he just balanced his ass on the edge.

Once the fire was crackling, Oromir dug out his familiar flask of brandy, took a sip, then passed it to Jolan.

"Seems so long ago, back in that barn, when we did this the first time," Oromir said.

"Yeah."

They exchanged a few sips in silence.

"What's wrong?" Oromir asked. "You look sad."

Jolan took a sip before answering. "The longer I live in this world, and the more things that I see, the more I feel . . . overmatched."

"Overmatched," Oromir repeated. "In what way?"

"All ways, I guess." Jolan sipped the brandy again. The warmth in his bloodstream gave him the courage to keep talking. "I spent the first half of my life helping the smartest man I knew try to stop a plague in Otter Rock, and we got nowhere. We failed. And when I left, I wanted to help people. Use the things I learned to make this world . . . better. But somehow all I've managed to do is save the lives of killers. Their hearts are so hardened and cold."

"You're talking about wardens and widows. People like me."

Jolan looked up, saw the sadness in Oromir's eyes.

"No, Oromir. Not like you. You still name your horses. You're not like the others."

"Not yet." He sighed. "But I worry about it. Maybe it's just because I'm younger. What will I be like in ten years, leading this life? Or twenty? Cumberland cares about us, I know that much. But sometimes he seems so . . . empty inside. Like whatever joy he had—true joy—died a long time ago, along with the Bershad lords."

Oromir held out the flask of brandy. But instead of taking it, Jolan took his hand. Squeezed it.

"Do you remember what you asked me in that barn? About what I . . . you know . . . think about."

Oromir looked embarrassed. "I shouldn't have asked you that. It was crass."

"I think of you," Jolan said quickly. "I think of you all the time. The way you brush your hair off your face when you're watching a bird in the sky. The way your hips move when you ride. And the way your fingers rest on the reins or your sword or my hand. It's always you."

Oromir had such a serious look on his face that Jolan thought he'd said something wrong. But then Oromir's eyes welled up and a tear fell down his cheek.

"Come here."

Oromir wrapped him into a tight embrace. For a moment, they just held each other. Then Oromir took Jolan's jaw in his callused hand and kissed him.

Jolan had never kissed anyone before. Oromir's stubble was rough against his face, but his lips and tongue were soft and wet. He tasted like brandy and spearmint. Jolan placed his hands on Oromir's waist. Let his thumbs explore the ridges of his hips.

"That tickles," Oromir said, breaking away.

"Oh! Sorry . . ." Jolan tucked his hands against his own chest.

"It's okay," Oromir said, laughing, then put his hands on Jolan's shirt. "Here, let's get this off. It's wet."

Oromir unfastened the button of Jolan's shirt with easy dexterity and pulled the garment over his head. Jolan felt self-conscious. They were the same age, but where Oromir was all wiry muscle and lean strength, Jolan was bony and awkward. His chest looked like a boy's chest. Oromir ran his hands along his collarbone and rubbed his shoulders, then kissed him again on the mouth, jaw, and neck.

Before Jolan realized what was happening, Oromir had guided him back into the enveloping softness of the bed. The blanket was torn and covered in splinters, but it didn't matter. Oromir's skin was burning with warmth. Jolan rubbed his hands along his strong arms and back.

He shuddered as Oromir's hand drifted down past his belly button, then undid his pants. Drifted farther. He gasped as Oromir touched him, teased the tip of his cock with the same dexterous fingers Jolan had been watching for weeks as they fastened buttons, held ale mugs and horse reins. And now they were on him, making his entire body tremble. All of a sudden, the hand was gone again and Jolan was aching to have it back.

"The first time can go by fast," Oromir whispered in his ear, then sucked on the lobe. "We should make it last."

Oromir lifted his hips and pulled his own leather riding pants off. Jolan found himself momentarily frozen as he watched the young warden strip naked in front of him. He had a hard time looking away from his cock.

"You're making me blush, Jolan," Oromir said with a laugh. "C'mon, I know you've seen plenty before. Gods, you've been helping Willem with his cock rot since we met."

"Don't make me think of cock rot right now." Jolan smiled. "And it's different this way."

Jolan pulled his own pants off, fighting how vulnerable it made him feel. Then he lay down alongside Oromir and started kissing him again. He did his best to casually move his own hand lower and lower—trying to make it seem like his every thought and heart fiber wasn't focused on the place his hand was going to arrive.

When it did, Oromir let out a long, almost surprised breath. Jolan wrapped his hand around Oromir's cock and stroked it. He nearly blurted out how much different it felt than touching his own, but realized that wasn't a very romantic comment. Instead he just kept on touching and kissing and pressing his body into Oromir, who did the same things back. For moments or minutes or maybe hours, Jolan got lost in the sensations of their bodies touching. And the tastes of Oromir. His mouth. The sweat on his skin.

Oromir was right, the first time didn't last very long. But the second and third times did.

———

Oromir fell asleep first, snoring lightly with his head nestled into Jolan's armpit. Every few minutes he would shift a little, or scratch the tip of his nose, then go still again.

Jolan fought against sleep for as long as he could. If he fell asleep, it would be over.

His life had been dominated by other people's ailments for as long as he could remember. Defined by cures and tonics and the weights of herb packets. And after the apothecary, it had been defined by the pursuit of a lofty goal—to find an explanation for what he saw the day the Flawless Bershad killed that dragon. For the first time since it happened, Jolan didn't care about the answer. He only cared about staying near Oromir for as long as possible.

As if he could hear his thoughts, Oromir opened his cool blue eyes.

"I don't think I want to be a warden anymore," he whispered.

"Then don't be," Jolan said. "Once this is done, we can disappear. Find some little cottage in the woods and live there. It'll be just you and me. Peaceful. Safe."

Oromir smiled. "Yeah. I'd like that."

He went back to sleep. Jolan studied the line of his ribs and hip. Fought against the drowsiness that was flooding his body. There were still a few hours left in the night. A few hours to hold on to this feeling.

Jolan closed his eyes, just for a second.

The next thing he knew, dawn was streaming through the cabin's window and Iko was shouting from the top of a tree she'd climbed.

"More skyships on the horizon!"

40

VERA

Almira, Floodhaven, Castle Malgrave

Osyrus Ward's machine summoned the entire Balarian armada to Floodhaven during the night. Twenty-eight skyships.

They hung like black storm clouds, lashed to the ground by anchors that Osyrus Ward's machine had compelled them to drop in the harbor. There was no movement on the decks. No sign of life.

Despite Vera's protests, Kira had insisted that she go with the boarding party to Actus Thorn's skyship, the *Black Clock*.

"I need to see his fate with my own eyes," she'd said.

Decimar's men crewed the *Blue Sparrow* and ascended to an even height with the *Black Clock,* then Vera, Kira, Osyrus, and Decimar boarded via a thick gangplank.

Inside the ship, each man had died the same way: The clock on his chest had exploded inward, tearing his chest cavity to shreds and, in many cases, spraying his innards all over the wall and floor behind him.

"Gods, this is foul," Kira said, holding a silk scarf over her mouth. "Why do they smell so bad? I thought you said that they only died a few hours ago. Don't corpses take longer to fester?"

"They aren't festering yet," Decimar said. "People usually shit themselves after they die."

"Gods," Kira said again. "Ending lives is a disgusting process."

"I think it's fascinating," said Osyrus Ward, bending over to examine a man's ruined chest. He dipped one knobby finger into the open cavity. Rubbed the blood between finger and thumb. "Ever since Mercer Domitian was killed, I have been forced to spend most of my time creating simple machines that mimic life with clockwork and pistons and steam. But that's all a machine will ever do on its own. Dumb imitation. The possibilities are far more interesting when you bind the two. Mechanical and organic, fused together in a perfect harmony." Osyrus looked up from the corpses, eyes bright with passion. "I would greatly appreciate access to these corpses for my research. It has been quite some time since I was given the opportunity to study so many fresh human specimens."

Kira hesitated. "They had to die, but there is no reason to disrespect their bodies. They should be given seashells."

"When we began our work together, you promised me that you would provide me with the materials that I need for my research. It is time for you to keep that promise, Empress."

Kira screwed up her face in disgust. "What are you going to do with them?"

"Disclosing my methods was not part of our agreement."

"Very well," she said softly. "Take them."

"You are most generous," Osyrus Ward said cheerfully. "We should proceed to the main deck."

They found Actus Thorn's corpse splayed out across a large map of Terra. His blood stained the countries and the calculations that were scrawled across the realm. Thorn was still wearing his military breastplate, but unlike all the other dead soldiers on the skyship, his hadn't imploded and killed him.

His throat had been slit.

There was a flicker of movement from a shadowy corner. Vera shoved Kira behind her while simultaneously drawing *Owaru* and throwing it at the figure. Her blade banged off a steel bracer with a metallic clang. She drew *Kaisha* and shifted into a defensive position.

"Decimar."

The longbowman had an arrow nocked and drawn a heartbeat later.

"There is no need for violence!" Osyrus said quickly, moving between her and the shadowy figure. "Come forward."

The man stepped out of the shadows, so Vera could see his face. He was wearing black armor and red face paint, but she recognized his features and the rings in his hair.

"Gyle," she said. The Wormwrot mercenary who'd helped her steal the dragon oil.

"Aye. So much for a friendly greeting amongst old coworkers, yeah?" He rubbed the forearm that he'd used to block the dagger. The bracer was badly dented and would need several hours with a blacksmith. "Gods, you throw hard, woman. Lucky I got myself some cat reflexes or that would have divided my fucking face."

"I see that you elected to put on your Wormwrot colors," Osyrus said, motioning to red paint on Gyle's cheeks.

"Aye. Vergun's orders."

"He always had a flair for the dramatic. Very intimidating. All went according to plan, I assume?" Osyrus asked, leaning over to examine Thorn's corpse.

"Oh yeah, sprung off just like you said. Wasn't no good way to get to Thorn during the flight, but once the breastplates started poppin', it was easy. Strode in and put a big leak in his food pipe."

Gyle pantomimed the process of sawing a man's throat open.

"Why didn't Thorn's breastplate explode?" Kira asked.

"Our dearly departed prime magnate was a very recalcitrant man. He outfitted his troops with the newly designed breastplates, but refused to upgrade personally, opting instead to continue wearing the same hunk of metal he had during the Almiran invasion thirty years ago. Not a major obstacle, though. An old-fashioned mindset simply calls for an old-fashioned solution."

He pointed at Gyle, who smiled. "Stowaways and backstabbing in the dark. Just my style."

"It's dirty business," Kira said mildly. "But so was shooting a bunch of lords and wardens in the back while they were eating dinner." She looked around the room. "And both tasks were necessary."

"I agree," Osyrus said, bowing his head. "You now have twenty-nine ships at your disposal. I am happy to provide my acolytes as intermediary crew until we can consolidate manpower and train our own, loyal troops. What will you do with your new fleet?"

"Disarm it," Kira said.

"Disarm?" Osyrus asked. Surprised for the first time that Vera could recall. "Why would we do that?"

"I will not continue down the path that my father and Mercer and all the other rulers of Terra have cleared for me. Look at where it has led. The whole world is on fire, and I will not stoke the flames. Remove the explosives and the archer stations and anything else that can be used for destruction. These are war frigates no longer. They will become beacons of peace and prosperity in the realm of Terra."

She turned to Vera. "First, we will unite Almira. Then we will open trade lines with the other countries of Terra, one by one. I am sure that whoever now rules Balaria is someone that I know. And Okinu is my aunt. I can do this." She paused. "I will fix the mess that I created when I ran away with Ganon."

Osyrus began twisting his beard into greasy knots. "A noble goal, Empress. But even the first step of uniting Almira will prove difficult. The small lords of the Atlas Coast will likely support you without much convincing—the Malgrave name always carried water in that province. But the Daintree jaguars have been in full revolt since the summer. And that jungle is the one place in Terra where the skyship's strength is diminished by the canopy. Perhaps if we began with a show of force, we might be able to—"

"No. The jaguars rebelled against Linkon Pommol. Not against me. We'll send emissaries to their leadership, inform them that Pommol and his government no longer exist, and offer a parley. I'll make peace with the Dainwood, then everyone else."

Vera glanced at Decimar, who gave her a satisfied nod. Kira was a long way from fulfilling the promises that Vera had made on her behalf back in that kitchen, but she'd taken the first step.

Osyrus stopped twisting his beard. Gave a smile. "Well, who am I to stand in the way of a realm-wide peace? I am just glad that my ships may serve as tools toward such a magnanimous purpose."

"Good, Osyrus. I am glad I can count on your support."

"Gyle," Osyrus said pleasantly. "Please wait for us outside."

The mercenary gave a nod, spat on the floor, and left—closing the hatch behind him. Vera listened for footfalls and gauged that he was three strides to the left of the door. She made a mental note to leave on that side of Kira.

"There is also the matter of the Wormwrot mercenaries we now have in Floodhaven."

"Mercenaries? Plural?"

"I planted stowaways on the larger ships in the unlikely event there were survivors. Assuming there were no complications, we now have half a score of Gyle's comrades at our disposal."

"A score of unpredictable killers, you mean," Vera said, remembering Rike and Wun from Balaria. "They're a liability behind the walls of Floodhaven."

"Agreed," Osyrus said. "I propose we send them beyond the city walls." He paused. "The *Time's Daughter* crashed in that eucalyptus forest for unknown reasons. But it was carrying the first prototype Kor engine. She has by far the largest cargo capacity and fuel longevity in the fleet. Losing her is a great forfeiture to us, since she would have been able to transport enormous amounts of food to the far corners of the realm. But Wormwrot could salvage the ship at dawn."

"Yes," Kira said. "I agree, we must salvage the ship."

Vera glanced at Decimar. He shrugged. "I'd take the *Blue Sparrow* and do it with my men, but that leaves the castle vulnerable."

And if the castle was vulnerable, so was Kira.

"Very well," said Vera. "Give the Wormwrot men horses and send them to the wreck."

"Time is of the essence, I'm afraid. The longer that ship stays in those woods, the greater chance that her machinery will be damaged by animals or pillaged by locals. As I said, my acolytes are all trained pilots. They can ensure that Wormwrot salvages all valuable technology."

"We need the *Time's Daughter*," said Kira. "If not the entire ship, then the engine."

Vera chewed on the inside of her cheek. Those mercenaries were Osyrus Ward's creatures, just like his gray-skinned acolytes. She did not like giving them such independence and control. But she didn't like any of the alternatives, either.

"Do it."

41

JOLAN

Almira, Wreckage of the Time's Daughter

"How many ships?" Cumberland barked up to Iko.

Everyone was outside the wreckage, looking up at her.

She paused to count.

"Twenty-nine."

"Attacking the city?"

"No. Just hovering over it."

"If they came all this way, why wouldn't they attack?" Willem said.

"Because they were all wearing their armor like Quinn," Jolan responded. "They're all dead."

"Some kind of rebellion?" Sten asked from his seat by the burned-out fire.

"Septimus mentioned that there was unrest amongst the Balarians," Jolan said.

"Who's Septimus?" Willem asked.

"The *navigator*," Jolan said. "The one that Shoshone k—"

"Black skies," Iko hissed from the tree.

"What?"

"One of the ships *is* moving now." She paused, watching. "And it's heading directly for us."

"How long?" Cumberland asked.

Another pause.

"I'd say we have about thirty minutes."

"Shit," Cumberland muttered.

Iko dropped down from the tree. "Plan?"

"No time to run in a way that won't leave a shitload of boot prints. Not with Sten's leg. Even a half-blind Balarian will be able to track us. But we're going to be outnumbered bad in a fight."

"That's never stopped us before," Willem said.

"What if we can do it without a fight?" Jolan asked.

Everyone turned to him.

"No fight?" Willem asked. "That ship's gonna be throwing a shadow on us real soon, and whether it's full of Balarians or some other manner of asshole, I doubt they'll be friendly to a bunch of jaguar wardens and a Papyrian widow."

"But they'll be friendly to me," Jolan said. "A boy. An alchemist. Alone in the wreckage and the corpses. Or looking that way, at least. I can talk my way out of this."

Cumberland sucked on his teeth. "Don't like it."

"Neither do I," Jolan said. "But it's the best chance we have to get through this without bloodshed."

They looked at each other, then at the landscape.

"That ridge has good cover," Willem said.

"In range of my sling," Iko continued. "And your crossbow. It could work."

"So we're the overwatch . . ." Willem said, then looked to Cumberland and Oromir.

"And we are the corpses," Oromir finished.

"What about this one?" Willem said, giving Garret's bindings a yank.

"This is going to be simpler with fewer elements," Iko said. "We can't trust him, so we should kill him."

"Agreed," said Willem.

But they both looked at Cumberland to decide. Cumberland turned to Jolan.

"You know him. You decide."

Now that the decision did fall to Jolan, he wasn't so sure that he wanted it. He glanced at Oromir, whose jaw and lips were tight. He shook his head once, then said softly, "He *is* dangerous, Jolan."

Jolan's heart sank a little. He didn't know what he'd expected from Oromir. But he'd wanted something else.

Lastly, he turned to Garret. Whose eyes were as cold and unknowable as ever.

"Don't kill him. Bring him up to the ridge and chain him to a tree, where he's out of the way."

———

They made their preparations as quickly as they could. Jolan had just barely gotten himself situated on Quinn's corpse when the airship came into view over the trees and threw a shadow over everything. Black ropes dropped to the ground with a thump, followed by twenty armed men in black armor. All of them wore red face paint, which Jolan had read in a history of war was a common practice with mercenaries from the far side of the Soul Sea. So, there had been a Balarian coup. But who were they serving? Who had hired them?

Jolan raised his hands over his head while the men surrounded him. Oromir was three strides to his left, playing dead.

"I'm not armed!" he said, raising his voice so he could be heard.

"The fuck you doing out here, boy?" one man asked, speaking Almiran with a Dainwood accent. He was a local. Or had been, at one point.

"I'm an alchemist."

"Didn't ask for your vocation. Asked what you're doing sitting on a corpse in the middle of nowhere."

"I have a business proposition for you. I speak on behalf of my master, a man named Morgan Mo—"

"Shut up for second," the man said. "Rike. Wun. Full perimeter check. Everyone else inside the ship for salvage."

Two massive Lysterians headed into the woods. Most of the soldiers headed into the gaping hole in the side of the ship.

The man turned back to Jolan.

"So what is it that you're doing perched on that corpse? Trying to pretend you weren't pillaging the ship?"

"There's no reason for me to go inside that ship. Everything I need is out here." He motioned to the dead bodies they'd laid out in front of Jolan.

"Corpse robber."

"Alchemist. Like I said. My order can do a lot with a corpse. Dentistry. Tissue replacement. General anatomical study and the charting of different diseases' impacts on organs."

"Blah, blah, blah. Arrive at the point, kid."

"Very well." Jolan paused, dug into his pocket. Came back with a handful of coins. "My master would like to buy one of the corpses."

The man squinted at the coins. "How's it you've managed to get yourself in the position to purchase dead bodies so quickly?"

"We run an apothecary just over that ridge," Jolan said, the lie coming easy and natural. "Heard the crash last night, and my mas-

ter sent me to check on survivors. If there weren't any, he told me
to bring back a good dead body on my sledge."

Jolan motioned to the half-finished sledge they'd built in a
hurry. Sten was already loaded inside and pretending to be dead.

"You got a few options here. What's special about that one?"

"He was showing signs of liver cirrhosis. My master has an interest in the effects of the disease, which will be evident in a post
mortem surgery."

"Post what?"

"After he's dead."

"Hm. Well, boy, as it turns out, *my* master has a pretty keen interest in dead bodies, too. You bookish types are all pretty strange
when you get up close and scrutinize the measure of your habits."
He glanced at the gold. Then back at the two men behind him, who
both nodded approval of the proposition. "But letting go of one
croaker ain't gonna get noticed, don't think. Let's have that coin."

Jolan handed it over. Heart racing when the man came close.
His fingernails had blood and grease caked beneath them.

"There. You got your trade. Get lost then, yeah?"

Jolan nodded. Hustled over to the sledge. It was half built, but
put-together enough for him to drag it into the forest and wait for
the ship to depart. He pulled the makeshift straps over his shoulders. Prepared to haul it into the nearest overgrowth.

Five soldiers emerged from the ship. One of them shrugged.
"Ain't in there, Gyle."

"Fuck you mean? The ship flew itself out here, didn't it?"

"Sure, but the engine tray's been yanked out. No Kor inside."

"No Kor, huh." He looked back to Jolan, who was cursing internally and trying to haul the massive sled away as quickly as possible, but not getting anywhere fast.

"Hold up, boy. You go in there?"

"No," Jolan said, stopping.

"See anyone come out?"

"No."

"We got all kinds of boot prints in the wreckage," said one soldier.
"Beds all used up, too. Like someone spent the night. Recent, like."

"I don't know anything about that."

"Uh-huh." Gyle rubbed his beard. "That is all fine. But I'm

gonna need to search that sledge of yours and make sure you didn't sneak off with something a little more valuable than a dead body." He drew a knife from his belt and began picking his way between the bodies.

Jolan twitched. Sighed. "I tried to do it peacefully," he muttered.

"I know," Oromir said, opening his eyes.

"The fuck?" Gyle asked, startled at the voice.

Oromir sprang up and stabbed him through the center of his breastplate.

The two mercenaries who'd been with Gyle lifted their weapons. One's head exploded a heartbeat later. Willem's bolt thumped into the other man's chest, slamming him on his back.

"Run, Jolan!" Oromir hissed, then yanked his sword free from Gyle's chest and rushed the group of soldiers—outnumbered five to one. They angled up against him, grinning at the overmatched idiot.

One of their heads exploded. A second took a bolt to the belly and doubled over.

Behind them, Cumberland rose from beneath a corpse and ran his greatsword across the backs of two men's thighs. They crumpled, and he took their heads off with the backswing.

The remaining mercenary—who was now surrounded and, for the moment, outnumbered himself—charged Oromir.

"I said get clear!" Oromir shouted at Jolan. Then launched into a set of lightning-fast parries. "Now!"

Jolan sprinted up the ridge. The screams of steel on steel hammered through the dawn air while he climbed the hill, back to Willem's position. When he got there, Willem was aiming his crossbow, lips twitching with irritation. Jolan looked back at the skyship's wreckage to see the ten remaining mercenaries pouring out of it and surrounding Oromir and Cumberland.

Willem fired a bolt, but it landed far short of the closest mercenary.

"Fuck," he hissed, reloading the weapon. "They're too far away."

"We need to get down there," Iko said.

"Yeah." Willem put a hand on Jolan's shoulder. "You need to run."

"No."

"It's four on ten. This will get ugly. Go, Jolan."

"I won't. Not with Oromir down there."

Willem cursed. "Fine."

Then he pushed his crossbow into Jolan's chest.

"It's loaded. You just have to point and squeeze this trigger. You'll only have the one shot, so make it count."

"Shoot at what?"

"Anyone who comes up this hill that ain't us."

With that, Willem and Iko ran toward the fight.

Jolan watched in frozen horror. Cumberland and Oromir were surrounded. About to be cut down like lambs.

Then Iko released a bloodcurdling war howl as she sprinted across the field, moving twice as fast as Willem. Both her daggers were drawn. Five mercenaries broke off to meet her, giving Oromir and Cumberland a fighting chance.

Iko hit the line of soldiers at a full run, ducking and dodging and stabbing. She was wrestled to the ground by two seething men. They became a tangle of limbs and flashing blades and Jolan couldn't tell who was who, or who was winning.

Willem reached the fray a moment later, throwing one of his war hatchets at a tall mercenary, who blocked it with his shield, then tackled Willem. Pressed him into the mud with his shield, snarling. Willem drew his second hatchet and started hacking at the man's thigh and ribs.

Jolan turned back to Iko. His heart sank.

It took four men to kill her. Three to pin her down, and one to stab her through the heart with a spear. When it was done, the men who'd held her in place stumbled away and fell to the ground, clutching wounds at their throats, armpits, or groins. They bled out in seconds.

"No!" shouted Willem, who'd finally killed the mercenary and shoved him to the side. He charged the spearman who'd killed Iko. Split his skull apart with a vicious hack and a wild yell.

But it didn't change anything. She was gone.

Willem charged toward Oromir and Cumberland, who were still fighting the other five mercenaries. He screamed as he joined the vicious fray.

This was Jolan's fault. If he'd said something different. Something better. Tricked Gyle.

If he hadn't come up with his stupid plan to begin with.

If. If. If.

"Jolan!" came a hiss from behind him. Garret.

He twisted around. Garret jerked his head farther up the hill, where two massive Lysterians were sneaking out of the forest.

"No," he whispered. They'd snuck around.

Jolan aimed his crossbow at them.

"There are two of them," Garret whispered.

"I can count."

"You have one bolt."

"I *know*."

"Set me free," Garret said.

Jolan's mind swarmed with panicked thoughts.

"Set me free, and I will kill them."

"I don't . . ."

The men were fifty strides away now, moving faster now that they'd heard the sounds of fighting.

"Jolan, there's no time. Do it."

With a curse, Jolan dropped the crossbow and moved to Garret, fumbling with the key to his chains.

"That a kid?" one of the soldiers muttered in Lysterian. They couldn't see Garret yet.

"Yup."

"You!" he called. "Come out where we can see you."

Jolan fit the key in the lock.

"Come on, now. Won't hurt you none, boy."

Turned it.

Garret was up and moving before the chains had fallen to the ground. Walking directly at the men—steady and deliberate. Holding his hands out to his sides.

"Hold up there," said the closest Lysterian, putting up a hand.

Garret kept moving forward. Didn't say anything.

"So that's how you wanna die, asshole? Fine." The Lysterian bulled forward. Tried to stab Garret through the chest. In one fluid motion, Garret dodged the sword, snatched it from the man's hand, and cut his head off with it.

The other Lysterian approached with more caution. His face was grim.

"That was my brother," he growled.

"I don't care," said Garret.

The Lysterian attacked, but Garret darted forward—moving far quicker than his opponent—and cut off the man's sword hand during his backswing. Garret sliced his hamstring open, forcing him to his knees.

Before the Lysterian could so much as scream, Garret cut his head off, too.

Garret marched back to Jolan, yanked the Kor from his satchel, and headed for the undergrowth.

"Wait," Jolan said. "You can't just take it."

"Yes, I can."

The sounds of fighting were still ringing out behind Jolan. That meant it wasn't over. Not yet.

Jolan picked up the crossbow, came around in front of Garret, and leveled the weapon.

That stopped Garret, but he didn't seem scared. "What are you going to do with that?"

"We need the Kor."

"A lot of people need it, which means it's worth a lot of money."

"So, you're just a common thief now?"

"Move."

Jolan shook his head. Placed his finger on the metal trigger. "They *saved* you."

"No. They wanted to kill me. *You* saved me. And now I have saved you, which makes us even. Those wardens spoiled my work, which means I'm spoiling theirs and taking the orb."

Garret stepped forward. Slow and confident.

Jolan tried to fire the crossbow. He really did. But before he could summon the courage—or whatever quality is required to kill a man—Garret put a hand over the mechanism and took the weapon from him, then slammed the butt into Jolan's mouth. He hit the ground with a grunt. Tasted blood. A moment later he felt the metal irons clamping around his wrist and locking.

"No!" Jolan shouted. "Stop!"

Garret headed toward the trees, but Cumberland came up the path before he disappeared into the jungle.

"I heard screaming," Cumberland said, seeing the dead bodies. "What happened?"

Jolan pointed at Garret with his bound hands. "He took the Kor."

Cumberland turned his gaze to Garret.

"Gray eyes," he called. Garret turned. "Can't let you take that."

"Yes you can, old man. It's not worth dying over."

In the distance, Jolan could hear steel ringing out. Oromir and Willem were still fighting.

Cumberland moved toward Garrett. Swung his bloodied sword into an attack posture. "Won't ask again. Drop it."

"Have it your way. But I warned you."

Garret slipped the crossbow around from the small of his back and fired it. Cumberland twitched left so the bolt glanced off his breastplate. Garret was on him a moment later, raining down a flurry of blows with his sword. Cumberland parried and dodged, then beat Garret back with a series of his own rapid strikes. Their swords moved so quickly that Jolan couldn't follow the movements, just hear metallic clangs ringing out faster than his hammering heart.

And then, without warning, it was over.

One moment, they were matching each other blow for blow, the next Garret thumped Cumberland in the mouth with the pommel of his sword, then ran the blade through his heart.

"No!" Jolan shouted, voice cracking in his throat. He yanked on his manacles as hard as he could. Felt the skin break. Didn't care. He yanked and he screamed and then yanked more. His vision blurred over with tears. But he kept on screaming—a wordless, tortured wail.

"Jolan!" came Oromir's voice from far down the hill. "We're coming!"

Garret looked at Jolan. "I told you that it was a mistake to save my life."

Then he disappeared into the jungle.

Jolan sat there trembling and yanking on the chains until Oromir and Willem came running up the muddy road.

"What happened?" Oromir asked. He hadn't seen Cumberland yet.

"Let me out," Jolan cried. "Let me out so I can save him."

Cumberland was still moving. Trying to reach for his sword with a weak hand. Oromir finally saw him.

"Gods. Fucking gods." Oromir moved fast, grabbing the keys

from the ground and unlocking Jolan. As soon as the irons clicked open, Jolan ran to Cumberland.

Blood was everywhere, pooling in the muddy rut where Cumberland had fallen.

Jolan surveyed the wound as Morgan taught him. Panic rose in this throat. Cumberland had been stabbed just beneath the solar plexus. Garret had yanked the blade upward, where it tore into lung and heart. Blood surged from the wound in so many places there was no way to identify the source.

Cumberland's eyes were wide open. He tried to talk but blood came out instead of words.

"Don't talk," Jolan said, tearing open his satchel. Ramming the sealskin gloves on and pulling out his scissors. He cut Cumberland's breastplate and shirt off. "I can fix this. I can fix it."

He tried to remember the *Guide to Field Surgeries.*

Find the source of the bleeding. Stop it. If there are multiple sources, start with the largest and repair them one at a time.

"I can't see anything," Jolan said, poised over the wound with his stitches ready.

Clear the field.

Jolan snatched his gauze from the satchel.

"Open your canteen," he said to Oromir as he packed the gauze into the wound to soak up the worst of the blood. "When I remove this, pour it over the wound."

"How much?" Oromir's voice was shaky as he pulled the stopper off his canteen.

"As much as it takes so I can fucking see." His voice cracked. "I *have* to see."

Jolan removed the saturated gauze. Picked up his stitches.

"Now."

Jolan watched as the water went into the wound. Cumberland jerked in pain. As the liquid splashed into Cumberland's chest, there was a moment where it washed his organs clean. Jolan could see the top of his stomach, the bottom of his heart, and the edge of his blue lung.

"That's enough," Jolan said, eyes focused.

Once Oromir stopped pouring, the wounds started pumping blood again, allowing him to identify the bleeds.

Jolan started stitching.

He moved as fast as he could—closing one wound, then moving to the next. Before long, his arms were covered from fingers to elbows with Cumberland's blood.

"Jolan . . ." Cumberland whispered.

"Don't talk," he said. "I can fix this. I can fix you. I can . . ."

"Stop." Cumberland took Jolan's hand. His fingers felt like they'd been submerged in an icy lake for hours. "It's all right."

Jolan looked up at Cumberland's face. His skin had gone pale and waxy. Lips blue. Then he looked at his chest again and saw that his heart was barely beating.

"I'm losing him."

"No," Oromir said. He turned to Jolan with tears in his eyes. "Fix it!"

"I'm trying," Jolan hissed, fingers moving as quickly as he could make them.

Oromir squeezed Cumberland's hand. "You can't go. You can't die."

"You were always gonna outlive me, Oro. That's the way this shit works."

"I told you to fix it!" Oromir shouted at Jolan.

Jolan looked at the wounds. Helpless. Willem had come up behind them.

"No," he muttered, then dropped to his knees.

"Get the Gods Moss!" Jolan barked.

"The what?"

"Move." Jolan shoved him out of the way and dug into the satchel until he found the metal box filled with the moss he'd scraped from the deepest part of the Dainwood warrens. Pushed all of it into Cumberland's wound.

"What are you . . ."

"I've seen it work!" he screamed, lips trembling. He was crying so hard he could barely see. "I've seen magic before. It will work. It *has* to."

Cumberland pulled Oromir close. Struggled to eke out the words. "Don't . . . don't be . . ."

His mouth hung open, the last word dying on his breath. Jolan's eyes blurred with tears. Cumberland's hand went slack in Oromir's fist.

"No! No, no, no, no."

Jolan pressed against the moss. Waiting for the miracle at Otter Rock to repeat itself. Frantically searching for a sign of life in Cumberland's body.

But it never came.

PART IV

42

BERSHAD

Ghost Moth Island, Naga Rock

Plink.

The sound of metal being dropped against metal woke Bershad up.

He was on his belly. Laid up on a rickety cot that smelled of pus and sweat. A man grunted with effort. Bershad felt a sharp pain in his back—as if someone was pinching a massive pustule—and then relief as the pressure was released and something cold was removed from his left shoulder blade.

Plink.

Bershad remembered the rushing river. Mouthfuls of red, putrid water. All those bolts in his chest and back—the last remnants of Gods Moss struggling to heal the wounds as he was carried down the bloody cataracts. Somewhere in that mess, the mushroom had floated down next to him. He'd grabbed it. Clung to the edge as the current took him over a rushing waterfall.

Everything went black when he hit the sea.

Plink.

"How many is that, Cormo?" asked a man who spoke Papyrian with a Ghalamarian accent.

"Twenty-three. Still got a few left that I can't get out. Bastard's bones healed over 'em somehow."

The first man whistled. "How's he still alive?"

"Fuck if I know, Boris," said Cormo, grunting as he pulled another bolt from Bershad's back. "But given all the shit the Flawless Bershad has survived, a bunch o' bolts wouldn't logically pose a major hurdle."

Plink.

"Ain't nothing logical about any of this," Boris said. "I don't like it."

"Good for you. Come down to do anything besides spread your discontent?"

"Kerrigan wants to know if he's awake. She wants to do his interview."

"Let's find out."

There was a pause. Cormo dropped whatever rusty metal tool he'd been using into a bucket of water, which smelled like it was half filled with horse piss, and then bent down so his face was a finger's width from Bershad's nose. Cormo was in his late forties. Bushy mutton chops covered meaty jowls and about half of his blue bars. His head was shaved and there was a jagged scar running across one side of his skull. Looked like it had been done with a fork.

"You awake yet, lizard killer?" he asked, switching to Almiran and smiling. All of his teeth were black.

"Where am I?" Bershad rasped. His throat felt like a dried bone with the marrow bored out.

"Naga Rock!" he said, clapping Bershad on the shoulder, which caused a shock of pain. "Subterranean home o' the Naga Killer Corsair Company. You are our prisoner."

"How long?" Bershad swallowed, trying to get his throat wet. It didn't really work. "How long have I been here?"

"A decent stretch. I been working on these bolts for, oh, don't even know how many days. They're wedged mighty deep, so I took lots of breaks." He turned to Boris and switched back to Papyrian. "Man's awake. Appears to have cheated death once again."

"Is he really . . . you know?"

"You see any other exiles wandering the halls with an arm like that?"

"Fucking hell. What are the chances of fishing the Flawless Bershad outta the Big Empty?"

"Not high. But let's have less wondering about long probabilities and more trotting down to Kerrigan and giving the news." Cormo squinted at Bershad. "I can take him up in a few ticks, I'd say."

"Yeah, yeah. I'm off then."

Boris left. Cormo pulled his pliers out of the water. "I can take one more run at those stragglers if you want," he said, switching back to Almiran.

Bershad shook his head. A few bolts in his back didn't matter, and he remembered what Goll had told him about how Cormo had earned those bars. He figured that if this idiot had sawed off the wrong leg of some general, the less healing he inflicted on Bershad the better.

"Water."

Cormo sucked on his teeth. "Poor luck there. Drinkable water ain't exactly a cheap commodity in Naga Rock. Or a priority. But we got enough ale to drown a dragon. Good stuff, too. None of that cheap rice wine piss that Papyrians like so much."

"Fine."

Cormo helped Bershad sit up on the cot, which sent a thousand needle shocks of pain through his body. He tried to get his bearings. They were in a cramped room with a low ceiling. Lit by three dirty lanterns and a fire in the corner that was almost down to embers. He smelled seawater and snails. The walls were carved directly from the rock and looked like they'd been dug out by a massive claw.

They were inside a dragon's lair. Must be a Naga Soul Strider— nothing else was big enough.

Cormo handed Bershad an earthenware jug with the stopper already pulled. The jug was cold and smelled of seawater. The pirate must have been keeping it in a tide pool or something. Bershad took a long, deep drink. Nearly finished off half the jug in one pull.

"It's Leeroy's outfit that found you," Cormo said while Bershad drank. "They were returning from a reaving—already planning which companions they'd go see first—when you plopped into the ocean, falling down the Bloody Sludge waterfall like a piece of flotsam, clinging to one o' the big mushrooms. The decision as to whether they get the Exile's Reward for that is still up in the air. Accidentally coming across a lizard killer doesn't happen often." Cormo burped. Thumped on his chest a few times. "Leeroy said both your legs were broke when he fished you out o' the water, but he's an idiot. They're just bruised to shit is all."

Bershad looked down at his legs, both of which were completely black and purple. Fixing those bones and fusing a few bolts to his skeleton must have been the last bit of healing the Gods

Moss managed. That meant his current injuries weren't going away anytime soon unless he could get some more warren moss.

Bershad tried to reach out with his senses and see if he could feel the Nomad. But the limestone walls of the cave were too thick. The world beyond the rock was closed off to him.

"How do I get out of this place?"

Cormo took the jug. "Not so fast. Kerrigan decides the fate of every exile that winds up at Naga Rock. Being the most famous lizard killer in Terra don't make you exempt."

Bershad pushed himself up from the cot. "I'm leaving."

"No. You are not."

Bershad ignored him. Crossed the room. The rusty tools were a few strides away and would make decent weapons.

But he only made it halfway to the tools—stumbling from the pain that shot up both legs with each step—before Cormo's meaty hand clamped around his shoulder and shoved him back onto the cot. Bershad was weaker than he'd realized, and the pirate overpowered him as easily as a jaguar ambushing a baby goat.

"None o' that now," Cormo said. "We got orders not to kill you, but in Kerrigan's outfit that means we ain't supposed to do it for no reason. You give me cause, I'll slit your fuckin' throat. And believe me, I will keep sawing till I'm sure you're dead. Clear?"

Bershad glared up at the man. He had a massive belly, but the rest of him was packed with meaty strength. Bershad couldn't take him in a fight. Not in this state, anyway.

"Clear."

"Good! Now let's have one more drink before we head up to Kerrigan."

He twisted around on his stool, reached into a bucket filled with cold seawater, and produced another earthenware jug of ale. Held it out. Bershad decided that if he couldn't murder his way out of here, he might as well make friends. He took the drink.

"You speak Almiran pretty well for an asshole pirate," he said after taking a pull and passing it back.

"*Corsair*'s the preferred term around here, but I don't have a stick up my ass about it as much as the others." Cormo shrugged. "Anyway, in Terra, a good corsair's gotta speak most o' the tongues. Makes it easier to threaten people into good behavior, see? Most o' the morons who board ships for a living barely speak one language, so they gotta growl and shout and break teeth or crack skulls to get people in line, which is a hassle." Cormo's face darkened. "But if you use a man's native language to whisper into his ear, tell him that if he so much as twitches a finger in an odd manner, you'll cut his daughter's head off in front of him and use it as a piss pot, well, that man'll do pretty much anything you say. Hell, he'll help you load all his shit onto your shallop and thank you for it in the end."

Cormo's face brightened again, as if he'd told a somewhat racy joke rather than revealed a horrific criminal habit.

"Yep, strong communication skills make the entire process a lot easier! That's why the Naga corsairs get through most reavings without a drop of blood spilled. It's Simeon and his crew up north that's always leaving behind a mess and giving Ghost Moth Island the black reputation. Well, them and the demons behind the bone wall."

"I heard it was nice back there. My original plan was to cross over and build myself a summer home."

Cormo laughed.

"You're funny, dragonslayer." He scratched at his ragged beard. Then considered the jug for a moment. Corked it and put it back in the tide pool. Then he dug up a brown, threadbare shirt and threw it to Bershad. "Put that on. We best get you over to Kerrigan for the interview. You'll get a look at Naga Rock on the way. Trust me, it leaves an impression."

———

Cormo was right.

Naga Rock was made from a long series of interconnected tunnels that had been bored out of the ground by an industrious dragon. And it definitely left an impression. The tunnels were all at least ten or fifteen strides high and, at times, wide enough to drive three wagons through at the same time. Given the fact that people lived there, the dragon obviously hadn't been around in years. But Bershad could still smell the distinct, feral remnants of the great lizard's scent on the walls.

Every few hundred strides, the tunnel that Cormo led Bershad down opened into a larger chamber. Each chamber seemed to have been outfitted for a specific form of commerce or entertainment.

The first chamber they reached had a meatmonger on one side hawking sausages and an old woman selling donkey's milk on the other. Both vendors had blue bars on their cheeks.

"Ale's free in the Rock," Cormo explained, motioning to the enormous barrel with a spigot in the middle of the chamber. "Meat and milk ain't. Prices are murderous, too. Supply and demand, Kerrigan likes to say."

The next chamber had an uneven stage built on one side, and dozens of cushions laid out on the other for people to watch the show. Only a handful of people were in the audience, but the performers were carrying on with the enthusiasm of actors inside of a crowded Balarian amphitheater. From what Bershad gleaned during their walk though, this one was about a teenage boy who accidentally gave his sister a love potion.

Bershad was just glad the play wasn't about him.

"Kerrigan booked a theater engagement?"

"Not exactly," Cormo said. "We captured 'em on their way from Lysteria to Ghalamar. They didn't have much coin, so we let 'em pay for their freedom in shows. Kerrigan offered to let them pay it off whoring—way faster, even for the men—but they refused. Artists, right?"

"Surprised they got a choice."

"Kerrigan's a different breed of outlaw. Everybody has a choice o' some kind in Naga."

"They didn't get a choice in terms of coming here to begin with."

Cormo shrugged. "Yeah, well. Life's imperfect."

The next chamber they passed was a bakery, with fresh rolls hot from an oven. The one after a smithy with more than twenty swords on offer and a hole bored straight through the ceiling that was providing ventilation. Bershad lingered beneath the hole as long as Cormo allowed, trying to get a whiff of the world above— hoping to pick up his connection to the Nomad—but the fumes from the furnace were too strong. All he got was smoke and dust.

Bershad tried to count the people they'd passed, too, but lost track around eighty or ninety. He figured about half of them were exiles.

"It really is a whole city," he muttered.

"More like a decent port town in my opinion," Cormo said.

Regardless of size, it was the only settlement Bershad had passed through in fourteen years where every citizen didn't ogle him as if he was a cave goblin. Down here, with his arm covered, he was just like everyone else.

Cormo motioned down a wide tunnel as they walked past. "The children's bunkhouses and private quarters are down that way, but you've slept enough for a while, I think."

"How many children live in Naga Rock?"

"Oh, enough to cause mischief and strife amongst the rest of us. The little band of Lysterian kids stole my Balarian watch yesterday. They take pleasure in ransoming the treasures of adults back to them—practice for the corsair life ahead of them, I suppose. I'm waiting to be presented with their terms. Last time I had to show them my entire collection of golden teeth before they'd give me back my week's portion of bread. Most people think it's cute, but it's a fucking pain in my ass."

They reached a long straightaway. This stretch of tunnel had dozens of shallow chambers carved into its sides. Each chamber's entrance was protected by a locked gate made from thick iron.

"These are the plunder rooms. Mind that your fingers don't get sticky in here."

Judging from the smells emanating from behind the gates, the corsairs had stolen something from every corner of Terra and packed it into a different cubby. Crates of frankincense and cinnamon filled one chamber. The next had dozens of white sacks emitting the floral smell of opium. Bear furs from eastern Ghalamar were stacked to the ceiling in another.

Past that, there was a briny tide pool filled to the brim with Pargossian blue snails. Their iridescent shells glowed in the water.

"Those little things are my favorite," Cormo said, jerking a thumb toward the pool. "But there's been problems with mysteriously depleted inventory. Kerrigan moved most of the stash to a deeper level and says the next man that goes for an unsanctioned snack loses an ear. Stiff price to pay for a bite to eat, but still tempting. Ears don't really do much 'cept hold earrings. And I'm not a man who puts much stock in jewelry."

Farther down—past a king's ransom in rare furs, spices, and gems—there was a chamber that was twice as large as the rest. It was protected by a thick slab of steel rather than an iron gate and guarded by two stern-looking exiles in full armor. Bershad could smell the piney scent of dragon oil harvested from a Ghalamarian Green Horn wafting out from behind the steel door.

"Your outfit's pretty successful," Bershad said.

"Kerrigan's got a gift for making plunder multiply. Hell, most of the shit we just passed wasn't specifically stolen. We exchange our stolen loot for clean goods with proper merchant records, then trade those for an even larger profit on our way home. Kerrigan has the whole thing worked out with a bunch of customs agents in the realm. Doubles the take and halves the risk. Hard to argue with that logic, right? Look at all this shit!"

He looked around the room. Sighed happily.

"Yeah. Seems like a completely separate life when a belly full of rat meat was a good day."

"During your exile, you mean?"

"Aye. Nasty business. Chasing lizards all day. Sleeping outside at night. No roof and no comforts. Always on the lookout for soldiers with an eye for truant lizard killers. Or just run-o'-the-mill assholes who don't like exiles on principle."

"You never fought a dragon?"

"Fuck no. Drew a writ for a Stone Scale up in the Razorbacks and decided to head in the complete opposite direction. My forsaken shield stole my boots while I was asleep and abandoned me. It was bad times. I was getting ready to eat my donkey when Kerrigan scooped me up."

"What happened to your donkey?"

"Oh, he's here with the rest o' them."

"Rest of them?"

Cormo smiled. "I suppose we got time for a detour." He motioned down another tunnel. "This way."

It only took a few dozen paces before Bershad picked up the smell of hay. That was followed by the sound of rustling hooves and hee-hawing brays. The familiar sounds put a lump in Bershad's throat.

The passage opened into a large, well-illuminated room that had been converted into an animal pen. There were at least two scores of donkeys milling around the grounds—munching from ample piles of hay or barrels of apples. Sniffing and nipping and braying at each other.

"Where you hiding, Ghalleyhad?" Cormo called, scanning the animals. "Ghalley? Come say hello, you salty bastard."

After a few more calls, a black donkey with white ears separated from the group and clopped over to the waiting Cormo. The corsair rubbed the donkey's muzzle, which was peppered with gray hairs.

"Most o' the exiles have already lost track of their mounts by the time someone from Naga finds them, but there are exceptions. Everyone's allowed to take their donkey with them if they want. Ghalley's food and fresh water comes outta my portion of the reavings, but I don't mind the cost. This grumpy bastard kept me warm on more than a few bad nights." He patted Ghalleyhad's belly. "More than a few."

Cormo turned to Bershad. "What was yours named?"

"Alfonso," Bershad whispered.

"A good name."

Cormo stood. Bershad could tell the pirate had another question coming that he wouldn't be in a rush to answer, so he got ahead of it.

"How much further to Kerrigan?" Bershad asked.

Cormo studied Bershad a moment. Then gave a little nod of understanding. "We're almost there. Follow me."

They left the donkeys and moved through a few more chambers in silence before turning a corner, where the tunnel opened into a massive chamber. It was as tall as Castle Malgrave and wide as a Floodhaven city block.

Wooden scaffolding was erected everywhere, creating a complicated series of stairs and walkways that led up, down, and across the wide chasm. The cavern floor was flooded with seawater—the salty brine filled Bershad's nose—but he didn't see a route to the ocean. The cave must be filled by an underwater channel.

But the most noticeable part of the cavern was the structure in the center, which was suspended in the air by hundreds of hemp ropes that were pinned to the limestone walls.

The building was shaped like a massive wasp nest—conical, and wider at the top than the base. It was made entirely from cedar planks that had been molded and warped and bent, then fit together in a seamless pattern that spiraled upward.

"We call it the hive. Nobody knows who built the thing,"

Cormo said, scratching his head. "Apparently, it was just floating in the water down there when Kerrigan arrived. She personally kidnapped a Balarian architect to truss the thing up like that. The onion-faced bastard said that whoever made it was a genius in terms of construction. He'd never seen its equal."

Bershad had. But he didn't say anything about Kasamir. No point.

"Anyway, Kerrigan likes doing the interviews in there 'cause there ain't but one way in and out. She sleeps up there for the same reason. But if it were me, I wouldn't get an ounce o' rest in that contraption. I'd just be wondering if the whole thing'll go crashing into the fucking water below at any given moment."

"How do we get inside?" Bershad asked.

"Oh, it's a process. Follow me."

Cormo led him down one of the wooden scaffolds. The boards shifted and swayed from their weight. They descended until they were below the hive, then took a bridge across until they were directly underneath. The slats of the hive were made from polished cedar but had been treated with sap from a rubber tree. Bershad could smell it. There was a single, wooden trapdoor about twenty paces above them.

"Ho!" Cormo called, cupping his hands around his mouth to help his voice carry the distance. "I brought the Flawless Bershad!"

The trapdoor snapped open and a man appeared with a long-ranged crossbow—each bow limb the length of an antelope horn. Looking down the barrel of the bow made Bershad's wounds tingle.

The sentry considered them for a long moment, then dropped a rope down, which writhed like a tree snake as it unfurled. The bottom settled so it was exactly one pace above the floorboards at Bershad's feet.

"Kerrigan just wants Bershad," the guard called down.

"Good," Cormo muttered. "Hate that climb. The way the fucking rope sways is unsettling." He clapped Bershad on the shoulder. "Good drinking with you."

"Yeah," Bershad said. "Thanks for pulling out some of the crossbow bolts, I guess."

"Don't mention it." Cormo clasped Bershad's hand at the wrist, then leaned closer. "Free piece of advice, though. Don't fuck about up there. Kerrigan doesn't suffer assholes or salty demeanors. And she keeps the best fighters in Naga Rock up there with her for protection. Might be they don't hold a candle to your lizard-killing record, but they put in some hard, bloody work in their day, and they'll send you down the river right quick on Kerri's orders. That'd be a damn shame. If you get yourself killed, then all these blisters I got on my thumbs from sortin' you out'll be for nothing."

Cormo held the rope as Bershad started to climb, but when he was halfway up, the rope started swaying more. He glanced down and saw that the corsair had disappeared.

The sentry guarding the hatch stepped backward as Bershad came through, the crossbow trained on Bershad's skull.

"Gonna be honest," Bershad said. "I'm getting real fucking sick of people pointing those things at me."

The crossbow didn't have all the machinery and gears like the ones Simeon's men carried, but it was still loaded and the bolt was still pointed at his face.

"Uh-huh," the man said. "Behave yourself, and pointing is where it'll stop."

He was an exile. Had such bushy eyebrows they were basically connected to his beard. He wore a scaled breastplate with no sleeves, so the five dragon tattoos on his wrist were on full display. Two Red Skulls and a trio of Blackjacks. Not bad.

Bershad figured there was a fifty-fifty chance he could snatch the bow and beat the man to death with it before sustaining a serious injury, but then he'd still be in the literal heart of a pirate hideout he couldn't properly navigate, surrounded by talented killers.

"Where to, then?"

The man used the crossbow to motion Bershad toward a narrow wooden ladder that led to the next level of the hive. The chamber above was filled with five more armed guards sitting around the perimeter of the room. All of them with blue bars and multiple dragons tattooed to their wrists. All of them with crossbows of their own. They'd arranged themselves so they could fire at the ladder without worrying about hitting each other in the crossfire.

There was a small cast-iron oven with a steel kettle for tea on top that smelled of fennel and nettles. A few puffy cakes were cooling on a shelf. There was also a large basin full of fresh river water and three smoked salmon hanging on a line. The food made Bershad's stomach turn over—he realized that he was starving.

"Keep moving," the sentry grunted, motioning to another ladder.

The next chamber was wider still and filled with ten corsairs. The floor was covered with a soft Balarian carpet that reminded Bershad of the stuff he'd seen in the Balarian palace. Silk drapes hung on the walls and there were massive pillows laid out in small circles that could work as beds or sofas or both at the same time. A large opium pipe was placed in the middle of each pillow circle, and incense burned everywhere. The place smelled like dragon oil and myrrh.

"One more, then." The sentry motioned to a final ladder on the far wall. He didn't move to follow Bershad to the next level.

Bershad ascended, and found himself in a large room that seemed to be part office, part archive, and part bedroom. The chamber was illuminated by a hanging chandelier made of glass. One side was dominated by a massive wood shelf that looked like a wine rack, but each cubby was filled with a thick leather scroll. The opposite side had a simple but comfortable-looking bedroll on the floor. A few books and candles were laid out next to a buckwheat pillow.

A low, rectangular table made from polished cedar was in the middle of the room. The surface was bare except for a candle and a scroll that was weighed down by four perfectly round, black stones at each corner.

And behind the table, a woman was sitting cross-legged and marking the scroll with a quill.

"Welcome, Silas Bershad." She spoke Almiran with an articulate voice. "I'm Kerrigan la Custar. Captain of the Naga Killer Corsair Company and mayor of Naga Rock."

Kerrigan had the obsidian-black skin of a Dunfarian. A close-cropped mohawk that was dyed bright blue. The rest of her head was shaved. Features smooth and round. She wore a simple leather jerkin and pants.

And she had a thick blue bar running down each of her dark cheeks.

"You're a dragonslayer."

"Points for observation. Yes. Although I am not nearly as famous or prolific as you." She held up her left arm, which was corded in wiry muscle. Only one dragon was tattooed there—a well-drawn Naga Soul Strider. "Do not worry, the bars themselves mean nothing in Naga Rock. All exiles are given an opportunity to join our miniature but prosperous nation."

"I've heard."

"Then you must also know that before we go any further, an interview is required. Please." Kerrigan extended an arm to a reed mat on the far side of the table. "Make yourself comfortable. I've been looking forward to speaking with you ever since I heard you'd arrived. We exiles of Terra share a bond."

"We share a set of ugly tattoos."

Kerrigan's smile faded slightly. "Have you ever met another dragonslayer face-to-face before?" she asked.

"Let me save you some time. I know all about your interview process and your lizard-killer sanctuary. I'm not interested. And I don't have time to sit and chat about the particulars of why. Just show me the door, I'll limp through it, and that'll be the end of it."

"Oh, but you *do* have time for a chat," Kerrigan said, voice sharpening. "Because you'll never leave this room alive unless you answer each of my questions with as much detail as possible, and I like the details that you provide. You clearly aren't a stranger to crossbow bolts, but my men *will* put enough of them into your body to kill you if I give the order. Understood?"

Bershad glared at her for a moment. He didn't have a choice.

"Fine."

"Fantastic. Now, have you ever met another dragonslayer before arriving on this island?"

"That always the question you start with?"

"Yes. Answer it."

Bershad sighed. "Sure, I've met one. Maybe seven or eight years ago, an impatient small lord put out two writs for one Needle-Throated Verdun and we both showed up the same night. Didn't have much to talk about, though. He was a cattle thief who'd gone insane from cock rot." Bershad tapped his temple. "That shit will spread everywhere if you let it. He spent the whole night huddled by a low fire, muttering meaningless words to his donkey and chewing on his fingernails."

"Interesting. Most of the exiles I interview have never met another blue-barred face until arriving here. Strange, isn't it? The dragonslayer custom means so much to this realm, but there are so few of us around."

"Short life expectancies will do that."

"Indeed." Kerrigan adjusted one of the rocks weighing down the scroll ever so slightly. "What happened to him? The cock-rotted dragonslayer."

The poor bastard had arrived an hour before Bershad, so he'd made the first pass. He pissed himself as soon as the Verdun appeared. Tried to run away. Got his lungs clawed out for the trouble. Bershad killed the lizard the next day. He remembered that a swatch of the criminal's sore-covered skin was still lodged underneath the great lizard's claws.

"The same thing that happens to all dragonslayers eventually," Bershad said.

"But not to you. Or to me. Or anyone else living in Naga Rock."

"That's your sales pitch, then? Safe harbor and safe haven?"

"Correct. At this juncture, I generally inquire about the circumstances in which you acquired your bars, and the length of time you've had them. However, in this case I already know the answer to both those questions."

Bershad scratched at a massive scab on his forearm left over from a crossbow bolt. "How long have you had yours?"

"Ah, now there's the one way in which I've surpassed your legend." She tapped one cheek. "These were needled into my skin sixteen years ago at the Argellian customs house. You know it?"

"I do. Last time I saw it, a Red Skull was tearing it apart."

Kerrigan snorted. "Good. What happened to the dragon?"

"I killed it."

"Of course you did."

They sat in silence for a moment.

"What was your crime?" Bershad asked.

Kerrigan opened her palms. "Bringing a pair of dark-skinned tits and a lot of money to a port of Ghalamar."

"That right? You sure there wasn't a little piracy involved, too?"

"A fair assumption. But my exile turned me into the criminal, not the other way around. I used to be a law-abiding merchant with a fleet of ten trading galleys and a rather wonderful villa back in Palmunatra, the jewel of Dunfar."

"You must have done something," Bershad said.

Kerrigan snorted. "Oh, are the laws of Terra historically packed full of unsullied justice in your experience? All I did was spill some wine on the baron of Argel's carpet and refuse to suck his cock in exchange for a lower tax rate. I've interviewed hundreds of wayward exiles. Most don't deserve the punishment they received."

"But you kill the ones who do."

"When necessary," Kerrigan admitted. "But everyone who comes to Naga Rock is given a choice."

"A choice," Bershad repeated. He thought of the tattooed faces he'd seen in those bushes by the red river. Some were grizzled, hard faces. But others had been too young to have spent ten years marauding for the alchemist.

They were new.

"I get it," he said. "The options are a quick death in this massive acorn thing, or joining Simeon and his blackhearted murderers who feed the alchemist's lust for prisoners while you run your little city in peace."

Kerrigan narrowed her eyes, like a cat who'd just spotted a wounded bird in a tree. "How do you know about the alchemist?"

"Doesn't matter. Because I deserve my bars. Nobody'd argue different, given how Glenlock Canyon went down. And I want to be sent to Simeon."

"You have a mind to join his band of vicious murderers?"

"I have a mind to kill him."

"No. Not so fast. I need some detail here, starting with why you came to this island to begin with. It clearly wasn't for sanctuary." She raised a hand before Bershad spoke. "Lying to me now is a choice you make. One that will have lethal consequences."

Bershad sucked on his teeth. "I came here with Ashlyn Malgrave. We were looking for Ghost Moth dragons and a crazy man's research. Things didn't go so great. She's imprisoned by Simeon up north, along with my friend and some of your crew. Goll. Vash. Wendell."

The curiosity on Kerrigan's faced disappeared. Replaced by a cold, simmering rage. "How did that happen?"

"We ran into your men by some lake. I killed a bear that was about to kill them, so they agreed to take us to the bone wall."

"Did they also tell you that was forbidden?"

"They did. But seeing as I'd saved their lives, they were open to bending the rules. Especially Goll."

"Fucking Lysterians and their blood debts. You know that's the fourth time he's put one on himself? The last one was a Pargossian witch doctor who pulled a splinter out of his infected foot. He disappeared for two months retrieving some rare bird's egg from a remote mountain peak to repay the favor. Pain in my ass. Nothing like an archaic tradition to make otherwise intelligent people act like morons."

"You and Ashlyn would get along."

"Glad to hear I have a witch queen's tacit approval." She waved her hand. "Continue."

"We reached the wall, but ran into some trouble there. Had to break our way through. Long and short of that story is that we killed this alchemist named Kasamir, along with his mushroom-giant thing. That woke up a bunch of infected people he buried in the ground, so we had to get moving. On the way out, Simeon stopped us, filled me with bolts, and took everyone else prisoner."

Kerrigan's eye twitched a little. "You fucking morons. Do you have any idea what you've done?"

Bershad pushed a finger into one of the crossbow wounds in his belly. Winced. "Yeah. Tried to save the world and bungled the job pretty good."

"Bungled? *Bungled* is not the word I would use. I've kept the peace with the alchemist for a decade while Naga Rock prospered. It was a delicate and treacherous balance—every day it could have fallen apart—but I held it together. For ten. Years. And you've pissed it away in two weeks. Put one thousand and sixty-three souls in danger."

"Might be I did. But you're the one who built a whole city on the precipice of doom, and laid the foundation with Simeon's murderous gang."

"No other place in Terra would have us."

Bershad shrugged. "I'm just saying that it's some hypocritical dragonshit to try and lay this all on me. Plenty of blame on both sides of your polished table."

She glared at him, but didn't argue the point any further. "The creatures will be coming for us. The alchemist promised they would come to Naga Rock and eat every last man, woman, and child if we ever broke the pact, or if he ever died." She chewed on her lip. "We'll evacuate. No way around it."

Bershad remembered the creatures he'd seen digging their way out of the ground. Then he imagined the members of that theater troupe trying to fight them. Yeah. Running away seemed like the right move.

"What about your men that Simeon's got prisoner?"

"They're the idiots who caused all this. Or helped you cause it, anyway. They deserve whatever fate Simeon has for them."

Bershad shrugged. "Maybe. But if you'll give me a boat and a weapon, might be I can get them back, along with my friends."

"You're half crippled. You aren't rescuing anyone."

"That'll change if you've got a spare pinch of Gods Moss somewhere amidst all that treasure."

"What, you got a case of fire piss you wanna cure before you go and get yourself killed?"

"Do you have the moss or not?"

"I'm rich and I am well supplied," Kerrigan said. "But I'm not *that* rich. And nobody living on a haunted island in the middle of the Big Empty is that well supplied."

"Then I'll go like this."

"You have four crossbow bolts poking out of your back."

"So? It's my life to cut short. You were vaguely planning on killing me anyway."

Kerrigan weighed that. Chewed her lip some more.

"You really came up here with Ashlyn Malgrave? Okinu's niece?"

Bershad saw where Kerrigan's thoughts were going. If she really intended to abandon her little city, she needed another safe harbor. And having Ashlyn vouch for her when they came to Papyria was about her only option.

"I did. And Ashlyn remembers the people who help her."

A little more lip chewing. A little more internal debate.

"There's another way to get them back. Parley."

"Simeon didn't strike me as the negotiating type."

"He and I have a history. He was my forsaken shield."

Bershad frowned. "How'd that happen?"

"When you get exiled in Argel, they give you the pick of the dungeon for your companion. Usually you get half-dead thieves who've been rotting in a cell for weeks, but I was lucky. Simeon had been arrested a day earlier for allegedly crossing the Line of Lornar and was set for execution the next day."

"Argellians love their Skojit executions."

"Indeed. My thinking was that a hulking killer like him might come in handy, and I was right. We drew the writ for the Naga, and after I killed it, Simeon helped me escape. We founded this place together. And when the alchemist made the offer. Well." She swallowed. "Let's just say that we have unfinished business I'm inclined to complete."

She glanced at a clock on the wall of the hive.

"The evacuation takes time. A few days at least to load everything onto the ships. While my crew is doing that, I'll sail north and see if I can talk some sense into Simeon. Goll and Vash fucked me over here, but they're still my people."

Kerrigan gave a sly smile.

"And I never turn down a chance for a queen to owe me a favor."

43

CABBAGE

Ghost Moth Island, the Proving Ground

Cabbage was so hungover that the Proving Ground alarm bell felt like someone was pounding nails into his temples. He rolled over on his cot. Pulled the moldy straw pillow over his head and squeezed. Tried to muffle out the bell, and when that didn't work, gave some serious thought to pressing a little harder and attempting to smother himself.

"Up, Cabbage," came Howell's raspy voice.

Cabbage didn't respond.

Howell came over and dropped his heavy dragon-bone shield on Cabbage's foot.

"Ow!"

"I said get up."

Cabbage rolled over. Squinted up at the gold-toothed pirate. "That fucking hurt."

Howell raised his Naga spear—barbed tip jagged and threatening. "Hurt as much as me slicing off a few fingers? 'Cause that's what I'll take as punishment for slow rousing, seeing as your ears have already gone for a walk."

The crazy alchemist had given Simeon the shield and spear along with the armor. Simeon had fought with them for years, but a few summers back, Howell had saved Simeon's life during the raid of a Dunfarian spice carrack that turned out to have fifty royal guardsmen waiting in the hold. Classic ambush. The particulars of Simeon's salvation were a matter of debate—neither Simeon nor Howell talked about it—but when they came back to Ghost Moth Island, Simeon promoted Howell to first mate and he gave him the shield and spear as a reward.

In Cabbage's experience, their Skojit captain was a mean bastard all the way down to his bones. Saving his life was the only known way to win his respect, and his respect came with great reward. Cabbage had seen Howell use that spear to skewer fully armored Almiran wardens like they were roasted steaks. And that shield had withstood a hundred sword blades and arrowheads without taking so much as a scratch.

Sadly, Cabbage had never had the chance to earn that kind of gratitude from Simeon. Or, if he had been given the chance, he hadn't recognized the opportunity.

"Are we under attack?" Cabbage asked.

"Naw. Kerrigan showed up with a parley flag. But Simeon wants everyone up on it."

"Why? It's a parley."

"All the excitement lately, he smells trouble. Now get up. Gear up. And get down to the dock."

———

Cabbage puked twice in his shit bucket, then went to the big cistern and took a few big swallows from the potato liquor to get his head right. Grabbed his crossbow, then headed down to the docks with the others to meet the captain of their southern counterpart.

Calling it a dock was generous. More a scattering of rotten planks thrown haphazardly over ancient iron pylons where they lashed their shallops. Simeon was never one for general upkeep and maintenance to anything besides weapons and armor. And seeing as the alchemist was the only bastard who could repair most of their gear, even that had gone by the wayside.

Simeon was already there. Hands on his hips. White armor glowing in the sun. Howell was next to him. Kerrigan's shallop had just about reached the dock. There were six oarsmen digging to shore at speed, which wasn't that fast, likely due to the three big cargo chests they were hauling. Behind her, there was an anchored frigate flying the blue parley flag.

Kerrigan hopped off her shallop and skipped across the decaying dock—arms open to show she had no weapons on her.

Simeon gave her a long once-over. Sniffed. Spat. "Been a long time, Kerri."

"Yes," she agreed. "Last cause for a parley was when a squall knocked that Papyrian warship into eyesight of the island last year and we had to tool up together."

"Aye. That was a good fight."

Kerrigan didn't say anything. Guess she wasn't much for reminiscing on violent times. Cabbage scratched at the place his ears used to be, trying not to dwell on the fact that if he'd stayed quiet when it came time to choose crews way back, he'd probably still have them attached to his head.

"So what brings you up my way?" Simeon asked, all pleasant and helpful in a way that made Cabbage's cock shrink. Simeon was always in the best of moods when the threat of violence loomed close. "Doesn't seem like you made the trek just to get nostalgic with your trusty forsaken shield."

"There's been some trouble. Outlanders from Papyria showed up. Broke open the bone wall and killed the alchemist."

"Yeah, I heard something to that effect."

"And that doesn't strike you as news worth discussing? There's a hole in the bone wall the size of a Balarian highway. Kasamir's creatures have already started coming through. You understand? Naga Rock is finished. My people are evacuating right now."

Simeon shrugged. "That's your problem. The mushroom people don't cross the Bloody Sludge, so I'm good here. And don't think you and yours can shack up with us. We like plenty o' space."

"Simeon. Don't be a prick. If the alchemist is dead, there's no more point to it all. No need for the reavings. The murders. You can let it go."

"There's always a reason. You just never understood it."

"What are you talking about?"

"You thought I was willing to carry the alchemist's black work so you could build your little city of rutting exiles. Run your grand experiment in free governance. I could give a fuck about Naga Rock. I made the pact because I wanted to kill as many low-landers as I could. That's what I've been doing, that's what I'm gonna keep doing. Some dead alchemist don't change shit."

Cabbage wasn't particularly surprised to hear that kind of wickedness coming from Simeon's mouth. He hadn't thrown in with Simeon's crew to protect Naga Rock, either. He did it for plunder. But killing for pay and killing for the sheer joy of it were two vastly different things in Cabbage's opinion.

Kerrigan's face changed. "I'm sorry for what happened, Simeon. Sorry what your end of the deal cost you."

"You're sorry now, maybe. Now that your city's about to get overrun with those creatures. But it was worth it before, yeah? One ruined Skojit soul—along with the greedy bastards who followed me—in exchange for all that comfort and redemption and care beneath the ground. So fuck your remorse, Kerri. I don't want it. And I ain't leaving this island."

"That's your choice." She licked her lips. "But I believe you have imprisoned several members of my crew. I came to collect them."

Simeon smiled. "You always were a well-informed fox, Kerri. Always full o' knowledge. Who's feeding you information this time?"

"That doesn't matter."

"Guess not." Simeon shrugged. "You can have your corsairs if you got the coin for 'em."

She waved at the chest she'd brought. "Five hundred a head do it?"

"Fine."

"I have two more chests. One full of rubies. The other emeralds."

That was worth ten, maybe fifteen times what she offered for the captured corsairs. As a younger man, that kind of plunder would have quickened Cabbage's heart. But not anymore. Turns out you can get tired of anything—even riches—when your life's defined by brutal violence and wet feet.

"Kerri, when a man agrees to an offer, you generally don't reveal that you were willing to pay more."

"It's not for them. It's for the queen you caught. Two chests of gemstones is about the going rate for a queen's ransom. Figured I'd save you the trouble of running lines into Papyria. Always a risky business, what with widows in the mix and all."

Simeon narrowed his eyes. Rolled his shoulders. "Now I really am curious where all this knowledge came from." He sniffed. "Thinking maybe I got a rat in my crew."

"Yes or no, Simeon."

Simeon studied the sky for a few moments. Smiled at something.

"It's gonna be a hard pass. Don't care how many gems you got on offer. That little queen's proven herself to be quite the tinkerer of the alchemist's toys. Only thing that's getting her out of my basement is the long swim."

"Or violence," Kerrigan said.

Simeon smiled. "You got a band of fifty, sixty killers hiding in that dinghy?"

"No."

"Then fuck off." He pointed a finger at her. "Push me on it again, and I will slit the throats of your crew members while you watch. Kid included. You know I'll do it."

Kerrigan tapped the buckle of her belt in a steady rhythm while she considered her options.

"Just my crew, then."

———

Simeon glared out at the sea until Kerrigan returned to her frigate, pulled anchor, and headed back south around the jagged coast. When they were gone, he waved a hand at the chest of newly acquired gold.

"Divide that up," he said to Howell. "And double the guard on all our watches, starting now."

"Yeah, boss."

"Double?" Cabbage asked without really thinking. "What for?"

"For a supposedly smart bastard, you are impressively stupid sometimes, Cabbage. Think about it."

Cabbage scratched the spot where his right earlobe used to be. "Dunno, boss. It's late in the season for trouble with the Nagas. And the Ghost Moths don't come here no more."

Simeon sighed. "Howell. Educate the educated man."

The first mate gave Cabbage a sneering, golden smile. "Ain't no way that Kerrigan came up here with two chests of precious stones for the Malgrave queen, and is just gonna call it quits 'cause Simeon gave her the cold shoulder. Gems didn't work, so she's gonna make a pass with steel."

"By herself? Thought you said she wasn't much of a fighter?"

"Naw. Not personally," Simeon said. "But that conniving bitch's always got a demon in the shadows behind her who's willing to do the black work on her behalf. I'm the prime fucking example."

"Who's she got that'll take a run at us? Them corsairs are kinda lightweights, yeah?"

"Lightweight. Heavyweight. Don't matter if they get their steel through your heart. We just need to be ready for 'em when they show up."

Everyone headed back to the Proving Ground. Cabbage was planning to sidle off and burn his hangover away with some more of the potato liquor, but his sulking caught Simeon's eye.

"Cabbage. With me."

"Where we going now?"

"Down to the queen, you earless fuck."

"Oh. The helmet."

"Finally figured something out your own self. I'm impressed."

"Think maybe I can skip it, boss?"

"You got somewheres else to be, Cabbage?"

"Naw, boss. It's just . . . I got a nasty hangover, it burns to all hell when I piss, and . . . well . . . she just scares me is all. Them cold blue eyes and that damn scowl. And I don't like that black thing snaking around her arm, neither. It's fucking unnatural."

"Gods, but you are a coward. You're also the only one who can read the alchemist drawings. So, I need you there to make sure she ain't tried something funny with that helmet."

In another life that Cabbage was very careful to avoid thinking about, he'd been a watchmaker's apprentice in Burz-al-dun. He hadn't done more than a handful of years before circumstances conspired against him and turned him outlaw, but he'd made it far enough to read a Balarian schematic.

"I can read a clock schematic. But that doesn't mean I under-stand all the shit down there. Compared to a clock design, the al-chemist pages may as well be instructions for building an entire fucking planet from scratch."

"Just follow me, and try to grow a pair o' walnuts on the way, yeah?"

44

ASHLYN

Ghost Moth Island, the Proving Ground

When Ashlyn was done stitching up the final incision she'd made in her own arm, she bandaged the wound with a strip of cloth from her shirt. Winced at the pain as she tightened it.

Felgor swallowed. "I can't believe you just spent a week carving your own arm up."

"It was necessary. And don't forget that I finished the helmet, too."

"Didn't it hurt?"

"Yes."

Ashlyn flexed her wrist, experimenting with the feel and place-ment of the lodestone, which pulsed with a gentle but steady mag-netic charge every time she flexed her forearm muscles. Before she'd gotten very far, the lock on the outer door of the workshop clicked and snapped as the seal unlocked.

Simeon came through with the earless pirate in tow, who looked and smelled like he'd spent the night swimming in a vat of potato liquor.

"All finished?" Simeon asked.

"As ordered."

She motioned to the helmet, which she'd placed just beyond the bars of her cage. The piece of armor had three major parts—a skullcap carved from a juvenile Ghost Moth's knee joint, and two faceplates made from a dragon scale that had been sheared in half. Like the rest of Osyrus Ward's work, it was simple and functional. But Ashlyn had to admit there was an elegance to the design.

"What happened there?" Simeon motioned to her bandaged arm.

"Minor accident." Ashlyn shrugged. "But better than losing a thumb. Then I wouldn't be any good to you, and you would cut Felgor in half."

Simeon made a noncommittal grunt. Studied the helmet.

"Try it on," Ashlyn prompted.

"Such eagerness," Simeon chided. "Not becoming of a queen. Cabbage. Check it out."

The earless pirate swallowed with some effort, then grabbed the helmet and gave it a once-over, checking the inside and outside with the random attention of somebody who had zero understanding of what he was looking at.

The three pieces were bound together by a complicated lattice of metal wires and gears that tightened or released based on the lodestone's shifting orientation. Ashlyn had set the faceplates to remain open until the helmet was attached to the rest of the armor. Once they were connected, the loop would close and the faceplates would connect, creating an impenetrable set of armor.

"Can I see the schematic?" he asked Ashlyn.

She slid the papers through the bars without a word.

Cabbage riffled through the papers, moving far too fast to be absorbing the information.

"Seems good, boss."

Simeon didn't move. So Cabbage trotted the fifteen paces back to him before handing the helmet over.

Ashlyn twitched her wrist just enough to probe the lodestones she'd implanted in the helmet. She could feel it react to the one in her body, but it was too weak to manipulate until he put it on and connected it to the armor's lodestone field.

Simeon took the helmet. Tapped a dragon-scale finger against the skullcap three times.

"You know where I just came from?" he asked her.

"Are we going to play the rhetorical question game now?"

"Watch the sass, Queen. You got some leverage what with the value of them fingers, but you don't have an unlimited amount. And I am notorious for violent impulses."

Ashlyn pressed her lips together. "Where did you just come from, Simeon?"

"A parley with Kerrigan. She paid the ransom on your Naga Rock traveling companions. Made an extremely generous offer for your royal hide, too."

"Which you denied."

"Obviously. But what's bothering me is how she knew about you at all. I've had the occasional runaway from my outfit over the years, but nobody's missing at present who was down by the Bloody Sludge."

Ashlyn shrugged.

"And something else's been nagging at me," he said. "There was a dragon circling the frigate that Kerrigan rode up here."

That got Ashlyn's attention. "What kind of dragon?"

"One o' them big gray bastards."

"A Nomad." Her pulse quickened. *The* Nomad. "So?"

"Oh, it's just unusual. We get Nagas up this way with frequency. An occasional Milk Wing. But never one of the wandering smokies."

Simeon paced around the cage, but he didn't get closer to her.

"Careful, Simeon," said Cabbage. "There's a few pressure plates over—"

"I know where the fucking plates are!" Simeon snapped, silencing Cabbage.

So, the floor was booby-trapped. Good to know.

"Now, I normally wouldn't pay an errant lizard much mind—especially since the dragon fucked off south with Kerrigan's frigate," Simeon continued. "But I seem to remember that same dragon swooping through the mire above the Bloody Sludge, too. Plus, there's a fog setting in on the evening tide. No way to know where that lizard is exactly until dawn burns it off."

"I wouldn't worry. Nomads aren't typically aggressive to human settlements."

"Ain't the dragon in particular I'm worried about. We got more ballistas on the tiers than an Almiran's got rings in his stupid hair. But I'm a mite curious about what's got such a fixture on that lizard's attention. Thought you could shed some light."

"Could be any number of things," Ashlyn said. "The sails of the frigate. The topography of the coast. Or it could be a simple fluke of—"

Simeon snatched a knife from Cabbage's belt and threw it at Felgor. It missed his face by a hand's width and thumped deep into a wooden desk behind his cage, quivering.

"Tell another lie, and the next one goes through his forehead. And don't think I won't resort to more savage methods of coercion to ensure you remain a productive worker. You might need your hands, but you don't need your toes, your feet, or any part of your legs for that matter. And I will take them from you one at a time."

Ashlyn tensed her body. Tested her pull on the helmet again. The magnetic field strained and shuddered, but it was too weak. She needed him to put it on, and to do that she needed him to be alarmed. Scared, even.

So, she decided to tell him the truth.

"The dragon is following the Flawless Bershad."

Simeon narrowed his eyes. "If that's true, then he's got an awfully mobile corpse. We porcupined that asshole by the Bloody Sludge."

"You filled him with bolts, but you didn't kill him. He'll be coming for me and Felgor. And you."

Simeon wiped a hand through his dirty hair. "Cabbage, what do you think about that notion?"

The earless pirate once again struggled to swallow. "Uh. Well. She and Silas Bershad were to be married way back. Things went to shit with the exile, but there's lots of Almiran plays about them. They were lovers."

"Lovers, is it?" Simeon smiled. "Might be he is mounting a rescue, then. The lonely heart getting all forlorn and shit. Hm. The Flawless Bershad, coming my way with heroics on his mind."

He rolled the helmet over in his hands a few times. Looked down at it. Seemed like he was finally about to put it on. Ashlyn straightened her back and loosened her shoulders. Got ready.

"This here's good work. And because of it, I'll most likely peel the skin off your lover's bones before he gets to you, but I best tighten security up all the same. Wouldn't want my new tinker queen to go missing."

Simeon moved to the machinery on the far side of the room. He lifted a circular metal plate and placed his right glove—the one that Ashlyn hadn't fixed—inside the big socket behind it.

"You had bad luck, Queen. If Bershad was left-handed, he'd have broken this glove when he came at me. And then I'd have been forced to cough up everything you needed to get to the pit that you're so curious about. As it stands, you got what you wanted anyway. For a time. Enjoy the horror show underneath, Queen. I'll come collect you when your lover is dead."

He twisted his glove.

The floor underneath Ashlyn opened, and she dropped into the darkness.

45

JOLAN

Almira, Wreckage of the Time's Daughter

Oromir didn't speak to Jolan. He didn't even look at him. Just put seashells in Cumberland's and Iko's mouths and saw to their burials in cold silence. Willem helped him dig. Sten wept from the half-finished sledge.

When it was done, Oromir started gathering supplies with the same cold efficiency that Shoshone had employed when she left the night before.

"Oro?" Jolan asked, following him around like an idiot.

"Don't call me that."

"Sorry. But where are you going?"

"To hunt down and kill that gray-eyed fuck."

Jolan started gathering his own supplies. Picking up random bits of food. "I'll go with you."

Oromir snatched a piece of salted pork from Jolan's hand. Stuffed it in his own pack.

"You'll just slow me down."

He turned around. Kept packing. Jolan stood with his shoulders hunched and tried not to cry.

"I'm sorry, Oromir. I tried to save him. I tried everything I knew."

"It never would have happened if you hadn't made us spare your friend's life."

"He isn't my friend. Don't do this."

"Do what?"

"Leave me behind. You said . . . the things that we said to each other last night. That we'd live in a cabin in the woods together. Remember?"

"That isn't happening. That was just . . . shit you say after you fuck. It didn't mean anything."

"It meant something to me."

"I don't care."

Oromir headed for the woods. Willem was standing next to the sledge.

"You coming?" Oromir asked.

Willem shook his head. "Sten needs help."

"Fine."

Oromir moved past him.

"Chasing a scrap of vengeance through those woods won't do any good," Willem called. "It's not what Cumberland would want."

Oromir stopped, but he didn't turn around. "He didn't want to die, either. But it happened."

Jolan was crying so hard that he couldn't even see Oromir disappear into the woods. He kept on sobbing—head hung between his knees—while Willem finished making the sledge for Sten. When it was done, Willem came over and put a hand on Jolan's shoulder.

"It's time to go."

"Where?"

"I know the alchemist station that Shoshone talked about. Frula's place. We'll go there."

"What does it matter anymore?"

He took out a roll of paper meant for a pigeon's leg. He must have taken it off Iko's corpse.

"Gotta get this to Papyria. Otherwise Cumberland and Iko died for nothing. I can't let that pass." He motioned to the sledge. "Will you help me with Sten? I can't lug him to the Dainwood on my own."

"Yeah," Jolan said. "I'll help."

46

BERSHAD

Ghost Moth Island, Western Coast

Bershad knew from Kerrigan's face that Ashlyn and Felgor weren't with her.

He helped everyone else out of the shallop and onto the frigate.

"Flawless!" Goll shouted, throwing him into an embrace. "I knew you would survive."

"Careful around the bolts in my back, yeah?"

"Ah. Yes. Sorry."

Vash and Wendell came up next. Vash gave him a nod. "I'm not sure where Ashlyn and Felgor are," he said. "But I think they're alive."

"You two okay?" Bershad asked.

"It was horrible," Wendell said. "They put us in chattel cages and made us eat pig slop. And at night we could hear the creatures moving around beyond the forest. And Simeon's crew are drunk and mean and—"

"We're fine." Vash looked around the ship. "Glad to be safe, finally."

Kerrigan came aboard last.

"Sorry," she said to Bershad. "I did what I could."

"I know."

Bershad scanned the fortress that was built on the far side of the bay. It wasn't like any stone-and-mortar tower or holdfast that Bershad had seen in Almira or Ghalamar or even Balaria. The structure was comprised of stacked, dull-gray slabs of iron that got progressively smaller with each level, forming a series of fortified tiers. There was no decoration or design. Just hard angles and cold metal.

"Just need one favor." He pointed to the tip of a jagged peninsula that provided good cover. "Mind dropping me in a shallop right there?"

"So you mean to go through with it?" Kerrigan asked.

"I do."

"Your legs are still mostly bruises."

"They're getting better," Bershad said. Kerrigan had found some Crimson Tower moss in her stores, and Bershad had mushed it into a paste and rubbed it on his legs. It wasn't perfect, but it was better than nothing.

"Go through with what?" Goll asked Bershad.

"I'm not leaving Ashlyn and Felgor behind."

"I see." His face turned serious. "I will accompany you."

"No you won't," Bershad said.

"You cannot talk me out of this decision."

"It's going to involve swimming across that harbor in the middle of the night."

Goll's mouth opened. Closed. "But the blood debt."

"That'll just have to wait for another time," Bershad said.

Goll sighed. "At least let me wait with you on the boat. It won't be dark for hours."

"Fine."

"If you're going to sit with him on that shallop, so am I," Kerrigan said.

"Why?"

"Because I just spent a small fortune buying you back from Simeon. No way am I going to let you drown yourself trying to follow your new friend. And don't pretend like you weren't going to try it. You idiot Lysterians would jump down a Red Skull's throat to fulfill a blood debt."

Goll shrugged, all innocence. "Does anyone on this ship have a jug of decent rum they're willing to part with?"

———

An hour later, Bershad, Kerrigan, and Goll were alone in the shallop. Goll passed the time by drinking his borrowed rum and telling stories about Lysteria. He pissed off the side of the boat every hour or so. When nightfall was about twenty minutes away, Bershad started to get ready.

Along with the rum—which was mostly depleted—Goll had scrounged up a big vat of tar that the corsairs used for night incursions. Bershad started rubbing it on his face and arms and back, careful to avoid the crossbow bolts.

"It won't wash off in the water?" Bershad asked as he covered his tattooed arm.

"Wouldn't be much good to us if it did," Kerrigan replied.

Bershad continued coating his body. The stuff was sticky and thick. Getting himself fully covered was going to take a while.

"Got a question for you, Kerrigan," Bershad said to her.

"Yeah?"

"How did you kill that Naga Soul Strider?"

Kerrigan looked up at him. "You're about to try and fight your way through scores of the most well-armed, most dangerous pirates in Terra, and that's what you want to know?"

He shrugged. "I always figured that if I drew a writ for a Naga, that would be the end of me. Curious how you came up on the winning side."

She glanced at Goll. Raised an eyebrow.

"I am also curious. Cormo was convinced that you played it a song with some Dunfarian flute that made it go to sleep underwater and drown itself. But that doesn't make sense. You don't play the flute."

Kerrigan sighed. Turned back to the water, then responded softly. "I poisoned my donkey."

Bershad frowned, confused. "What?"

"Before I was arrested, one of the ships that I brought to Argel was carrying ten barrels of bilo-barb poison. It's derived from the venom glands of a rare dragon called a Dusk Greezel that only lives on the smallest of the Southern Islands. You can trade a small jug of it for two good horses."

"Sounds rare."

"Not as valuable as Gods Moss, maybe. But it's in the same general region of profit potential, and a little easier to procure. All the same, smuggling a whole barrel of it onto the ship that took me to Ghost Moth Island nearly bankrupted my crew. But they did it anyway. One last favor for their doomed captain. Funny how nobody notices one extra barrel on a big ship."

Kerrigan licked her lips.

"We found the Naga hunting just east of this island—picking seals off a cluster of rocks. The soldiers didn't know why I asked for my donkey and the barrel to be put into my sloop when they sent me digging out into the ocean after the great beast. They didn't much care, either. I was a dead woman." She lowered her voice. "It wasn't an easy thing, making the poor beast drink the poison. They're stubborn creatures. But once I got some in his belly, he died quick."

Bershad swallowed hard. Tried not to think about Alfonso. Failed. He scratched at the corner of his eye, then motioned for Kerrigan to keep going.

"Once the donkey was dead, I poured the rest of the poison down his throat. Then it was just a matter of dropping the carcass into the right current so that he floated right into the Naga's hunting ground. The lizard ate him in a single bite. Maybe a minute later it crashed into the ocean." She tapped the dragon on her forearm. "One of the sailors put this on me that same day."

"How'd you avoid being sent after another?"

"The soldiers lashed the Naga's carcass to their hull. Since there was no lord on the boat, all the oil was theirs for the taking. They celebrated their good fortune by getting drooling drunk on rice wine in the hold below." Kerrigan smiled, remembering. "Then one of them got cold and decided to use some fresh dragon fat to warm up."

It took Bershad a moment to understand. "The poison."

"Yeah. The Naga was so pumped full of bilo-barb that her fat turned the lower deck into a bladder of noxious fumes. Killed everyone in a fit of bloody shit and vomit. The only survivors were me and Simeon and the five shivering soldiers who'd been guarding us above deck. Simeon took care of them. With all the confusion, it wasn't much of a fight.

"When the sun rose the next day, we had a ship of our own and an entire island to ourselves that everyone else in Terra was afraid to visit. Deciding our future didn't take long. I sold the blighted dragon oil in Himeja and used the profits to hire our first crew. Started snatching exiles from the clutches of Terra. And when the alchemist showed up and made his offer . . . well . . . Simeon took the dirty path so I could walk the clean one. We've had our disagreements over the years, but the only reason I'm alive and that Naga Rock exists is because of Simeon."

Kerrigan looked away. The sky darkened. All three of them went quiet.

As soon as the ragged outline of the fortress started getting hazy, a series of dragon-oil lights turned on, casting a swath of illumination across the harbor.

"He doesn't usually run the lanterns," Kerrigan said. "Guess my little parley spooked him. No way we can row you much closer than this. Sorry."

Bershad scanned the water. Figured it was about two leagues to the base of the cliff, where he could climb up to the backside of the Proving Ground.

"This is close enough."

Kerrigan pulled out a Papyrian lens and studied the fortress, moving from one spot to the next in a careful order.

"Nineteen sentries, looks like."

"Twenty-four," Bershad corrected. The Nomad had expanded her gyre to give him a good feel for the men running their loose patrols along the metal tiers. He stripped off the rags that he'd been wearing since he woke up in Naga Rock. His connection to the dragon was stronger when his flesh was exposed. He covered his legs and feet with the tar.

"Your skin might be covered, but those hair decorations are gonna sparkle like pearls in the lights. You as sentimental about those things as every other Almiran I've met?"

"Give me your knife."

Bershad took his own hair in a tight ball and sliced it off with three quick strokes. Left the mess of tangles and rings and amulets in the bottom of the boat.

"I can save 'em for you if you want," Goll offered.

"Don't bother. I don't need them anymore."

Bershad used a length of fishing line to tie the knife to his thigh. No point in taking more weapons. This outnumbered, and without any Gods Moss, he was a dead man if he needed more than a knife.

"Simeon has a few skiffs by the dock with decent sails," Kerrigan said. "Once you have your friends, you need to get to one of those skiffs and get clear before daybreak. I'll hang back with one frigate till midday, waiting for you. If you actually manage to pull this off, I wanna make sure the queen of Almira attaches my face to the credit."

"Got it."

Bershad stepped onto the gunwale, which sent a shock of pain up both legs. He stumbled backward with a grunt and a curse.

Goll watched him with concerned eyes. "You sure you can do this, Flawless?"

"No," Bershad said.

Then he dove into the freezing ocean and started swimming toward the coast.

47

ASHLYN

Ghost Moth Island, Beneath the Proving Ground

Ashlyn landed on something mushy and wet. Rolled off it and banged her knee against a rock. The hatch above snapped closed, leaving her in darkness.

No. Not darkness. Not completely. She noticed a blue-green light emanating from the ground and walls. She crawled toward the closest source of light, careful on her injured knee, and examined it. A bioluminescent mushroom the size of a coffeepot. She recognized it as one of the species that had grown in Kasamir's garden.

This wasn't her first time in a cave with poor lighting. She sat up. Crossed her legs. And stayed still for about ten minutes, waiting for her eyes to adapt. Tried to use her other senses to get some semblance of orientation. The air was thicker here. Humid and warm, like one of her greenhouses back in Floodhaven. There were rustles and flickers of squirming movement in the shadowy pits and corners. Crabs and cave toads, probably.

A larger shape seemed to materialize in the gloom about twenty strides in front of her. Ashlyn squinted at it, trying to decide if it was a big rock, or something else. When her eyes finally adjusted enough for her to identify it, her pulse went wild.

It was a Naga Soul Strider. Scaled hide arching high. Tail wrapped around its body.

For a moment, Ashlyn thought that Simeon had dropped her into a quick and brutal death. But the dragon didn't stir. It took Ashlyn a few heart-pounding seconds of stillness to realize it wasn't breathing. Dead. And perfectly preserved, same as the Ghost Moths.

She got up. Walked around the head. It was a juvenile male. There was a ballista bolt lodged in its forehead, and its tail barb had been surgically removed. Ashlyn realized this was where the spear that Howell carried must have come from. Dozens of rubber tubes were connected to his body. They ran farther into the darkness of the cave, out of sight.

Ashlyn followed them.

She could see much better now. Machinery dominated the cavern floor, but the walls were overgrown with tangled vines and sprawling plants. They weren't healthy—all wilted leaves and drooping petals. But they shouldn't have been able to grow down here at all. Not without light, and only tiny pools of brackish water as sustenance.

As before, the tubes from the dragon converged on a single spot. But this was different from Kasamir's garden. In place of a metal table, she found what looked like a misshapen alabaster tree. Trunk bent. Dozens of thin branches sprouting off it, each blooming with vibrant blue and red leaves that fluttered in the damp cave air. Pale salamanders crawled amid the foliage.

Ashlyn circled the tree, trying to think of what species it could be. But when she got to the far side, she stopped in her tracks.

This wasn't a tree. It was a woman.

Ashlyn could make out the familiar outline of hips and breasts and collarbones. And a face with Papyrian features. Small nose. Black hair. And dark, oval eyes that were looking back at her, full of life and recognition.

"Beautiful, isn't it?" the woman said in Papyrian.

Ashlyn jerked back a step.

"Apologies," the woman continued. "I know how alarming I am."

Ashlyn forced herself to stay calm. Examine the woman. Get

details. Whatever had occurred here, this wasn't the overrun fungal infection that had afflicted the others that she'd seen on the island. The woman's body had been altered in incredible ways. Her skin was pale and smooth like petrified wood. Covered in blooming blue flowers. Winding threads of roots and moss ran along the curves and crooks of her torso. The branches—if you could call them that—grew off her back and shoulders, but there was something elegant about them. Natural, despite how strange it looked. Nothing like the lumps and deformities that plagued Kasamir's giant. Still, unnatural things had been done to her. A large part of her torso had been surgically removed and replaced with a gray metal alloy. Her left arm was missing. A tangle of moss-choked vines hung from the stump like blood vessels.

"Who are you?" Ashlyn asked.

"Gaya," she said. "Although I am not sure there is enough humanity left in me to use that name anymore. He always called me Specimen 88."

"He," Ashlyn repeated. "Osyrus Ward?"

"Yes."

"How long have you been down here?"

"I am not sure how long I was imprisoned by him. But it has been thirty-one years, one hundred and three days, and eleven hours since he left." She smiled. "I count my heartbeats to pass the time. There is not much else to do."

"I'm sorry."

"Apologies are a waste of breath," Gaya said. "Who are you?"

"Ashlyn."

"Not a Papyrian name, even though you have a Papyrian face."

"My mother was Papyrian, but I have an Almiran father."

"Ah." She swallowed. "Tell me . . . how did such a curious half-breed get herself thrown into this pit?"

"Okinu sent me here to find out what happened on this island."

"So many of us dispatched into Osyrus Ward's nightmare because of the Eternal Empress's orders." She paused. "After all this time . . . I assumed she had given up. She told me that I was her last hope. And I failed her."

Ashlyn absorbed that. "You're the widow."

The woman nodded. "I was the best. But on this island—in his domain—I was no match for him. Nobody was. We were all just flies that got caught in his merciless, metal web."

"I've read some of his notes, up above. He said that you were the key to everything. Do you know what he meant by that?"

"He took great interest in my body, and the transformation. The bloom, he called it. But he never said why. Only that I was . . . an anomaly. A Seed. I suppose the name fits. Everything that is alive in this room grew from my body."

Gaya's legs were rooted to the ground. The foliage around her radiated outward in an explosion of moss with blue flowers in it. Ashlyn hadn't connected everything until that moment. Hadn't realized what this was. Blame the darkness. The dragon. Or the fact that this place wasn't as fecund or lush as she was used to, but the pattern of the ecology was unmistakable, along with the Gods Moss that grew from Gaya's body.

"This is a dragon warren."

"Yes. A stunted one, but still a warren."

"Osyrus did all of this to you? Forced your body to change?"

"Not exactly."

"Tell me then, exactly. Tell me everything. From the beginning."

"After all this time, what does it matter?"

"Osyrus Ward is still alive. And his nightmare has spread across Terra. I came to this island to find a way to stop him."

Gaya hesitated. "You're not a widow. And you're not a soldier. What makes you think you can succeed where all of us failed?"

"You failed because you tried to fight him your way. On your terms." Ashlyn touched her arm. "I can fight *his* way. But there are pieces that I'm missing. Pieces that he left behind. Please. Tell me what happened. The more I understand him, the bigger the threat I can become."

Gaya blinked.

"I came with eleven soldiers. Veterans, all of them. We landed on the island and found the landscape defiled. The rivers ran red with rust and bloated rodents. Whole sections of the forest were blasted and blackened. And there was . . . evidence that the previous incursions had failed."

"What evidence?"

"Corpses. Some of them had gone to rot where they'd fallen.

Shot by bolts, mostly. But others were bulging with a strange fungus. Wandering around like . . . demons. Their muscles and hands were torn ragged from some kind of labor. We didn't know what he made them build until we found the fortress."

"The Proving Ground."

Gaya nodded. "I went in alone. Snuck through his workshop of horrors. All those caged abominations, clawing and scratching and screeching to be free. Or to be killed." She paused. "I've sent sixty-seven souls down the river. Infiltrated cities and villas and castles. Come and gone like a bad rumor. But this place . . . everything in this place is connected. Reactive to intruders. I hadn't stepped on a pressure plate in twenty years. But I never saw it coming. Perfectly disguised. The dart hit me in the jugular with surgical precision. I blacked out, and woke up in a cage. That's when the real horrors began. First there were needles. Yellow fluid he injected into me. And then . . ."

She stopped talking. Ashlyn remembered the bloodstains on the floor of the cage above.

"He started putting things inside of you," Ashlyn said.

"They were small, at first. Little orbs, just beneath my skin. But when the wounds didn't fester, he put them deeper. Then he started doing other things. Siphoning blood. Cutting me. Shallow. Then deep. Down to the bone. And he knew . . . he knew what the moss did to me."

Ashlyn's breath caught in her throat.

"What does it do?" she asked, voice choked into a whisper.

"Far more than it should," Gaya said. "For years, it was my secret. My edge. The reason that I came back from so many missions that should have killed me. Once Osyrus saw it, he was relentless with his torture. He would heal some wounds with moss and leave others open for days. Weeks. I pulled back from my body. Ignored the pain. Counted the minutes and hours and days using my heartbeat as an anchor. An old widow's trick to avoid going into shock.

"Eventually, my men tried to rescue me. He lured them here with my screams. And filled them with darts when they arrived. Took them down that tunnel behind you one at a time." Ashlyn turned. There was a workstation there. Old and rusted machines, long stilled. Beyond the machines, there was a roughly hewn tunnel leading farther into the ground. "The first Naga arrived soon after that. Started circling this place. I couldn't see him, but I could feel him. There was so much pain, blinding and constant, but his presence was the first thing that had felt good in so long. We were drawn to each other. But when the Naga came down to me, Osyrus Ward killed him."

Ashlyn fought with every ounce of her self-control not to panic. Because Gaya was describing the same things that were happening to Silas. And that meant that all of this would happen to him in time.

"And after that?" Ashlyn asked, struggling to keep her voice even.

"Osyrus drew more blood. Took more . . . pieces of me. He kept muttering about scope and scale and filtration. But the more he hurt me, the more Nagas were attracted to this place. Five. Ten. Twenty. I could feel them burrowing into the earth, looking for me." She swallowed. "The Nagas started getting aggressive. Harrying the tiers above. That's when Osyrus sealed the roof. Buried me with layers of metal and machines. I couldn't feel them after that. Couldn't feel anything. And that's when the bloom happened."

"Can you describe how it felt?"

"Yes. I felt a burning pit in my stomach. I begged him to stop. Told him something was wrong. But he didn't care. I don't . . . I don't think he knew what would happen, either. When he cut off my arm, it started. I thought I knew what pain was before. But to feel my body changing like this . . . expanding. Veins wrapping around the earth and stone. My blood turning to moss." She blinked. "The physical pain was bad. But to feel your body transforming. Becoming something that you don't understand. That is true agony."

She went quiet a moment. Looked up at the spiraling tendrils and wild plants along the ceiling.

"Osyrus was enthralled. He scratched his fucking notes for hours and hours. The grating sound of that quill made me sick. Then it was more needles. More knives. Eventually, he started taking organs out of me." She winced. Looked down at the metallic patches on her torso. "I don't know why I didn't die after that. I don't know . . . anything, besides the fact that I am an abomination."

A tear fell from Ashlyn's cheek. She wiped it away, but Gaya noticed.

"You've kept a tight grip on your emotions so far, Ashlyn. Which means that sorrow's not for me."

"There's someone that I care about who has survived fatal injures for years. And a Gray-Winged Nomad has been following him for almost a month."

"I see. It is his beginning. And my end. Fitting, I suppose. Although I am not sure there is an end for creatures like us. Just an endless loop of suffering and decay and rebirth."

Ashlyn blinked the rest of the tears out of her eyes. Took a breath. She'd come a long way for answers. She needed to get as many as possible.

"What did Osyrus Ward do with the organs that he extracted?"

"I do not know. Everything that Osyrus took from me, he moved down that tunnel, where my men were." She paused. "They screamed for weeks. Just as I screamed. And then one day . . . nothing. Osyrus left soon after. But he wasn't angry. Driven, more like. Focused."

Ashlyn looked at the tunnel. The luminescent mushrooms gave it enough of a glow to see the first turn. From there, it was impossible to tell what waited for her.

"You came for answers," Gaya said. "Go get them."

Ashlyn picked her way through the tangled vines that sprawled across the uneven ground. Before she reached the tunnel, she stopped at the workstation. It was almost entirely covered with overgrown plants, but beneath the fecund mass, Ashlyn could see various rusted tools. Needles as long as her arm. Saws and scalpels. She pulled a thick bundle of roots aside, and found a few decaying notes.

The light of the glowing mushrooms was weak, but if she tilted the note at just the right angle, the ink reflected off the light and became legible.

2 Farrin—224

- *Specimen 88 attracting Naga Soul Striders at an increasing rate. Killed one. Sealed area to prevent lizards from interrupting my work. Illumination by dragon oil would be toxic in sealed space, so planted some of Specimen 01's luminescent mushrooms. And he said I was a poor steward of plants.*

- *Breakthrough. Interwoven in the Seed's biology is the mechanism that creates the dragon warrens. Transformation is spurred by a critical mass of physical trauma. Impossible to pinpoint the causation apex without further experimentation on future specimens.*
- *Process thrilling to witness. Akin to a caterpillar's transformation into a butterfly, but external and extremely rapid. Violent, even.*
- *Assume there is a symbiotic relationship between the lizards and the Seeds that makes the bloom area a viable breeding ground. Interesting, but not useful to me on its own. I seek to surpass nature's disgusting and random intricacies. Understanding them is simply a means to an end. But understand them, I must. Beginning exploratory surgeries on the bloomed Seed tomorrow.*

She peeled away more notes, resisting the urge to gag when she saw that the sheet beneath was soiled by squirming maggots. She brushed them aside.

17 Farrin—224

- *Vivisection of 88 complete. Bloodstream mutated into the most potent Gods Moss I've ever encountered. Possible that age of the substance is correlated with efficacy. Organs underwent a transformation akin to petrification, however they retain an altered functionality. The lungs produce air, almost like a miniature greenhouse. The heart brings nutrients through the moss veins. The liver culls infection.*
- *A curiosity. Cognitive function of 88 unaltered after bloom. Suggests brain did not undergo petrification, and is somehow preserved in its original state. Requires further study and research into possible applications.*
- *During the transformation, 88's body excretes a perfectly clear liquid, which is then stored in petrified organ cavities, not unlike a tortoise storing water in its bladder. Extracted the liquid from the following organs, in the following amounts:*

    — *Heart: 3.4 pints*
    — *Liver: 2.3 pints*
    — *Lungs: 0.2 pints (respectively)*
    — *Kidneys: 1.9 pints*

Ashlyn looked back at Gaya, and the holes in her torso that Ward had patched with alloy and iron and bolts.

- *Initial testing of the liquid on bacteria cultures reveals an incredibly potent level of sterilization potential. Makes my Gods Moss and Cordata slurry look like dragon shit in comparison. This is the missing piece! A flicker of perfection hidden amidst the ruination of these peculiar meat sacks. These Seeds.*
- *Disinfection is just the beginning. I will take the flicker and convert it to an eternal, pristine flame.*
- *Shifting trials to the eleven remaining human specimens. The last that Okinu will send, I think. Must create a clean workspace for them—one that cannot be corrupted by my previous failures.*

Ashlyn put the paper down. Looked at the tunnel again. It twisted to the right, but a track of glowing mushrooms ran along the ceiling, offering enough light to navigate.

She went inside.

48

CABBAGE

Ghost Moth Island, the Proving Ground

Cabbage had drawn the flex patrol for the night watch. That meant two unfortunate things. First, he had to travel through the upper levels of the Proving Ground to reach the tiers, and those levels were fucking horror shows. He'd repeatedly asked Simeon if they could clean all the disgusting crap out, but Simeon always refused and told Cabbage that he had the wrong type of blood for this work.

Second, Cabbage had to spend the whole night walking up and down the Proving Ground stairs, checking on everyone's post to make sure nobody fell asleep or got drunk on the sly. Worst assignment you can draw, on the worst shift you can work.

Typical.

Howell used dice to create the crew assignments. Supposed to be random that way. But Cabbage seemed to draw the shit duties more often than not, and he was starting to wonder if the dice were loaded. Cabbage had a theory that Howell was jealous of his tapestries, and possibly seeking vengeance in the form of shit duties.

Doubting Simeon after the parley hadn't won him any favor, either.

Cabbage's ankle was screaming at him as he limped down the steps to the sea rail. He'd broken it three years back, racing across an ice-slick deck to behead a Ghalamarian merchant who'd taken Gnut by the throat. Cabbage had slipped before he reached the bastard and snapped the ankle. Gnut had died, and his cursed anklebone never healed right.

In addition to the consistently dodgy ankle, Cabbage hadn't had time to finish fully drying out his socks before starting his shift. So there was a cold squelch against his skin to go with each shooting pain in his shit joint.

Nights like this made Cabbage rehash the wisdom of joining Simeon's crew.

The plunder was good, no denying. Cabbage had squirreled away fourteen thousand and twenty-two gold pieces over their ten-year stint of marauding and murder, with another sixty-two coming from the prisoner exchange with Kerrigan. Plus he had his tapestries, taken from an Almiran envoy boat. The Malgrave dynasty alone was probably worth five thousand gold. Although he'd never sell those. Well, maybe the Hertzog one.

Point being, Cabbage was rich. But there was no amount of plunder that would regrow his ears.

Three years back, he'd thought about deserting down to Naga Rock, where there were apparently spiced meals, theater troupes, and feather beds, but it was hard to summon the courage. Simeon had personally caught the last man who went for a walk. Torn his arms off and beat him to death with them. Not that he was gonna live long without arms.

Still. It was a shitty way to die just for wanting to see a funny show and sleep on something besides moldy hay.

But from the way Kerrigan was talking, Naga Rock was no

more. He'd missed his shot at a better life. Now there was nothing to do but pass another miserable winter in this cold metal shithole with too much to drink and not enough to eat, listening to the mushroom people rooting around in the forest across the Bloody Sludge.

And in spring, the killing would start again.

While he was pondering his plight, Cabbage came up on Frost, who was manning the sea rail ballista and huddled up in a Lysterian cloak to stave off the autumn chill. Cabbage was envious of the garment. Lysterians made the best cloaks.

"Cabbage."

"Frost." He sidled up. Looked out over the black expanse. "Catch sight of anything?"

"Some lizard's been circling, but it's staying up in the rafters. Deep outta range."

"You see what kind?"

"The big kind."

"Because Simeon's all worked up over some Gray-Winged Nomad. Was it a Nomad?"

Frost just shrugged.

"You heard them outlanders killed the alchemist?" Cabbage asked.

Every man in Simeon's crew had made the chattel run a dozen times, so they all knew the drill. Wasn't no pact with demons or open pit to hell. Just that crazy alchemist burying people alive in the middle of the island and keeping their crew rich in weapons and poor in everything else.

"Heard it."

"And?"

"It's dragonshit."

"How do you know?"

"Because Simeon's walking around with that shiny new helmet. The alchemist was the only one who could work that machinery shit."

"Naw, Ashlyn Malgrave made that for him."

"The ransom queen? I heard she was a witch. Fucked a bunch of Almiran forest demons or something to get lightning magic."

"Dunno about that, but she's a good tinkerer."

"Huh. Well she can tinker my dick whenever she wants."

Frost grinned, looking to see if Cabbage would follow suit. He didn't.

"If the alchemist *is* dead, do you think we'll move on? I mean . . . not right away. But maybe in a season or two? No reason to stay here with all this weird crap without the alchemist to fix it."

"Don't be stupid. We're never leaving this island, man."

"Why not?"

"How many death sentences you got on your head?"

"Two," Cabbage admitted. Papyria and Ghalamar. They all had them in Ghalamar, though. Simeon loved killing Ghalamarians.

"I got four. And Simeon's got one pretty much everywhere you can earn the bitch. They won't even let him into Taggarstan anymore. Taggarstan, man. They would let one o' them mushroom people in if he had coin to pay for his drinks. You best accept that this hunk o' metal is the only safe harbor left to our lot."

"Well, I hate it up here."

"Should have thought about that before you made the pact."

"But the pact is dead."

"Some agreements outlive the related parties, you know?"

Cabbage scratched at his ruined ears. "I do."

He left Frost to his post, and made the rounds along the Proving Ground. Up the steps. Check on Roli and Carl. Down the stairs. Check on Ufrith and Laith. And on it went. Carl was drunk and pretending not to be, but everyone else was doing their job.

But when he came back around to Frost, he was gone.

"Frost?" Cabbage called.

The only response he got was a gusty howl of cold air.

Cabbage looked around the tier. Other than the unmanned ballista, all he saw was rust and lichen.

He headed back up the stairs, cursing softly at his shitty ankle.

"Ufrith!" he huffed as he neared the top of the stair. "Did Frost come up this way?"

He summited. Looked around. But Ufrith was gone now, too.

"Ufrith?"

Nothing. Shit.

Where could Ufrith have gone? Cabbage had just seen him on his way down to the sea rail. He'd flipped an obscene gesture as Cabbage passed.

He searched the area where Ufrith should have been standing. This time, along with the rust and the lichen he found a trail of blood.

Just a few drops at first, then a steady, long stream that could only come from an open wound.

Cabbage unslung his crossbow. Yanked the bolt back to put tension in the first round. He'd learned the hard way you can't leave the thing wound tight for too long. On one of his first reavings, he'd left his bow armed overnight because he was afraid he wouldn't be able to work the complicated thing in the heat of the moment, then when he did finally shoot it at some Balarian soldier, the bolt barely had enough power to dent the breastplate.

That Balarian would have killed him. But Simeon was there. Saved his ass.

Cabbage followed the blood. Moving slow. Careful. Checking each shadow, praying that Ufrith would appear holding a rag over his hand and bitching about a misfire or something. That happened more and more these days. Just last week Jackal had lost a thumb after trying to calibrate a crossbow that started shooting practically sideways after he dropped it during a rough boarding.

Something twitched in the shadows ahead. A big, hulking shape.

"Hey!" Cabbage shouted, raising the crossbow. "Who's that?"

No response.

"Respond or I fire."

The hulking shape moved out of the shadows, revealing an all-too-familiar set of armor. The Ghost Moth scales were glowing in the moonlight. Cabbage relaxed his trigger finger.

"Hey, Simeon."

"What have I told you about hesitating, Cabbage?"

"That it'll send me down the river one day." He lowered the crossbow. "But if you'd been someone else in our crew . . . a shot in the dark would have killed you."

"A slow response on a foggy night will send a man down the river, too." Simeon ran a gloved hand through his greasy hair. The new helmet was attached to a hook on his hip. "What's got you all wound up?"

"Probably nothing."

"Spit it out, Cabbage."

"Frost and Ufrith, uh, they're not at their posts. But they probably just went for shits."

"Huh." Simeon looked down at the blood trail. Rolled one of his shoulders. A clattering of dragon scales followed, like a crowd of men cracking their knuckles.

"Thought maybe Ufrith clamped his finger down on the jam of his crossbow. Happened to Jackal last month and bled like a stuck goat. Anyway, I'll give 'em an earful when I find 'em but we—"

He was interrupted by something falling off the top tier and landing between them with a splatter.

Ufrith. His throat sawed open from ear to ear.

"Well, Cabbage. Your theory has been debunked."

"Aeternita's mercy. What do we do?"

By way of response, Simeon unhooked the helmet from his hip and slid it over his head. There was a metallic thump, then a whir of internal wires as the machinery tightened. The two halves of the faceplate shifted together—hiding Simeon's face.

"Find the fucker who did this and kill him."

A moment later Simeon was climbing up the side of the Proving Ground—dragon-scale gauntlets screeching against the steel as he scaled the heights faster than a Balarian monkey.

"Anything?" Cabbage called after he disappeared into the fog above.

"Nothing." Simeon's voice was muffled by the helm.

There was a scream on the far side of the Proving Ground. Then the metallic snap of crossbow bolts firing.

"Cut him off on the eastern side," Simeon hissed from above, then clomped off into the darkness.

"Bloody hell," Cabbage muttered, checking his bolt jam again for no reason. Not like its status had changed in the last minute. Then he worked his stubborn legs into a rough trot around the tier. Cabbage was grumpy, cold, and a bit of a coward in general. But he followed Simeon's orders without a whiff of second-guessing. Otherwise the whole world went to shit.

The eastern side of the Proving Ground was lit up a little better than the seaward side. There were two, twin dragon-oil braziers burning down at the main gate, and their light ignited the tiers above. The outline of a man emerged. Cabbage raised his crossbow. Aimed.

Don't hesitate, he told himself, while doing exactly that. *Don't hesitate. Don't—*

A moment before squeezing the trigger, he pulled up short, recognizing Carl's familiar and drunk, stumbling gate. Although he was stumbling an awful lot more than he had been a few minutes ago.

"Carl?"

"Hey, Cabbage," he said, continuing forward another step or two. He was clutching his left side with his right arm.

"You all right, Carl?"

"Naw." He stopped. Checked the place along his rib cage. "Naw, don't think I am. Fucker came out of nowhere."

He collapsed in a heap. Cabbage ran over, forgetting to keep his guard up. There was a stab wound between the slats of Carl's rib guard. Blood pouring out. Cabbage could tell from the power of the bleed that his heart was probably cut in half. Nothing to be done but stay with him while he died.

"Who did it?" he asked.

"Some naked demon."

"One o' the mushroom people, you mean?"

"Naw. Never seen someone like him. Skin's all black. Had spikes sproutin' out his back. Scary bastard."

Carl died.

And when Cabbage looked up, a naked man who was covered from head to toe with night tar and holding a wet fishing knife was standing in front of him. Broken crossbow bolts sprouted from his back.

"Fuck," Cabbage said, hefting his crossbow. But before he could get it level, the man rushed forward, ripped it from his hands, then rammed it into his stomach, knocking the wind out of him. He puked on the ground next to Carl's corpse. White, chunky leftovers of the night's porridge.

The man stood over him. He recognized those green eyes—the color of midsummer moss, swimming in a sea of dark. Not a demon.

That was the Flawless Bershad.

"Don't. Please."

Bershad didn't say anything. Just raised the crossbow and aimed it at Cabbage's face. He was about to squeeze the trigger when some flicker of movement caught Bershad's attention. There was a loud slam of boots on the metal tier. Bershad raised his crossbow to the noise and released a bolt.

But there was no soft thump of bolt piercing flesh. No scream or groan. Instead, Cabbage heard the hollow snap of the bolt breaking against dragon scales.

Simeon was on Bershad a moment later, swinging his fists in a rattle of churning gears and clacking scales. His red hair flooded out the back of the helm and flailed around like a fox's tail. Bershad dodged the punches, and when Simeon went to take him in a bear hug—one of his favorite ways to vanquish people—Bershad ducked, pressed the crossbow against a seam in his armor, and fired a second bolt.

Simeon grunted. Elbowed Bershad in the face, which sent him stumbling backward a few paces. His nose and ear started bleeding. Eye swelling. They glared at each other.

"You ain't easy to kill," Simeon growled from behind his helm. "But that don't mean you got the muscle to put me down."

"You're right."

A flash of gray cut through the blanket of fog. Dragon talons snapped down and raked Simeon across his back. Put him on the ground. Cabbage closed his eyes and waited to be killed by either dragon or dragonslayer. But neither happened.

"Open your eyes, you coward," Simeon growled.

Cabbage obeyed. Despite the fact that Simeon had just been struck by a dragon, he was already back on his feet and squared for a fight. But the tier was empty.

"Slippery bastard," Simeon muttered.

"Did he ride off on the dragon?" Cabbage asked, finally getting up.

"Don't be a moron." Simeon went over to the railing, wincing and rubbing the place the dragon had mauled him. He ignored the bolt that was sticking out of his side. Turned around and looked up to the top level. "He either went up, or down."

"Which one, you think?"

Someone below them fired a crossbow bolt. Cursed. Then there was a wet splatter followed by a long gurgle.

"Down." Simeon hopped over the railing. "On me, Cabbage."

"It's a *long* way down, boss."

"Take the stairs if you ain't got the walnuts for a little jump."

And then he was gone into the fog.

"Fuck. Fuck. Fuck," Cabbage muttered, drawing his sword and heading for the stairs, taking them two at a time despite the screaming protestations of his ankle.

When he got down to the open area in front of the main gate, there were four corpses scattered around the yard. Simeon was crouched in front of a fifth man, holding his guts in for him.

"You sure he went into the woods?" Simeon asked.

"Aye, boss. Naked fucker pulled my guts out then drug Ezra off that way."

He pointed east. Straight into the wilting forest that dipped down into a deep valley before hitting the Bloody Sludge.

"I see his footprints," said Simeon. "Crazy asshole isn't even wearing boots."

A crowd was developing by then—everyone had come off the tier after hearing the commotion. Simeon's crew were good sailors and good killers, but they were shit when it came to defensive discipline.

"What's the situation, boss?" said Howell. A few of the men stepped aside to let the veteran warrior pass. The dragon-bone shield was slung over his back. He was carrying the Naga spear all casual in one hand, despite the situation.

"The lizard killer's alive. He ran off into the wilts with Ezra." Simeon pointed. "Let's go kill him."

That was the thing with Simeon. Nobody was calmer in a head-on fight. Focused and murderous and full of deranged joy. But he got frustrated by subtlety and deception. Drove the bastard mad. Turned him into an idiot.

"He's baiting us," said Cabbage.

"Don't fucking care. He dies tonight."

The men gave a rumble of battle grunts. Cabbage was less enthusiastic about the prospect of chasing a naked and angry Flawless Bershad through the wilted forest.

"Shouldn't some of us hang back?" Cabbage asked. "Form a perimeter so he can't sneak back through and steal the queen?"

"You turning coward on me, Cabbage?"

"Naw, boss. Just trying to think it all through a little. He came to get the queen, not to gut Ezra in the wilts."

Simeon looked at Howell, who gave a begrudging nod. "The earless fuck has a point, boss."

Far off in the forest, a bloodcurdling cry rang out. Ezra.

"Fine," Simeon snarled. "I'll go out alone. Howell, you're in charge o' defenses here. Do not lose track of my tinker queen."

"Aye, boss."

There were murmurs of agreement. Simeon barreled off into the woods at speed—pale armor swallowed by the darkness. The men looked to Howell for orders, which he started rattling off in quick succession.

"Butcher. Kenpo. Trundle. You're on the main gate. Echo, get down to the queen's cell and stay outside. Turtle. Keen. Get an irregular sweep of the western wall going. Shadow and Weasel, work the east. I'll head to the centrifuge and monitor the alarms. Anyone gets into trouble, find a trap and set it off. I'll come for you."

Whoever had built the Proving Ground had riddled the place with booby traps. The alchemist had shown Simeon all the locations, but he'd decided to leave them armed and force the men to work around them. Said it made the place less inviting to the Papyrian military.

That was true. But it also made it extremely hazardous to a wandering drunk man. Over the years, at least a half score of men in the crew had perished from placing a wobbly foot in the wrong spot in the Proving Ground.

Howell continued giving orders. The men bounced into action. Cabbage waited for his orders, which arrived last, and were predicated by a shiny smirk from Howell, which did not bode well.

"Cabbage, go run the sea rail again then report back."

Of course Howell would give him the job with the most steps. Howell knew about his dodgy ankle—Cabbage complained about it more than he should—but in this case he didn't mind the shitty assignment. He figured it was better to torment a single joint than open himself up to the possibility of his entire viscera getting yanked out of his stomach like Ezra.

"Aye, Howell. I'm on it."

Cabbage began the climb. Now that he'd been running around, his ankle was sending spikes of pain up his leg with each step. But the nervous knots in his belly slowly loosened as he got farther away from the woods, and the possibility of disembowelment via fishing knife. That was the closest he'd come to dying in a while. And once again, it was Simeon who saved him. For such an objectively evil bastard, the man looked out for his own.

Once Cabbage was relaxed enough to realize he had to piss, the feeling came with considerable urgency.

He made his way up to the very top of the Proving Ground to relieve himself. Something about pissing off high places made him feel the way he imagined a king might feel. He got to his favorite spot, undid his trousers, and let things fly. Cabbage wondered what country he'd prefer to be the king of. Lysteria and Ghalamar were both conquered, so they were out. Papyria didn't have kings. Almira was a muddy shithole. Pargos, maybe. The Alchemist Order had a big library there. Maybe as king he could hire one of them to make a potion that'd regrow his ears.

Cabbage stopped pissing. Something was wrong. He frowned. Turned around.

The top hatch was open.

The hatch itself was an exhaust vent that was built to flush toxic fumes out of the Proving Ground, back when some crazy bastard was doing all his experiments. Simeon's crew always kept the thing closed on cold nights because it shuttled freezing air through the barracks.

That being said, the occasional pirate was known to sneak away from his post and steal a nap in the upper tunnel. Pig, in particular, made a habit of it. And Cabbage hadn't seen Pig all night. But he would have closed the hatch behind him if he was stealing a nap. 'Cause of the drafts.

With a growing sense of unease, Cabbage made his way over to the open hatch. Peeked inside.

There was a substantial puddle of blood on the floor beneath. Cabbage seriously doubted that the previous owner of the blood was still alive.

Flawless Bershad must have come back up this way. Seemed impossible. But Cabbage had trouble conjuring a more likely explanation.

Cabbage would have liked to think of himself as the type of pirate who'd redraw his steel and go searching the dark tunnels of the Proving Ground for the naked bastard who had murdered anywhere from eight to ten of his comrades. Kill the legendary fucker or die trying. Cabbage wanted to be that pirate. But somewhere between losing his ears and spending a decade of his life with wet feet, his disposition for seizing the initiative had soured.

He slammed the hatch shut. And decided to pretend for the rest of his life that he'd never seen it opened.

49

BERSHAD

Ghost Moth Island, the Proving Ground

Bershad waited in the shadows to see if the pirate whose piss smelled like pure potato liquor would follow him down the hatch. But after looking at the pool of blood for a while—body flooding with the acrid smell of fear and doubt—he closed the hatch. Headed back down the side of the building at a casual pace and dwindling level of concern that made it clear he wasn't about to raise any alarms.

"Smart choice," he muttered.

When Bershad dropped down into the hatch, he'd found a napping pirate with thick jowls and an upturned nose. Cut his throat. Presently, he took the dead man's crossbow, crammed his corpse behind the ladder to the roof, and headed deeper into Osyrus Ward's bunker of horrors. He followed the narrow tunnel for a few dozen paces before finding a place to drop down into a main corridor.

The place smelled of chemicals and rot. Rust and singed hair. The hallway he dropped into was lined with glass cages, each one with a different dead animal inside. Bershad passed a mantis with front pincers made from copper. A tarantula with wings made from glass and wire.

Then came the rats. Hundreds of them.

Some had metal limbs and tails. Others had distended, broken bellies with tiny gears spilling out. Their eyes replaced with red nubs that were connected to acorn-sized lodestones by copper wires.

The animals were long dead, but they twitched in little increments, making the long hallway itchy with artificial movement
that the Gray-Winged Nomad didn't register. The dichotomy of
seeing movement that he couldn't feel with the dragon's senses was
disorienting and confusing. Gave him a headache.

———

Bershad descended farther into the stink and the dark. Climbing
down decrepit ladders and narrow stairwells. Slinking along more
hallways and chambers lined with Ward's madness. It was easy to
avoid the handful of pirates who patrolled the corridors. Most of
the assholes were outside, trying to prevent him from getting in.

A few levels down, Osyrus Ward's experiments turned to
human subjects. Papyrian soldiers, judging from their rotting armor.

He passed a man with all of his organs cut out of his chest and
stowed in putrid jars. The jars were attached to tubes that ran back
into the dead man's chest cavity. Just like the rats, the man was
long since dead.

The farther he descended, the duller his connection to the Nomad became. But it was still strong enough for him to feel two
heartbeats itching against his skin as he approached yet another
ladder. They were coming from the opposite direction at a brisk
walk.

Not worth a fight. He ducked into one of the experiment
nooks—hiding behind a man who had had his entire spine exposed and hundreds of wires attached to the vertebra. They connected to two long slabs of curved dragon bones that looked
suspiciously like they were meant to be wings.

"What's the fuss?" the first pirate asked. His breath reeked of
tobacco and chicken.

"Simeon's all fired up about something," said the other, who
was all rum and sausage. "Says we're under attack."

"Military? Been a while since they caught a whiff of us."

"Naw. Some naked lunatic, apparently. Killed a bunch of men
then ran off into the woods with Ezra's guts wrapped around his
junk."

"You're fucking with me."

"That's what Cabbage said. He's generally truthful, except
when he's bragging about the value of those fucking tapestries."

"You seen the one of Kira Malgrave? Only thing covering her bits is a piece of fruit. And it ain't a big piece if you know what I mean. One o' them miniature peaches from the Dainwood that—"

"I've seen it. C'mon. We got our orders. Everyone's meant to secure the perimeter while Simeon flushes the naked bastard out of the woods."

Their voices faded. Bershad waited until they were completely out of range, then continued his descent by climbing down a long series of vertical pipes. They were still giving off warmth, and by the time Bershad reached the bottom, he was gritting his teeth from the pain of burning palms and feet.

The room at the bottom of the Proving Ground was circular and far more open than the tiny chambers and narrow hallways he'd come through. There was a dome made from black cement in the middle. The dome had a single, circular door made from bronze and locked with a Balarian seal. Bershad could just barely feel a single heartbeat on the far side.

There was one sentry out front. He smelled like sawdust and cheese and he was picking his ass with one hand, holding his cross-bow slack in the other.

Bershad shot him in the face. Came out of the shadows.

He looked up as he crossed the open space. Above, there was a long pillar that led up through the bowels of the Proving Ground. It seemed as if it had once been an open window to the sky, but the opening had been sealed by a thick metal plate that was attached to dozens of hydraulic pipes.

The design of the space reminded Bershad of Kasamir's garden, except the mushrooms and hanging plants were replaced with dark machinery, and the sky was covered, not cleared.

He searched the man he'd just killed, digging through pockets until he found the round seal. He slipped it into the mechanism. There was a rusty rattle inside the guts of the door, then a pop of retracting tumblers as it opened.

Felgor was on the other side.

He was hanging in a cage, arms folded in his lap. The Balarian squinted back at Bershad for a moment before recognizing him.

"Oh. Hey, Silas. Nice haircut."

Felgor produced two small tools from up his sleeve and started messing with the lock on the front of his cage.

"Are those chicken bones?" Bershad asked.

"Yep. Almost got this charmed. Just stay there, and I'll be right with you."

"What happened to Ashlyn?"

"Uh, that's a real long, weird story. But it ends with her getting dropped into a big pit beneath that cage." He motioned to a larger, domed cage to his left. "Floor dropped out, then sealed up behind her."

Bershad looked down at the floor. He took a breath—did his best to coax the Nomad a little lower, which she stubbornly obliged for a few heartbeats. No good. He couldn't sense anything beneath this room.

"I think she's okay, though," Felgor continued. "Simeon wants her alive. When he heard you were coming, he dropped her in for safekeeping in case you got down here. Which I guess you managed. Congratulations? They were all skeptical."

"How do I open it?" Bershad said, taking a step forward.

"You can't. The system is a closed magnetic field with structural pressure from the whole building. Applying the opposite magnetic charge is the only way to open it."

"You're just repeating something Ashlyn said, aren't you?"

"Which means it's probably correct. And don't come any closer until I can get out of this cage so I can make sure you don't trigger a—"

Felgor was interrupted by Bershad stepping on a metal tile. There was a click, then a bolt plugged him in the shoulder. Bershad grunted. Went down on a knee. That triggered a second bolt that fired from somewhere above, pegged him through his right foot, pinning him in place.

"Pressure trap," Felgor finished. "This room's riddled with 'em."

"Why didn't you warn me?" Bershad hissed through gritted teeth.

"I was getting to it. You kept asking other questions."

Bershad tried to yank the bolt out of his foot, but with all the blood, his hand kept slipping.

"Fuck's sake," he muttered, trying again and failing again.

"Just hold tight," Felgor said. "I squirreled away a little—"

"Quiet," Bershad hissed, turning back toward the door to the hatch. Three heartbeats were moving toward them with a purpose. "People coming. Three of 'em."

"Might be you wanna hide?"

Bershad looked at the distance between him and the nearest shadow. Judged it against the speed of the three men, plus the fact there was a bolt through his foot.

"No time."

He ripped the bolt out of his shoulder and snapped it in half. Got onto his belly, hiding the bolt tip underneath him. He wedged the shaft and fletching between two fingers, then held it against the back of his head, making it look like the rest of the bolt was buried six inches through his skull, not clutched in his other fist. He settled down into a pool of his own blood.

"Ah. Playing dead. Good strategy."

A moment later, the thump of boots pounding onto the metal floor sounded from outside.

"Echo's dead," one man said.

"Solid fucking observation, Gill."

"Workshop door's open, too."

"You can't rightfully trigger the dome's seventh pressure plate without going inside the dome first, can you?"

"I dunno, Howell. Maybe the Balarian that Simeon hates so much sprung his cage."

"Let's find out."

They both approached, cautious and slow. Bershad took a deep breath in. Held it.

"Hey guys!" Felgor called cheerfully. "Some idiot broke in and got himself killed."

"Shut your fucking mouth or I'll put a bolt through it," Gill hissed.

"Rude."

There was a silence while they scanned the room.

"Fuck. Is that him?" Gill asked.

"Seems so," Howell responded.

"But I thought Simeon was rooting him out of the woods?"

"Either there are two naked men all mucked up in night tar with a mind for violence tonight, or the asshole slipped through."

"Pretty clever."

"Man's got a bolt in the back of his head. So, he's not that clever."

They both approached.

"Give the clever bastard another bolt for good measure," Howell said.

"Aye."

Bershad stayed still as he heard Gill lifting his crossbow. Stayed still as the pirate's fish-crusted fingers pressed against the trigger.

But just as Gill pulled the trigger, Bershad jerked his head to the right.

The bolt shattered on the ground. Shrapnel sprayed into Bershad's face and punctured his neck.

"Fuck!" Gill shouted. "He's still alive."

Bershad rolled onto his back—tearing his foot free in the process—and threw the tip of the bolt at Gill, catching him in the mouth and sending him stumbling backward. Bershad shot up and tackled Gill. Ripped the bolt out of the pirate's cheek and rammed it through his throat.

Before he could pull it out, Howell was on him with a spear thrust. Bershad dodged. Backed up. Drew his knife from its fishing-line sheath. Howell had that dragon-scale shield tucked up in a tight guard. Spear ready to lash out with a thrust if Bershad got closer.

"I remember you from the river," Bershad growled, pressing one hand against his neck to stanch the bleeding from the bolt shrapnel.

"Aye." Howell studied him. "Simeon wanted you for himself. He'll be pissed when he finds out I'm the one who crammed the shell in your mouth."

"Careful. I'm not dead yet."

"No. But you're approaching at speed. All I gotta do is wait a few ticks while you bleed out on your feet."

That wasn't wrong. And it gave Bershad an idea.

He wavered. Dropped to his knees. Let his head wobble.

"Coward," he muttered.

Howell didn't respond, but he lowered his shield enough for Bershad to get a look at his smiling mouth full of gold teeth.

Bershad whipped his fishing knife through the air. Split Howell's face from nose to chin. He crumpled to the floor.

"Shit, Silas," said Felgor. "That was a good throw."

"Yeah." Bershad turned to him. He was woozy. Vision blurry. He stumbled and fell over. "Need some . . . need some help."

"Fear not," Felgor said, resuming his work picking the lock of his cage. "I'm on the cusp."

"No . . . time for bone picks," Bershad said. "Where's the key?"

"There's always time for greatness," Felgor said. "Just need to . . ."

Something clicked.

"Yes. Yes, and then here . . ."

Another click.

"Last one . . ." Felgor squinted and stuck his tongue out of the corner of his mouth as he slipped the bone deep into the slot. Twisted. The lock rumbled with clanks and metal ticks, then the entire thing spun once and opened like a flower blooming in spring.

"Victory!" Felgor shouted, hopping down from the cage. "You're a witness!" he said, pointing at Bershad. "The legendary Felgor does it again! Picked a Balarian seal with a fucking chicken bone. Someone's gonna write a song about this. I can feel it."

"Felgor," Bershad gurgled, mouth filling with blood from his throat wound. "Help."

"Right, right," Felgor said, shuffling over to Bershad on an irregular path. "Ashlyn kept a close watch on me nicking the Gods Moss, but I did pinch some Crimson Tower nuggets a while back." He crouched down. Produced three vials of bright red moss from somewhere in his coat. "Just try not to choke on your own blood before I can sort you out."

He started filling Bershad's various wounds with the moss.

"I don't even know why I stole these," he said while he worked. "Not like there's anyone to sell them to. I'd like to take credit for the foresight, but that's hot air. Mostly it's just a compulsion at this point. I can't help myself. Like the saps who can't get outta bed without a pint of juniper liquor. Except my booze is thievery. And gods, it is strong stuff."

Twenty minutes later, Felgor had packed the worst of his wounds with the moss, then wrapped them in strips of the dead men's clothes. Bershad could feel the burning warmth of his body healing, but it was going slow.

"How do we get to Ashlyn?" Bershad asked.

"Yeah, so there's a bit of an issue on that front. Far as I can tell, the only thing that can get that floor to open again is Simeon's right gauntlet. That's what he used to drop her in there."

"Great," Bershad muttered. Then checked the wound in his throat. It was still bleeding on the outside, but it had sealed internally. "Well, let's go find him."

"You sure you're up for that? You're looking pretty raw."

"I'm fine."

"You got blood coming out of a dozen places."

"I said I'm fine."

Bershad took a breath. Focused his senses again. Still nothing coming from below—not even a rat. Something was blocking the Nomad's reach. But when he looked up at the ceiling he could feel the vague sizzle of the pirates overhead—they weren't clustered around the front entrance anymore, but had instead started running varied patrols along the different levels. Must have dawned on them that he wasn't back in those woods after all.

"So what's the plan?" Felgor asked.

The sun would be up in less than an hour. Whatever they were going to do, it needed to happen fast. But Bershad had an idea.

"First, we need to get you to a boat."

Bershad picked up Gill's crossbow. Slung it over his shoulder, wincing at the pain the strap put on one of his many wounds. He picked up the dragon-bone shield and situated it on his off hand. Gave the spear a few practice thrusts.

Good balance. Better than his old dagger.

"Stay exactly two paces behind me at all times," Bershad said, heading for the open door. "Stop when I stop, move when I move."

"So, your plan doesn't involve putting on pants?"

"No."

"Could we maybe restrategize so that it does?"

"Just follow me, Felgor."

50

ASHLYN

Ghost Moth Island, Beneath the Proving Ground

After several turns, the roughly carved tunnel ended at a gray metal door. No lock. Just a circular latch. Ashlyn pulled it open without hesitating. Inside, there was a spherical room illuminated by the sallow pulse of chemically activated dragon threads. They were embedded in the walls like the blood vessels of an egg. There was another workstation next to the door. An array of clean surgical tools were arranged in a line. Sealskin gloves next to them. Unlike the rest of the Proving Ground, there was no rust or plant growth in here. It had stayed pristine for all this time.

Well, *pristine* was perhaps the wrong word. There were ten men suspended from the ceiling by steel cords.

They all had a heavy mechanical apparatus attached to their backs, with two glass orbs over each shoulder that were blackened by burned dragon-oil residue. The first hanging man's body was undamaged, but his skin had a strange, gray pallor. The same color as a pill bug.

The others had assorted injuries. Blown-open kneecaps. Cracked teeth. Distorted and broken necks. One of them was cut in half just below his ribs. Metal tubes and wires hung from his chest cavity. Dozens of acorn-sized lodestones were implanted along his exposed spine. There was no sign of his legs.

There was also one empty place on the ceiling. Empty hooks.

"Ten men," Ashlyn muttered. "Gaya came with eleven."

It took her a moment to understand. After Osyrus left, Kasamir had come down here and taken one of the Papyrian soldiers for himself. Reanimated his corpse with Cordata mushrooms and used him as a personal automaton and bodyguard.

"Specimen 9009," Ashlyn said to herself, remembering what Kasamir had called the mushroom giant.

Ashlyn stepped beneath the bisected hanging man so she could see into his rib cage. His heart was visible and intact. She frowned, wondering why it hadn't gone to rot after thirty years in his chest. Then she saw something that didn't make sense.

The left ventricle was connected to the spinal column by a pipe.

Ashlyn went back to the workstation. Put on the gloves and grabbed a scalpel. She stood on her toes to reach the heart and carefully unscrewed it from the spine. It was heavier than a heart should be. Denser.

She took it back to the workstation and cut it open.

The heart was encased in natural human tissue and blood vessels, but beneath the layer of organic matter there was a wire mesh that gave the organ its shape. The muscle underneath the mesh was wrong—light gray, not pink. The texture a little too smooth. Ashlyn cut the mesh and muscle apart to find scores of lodestones the size of river pebbles embedded in the gray meat. When she tapped one of the lodestones with the scalpel, a little surge of current moved from her wrist to the lodestone, and then the entire heart gave a shuddering pump—attempting to push blood through an empty ventricle.

Osyrus Ward hadn't altered these men's organs. He had created replacements.

Ashlyn couldn't fathom how he'd accomplished such a thing. But there was a small heap of stained papers behind the men. She ducked beneath the hanging corpses and started reading.

---
12 Credo—223

- *Breakthrough. The Seed's fluid can be manipulated to grow artificial tissue around a lattice framework. The tissue requires a power source, but no sustenance to remain healthy. It is a closed system. Moreover, the fluid also prompts normative human tissue to bind with the machinery and artificial organs, which I previously assumed to be impossible.*
- *This is what I needed. Beginning trials tomorrow morning.*

Beneath that note, there were dozens of pages of diagrams and chemical equations illustrating how Osyrus grew the organs around a mesh framework and planned to embed them into human bodies. Ashlyn kept sifting until she found the results.

28 Lomas—224

- *Failure. All specimens perished within seventeen days of procedure due to various complications. Blood loss. Shock. Filtration system clogs. Power surges from the apparatus. But this is a failure of implementation and mechanism, not principle. Specimens accepted their organs without sign of infection, and achieved full corporeal function from them. The organs required no food or water to sustain themselves, and the specimens retained full mental faculties.*
- *This is the baseline. The skeleton upon which I will build my creations.*
- *Myriad improvements to the filtration and power systems required. Modules burn 2.9 pints of dragon oil per day. Not sustainable. Size and weight of the apparatus also severe hindrance. Two specimens exploded their kneecaps when ordered to walk. Must make everything more efficient.*
- *Designed a theoretical system that is fueled by a symbiosis of dragon tissue, human flesh, and lodestone fields. This would be perfect, but a far stronger elemental charge from the dragon tissue is required to make the system viable. At current levels, the damn things are just glorified lanterns. For now, a dragon-oil engine is the only path forward.*
- *A curious side effect: specimens developed a gray pallor to the skin after the procedure. Odd, and likely preventable. But perhaps I shall adopt it as my maker's mark. A signature upon my Acolytes.*

Ashlyn frowned. Turned to the schematic he referenced.

Osyrus was right—his proposed design wouldn't function without tissue that was four or five times stronger than his chemically activated threads. But if the rest of his discoveries were true, the weakness of his persistent charge was the only thing preventing Osyrus Ward from creating a functionally immortal person.

Ashlyn looked at the hanging men—their limbs blown out and broken. Faces contorted in pain. She remembered all the sadistic things that she'd seen on the island already. If this was the cost of immortality, it was too high. Moreover, Osyrus Ward's thesis was flawed: these organs and creations might not need food or water to function, but the process relied on extremely rare natural resources—

lodestones, this Seed fluid, and dragon threads. Ward could never transform Terra into a place free from suffering and death and decay. Not without drastically altering the environment or killing the vast majority of Terra's people.

But once she had that thought, she realized that Osyrus Ward would not see either requirement as a serious obstacle.

She stopped herself from spinning farther down that rabbit hole. Regardless of immortality's moral and practical implications on Terra, she was still stuck in this pit and needed a way out.

Beneath the schematic, there were a few more pages of Osyrus's final notes. She dug through, hoping for something she could use.

---

1 Noctar—225

- *Used all available seed fluid harvested from 88. Attempted to bloom Specimen 01, but failed, despite considerable and prolonged disruption to his body. Most likely explanation is twenty years attached to the preservation loop. Whatever the cause, his frail body now is weaker than Papyrian wine, and useless to me.*
- *To continue, I require more materials than this island can offer. It is time to leave.*
- *Priority One. Faster method of travel. If each dragon warren in Terra contains 8 pints of fluid, I have many long journeys ahead of me before I can build my next set of organs. Flight, I think. My filtration and power systems for the organs can be retrofitted into a combustion engine. The lightweight strength of dragon bone and hide is also a distinct engineering advantage. Will build a prototype here and use it to leave the island.*
- *Priority Two. Access to unbloomed Seeds. I must find a method that takes them to the cusp of transformation and holds them there, so they might produce the fluid in larger amounts. I cannot create a better world in 8-pint increments. This will likely take decades, given the rarity of Seeds and difficulty in identifying them. An inconvenience, but not an impossible obstacle.*
- *Priority Three. A place to work that is rich in resources. Balaria's capital is ideal. They have the quarries and kiln refineries I will need to build an apparatus that delays the bloom. The machine will be massive—an eternally spinning gear that can be seen for*

leagues. But I can always dress it up as something else. A source of power and industry. Not even a lie. Just an incomplete truth.
- *In addition, Balarian obsession with Clock God suggests a more receptive outlook to my work than the Papyrian empress. Religion is a powerful tool for manipulation of the masses. But have learned from mistakes with Okinu. Must make myself invaluable to Balarian emperor. Will ply him with simple machines and methods of control, but withhold full extent of inventions and my true purpose until the proper time. Until there is nothing anyone can do to stop me.*

The final note was dated thirty-one years ago. Seven months before Balaria closed their borders to outlanders.

15 Crima—230

- *Skyship prototype complete. Engine relies on lizard oil for fuel. A crude application. But the Ghost Moth spinal tissue requires advances before viability. Stored all unrefined strands on the ship for future trials, pending advances.*
- *Left Specimen 01 alive. Sentimental of me, perhaps. But he always wanted to live forever. No reason for me to stop him. Curious what he will do with the island when I leave. Bemoan his suffering as always, or free himself? I left him the tools, should he prove industrious.*
- *Plan to collect 5 gallons of Seed fluid, then travel to Balaria and resume work. Will revert back to insect trials. Focus on smaller apparatus. More efficient titration process. When perfect, will resume human trials.*
- *Packed all indispensable materials onto the prototype skyship. Forced to leave dragon bones and almost all of my notes on site. Pity, but the lodestones and spinal tissue take priority. They are the only things that cannot be replaced. I can always write more notes. And preserving dragon bones is easy. I just need fresh specimens. They are rare, but they cannot hide from me. Not anymore.*
- *Leaving tomorrow, assuming favorable wind.*

Ashlyn read the last part of the note over again, resisting the urge to tear it apart.

Osyrus had taken all the threads with him when he left. She'd come all this way, and for what? All she'd managed to do was endanger people's lives and find a way to generate a small magnetic field around her arm. That wasn't enough to break her out of this pit, let alone pull the armada of flying ships out of the sky.

"Fuck," she muttered. "Fuck. Fuck. Fuck."

Ashlyn allowed herself sixty seconds to fully panic. She let her mind sit, stunned and useless.

Then she took a few long, deep breaths. Concentrated.

If Osyrus Ward's horrors were the only tools with which she had to work, she would make good use of them.

She touched the bandage on her wrist. Even in its severely diminished state, the dragon thread produced more than a hundred times the energy of Ward's design. And it was getting stronger the more it spread through her body. That was why she overloaded his systems when she connected to them—they weren't designed for such a powerful boost to the lodestone charge.

That meant that if she built a system that could handle a stronger current, she could create magnetic fields on a scale that Osyrus never accounted for. It would be enough to get her out of this pit, for one thing. But that was just the beginning.

She turned to the surgical tools.

"At least I don't have to use a sharpened dragon scale this time."

Then she picked up a scalpel.

———

When it was done, Ashlyn went back down the tunnel to Gaya.

"You found my men?" Gaya asked.

"Yes."

"How did they die?"

"You sure that you want to know?"

"Widows do not turn away from consequences. They were my men. I want to know."

"Osyrus Ward used the fluid he took from your body to create a series of artificial organs that do not degrade with age or require outside sustenance. He implanted them in your men, but the process killed them."

"I see." She paused. Looked at what Ashlyn had done to her own arm.

The surgery had been painful and rushed. The metal contact plates were attached to her flesh in the rough shape of an armored gauntlet. The conductive copper wiring was messily braided between the implanted lodestones and her dragon thread.

"Did you find what you were looking for?" Gaya asked.

"No," Ashlyn said. "But I found what I needed."

"I suppose you'll be leaving, then."

"Yes." Ashlyn hesitated. "Do you want me to kill you before I go?"

"That's a kind offer." Her face twitched. The metal plates along her chest strained against her alabaster skin. "Yes, I suppose." She glanced up at the hatch that Ashlyn had fallen through. "Unless you have a way to tear the roof off this pit so I can see the sky again. The Nagas would come back to me, I think. I would like that."

Ashlyn thought back to the blueprints of the Proving Ground that she'd seen. The entire structure relied on lodestones for integrity. And they were all part of the same orientation system.

She smiled. "I can do that."

51

CABBAGE

Ghost Moth Island, the Proving Ground

Simeon emerged from the woods just as dawn was breaking. He was drenched in mud from the waist down, but the Ghost Moth scales on his chest were glowing in the early light. Cabbage always thought that was a strange contrast. Simeon's soul was scarred and black, but his armor was the stuff of divinity.

Simeon marched toward the front gate with a posture that radiated frustration and fury. Cabbage had been bullshitting with Lexine and a few others by the front gate.

"What'd you find?" Cabbage asked, knowing full well it wasn't the Flawless Bershad.

"Ezra's dead. Splattered all over the red boulder pile."

"He drug 'im all the way out to the boulder pile that fast?" Lexine asked. The pile of mined rocks was two leagues away, at least. "Doesn't seem possible."

And it seemed even less possible that he'd managed to double back and re-climb the Proving Ground, then slip inside. But this was the Flawless Bershad. Slayer of sixty-seven or sixty-eight dragons. Cabbage couldn't even remember the exact figure. Point being, impossible feats were part of his daily routine. Bastard probably shat diamonds, too.

"How are things here?" Simeon asked.

"Quiet, boss. No sight of anything coming outta the woods. No word from any patrols. A few pressure switches went off in the workshop a while ago. Howell and Gill went to check on them."

Simeon removed his helmet with a hiss and a whir. The unhappy expression on his sweat-sheened face made Cabbage's mouth go dry.

"A while ago. Define that."

Cabbage shrugged. "Dunno. An hour?"

"And you all have just been sitting out here with your thumbs up your asses since then?"

"Howell said he could handle it," Cabbage said. "What with him having the shield and spear and all."

"Crew o' morons, one bigger than the last," Simeon grumbled. "Gotta handle every fucking thing myself."

"We got an errant skiff!" Lexine shouted, pointing west, where the Big Empty was shimmering orange with the dawn light.

Cabbage squinted. Sure enough, a skiff with a bloodred sail was about a league out from the surf. There wasn't much wind, and he could just barely make out someone working the oars.

"Lens," Simeon said, shoving Cabbage out of the way and moving closer.

Lexine turned over his lens to Simeon, who gave the skiff a long look.

"Whaddaya see, boss?" Cabbage asked.

"Three people. Man rowing like his life depended on it. Two others I can't make out. One of 'em might have a bunch o' bolts in his back."

"The lizard killer stole the queen?" Lexine asked. "How?"

"By sneaking past you useless fucks while I was gone," Simeon hissed.

Cabbage decided it wasn't a good time to mention that if Simeon hadn't gone traipsing off into the woods with his blood all hot, he might have been around to stop the Flawless Bershad. Pointing that out seemed like a really good way for Cabbage to get his arms torn off.

"All of you, with me," Simeon said, already heading toward the winding stair that led to the docks.

Simeon took the stairs three at a time. Cabbage, Lexine, and the other two struggled to catch up. Cabbage had always had a deep-seated fear that he would die due to falling down a set of stairs. He wasn't sure why. But that fear—combined with his dodgy ankle—put him at the back of the pack when they reached the dock.

"Oars," Simeon growled, waving at the big pile stacked against the cliff. He was already moving toward the closest skiff, which was tied to one of the sagging, lichen-crusted pylons.

"On it, boss," Lexine said, trotting over. "Ain't gonna be no problem—with all of us rowing we'll have 'em in ten min—"

Lexine's optimistic prediction was cut short by a bolt through the mouth. He collapsed. Started twitching on the sand.

Cabbage was more or less exactly in the middle of the beach. Nowhere near anything resembling cover. So he just crouched down and searched frantically for the asshole who was waylaying them.

While he was searching, two more bolts fired. The other two pirates fell over dead.

Knowing the next bolt would be for him, Cabbage closed his eyes. Mind going blank with fear.

But instead of getting a bolt through the brain, he heard the familiar sound of a crossbow jamming. By Aeternita, what a wonderful sound. It was followed by the dry rasp-and-click of someone pulling the trigger again and again, which only made the jam worse.

"Misfire, is it?" Simeon asked, voice muffled by the helm. "Damn crossbows will do that when you fire 'em too fast. Make you look like a damn fool."

Simeon scanned the dock. "Gonna have to come out of your hole if you wanna finish this, lizard killer."

There was a silence. Murky water lapping at the rotten dock.

Then a twitch of movement in the shallows.

The Flawless Bershad rose from his hiding spot—naked body dripping mud. He tossed the crossbow. Raised the Naga spear from the muck. The dragon-bone shield was on his arm.

"Clever bag of tricks you showed, today." Simeon spat. "Didn't peg you for a man with some sneak to him on account of your idiot charge back by the Bloody Sludge. Burns my piss, but I respect the skill."

"Got no use for your respect."

"Uh-huh." Simeon smiled. Motioned to the weapons Bershad had acquired. "You kill the man who carried those?"

"That's right."

"Howell was my best."

"I didn't have much trouble with him."

"Dunno about that. You're looking pretty chewed up, lizard killer."

He motioned to Bershad's body. Along with the muddy water, there was a lot of blood dripping from fresh wounds.

"Had worse."

"So I've heard."

They circled around each other on the sand. Angling up.

"Gonna need that gauntlet from you," Bershad growled.

"Ah," Simeon said. "I get it now. You went down to the workshop. Relieved Howell of his weapons. And I'm thinking you got Felgor rowing his ass off with two dead members of my crew as cargo. Which puts you short the queen you came for. That sum things up?"

"More or less."

"Then make your pass," Simeon said. "Gotta say, most men who've fought me might as well have been naked for all the good their armor did them. Think you'll be the first to try it in the literal sense, though."

Bershad charged.

He didn't move that fast. One of his feet was obviously hurt. And he didn't do anything tricky with the approach—no big leaps or hops or other tactics you'd expect from a legendary dragonslayer.

But his first spear thrust shot out with such blinding speed,

Cabbage didn't even realize the attack had happened until he'd drawn the spear back into a guard. Apparently, Simeon didn't either, because he took the raking thrust across his chest with a pained grunt. Dragon scales sprayed across the sand.

Simeon came around with a powerful punch, but Flawless got the shield up. There was a crunch, and Bershad went tumbling across the sand, landing in a coiled crouch. The rut that his left foot dug in the sand was smeared with black blood.

Cabbage raised his crossbow. He had a clear view of Bershad's temple.

This was his chance to save Simeon. Finally.

And this time, he didn't hesitate. Fired.

Bershad's temple disappeared behind the shield. Bolt plunked harmlessly off bone. Bershad turned to him, eyes burning green with rage.

"Oh, shit."

Cabbage fired again. Bershad blocked it again.

"Shit. Fuck." He fired. Bershad smacked the bolt out of the air. "Shit. Fuck. Sh—"

Bershad slammed the spear into the sand, reached behind his shield, and flicked a knife at Cabbage. The blade caught him in the neck and sent him backward into the cliff. His vision cracked white and he went down on his ass. Cabbage prepared to bleed out before he realized that his collarbone had caught the blade. Stopped it just short of the big veins.

Simeon roared, then charged Bershad, who snatched the spear out of the sand and met him in a flurry of blows and kicked sand— both of them moving faster than snakes. Simeon's fists pounded off the dragon-bone shield. Bershad's spear shot out and scraped across Simeon's armor, sending more white scales flying.

They broke apart. Stalked around each other in a predatory circle. Both breathing hard. Gods, Bershad was scary to look at— all painted black with crossbow bolts poking out of his back like dragon spikes. He looked more like a demon than the alchemist's creatures.

"You're slowing down, lizard killer."

"So are you."

They were both right, and Cabbage couldn't tell who was hurt worse. Bershad was bleeding all over the place, but Simeon had plenty of bad gouges, too. Every scale on his right arm was covered in blood.

Simeon picked Lexine's sword out of the sand. Worked the grip a bit in his fist.

Cabbage hadn't seen Simeon use a weapon besides his fists since giving the spear to Howell. That wasn't a good sign.

Simeon raised the sword. "When this fight's done—and I've ripped your head off your fucking neck—I'm gonna use your skull as a piss pot for the rest o' my days."

Bershad twitched the spear in his hand. "Yeah."

They moved toward each other. Slow. Methodical.

Cabbage looked around. His crossbow was half buried in sand about five strides away. Still had one shot left, if he'd counted proper. And he could put it straight through the Flawless Bershad's skull. He just had to pick his moment.

When Bershad and Simeon were five strides away from each other, they both darted forward like slipped hounds.

Cabbage could barely follow the fight. Simeon came on in another careening wreckage of sword strokes that caught air or shield, but never Bershad's flesh. Each time Simeon gave him an opening, Bershad's spear snapped out from behind his shield, punching into Simeon's armor—shattering scales or scraping across them with an ear-crunching screech.

It went on like that for a few heart-pounding minutes. After a long flurry of offensive spear stabs, Bershad's back foot gave out. He went down on one knee, and Simeon lunged for a killing stroke. Bershad twisted his body so Simeon's sword cut nothing but sand, then slammed the side of the spear into Simeon's cheek. The blow disconnected one of the faceplates and sent it flying across the beach.

Simeon reeled backward—his face suddenly visible again. Both his lips were cut up. Cheek swollen. He spat a mouthful of blood onto the sand.

"You got salt, lizard killer. I'll give you that."

"All you got is that armor, saving your life over and over."

"Maybe. But the point is I got it."

Simeon threw a vicious downward stroke that Bershad caught with the shield. The sword broke in half—tip spinning backward into the surf. Simeon grabbed the lip of the shield and slammed it backward into Bershad's mouth.

Bershad ducked away, abandoning his shield to get some space. Simeon left it in the sand.

And that's what Cabbage had been waiting for.

He crawled over to his crossbow. Knife screaming in his collarbone. Snatched the weapon. Raised it. Aimed at the Flawless Bershad.

"Put that thing down, Cabbage."

"I got a clear shot."

"I know you do. But this is between me and the lizard killer now." Cabbage didn't move. "Boss?"

"Put. Down. The. Crossbow."

With great hesitation, Cabbage did as he was told.

"Cabbage doesn't understand," Simeon said, keeping his eyes on Bershad. "He never had the right blood for this work. But you have it, don't you, lizard killer?"

"I do," Bershad said.

Simeon nodded. "Things go your way, promise me you'll let the earless bastard live. Having the wrong blood for this black life ain't entirely a bad thing."

"I promise." Bershad paused. "This goes your way, send me out to the sea proper. No piss pot forged from my skull."

Simeon smiled. "Deal."

They angled up. Bershad adjusted the spear in his fist. Simeon rolled his shoulders, creating the familiar mechanical crunch. He was still holding the broken shard of sword.

They both hunched low. Prepared to charge.

And then the top of the Proving Ground exploded in a shower of broken metal.

Something shot up from the wreckage and into the sky, getting smaller as it rose, until it was just a dot. It stopped rising. Hung for a moment. Then started coming down.

Cabbage followed its meteoric fall, which ended almost exactly in the middle of Simeon and the Flawless Bershad. There was a blast of white sand. When it dissipated, Cabbage saw a person hovering three strides above the dock pylons, suspended by one arm, which was wreathed in machinery and humming with current. The pylons were shaking like Cabbage's hands the morning after a long night of drinking.

Ashlyn Malgrave.

"Fuck me," Cabbage muttered.

The pylons stopped shaking, and Ashlyn dropped her feet onto the ground with the grace of a dancer. She adjusted a black satchel that was slung over one shoulder. Looked at Bershad.

"What're you doing here?"

"Came to rescue you."

"Good job." She turned to Simeon. "Will you yield?"

"Fuck no."

"Didn't think so." Ashlyn started walking right at him.

Simeon raised his gauntlet. "Don't know what sorcery you got in that arm, Queen, but it ain't gonna stop my fist from blowing your skull apart like a melon when I punch you."

Ashlyn kept walking. "Sorcery doesn't exist."

When she was two strides from Simeon, she jabbed her metal hand out, then ripped it down. Simeon's head got sucked into the sand, as if a very powerful, invisible man had come up behind him and shoved his head into the earth. He was buried to his chin. Body still.

That seemed an awful lot like sorcery to Cabbage. He raised his crossbow. Aimed.

Don't hesitate. Don't hesitate.

Ashlyn turned to him. Opened her palm. "I wouldn't recommend it, Cabbage."

His finger trembled.

"If you fire that weapon, I'll return the bolt to you by way of your brain."

He dropped his crossbow.

"Step away."

He obeyed.

Bershad raised his spear and walked over to Simeon with the clear intention of murdering him.

"No," Ashlyn said, stopping him. "I need to know more about that armor."

"He needs to be alive for that to happen?"

"Yes. It's bound to his nervous system and can help me—"

"Don't need the details," Bershad said. "Just the directive."

He grabbed Simeon's ankle and yanked hard enough for his

head to pop free of the sand. Bershad looked out at the sea. Waved at the distant skiff. "Felgor has a Papyrian lens with him. If he's using it, he'll turn around and collect us. Kerrigan said she'd leave one frigate along the coast till midday."

"Who's Kerrigan?"

"I'll explain later." Bershad turned to Cabbage. The spear twitched in his hand.

"Please don't kill me!" he piped.

"Ain't gonna kill you, Cabbage. Simeon and I made a deal, remember?"

Cabbage gave a slow nod. Once again, Simeon had saved him instead of the other way around.

Bershad stopped talking. Sniffed. Turned east, back toward the Proving Ground, which was billowing black smoke from the destroyed sublevels.

"Shit. We got a problem."

"Pirates?" Ashlyn asked.

"No. They're all dead. But Kasamir's crops aren't."

He motioned to the forest that led to the Bloody Sludge. From where they were standing, they had a good view of the tree line, which was filling with deformed figures—bloated muscles and hanging, broken limbs. Mushrooms leaking from their chest cavities.

"Impossible," Cabbage said. "The demons don't cross the Bloody Sludge."

"They do now," Bershad said, glancing back to the skiff and then the trees. The creatures were swarming out of the woods at speed—loping toward the Proving Ground like wounded jackals. "Felgor isn't going to get back here in time. That hand of yours able to explode those assholes, too?"

Ashlyn shook her head. "They need to have Osyrus Ward's machinery implanted in their bodies. Lodestones. Those are Kasamir's creations—the ones that Simeon brought and he buried in his garden." She lifted her hand. "This won't touch them."

Bershad cursed. Raised his spear. "This can."

"You're falling apart," Ashlyn said.

"I am, but my nose is telling me you got something that'll change that tucked into your satchel there."

"Silas . . . you need to be careful how much you use it, or you'll be—"

"No time, Ashe. Give me the Gods Moss, then get to that skiff," Bershad said. "I'll slow them down."

Ashlyn produced a vial full of something green and blue. Gave it to him. Bershad emptied the contents into his mouth, and Cabbage watched in amazed horror as all the damage that had been done to his body healed in a matter of seconds. Nothing remained of the wounds except dried blood and a few fresh scars.

"For sorcery not existing, you two perform an awful lot of it," Cabbage muttered.

Bershad was already walking across the beach. He picked up the shield on his way.

"Don't wait for me. Soon as Felgor comes back, you shove off and get clear."

"How are you going to reach us?"

"I'll figure something out."

Then he was off at a run, heading directly at the big line of mushroom people that had just reached the top of the cliffside stair.

52

BERSHAD

Ghost Moth Island, the Proving Ground

Bershad charged the horde of creatures.

Some were soldiers. Wearing full armor and carrying swords or spears. Others had nothing but decayed rags hanging from desiccated skin. Spores and fungus burst from gashes in their guts.

Bershad couldn't kill them all, but he could get their attention. He didn't bother spearing the first wave of creatures coming down the steps—just bashed them with his shield, snapping dry knees and caving in half-rotten faces. Mushroom spores and black, infected liquid sprayed everywhere, filling his nose with the horrible reek.

When he reached the top of the stairs—a trail of twitching bodies behind him—he started using the spear.

A thrust to the face or spine seemed to drop the creatures in their tracks, so that was what Bershad started doing. One face, one spear thrust. Again and again and again.

They clawed at him—taking strips of skin and muscle off his bones. But the Gods Moss that Ashlyn gave him was stronger than anything he'd felt before—the healing kept pace with the damage, despite the fact that he was getting torn apart.

He pressed further into the horde. Screaming as he bashed with his shield and thrust with his spear, trying to attract as much of their attention as possible. He jumped onto a boulder and turned to the beach. Felgor had almost reached the shore. Ashlyn and Cabbage were wading out to meet him. Ashlyn was dragging Simeon through the shallows using whatever power she'd imbued to that metal hand.

He hopped off the rock. Looked around.

"Crap."

The creatures were swarming from all directions—jaws working, infected eyes weeping. He was completely surrounded.

If he cut back through them to the beach, he'd just undo the work of luring the creatures away from Ashlyn and Felgor. There was nothing else to do besides charge farther into the woods, away from the sea. Bershad hopped off the rock and sprinted east—feet pounding over the damp, black grass. Through mud puddles and over broken ground. He fought as he ran, but for every corrupted face or body he skewered, two more appeared in its place.

He reached the edge of the woods, which gave way to an incredibly steep downward slope that ended in a muddy ravine. Bershad turned. Whipped his shield across the faces of two attacking creatures, reducing their skulls to fungal mist.

Then a blinding, sharp pain rippled through his left side.

He looked down. A dripping green claw was sunk deep in his rib cage. The claw belonged to a decaying man in rusted Ghalamarian armor. Bershad tried to spear him through the face, but the point glanced off his jaw, sending the desiccated bone flying across the field.

The Ghalamarian twisted his fist inside Bershad's guts. Bershad lost his balance. Fell backward down the slope.

The Ghalamarian came with him.

They landed on a pile of sharp rocks. A large number of Bershad's bones broke. He heaved and wheezed, trying to draw air from his lungs. Having a monster claw still jammed through them wasn't helping. The Ghalamarian had landed on top of Bershad, but hadn't died. His rotten breath was hot on Bershad's face. He wrapped his free hand around Bershad's throat and squeezed.

Shoots of black, barbed fungus squirmed out of the Ghalamarian's infected arm, latching on to Bershad's mouth and nose and ears. Worming inside.

"Join us," the Ghalamarian growled, voice guttural and low. "Jooooin."

Bershad could feel his body trying to heal the damage, but the bastard kept rooting around in his chest cavity—the fungus spreading through his guts. This was too much pain. Too much damage. Even with a bloodstream full of Gods Moss, this was killing him.

His skin started to burn. He looked down at his forearm and saw small spires of moss protruding from his tattooed skin—blue flowers blossoming from the inky chests of the dragons that he'd killed. The forest ignited with the croaking murmur of animal and insect heartbeats, but the sensation wasn't coming from the Nomad above. It was coming from him.

His body hummed and heaved. The earth beneath him turned rich and warm and welcoming. Ready for him. He was on the precipice of something that felt terrible and wonderful at the same time.

"No," Bershad growled. "Not like this."

He stopped focusing on his own body, and instead reached higher, above the trees, into the sky, where the Gray-Winged Nomad was circling.

And he asked for her help.

53

ASHLYN

Ghost Moth Island, Western Coast

"What the hell was he thinking?" Felgor asked, helping Ashlyn onto the skiff. She'd already loaded Simeon using the lodestones in her arm. The unconscious pirate was so heavy, the skiff sagged deep in the surf, almost to the railing.

"You know Silas," she said. "He never thinks anything through."

"True."

"But it's working," Cabbage said.

Most of the creatures were swarming toward the forest where Silas had disappeared down into the ravine.

"Not quite," Ashlyn said, pointing to the beach, where ten of the ones Bershad had battered with his shield were on their feet again, lumbering toward their skiff.

"What do we do?"

"Shove off," Ashlyn said, bending down to open the black bag of materials she'd taken from the Proving Ground. "And get us into deeper water."

"That isn't going to be a quick process," Felgor warned, already working the rigging again. "Simeon's got us weighed down more than a greedy merchant's last carrack of the season."

"I know," Ashlyn said. "Just do the best you can. Cabbage, start shooting them when they get in range."

"I only have one bolt left."

"What happened to the rest?"

"I, uh, shot them at Bershad."

"Perfect."

"Can't you use your sorcery?"

"No. Not on them."

"What *can* you use it on, then?"

Ashlyn chewed her lip. That gave her an idea. She started rooting around in her bag. Found a lodestone the size of an apple.

"This."

The creatures were about twenty strides from their carrack, and up to their hips in seawater, but that wasn't slowing them down.

Ashlyn stood up in the carrack. Got ready to throw the stone.

"What are you waiting for?" Cabbage shouted.

"They need to be closer together," Ashlyn said.

"How much closer?"

She could feel the dense core vibrating low and steady, reacting to the magnet in her arm. She had to be careful. If this went sideways, Ashlyn would—at best—blow her own fingers off. At worst, the attraction would backfire and she'd push the metal through her own brainpan.

"Just a little more."

When they were almost within arm's reach of the stern, Ashlyn threw the orb toward them and activated every lodestone she'd implanted along her wrist.

The dragon thread pulsed. Made her teeth vibrate in her mouth. The closest mushroom person's head simply disappeared. Behind him, the water shuddered and rippled and the rest of the mushroom people were blasted apart in a massive explosion of bile and fungus. The ocean surged with an infected swamp of green sludge. The wretched smell of pus and infection filled her nostrils.

"If that wasn't sorcery, then there ain't no such thing as dragons or lies or sins, neither," said Cabbage.

They sailed in silence for a few minutes, drawing farther and farther away from the coast. Ashlyn stared back at the island, eyes fixed on the edges of the cedar forest.

"You see any sign of him?" Felgor asked, coming up to join her.

"Not yet."

But as the morning fog started to lift, she could see the Gray-Winged Nomad circling the forest, getting lower with each pass.

And just as its wings were about to start skimming branches, she dove.

54

BERSHAD

Ghost Moth Island, the Wilting Forest

The Nomad snatched the Ghalamarian into her claws and squeezed. Sprayed his corrupted organs in a dozen different directions, then plowed through the forest with the leftovers in her claws. Bershad heard snapping cedars as she skidded to a stop in the distance.

The Ghalamarian's claw was still inside of his chest—broken off at the elbow. Bershad used all the strength he had left in his body to rip it out of him. Then he just lay back. Went still while his body healed. Whatever had been happening to him seemed to have stopped. It took long minutes of ragged, shallow breaths before he didn't feel like he was drowning. A few minutes after that he had enough strength to move.

He got to his feet. Cracked his neck. Looked around.

The Nomad was picking at the remnants of the rotten Ghalamarian like a dog gnawing the last scraps of meat off a chicken bone.

"Stop that," Bershad said. "It's gross."

The Nomad looked up at him. Cocked her head. Then went back to nibbling the rotted bones.

Bershad sighed. Looked up at the rim of the ravine. Cursed.

There were scores of mushroom people up there. Some of them were already on their way down. More claws. More angry teeth.

Bershad still had his shield and spear, but his body had burned through almost all of the Gods Moss in his blood. No way he was cutting his way back up that ravine before he ran out. Meant he needed a faster way out to the sea.

He looked back to the dragon.

"Turns out I'm gonna need your help with one more thing."

55

ASHLYN

Ghost Moth Island, Western Coast

Ashlyn was still staring at the sagging tree line when Felgor banged their sloop up against the waiting frigate. Goll was there to help them aboard with powerful arms, but hesitated when he saw Simeon's unconscious body.

"Should I kill this one, Kerrigan?" he asked a dark-skinned woman with a blue mohawk, who was standing behind him with crossed arms.

"No," Kerrigan responded. "Get everyone on board."

"But he hurt Flawless."

"Do as I say," Kerrigan ordered. "Just make sure that Simeon is chained to a mast before he wakes up."

Goll grumbled, then hauled Simeon up, threw him against a mast, and started wrapping a thick anchor chain around his chest.

"So, I'm thinking you're the queen of Almira, that right?" Kerrigan asked Ashlyn when she reached the deck.

"That's right."

"You really fucked me over with what you did on my island."

"I know."

"Where is Flawless?" Goll asked, still wrapping lengths of chain around Simeon.

"He stayed behind to make sure we got clear," Ashlyn said.

Everyone looked back to the coast, which was now swarming with twitching bodies that stared at them from the shallows. Eyes full of hunger.

"No," Goll muttered. "No, this is not acceptable. I owe him a blood debt. If he dies, the debt will be forever unpaid. I will never reach my ancestors in the afterlife with that sin on my shoulders."

"Least you ain't already with your ancestors," Cabbage muttered, scratching at one of the holes in his head.

"Neither is Silas," Ashlyn said.

"What do you mean?"

"Look." Ashlyn pointed to a copse of wilted, shaking trees. "There."

The Nomad blasted out of the forest, heading straight up at first, then turning toward the frigate. The sound of her wingbeats boomed across the open ocean like a drum, but as she got closer, another sound rose above it.

Silas. Screaming his lungs out. He was clutched in her claws.

"By Aeternita's perfect tits," said Felgor. "He's riding a dragon."

"*Riding* is a generous description," Kerrigan said. "Looks to me like he's just hitching a rough ride. A *very* rough ride."

When the Nomad was directly above the ship, she dropped him. Silas hit the water at such speed that he skipped off the surface like a thrown stone, limbs and head flailing from the brutal impact. His naked body floated on the churning surf for a moment, then sank.

Without hesitation, Goll dove into the water after him. Disappeared beneath the waves.

"Uh, I might be misremembering, but didn't Goll say that he couldn't swim?" Felgor asked.

They all exchanged looks. Vash, Felgor, and Ashlyn all went into the water a moment later, swimming hard to catch up with the two sinking bodies.

Felgor and Vash dealt with Goll. Ashlyn grabbed Silas by the armpits and hauled him back to the surface—her arms and legs and lungs burning from the effort of pulling his weight. She came up with a sputter and wheeze, barely able to keep herself afloat. Someone grabbed her and pulled her back onto the ship.

Ashlyn doubled over on the deck, breathing hard. Nose and ears and mouth full of seawater.

"He's not breathing," Felgor said, hand on Silas's chest.

She stood up, motioning for everyone to back away.

Then she crossed the deck and kicked Silas in the stomach as hard as possible.

He vomited up a bucketful of red seawater. Started coughing. After he collected his breath, he popped his own dislocated shoulder back into place, followed by three of his twisted fingers.

"Oh, that is disgusting," Felgor said, covering his ears to drown out the loud pops.

Bershad ignored him. Looked around. Sniffed. "Everyone made it. Good."

Ashlyn put her hands on her hips, standing over Bershad. He looked up at her and smiled.

"What?"

"You have a nice ride?" she asked.

"Well, I tried to explain to the wild dragon that a gentle landing would be smoother on my delicate and scaleless body, but things got lost in translation somewhere along the way."

"Hey. Queen."

Ashlyn turned around. Kerrigan was glaring at her. One hand rested on the rapier at her hip.

"Yes?"

"Don't forget, the only reason you're standing on this deck instead of getting digested by a dozen of those monsters is because of me. Got that?"

She glanced at Bershad, who gave a nod.

"Yes. I understand."

"Good."

Kerrigan looked back at Naga Rock, and so did Ashlyn. The island was getting smaller with each passing second, but in the dying light, she could just barely make out the silhouettes of misshapen figures. Glowing eyes dotted the cliffside like infected fireflies.

Kerrigan turned to Bershad and Ashlyn. "And seeing as I lost my island to demons because of you two, I am thinking that you owe us some assistance when it comes to relocation."

"We do," Ashlyn agreed. "Make a heading for Himeja. I'll ensure that you and your people are given pardons and a place of your own. One of the smaller Papyrian islands along the eastern point, maybe."

Kerrigan considered that.

"Sharing a scrap of blood with Empress Okinu won't necessarily put her in a forgiving kind of mood for all the shit Simeon and I have pulled in her backyard. Giving over one of her islands sounds like a real stretch."

"Okinu is a pragmatist," Ashlyn said, lifting her arm so that Kerrigan could see what she'd done to it. "And I have something to give her that's far more valuable than a few islands."

Kerrigan chewed her lip a few more moments. Then turned to her pilot.

"Make for Himeja. And signal the other ships in the fleet. We all go together—I do not want stragglers or strays."

"Aye, Captain. Himeja."

Ashlyn turned to Bershad. "We need to talk. Alone."

Bershad nodded. "Belowdecks."

————

"You put a lodestone inside yourself?" Bershad asked Ashlyn after she explained what happened while she was Simeon's prisoner.

"No. I put twelve of them between the deep tissue and bone of my forearm, and linked them to the prongs of the dragon thread that is slowly spreading through my body."

"Didn't that hurt?"

"Yes. But it had to be done."

"Why?"

"We needed a way to combat those skyships. Now we have one."

"The plan was to get more dragon threads."

"There were none left."

"You're sure?"

"I'm sure. Osyrus took them when he left. He knows their potential, he just hasn't figured out how to unlock it yet." She blew out a long breath. Tried not to think about what he would do if he did. But one problem at a time. "Every skyship engine contains a system of lodestones, just like Simeon's armor. That means I can fight them."

Bershad looked at the machinery that she'd grafted around the wild black tendrils of dragon thread. The intertwining of flesh and metal and dragon thread was both impressive and unsettling.

"What's the range on that?"

"Five or six paces," she said.

"Ashe, in case you forgot, those skyships don't fly five or six paces off the ground."

"I'll figure something out, just like you did back there," she said. "There has to be a way to increase the range, and the answer is probably inside one of those ships."

"What're you gonna do, climb into one and go poking around?"

"I'll do whatever it takes to stop Osyrus Ward. The things that

I saw in that pit. The things that he's planning to do. Or already doing." She looked at him. "We *have* to stop him."

Silas gave a nod. "I'm with you."

He said it as if she'd just asked him to do something as simple as tracking a deer through a forest. But that was always his way. Easy acceptance of the most difficult and dangerous tasks. It was the safe, synthetic routines of civilized life that gave him trouble.

He sat down next to her. Put a hand on her shoulder.

"Osyrus Ward's work isn't the only thing that you found in that pit, is it?"

"No," Ashlyn said. She hesitated. Tucked a strand of hair behind her ear.

"It's all right, Ashe. You can tell me."

She swallowed. Looked at him.

"I found out why that Nomad has been following you. And it's awful."

56

VERA

Almira, Floodhaven, Castle Malgrave

Fourteen Dainwood wardens were brought into the same audience hall where Kira had murdered Linkon Pommol and his lords, although the blood had been cleaned up.

The jaguars' weapons and armor had been taken when they entered the city, but Kira had allowed them to keep their masks, which were hooked at their belts. Torches spat and crackled in the corners, which Kira had insisted be fueled with normal animal fat instead of dragon oil. To make it feel familiar, she'd said.

Decimar's archers were stationed in the gallery above, same as before. Although their orders were very different.

High-Warden Carlyle Llayawin bowed in front of Kira. Glanced at the archers before speaking.

"Most of my men said that my head was packed with dragonshit for accepting your invitation. Said you made porcupines out of the last lords to treat with you, and you'd do the same to me. They right?"

Kira smiled with understanding. "Some of my advisors warned me against this audience as well. But no, Carlyle. You are in no danger. My archers are simply a precaution. I'm the last living Malgrave. The only way to avoid joining my father and sister on the long swim is to be wary of betrayals."

Carlyle nodded. Seemed to accept that answer and relax a little.

"I served your sister during the siege of Floodhaven. And I fought by her side in the battle that followed. What Linkon and Wallace did to her is unforgivable." He swallowed. "It grieved me to learn of her death. For weeks, I clung to the hope that she had survived. Snuck away, somehow."

"I appreciate that, Carlyle. My sister always trusted you, which is one of the reasons that I was willing to make this peace offering to you. You're a better breed of Almiran than the men who died in this room."

Carlyle nodded. "What are your terms for peace?"

Kira readjusted herself on the dais, moving to business.

"I ask very little," she said. "You may keep sovereignty of the Dainwood, and decide who will rule from Deepdale for yourselves. You will pay no taxes of silver or gold to me, and you will owe no portion of your lumber sales to me."

"We will sell no more of the Dainwood for profit," Carlyle said, voice firm.

Kira nodded. "That is your choice, and will not be disputed."

Carlyle hesitated. "This can be sealed in a contract?"

"Of course. Valid from the birthing of the forest gods out of the Soul Sea to the end of time."

Many of the wardens nodded happily at Kira's mention of the gods. That was a lesson that her older sister never learned. Respecting the Almiran religion was one of the fastest ways to win their loyalty.

"Good. But if we are allowed to choose our own sovereign, and you do not want taxes or levies, what do you want from the Dainwood?"

Kira leaned forward. "My predecessor, Actus Thorn, brought the Balarian armada to Almira with selfish motivations and violent intention. The theft of the Clear Sky harvest was a terrible crime, and it will never be repeated. But there are thousands of innocent, starving people in Balaria who need food. All that I ask of the Dainwood is that you lend a portion of your rich crop yields to their aid."

"What happened to the crops you already took?" growled a young but rough-looking warden with long black hair.

Kira bowed her head in regret. "Those yields were taken by the aristocrats and military of Burz-al-dun. They never reached those who needed it most." She paused. "But the men responsible for that injustice are dead. I will not repeat their crimes."

"Why should we trust your word?" the warden continued. "You still got those fucking skyships. You still got those assholes with their longbows." He motioned to the gallery. "What's different?"

"I also have Almiran blood in my veins," Kira said. "But that isn't enough. Not on its own. All my life, I watched while my father and the high lords tore this country apart, one land squabble and skirmish at a time. My sister wasn't a warmonger, but she would have turned Almira into a dragon sanctuary if she had her way. I am different. I haven't come back to my homeland to bleed the Dainwood dry, or to let the great lizards run wild across it while people suffer. I've come to make it a prosperous and peaceful land."

Carlyle brushed a strand of hair away from his face.

"That sounds awfully nice," he said. "But just to entertain a hypothetical. What happens if we refuse?"

"That is your choice, and it will force me to search for a solution to Balaria's starvation problems elsewhere. We can live in harmony on opposite sides of the Gorgon River, I am sure. But you will forgo the protection that my armada offers. Both from foreign invaders and from the legions of dragons that will be returning to Almira come spring, forcing your farmers to keep one eye on the sky once again. With my help, every year will become a Clear Sky harvest. Without it?" She shrugged. "You will be on your own to face the dangers of this world."

Carlyle cleared his throat. "This is a surprise. Ashlyn was a famous lover of the great lizards."

"I am not my sister. My priority is the *people* of Almira. Not the dragons of Terra."

Carlyle's jaw worked back and forth and his shoulders tensed as he weighed his options. Eventually, his posture relaxed.

"I will need all of this drawn up in contracts. Reviewed by my stewards. But for now, how about we drink and feast on it, like proper Almirans?"

Kira smiled. "Agreed."

———

Twenty minutes later, drums were booming in the corner of the feasting hall and servants were everywhere, bringing jugs of wine and ale, platters of roasted boar and chicken and goat. The massive floor-to-ceiling stained-glass window on the western wall poured multicolored light into the large hall.

Vera sat to the left of Kira on the dais, looking out over the feast. Watching the wardens of the Dainwood laugh and drink and slap shoulders with the small lords of the Atlas Coast that Kira had already won over to her cause. Two of Decimar's archers stood behind Kira's chair. Osyrus was seated to her right. One of his acolytes loomed behind him. He took slow, rough breaths and scanned the sectors of the room in a steady, endless loop. Vera had insisted that he carry no weapons, but she couldn't deny the value of an extra set of vigilant eyes.

And, of course, Decimar and his men remained above on Vera's orders. There would be no massacre like Linkon and his lords, but she'd told them to keep their eyes open and their hands within reach of an arrow at all times.

"Do you know what this means?" Kira asked, smiling out at the crowd.

"That there will be quite a few hungover jaguars tomorrow?"

Kira snorted. "Well, yes. But there's a bigger picture! We've set a precedent for diplomatic resolutions, despite the skyships we could have used."

"You might not have used them, but I am fairly certain their presence played a part in this peace."

"Either way, now that we're allied with the Dainwood, we can return to Balaria with the rations we need to stabilize Burz-al-dun and Ghalamar. It's perfect."

"What about Lysteria? When Osyrus Ward called these ships to Floodhaven, they were dropping mayhem and destruction upon their country."

"I didn't give those orders."

"The Lysterians may not appreciate that distinction."

"It's a good thing that I can be very convincing."

Kira smiled at her again. Not the fake, beautiful smile that Vera had seen her use for her entire adult life. But a vulnerable, genuine expression.

"I've never seen you this happy before," Vera said.

"That's because I've never done something like this before. And it really means something! It's not some stupid feast or little victory over some fat minister who's mostly just hoping for a better look at my tits. This is real. And it will help people." She turned to Vera. Put a hand on her wrist. "And once things have calmed down here, you and I can go for a nice, long ride in my skyship. Just the two of us."

"What about a pilot?"

"Entras has been teaching me. He says I'm ready!"

Vera smiled. Squeezed Kira's hand. "All right, Ki. Just the two of us."

The acolyte took a step forward and leaned down to Ward's ear.

"Master," he rasped. "There is a drunken warden with a bad look in his eye."

It only took Vera a moment to find the man in question. It was the dark-haired warden who'd spoken up during the audience. He was on a bench to Vera's left, drinking ale the way a man fresh from the desert drinks water. But those things alone didn't bother Vera. It was the meat knife he was shifting between callused fingers with a singular focus.

"Yes, a very bad look," Osyrus agreed. "Please remove him from the hall."

"No," Kira said quickly. "I do not want to make a scene."

"Number Seven will be discreet," Osyrus said.

"That is not possible." Kira turned to Vera. "Please handle this. Quietly. Even a small altercation could put this entire treaty at risk."

Vera didn't like leaving Kira's side. But she liked the idea of Osyrus Ward's gray-skinned behemoth trotting through the ranks of wardens and snatching one by the back of the neck far less. She turned to the two longbowmen standing behind Kira. "Keep sharp."

Vera stepped off the dais and walked toward the drunken man, both hands on her daggers. The wardens all went quiet as they saw her approaching, but Vera didn't sense any fighters among them. Not tonight, anyway. They were full of meat and ale and they were happy.

"What's your name, warden?" Vera asked the man.

He looked up, eyes bleary. "What do you care, Papyrian?"

"We're allies now. Best get to know each other."

He glared at her a moment longer, then turned back to his mug and his knife. "Oromir."

Vera took a closer look at him. His face was scratched near the scalp—his fingers calloused and raw. He had the hungry and hollow look in his eyes of a man who hadn't seen a bed in a very long time.

"The war went hard on you, yes?"

"All wars go hard. 'Less you got yourself a fucking flying ship to hide inside."

"We're not hiding. And we're not here to keep fighting."

Oromir looked up again. "I've known a few widows. The only thing you lot are good for is killing. So don't come over and ruin my sulking with dragonshit words of peace. I know the truth."

Vera stepped closer. "You're drunk. And you are obviously upset. But you can stay if you give me that knife."

She reached out with one hand. Tightened her grip on *Kaisha* with the other. But the warden just grunted and handed the blade over.

"Take it. Ain't looking for trouble."

"Appreciated."

"One question for you, though. Since I'm being so reasonable."

"Yes?"

"Has a man come to Floodhaven in the last few weeks? A foreigner with gray eyes and a mole on his face, right here." He gestured to a place on his forehead. "He'd be armed, most likely."

"I haven't seen anyone who fits that description. And if he was armed, we would have arrested him."

Oromir grunted. Turned back to his drink.

Vera spun. Started heading back to the dais. But something caught her eye in the crowd. A serving woman who was also moving toward the dais, but there was a row of benches between them.

She was carrying a tray of sliced beef wedges. Something in her posture was wrong. Too coiled. Too careful.

The woman turned to Vera just before she reached the dais.

Dark hair. Dark eyes. A forked scar across her cheek and lips.

Vera had never met Shoshone Kalara Sun in person, but every widow knew what the empress's most prolific assassin looked like.

Shoshone gave a little nod of acknowledgment. Then she dropped her tray and drew a meat cleaver. Rushed toward Kira with the naked blade.

"Stop her!" Vera screamed.

The two longbowmen behind Kira reacted quickly—drawing swords and moving to intercept Shoshone before she reached the empress—but they were no match for the widow. She vaulted over both men, slashing one's neck open as she flew through the air and hacking the other in the back of the neck as soon as she landed. Shoshone coiled her body and launched toward the dais.

Kira screamed, frozen in her chair. Vera threw the cutting knife at Shoshone. She'd been aiming for her ear—a blade to the brain was the only chance she had for a kill shot from that distance—but she caught her in the meat of her shoulder instead. Useless, except to put one small hitch in the widow's murderous step. Vera followed her throw, leaping over a table and pounding across the room.

She drew her daggers just before she slammed into Shoshone.

Both widows landed in a heap to the side of the dais. Vera felt *Owaru* sink between two of Shoshone's ribs, but *Kaisha* slipped out of her hand and skittered into a corner. Almost immediately, Vera was hit with three concussive blows to her face, barely getting her arm up to block a fourth punch that would have collapsed her windpipe.

And then it stopped.

Vera got her bearings just in time to realize Shoshone had jumped off her and was sprinting toward the empress again.

"Shoot her!" Vera screamed at the archers in the gallery above, who had their bows drawn but hesitated. Shoshone was within three strides of Kira.

"Black fucking skies, shoot!" Vera cried as she lurched to her feet and followed Shoshone.

Three arrows plunked into Shoshone's back. The widow's step faltered again. She dropped her cleaver but somehow managed to stay on her feet. As she took another stumbling step, she yanked Vera's dagger out of her side and lunged forward, up the dais where Kira and Osyrus were still sitting.

Vera didn't have a good view of Shoshone's attack. But she saw the acolyte snap into action at the last moment—grabbing Shoshone by the wrist with blinding speed, trying to wrench the blade away. He was too slow.

The dagger plunged deep into Kira's stomach. Then her chest.

"No!" Vera shrieked, panic coursing through her body.

Vera hit Shoshone at a full run. Lifted her off the dais, through the stained-glass window, and toward the sea below.

They both ended up in the water. A tangle of surging, struggling limbs.

Vera grappled with the severely injured widow until she had control, then hauled Shoshone onto the stone quay with a furious grunt. She resisted the urge to shove Shoshone's face back into the water and drown her.

"Why?" Vera asked, breathing hard.

She'd expected attacks, but not from Papyria. Not from another widow. She didn't understand.

"Orders."

"Impossible."

Kira hadn't wanted to live beneath Okinu's yoke, but she hadn't done any harm to Papyria, either.

Blood was streaming from the arrow wounds along Shoshone's back. One of her legs had broken during the fall to the sea—the foot twisted in an unnatural direction. She was holding a hand tight against the place Vera had stabbed her.

"Okinu's word is law. You know this. Osyrus Ward—and all of his allies—are enemies of Papyria."

"Kira was trying to bring *peace* to Terra. She wasn't an enemy."

"Not directly. But that does not change my orders." Shoshone leaned back on the stones. Looked up at the sky. "See what they make us do to each other, Vera? The rulers of this fucking realm. Such wretched lives we lead."

Shoshone closed her eyes. Died.

———

Vera limped back to the castle in a fog. The image of her own dagger in Kira's chest was scorched into her mind. She tried to tell herself that the dagger hadn't hit any vital areas. But she knew that was a lie. Those were mortal wounds. Both of them.

She reached a postern gate that led back to the castle, but a flicker of movement caught her eye before she went through. She squinted in the dying light—working hard to get her battered and swollen left eye to focus, and failing—but swore she made out four figures moving along the dock. One in the lead. Three behind that were carrying something between them.

It was dark, and they were far away, but Vera recognized Osyrus Ward's wild hair and the queer masks of his acolytes.

They were going to the *Blue Sparrow*. Vera followed them.

When she reached the skyship, Osyrus was nowhere in sight, but two of Osyrus's acolytes guarded the dock. Otherwise it was empty. Vera had never seen them armed before, but these two carried long spears with jagged, barbed tips. The shape reminded Vera of a Naga Soul Strider's tail. The acolytes' grips and postures made it clear they knew how to use them.

"Vera the widow," one said. "Osyrus Ward requests that you come aboard."

"Is Kira alive?"

"Follow us. We will show you."

————

They took Vera belowdecks.

Vera had never been down to that part of the ship. The walls were made of metal and bone and they vibrated at a low hum that made her teeth hurt. The two acolytes moved through the different chambers in silence—opening the bulkhead hatches with a series of Balarian seals. They moved into a circular chamber that was hotter and larger than the other rooms. In the center, the pipes converged on a pedestal, where the Kor was placed. White threads pulsing with power.

There were also two acolytes prostrate on the floor. Black wires ran from their wrists to the apparatus that held the core. Vera couldn't tell if they were conscious or not.

"What are they doing?" she asked.

"Providing balance."

"What does that mean?"

"The Kor requires stability. Our bodies serve."

"How?"

The acolytes didn't respond. Just kept moving through the holds of the ship. The final hatch required a seal from each of them placed on either side of the circular door. They opened it, and motioned her inside.

Kira was laid out on a raised slab in the center of the room. Eyes closed. There were bandages woven around her belly and chest. Tubes were stuck into both of her arms. One tube had the crimson pallor of blood. The other a dark, mossy green. The tubes snaked toward the walls, which were dominated by complex machinery. Rattling pipes and churning gears and quivering wires sprawled around the room like ivy. Everything seemed to lead back to a massive glass centrifuge that was filled with that dark green substance.

Osyrus had his back to her, scribbling notes on a piece of paper. He didn't look up or stop writing.

Vera crossed the room. Put a hand on Kira's forehead. Her skin was clammy and cold and Kira winced at the contact, but didn't open her eyes. Slowly, Vera unhooked the clasp along Kira's ribs that held the bandage in place. Started to unwind the dressings. When the last bolt of fabric was removed, and her chest exposed, Vera sucked in a breath. Stepped back.

"Black skies," she whispered.

The wound was still open, her heart still torn. But there were beads of the green material collecting around the sliced ventricles, slowly pulling them back into place.

"Do not fret," Osyrus said, finally turning around. "She is alive."

"What are you doing to her?"

"Making sure that she stays that way."

"The blade pierced her heart," Vera said.

"And severed her spine, I'm afraid. Both grave injuries. Without careful attention to the healing process, she will never again walk, speak, nor breathe without the aid of these machines."

Osyrus motioned to the corner of the room, where Vera's dagger had been placed in a shallow copper tray filled with water, which was rusty brown from blood. He came over to the other side of the bed. "But Empress Domitian is a very special young woman. Her body can repair the damage under the proper conditions, which I have created here." He raised his arms and looked around the room. "Do you like it? Of course, I need to dress it up a bit more before the empress will feel comfortable. Plants. Moss. A nice teakwood for the walls, I think. Cover up all this grinding machinery, you know? But there is plenty of time for that."

"What are you *doing* to her?" Vera repeated.

"Come now, this is nothing you have not seen before. Her brother has the same condition. The only difference is precision and pace."

She studied the wound a little longer. Remembered what she'd seen Silas do in the dim hold of that riverboat on the way to Burz-al-dun.

It took her a few more moments to put the pieces together. Leon Bershad had been executed for fathering a child with Shiru Malgrave. That child had died at birth. But that didn't mean it was the only one they'd conceived together.

"Kira is Silas Bershad's sister," she said.

"Yes." Osyrus nodded. "Although her presentation of the anomaly is far cleaner. And full of far more possibilities."

Vera frowned at the wound. "Silas healed faster."

"Silas Bershad never took a wound like this. Kira's spine has been completely severed at the eleventh vertebra. Repairing the nerve pathways will take time. And careful strategy." Osyrus moved to the tank and shifted several dials and levers. "This is an unfortunate setback, but not wholly unexpected given our early departure from Burz-al-dun. Things have been quite chaotic since Kira's aggressive reaction to Ganon's discovery of her plans."

The implications of Osyrus's words didn't sink into Vera right away. She was staring at Kira's wounds. Mind locked down. But she gave them more thought as Osyrus continued adjusting his machines.

"Early departure," she repeated. "Meaning you always planned to leave the city?"

Osyrus stopped working. Turned to face her. There was an odd expression on his face. Half amusement, half malice.

"That is correct, Vera."

She felt the two acolytes behind her shift into fighting stances. Knew they'd kill her if she said or did the wrong thing. She kept her temper controlled. Keeping Kira alive was the priority, which meant that she needed to stay alive, too. But she also needed answers.

"You're the one who told Ganon what Kira was doing," she said. It wasn't a question.

"Correct again," Osyrus said. "At first, I assumed she would fail to build political support naturally. When her success became imminent, I intervened. I knew that Kira would have a strong reaction to Ganon's quashing of her plans, but not such a . . . decisive one. My expectation was that Kira would be forced to accept Thorn indefinitely, which would drive her to disenchantment with Burz-al-dun politics. When the time was right, I planned to quietly slip you and her out of the city, and back to Almira on the *Blue Sparrow*. That is why I had Decimar's crew held back from Lysteria and trained. Although they were meant to have embarked on five test flights before Kira came aboard."

"And Linkon Pommol?"

"Was to already be deposed before our departure, which would have made the procurement of the dragon oil my machine required far simpler. But you proved more than capable of overcoming that obstacle. Thank you for that, Vera. And rest assured, there are many more obstacles that you can help me with while I repair Kira's body."

"What obstacles?"

"We are betrayed, Vera. My acolytes killed most of the Dainwood wardens, but a small group survived and fled the city after the assassination attempt. Skulking back to their jungle like the cowardly animals they are, where they will continue to cause trouble for us. We must also deal with the remnants of the Balarian Empire. And you should know better than anyone that there is only one person in Terra who controls Shoshone Kalara Sun's hand."

"Okinu."

He nodded. "Perhaps Kira could have forged a peace with her aunt in time, but Papyria is our enemy now. We have no choice but to counterattack with the armada. As for the jaguars, they might be safe from the skyships beneath their forest canopy, but I have a way to deal with them, too. We will root them out, and establish Kira's empire while she recovers." He turned to her. "Will you help me do that?"

Vera very much wanted to put a knife through Osyrus Ward's heart, unplug Kira from the machines, and run away with her. But that would kill Kira. For the time being, she would do whatever was necessary to keep her alive. That meant making peace with Osyrus Ward's deceptions, and staying in his good favor until the right moment.

"Yes."

Osyrus smiled. "Good."

"What's first?" Vera asked.

"Oh. Before we do anything else in Almira, I would like to rearm the skyships and send them to Papyria, where they will make Empress Okinu pay for what she's done to Kira. And prevent her from trying again."

If Osyrus had suggested that yesterday, Vera would have opened his throat. Papyria was her homeland. Okinu was her sovereign. But Okinu had betrayed her. Vera had no choice but to do the same. The only thing that mattered now was protecting Kira, no matter the cost.

"Do it."

57

JOLAN

Almira, Dainwood Province

Sten died on the journey to the alchemist's research station.

Jolan didn't understand why. The broken bone was swollen and serious, but there was no sign of infection or blood clot. Nothing that would have made the wound fatal. But the warden was dead all the same.

"Wasn't your fault," Willem said after they'd given him a shell and a burial. "Him and Cumberland had been soldiering together for twenty years. You lose a friend like that, sometimes you just give up trying. Sometimes that's all it takes."

"It is my fault. All of this is my fault."

"We're wardens, Jolan. Dying on the end of a blade is part of the job description. And we're the ones who press-ganged you into this whole goatfuck of a mission. Ain't like you volunteered for the fucking thing."

"But I could have stopped it. If I'd let you all kill Garret like you wanted. Or killed him myself. I had the chance."

"Maybe that's true. But I could have come running up that hill with Cumberland when we heard you scream. Cumberland could have beaten that gray-eyed asshole when it came to steel. And all of us could have fucked off and left Sten to die, seeing as he did that anyway. That's war. Looking back on anything, you see a thousand ways you could have done better. But there's no such thing as second chances, so here we are." He spat. "Let's finish the job so I can see about drinking myself to death, yeah?"

It took them another two weeks to find the research station, which was—according to Willem—tucked into a hidden valley of the Dainwood with high forested hills on either side. Cold rain hissed from the sky in a constant drizzle that soaked the trees and the ground and them. Jolan's socks squelched with each footfall, and even though he knew damp socks were the road to toe rot and fungus and eventually amputations, he couldn't summon the energy to change and dry them when they came to a halt each night. Instead, he just found a halfway-covered spot underneath a tree and went to bed fully clothed, shivering.

Monkeys yelled at them from the upper branches of the Daintrees. All the birds and dragons were gone. Each day he felt worse, not better. The sorrow inside of him was festering. Consuming him.

The research station was built around a small lake—water still as a pane of glass. On the near side of the lake, there was a lone hut with smoke rising from the chimney. On the far side, there were three buildings—a hut, a greenhouse, and an apiary. Jolan could hear the low hum of the bees.

As soon as Jolan laid eyes on the greenhouse, he knew that an alchemist lived there. It was built with the same geometric hexagons that Morgan Mollevan had used when they built theirs at Otter Rock.

As Jolan and Willem made their way around the waterline, a plump, bald man in a gray robe came out of the greenhouse and met them. His hands were covered in soil and he was sweating.

"Morning. I'm Frula," he said, wiping his hands on his robe. Smiling with warmth. "What brings you two all the way out here?"

Jolan glanced at Willem. "We came for the pigeon. Shoshone gave us a message to carry on its wings."

"I see," Frula said, smile disappearing into a sorrowful frown. "There's food and drink in my cabin. Come. You look as if your spirits need refreshment."

———————

The inside of the hut was a tidy space with a wood-burning furnace in the middle and a ladder that led to a sleeping loft. Jolan and Willem took seats near the furnace, warming their hands while Frula made a pot of tea.

Jolan stared blankly at the hut's western wall, taking a moment to register what was on it. There were rectangular sections of cork hung in long strips. Upon each cork, there were scores of bees, pinned in place by the thorax. The bees were organized by the color of their pin—red, green, blue. "What are you studying?" he asked.

"Ashlyn Malgrave contracted me to learn more about the bee colony's methodology for selecting new hives."

"What did you find?"

Frula pointed to the wall behind Jolan. This one was dominated by paper instead of dead insects. There was a carefully drawn, but erratic, swirling pattern in the middle of each parchment page. Dozens of equations filled the edges.

"To document a bee's path is quite laborious," Frula said. "But like most things, there is an underlying system to the process. The colony's strategy is actually quite simple after you peel away the movement and confusion. When spring comes, and the hive must select a new location, they dispatch scouts to search the surrounding area. Each scout hunts for the best location they can find, and returns to make their report through a series of gestures. If two scouts disagree, they visit the locations in question together and make a decision. In time, the scouts settle on a single, ideal new home. And the hive moves."

"Interesting," Jolan said, thinking to himself that that would never work with humans. When two scouts disagreed they would probably just murder each other.

"You got anything to drink?" Willem asked.

"The tea is almost ready."

"Tea," he muttered. "Who the fuck drinks tea? Stupid Pargossian drink."

"I'm from Pargos."

"I want booze, old man."

"Well, I am currently brewing a batch of mead, but it has not yet finished the secondary stage. There are too many sulfates."

"Course there are," Willem muttered, then stood up and started riffling through Frula's rack of supplies. He found a bottle full of clear liquid in the back of a cabinet.

"What is this?"

"That's purified potato liquor."

"You said there wasn't anything to drink."

"You can't drink that. We use it for sterilizing wounds and killing bacteria on the beakers."

"Uh-huh." Willem yanked the cork off and raised the bottle, taking four long, deep gulps.

Jolan waited for him to throw up, which was by far the most likely result, but instead the warden just whooped really loud—like a man who'd just had freezing water dumped on his head—and then took a few more long swallows. Slammed the bottle down on the table.

It was half empty.

"Now. Let's have that pigeon so we can update the fucking empress or whatever and then get out of this shithole."

Frula cleared his throat. "I am sure you are weary from your travels, and carry an urgent message, but I wonder if you would like to include recent news from Floodhaven? I just returned from the crossroads market, and heard several grave updates."

"Updates?" Willem said, sniffing the bottle and drinking some more of it. "What kind of updates?"

"The leader of your army recently traveled to Floodhaven under a banner of peace."

"Carlyle went to make peace with Linkon Pommol?"

"Linkon Pommol is dead."

"Huh. Serves the skinny bastard right."

"Carlyle met with Kira Domitian, who took control of Floodhaven," Frula continued. "However, from what I hear, Kira has also been killed."

"Killed? By Dainwood men?"

"They say that it was a Papyrian widow who performed that assassination. A woman with a forked scar on her face."

Jolan and Willem glanced at each other.

"She dead as well?" Willem asked.

"By all accounts."

"And Carlyle? His wardens?"

"Some were killed. Others escaped the city and made it back to the Dainwood."

"So who rules Floodhaven now?" Jolan asked. "Who's left?"

"That is unclear. Some say it is the Balarians, but I believe that is simply a result of one skyship continuing to fly over the city. The others have since departed. I do not know where they went, but I believe all of this is information that Empress Okinu would value." Frula sharpened his voice. "Some of the skyships headed *north*."

"I see," Jolan said. Whoever controlled the skyships would be seeking retribution for the assassination. "I need a quill," Jolan said. "To make some additions to our message."

———

Jolan wrote the note to the empress of Okinu with a careful script, doing his best to control the shaking of his hand.

"Is it Everlasting Empress?" he muttered.

"Eternal," Frula corrected from his spot in the corner of the apothecary.

"Eternal," Jolan said, going back to the paper. "Right."

"Who cares about the titles?" Willem took a pull of mead, which Frula had opened early for him. Apparently, the alchemist had decided that sacrificing a little flavor was better than having the warden blind himself from continuing to drink the pure potato liquor.

"Titles are important to the highborn," Jolan said.

Willem shrugged. Looked out the window at the white apiaries.

"Don't you get stung all the time?" he asked Frula. Now that he was drunk, he wasn't sulking quite as much as he had on their way to the research station.

"They are accustomed to my presence," the alchemist responded. "These days, I can feel them start humming with anticipation if I am late with my harvests. They miss me."

"Huh," Willem said. "You alchemists are a weird bunch, I will say that."

Jolan finished the letter. Blew on the ink with a few steady breaths so it dried. Rolled it up and sealed it with a bee-shaped wax stamp.

When that was done, he took the pigeon out of its cage and attached the missive to its foot. They all went outside together.

Jolan swallowed. Summoned his courage. And lifted the bird into the sky.

There was a flutter of wings. A few fallen, errant feathers. And then the bird was beating across the sky, heading north over the forest. They all watched its flight—Jolan suddenly worried that a Blackjack would snatch it from the canopy, until he remembered that Blackjacks migrate to the Balarian warrens along with the Verduns, Greezels, and Nomads.

The pigeon turned into a small black dot. Then disappeared entirely.

"Our little messenger made it to the horizon safely, at least," Willem said.

"Yeah." Jolan looked down at his ink-stained hands. Then back at the sky. He tried his best not to think of Cumberland. Of Oromir. Failed. "What do we do now?"

"Don't know about you, but I'm not done with this fight. And opening the western coast for the Papyrians cost more than I wanted to spend." Willem shrugged. "Let's at least go meet the fuckers we cleared a path for."

58

BERSHAD

Realm of Terra, the Soul Sea

"How much longer to Himeja?" Felgor asked.

"We're close," Kerrigan responded without looking up from her chart.

"Got to admit, a few weeks on that terrible island have gotten me excited by the prospect of some civilization," Felgor said. Paused. "Even if it's one where I've got a death sentence."

Bershad gave him a look. "You have a death sentence everywhere, Felgor."

"Not Almira. Royal pardon, remember? Courtesy of Ashlyn Malgrave herself." He looked out at the sea. "I've only been to Himeja once, but they got a pretty decent castle in the middle. White Stag or Red Bird or something."

"White Crane," Ashlyn corrected.

"Yeah. What did I say?"

"Not that," Ashlyn said. She looked up from the equations she'd been writing on a scrap of paper. "I'm excited to see it, too. Papyrian architecture is nothing like Almiran work, which relies on granite blocks for everything. I used to pester my father every time an envoy was departing to allow me to go with them to see the stacked castles."

Bershad watched the coast of the Papyrian islands, frowning. Something didn't feel right. Even with their ship sailing three hundred strides off the shore, he could sense something strange in the forest, like every creature from bear to shrew was hunched down and afraid.

"You're sure that you've got enough pull to vouch for us?" Kerrigan asked. She'd been content with Ashlyn's promise for most of their time at sea, but now that they were within a few leagues, she seemed less confident. That was the third time she'd asked since they made landfall.

"I'm sure."

Kerrigan narrowed her eyes. Didn't look convinced.

"Dunno why you're so nervous, Kerri," said Simeon. "It's me who did all the killing."

Nobody had known exactly what to do with the murderous Skojit pirate they captured. Bershad wanted to kill him. Kerrigan wanted to extract some private form of penitence through long conversations. And Ashlyn wanted to study his armor.

They'd settled for leaving Simeon chained to the mast of the frigate for the entire journey back to Papyria. He didn't seem to mind much, despite the shit weather they'd endured. All he'd asked was to have one hand free and a bucket of snails to eat each day. Presently, he popped a fresh one into his mouth. Chewed loudly.

"Killers are as common as mushrooms," Kerrigan said. "But I've spent the last decade destabilizing Papyria's economy for my own profit," she continued. "Okinu isn't going to be rushing to turn over a private island to me."

"Please, nobody say mushrooms for at least a month," Felgor muttered.

"I think you can all stow your concerns for the time being," Bershad said as they came around a bluff and an acrid smell filled his nostrils.

"Why's that?"

He pointed ahead. They cleared a protruding boulder along the coast, and Himeja came into view behind it. The city was built along a great crescent harbor, but instead of seeing a big sprawl of cedar buildings with slate roofs and the famously elegant White Crane Castle of Himeja, all they saw was ruination.

Strange fires burned everywhere. Blue and smokeless.

"More sorcery," Goll muttered, surveying the scene.

There were dozens of blast marks—each one had turned a whole city block to splinters and rubble, with flickering blue flames in the middle that seemed to have almost splashed across whatever they were incinerating.

"The skyships came north while we were on the island," Ashlyn said.

The water of the harbor was black and filled with burning flotsam. Thousands of dead fish floated among the wreckage—the scent of their spoilage rising off the surface like a sickness.

The White Crane Castle was destroyed. Once, it had been supported by eleven or twelve long flying buttresses, but all except two had been broken—their beams falling into the buildings below and incinerating everything. The stacked tower was crippled and sagging—leaned up against the two remaining buttresses like a fallen tree that had caught in a tangle of vines before slamming into the earth.

The people of Naga Rock were flooding the deck. Looking at the scene. Muttering to each other. Cursing.

"Well, isn't this a proper goatfuck," Simeon muttered, grabbing another handful of snails.

"Is anyone alive?" Ashlyn asked Bershad.

He scanned the shoreline for a long time. The Nomad ran a few circles around the castle and city.

"Not many," he said. "Forty-three. And that number's decreasing with a purpose."

He turned to the south, where a lone pigeon was winging across the sea. It soared over the wreckage of the city and slipped into the castle's dovecote, which stood crooked and precarious atop one of the castle towers that was still standing.

"That's one of my birds," Ashlyn said.

Bershad nodded. "There's someone alive in the dovecote. Just barely, but their heart's beating."

Ashlyn scanned the ruined city. Jaw tensing and untensing.

"We need to bring as many survivors as we can back to this ship," Ashlyn said. "But the air is polluted with chemicals. Nobody should go ashore except for you, Silas." She turned to Simeon. "And you, if you're willing to help."

Simeon frowned. "Why me?"

"Because that armor has been poisoning your body for years. I'm not worried about incurring a little extra damage if it saves innocent lives. But if you'd rather save your strength and whatever time you have left for the next violent act, go right ahead."

Simeon glared at her. "I'll go."

"What are you going to do?" Bershad asked while Goll unchained Simeon from the mast.

"Head to the dovecote. I need to know what that pigeon brought back from Almira."

"What about the chemicals?"

"Don't worry about that. I'll be fine."

59

ASHLYN

Papyria, City of Himeja, White Crane Castle

Ashlyn had to navigate the wreckage of the castle to reach the dovecote.

She moved through the broken passageways and scorched rooms. The paintings on the walls were singed and burned. The lacquered furniture was sagging and melted. Corpses were everywhere. Skin and bone still sizzling. She looked for Hayden and Okinu.

She found them both in the dovecote.

Hayden was already dead. Ashlyn couldn't bring herself to look at what had happened to her body. Okinu was leaning against the far wall of the dovecote, half her face burned and bubbled. Only one eye was working—the other was clouded over with red and white film that reminded Ashlyn of blood mixed with milk.

Without moving anything except her good eye, Okinu appraised Ashlyn. "You're late."

Ashlyn bent down in front of her. Studied the scene. There were two other dead widows, and one corpse clothed in the gray robes of an alchemist. There was also a broken vial next to Okinu's hip—the remnants of a blue fluid dripping off the shattered glass.

"The alchemist gave you something to counteract the chemicals?"

"Some mineral-oil concoction. Makes my lungs feel like meat shanks. And all it did was delay the inevitable."

"Mineral oil and what else?" Ashlyn asked. She was exposed to the chemicals, too.

Okinu smiled, realizing why Ashlyn had asked. "Pragmatic as always, my dear niece. Good." Okinu swallowed, wincing and touching her throat in pain. "Mineral-oil base. Three parts nitrate of sodium, two parts calcium alabaster mixed over an open flame."

Ashlyn nodded. The materials were expensive but not as uncommon as Gods Moss. Kerrigan should have some back on the ship.

"Did you find what you were looking for on the island?" Okinu asked.

"No. I found something else."

Ashlyn showed Okinu the metal implants in her arm. The charred black line of dragon thread that sank beneath her skin and was spreading along her bones.

"That can destroy the skyships?"

"Not yet. But with some improvements and some time—"

"There is no more time, Ashlyn. Ward controls the skyship armada now."

"What about Ganon? My sister?"

"Your sister murdered her new husband and fled Balaria. For weeks, nobody knew where she was. Then she turned up in Floodhaven with Osyrus Ward at her side. Together, they called the Balarian fleet to Almira and took control over it."

"Kira ordered this attack on Himeja?"

"No." Okinu swallowed. "For the last thirty years, I have given all of my widows a standing order when I set them loose upon Terra—a mission that supersedes all others."

Ashlyn remembered the final letter that Okinu had shown to her, back in Nulsine.

"To kill Osyrus Ward."

"Yes. I suspect that's part of the reason that he hid for so long behind Balaria's impenetrable borders. But now that his plans are in motion, he was forced to expose himself."

Osyrus had never mentioned being afraid of anything in his notes, especially Okinu. But Ashlyn saw no reason to mention that.

"Shoshone has been operating in Almira for months. She learned that Osyrus Ward was in Floodhaven, and she did as I ordered. At least, she tried."

"Tried," Ashlyn repeated. "What happened?"

Okinu held up a pigeon missive, sealed with the bee crest of Frula, the apiary specialist she'd hired to study the insect's ability to make collective decisions. "This is why you came up here, isn't it?"

Ashlyn opened the note. She didn't recognize the handwriting, but whoever had written the message was well informed about the last few months of events in Almira. Ashlyn read the news once, then again because she didn't believe it.

"To have caused the death of my own kin," Okinu said softly. "An unforgivable act. I deserve what's come for me. And all because as a young woman, I wanted a fleet of dragon-bone ships. Funny."

Ashlyn ignored her aunt's philosophical ramblings. They didn't serve a purpose. Instead, she read this Jolan's letter again. He wrote that the western coast was temporarily unguarded, and asked for the Papyrian navy to come to Almira's aid as soon as possible. But the Papyrian fleet was boiling in the chemical slurry that Himeja harbor had become.

"Promise me that you'll stop him," Okinu whispered, voice filled with wrath. "Promise me that you'll kill him."

In the last two months, Osyrus Ward had taken control of the most powerful empire in Terra and used its resources to conquer Almira and destroy Papyria. She had no idea if she could stop him. No idea if it was even possible.

"I promise."

———

"This stuff tastes like a monkey's asshole," Simeon said, glaring at the half-drunk flask of the mineral-oil concoction. Ashlyn had brewed enough for herself and him. Silas didn't need any. Just some moss.

"I've eaten monkey asshole actually," said Felgor. "It's a delicacy in Clockwork City. Not bad, but not worth the coin in my opinion."

"Fine. Monkey shit, then. You eaten that, too?"

"No."

"I don't care if you drink it or not," Ashlyn said, staring out at the wreckage of Himeja off their stern. "But if you don't, you'll start shitting blood in a few hours, and you'll be dead in a few days. Your choice."

Simeon drank the rest of his portion without protest.

"Avoiding the bloody shits today is all well and good," Kerrigan said. "But I've got nine hundred and sixty-three souls in this fleet. Where are we going to go?"

"The western coast of Almira is open to ships for the time being. That gives us a clear path into the Dainwood jungle, which is the only place in Terra those skyships can't reach."

"Fuck Terra, then," Kerrigan said. "We'll cross the Big Empty."

"Only one in a hundred carracks comes back from that journey," Ashlyn said.

"Who said anything about coming back?"

"Still poor odds."

"If it's between the ocean and a fleet of flying ships carrying bombs, I will take my chances with the Big Empty."

Kerrigan crossed her arms.

Ashlyn shrugged. "Then take them. Just leave me your weakest ship and anyone who doesn't want to die of dehydration four weeks from now."

Kerrigan chewed on that. Turned to Bershad. "You're going with her?"

"The Dainwood is my home," he said. Left it at that.

Ashlyn turned to Simeon. "Even if Kerrigan runs across the Big Empty, we could use you in Almira."

"More rescue missions and good deeds?" he asked.

"No," Ashlyn said. "Killing Ghalamarians. A lot of Ghalamarians."

He ran a hand through his slimy-red hair. "How's that?"

"Osyrus will consolidate power as quickly as possible in Almira and the Balarian Empire. But the skyships can't penetrate the Dainwood canopy, especially not when the dragons return in a few months. If Osyrus Ward wants Almira, he'll have no choice but to send soldiers into the jungle on foot. But the Balarian army has become fractured trying to quell the Lysterian revolt. That makes Ghalamar the only part of the empire with healthy, loyal soldiers. Osyrus will send them into the Dainwood, I'm sure of it. And that's where we're going."

Simeon's face split into a dirty grin. "Then I go with you."

Everyone turned back to Kerrigan, who still didn't look convinced.

"You can promise me the western coast of Almira is open?"

"I can't promise you anything," Ashlyn said. "But if we still have warm blood in our veins when Osyrus Ward is stopped, I will do everything in my power to make sure that you turn the memory of Naga Rock into a rich and prosperous country. One where you write all the laws."

Kerrigan took a long time thinking, then turned to one of her men.

"Raise the sails. We go south."

60

CASTOR

Realm of Terra, the Soul Sea

"What's the matter, Castor, you don't like the view?"

"Not especially, no."

"Castor," Vergun pressed. "My second-in-command is not of much value to me if he does not have his eyes open."

With great effort, Castor opened his eyes. Tried to focus on something close. The gray-skinned men working levers and cranks. The glass of wine on the table to Vergun's left, which was shimmering from the skyship's engine vibration.

"It's not natural, being up in the clouds like this," he said, glancing over the gunwale, where there was nothing but open sky. The Soul Sea was hundreds of strides below.

"Times are changing. Natural. Unnatural. I am not sure the distinction matters much anymore."

Castor completely disagreed with that statement, but said nothing.

One of the grayskins approached, his black goggles impenetrable. None of Osyrus Ward's strange crew were armed—Vergun had insisted on that—but Castor tensed up all the same anytime one came close. He didn't trust the ash-skinned bastards for a second.

"Arrival in thirty minutes," the man rasped, voice distorted by the mask.

Castor once again found himself tempted to tear the mask free and look the strange man in the eyes. See who they really were. Although Castor had looked into Vergun's red-rimmed and sadistic eyes plenty, but it hadn't brought much understanding.

"Excellent," Vergun said to the grayskin, then turned to Castor. "The men are prepared?"

"Yes, sir."

Osyrus Ward had sent word three weeks ago that he intended to engage Wormwrot Company for a one-year contract. He wanted every soldier Vergun had available. And he wanted them now. The payment—half of which was delivered in advance—was extraordinarily high.

And so, they now soared across the Soul Sea on four infernal ships, the belly of each one filled with armed and armored Wormwrot mercenaries. All of them heading for Almira.

There were rumors of other ships, too. They'd been spotted all over Terra. Ghalamar. Lysteria. Pargos. Dunfar. Even Burz-al-dun was said to have a ship hovering over the palace—casting a long shadow.

All of them controlled by the crazy old man, Osyrus Ward. He'd conquered the world in a single winter.

The coast of Almira appeared on the horizon.

Castor had spent almost his entire life in Balaria. He'd grown up surrounded by desert and dried grass. Almira was so unlike his homeland that it felt like a different world. The lush, green landscape was blanketed in massive trees and rising fog. Even from so far above, the forests of Almira felt untamed and intimidating.

"What are your orders when we make landfall?" Castor asked, staring at the view.

"Ward has control of the city and the Atlas Coast," Vergun said. "But the Dainwood is in revolt, and the skyships can't get to them with that damn canopy in the way. We'll unload. Bolster the defenses of Floodhaven, then dispatch various companies into the forest."

"The Dainwood," Castor repeated. "You've fought there before?"

"I have."

"The jaguar's as hard as they say?"

Vergun's lips pressed tight together.

"Harder."

To their left, a grayskin pulled a lever. There was a hiss of steam and release of the piney smell of burning dragon oil. The ship started to drop altitude.

———

The experience of landing the skyship in Floodhaven harbor brought Castor close to puking on three separate occasions. His mouth was filled with spit and the only way he kept his breakfast inside his body was by staring at the Balarian coin that was melted into the butt of his sword and pretending that he wasn't moving at all.

The harbor was mostly empty. The only thing in the water was flotsam left over from Linkon Pommol's destroyed navy. The only thing on the docks were more of those gray-skinned creatures, all of them hauling gear and cargo to various places—their muscles bulging with an unnatural strength.

And Osyrus Ward.

He was waiting with a rictus smile on his face. Arms clasped behind his back. He was also wearing a new leather jacket. This one black with milky swirls of white. A week ago, the fact that Ward had preserved enough dragon hide for a coat would have astonished Castor. Now—after crossing the Soul Sea in a single afternoon aboard a heap of metal and dragon bones—it barely registered in his mind.

Vergun stood, tucking his falchion and dragontooth dagger into his belt as he disembarked from the flying ship. He went straight to Osyrus and, to Castor's surprise, bowed.

Osyrus's rigid smile widened.

"Vallen Vergun. Welcome back to Almira. We have a lot of work to do."

61

JOLAN

Almira, Dainwood Province

It was raining when the four ships appeared on the horizon. They weren't from Papyria.

"Those are pirates," Willem said, glancing at the sails, then going back to picking dirt from beneath his nails with a cracked seashell. They'd been waiting on the beach for a night and a day. Catching crabs. Cooking them in a small fire in the sand. Waiting. Willem had taken a large store of mead and potato liquor from Frula's. He had not been sober for more than a few hours at a time.

"How can you tell?"

"The black sails are a clue."

"Should we be concerned?" Jolan asked.

"Dunno. Getting killed by pirates, getting killed by Balarians." He cupped his palms and pretended to weigh the two notions. "Probably about the same level of unpleasantness, all things considered. Some tavern-rat in Glenlock told me there's an outfit up north that takes people alive and brings 'em to some island that's run by criminals. Walrus Killers. Or whales? Something like that. Maybe this lot can give us a ride out of this fucking mess."

"I can't tell if you're serious or not."

"Well, I also heard the same crew eats babies and uses their rib bones as cock piercings. Hard to know which story is true when you've two sides of a rumor coin like that."

Jolan gave him a look.

Willem sighed. "C'mon. Let's hide in the ferns and see who comes ashore."

The ships dropped sails, then anchors. There were a few minutes of hustle and bustle on the decks, and then a shallop dropped from the side of one ship and started digging to shore. Jolan counted ten figures huddled on the boat—most of them shrouded in dark cloaks to shield them from the steady, cold rain that seemed unlikely to stop anytime soon. The whole sky was swollen with gray, whirling clouds.

When the shallop reached the shallows, a tall man hopped out and scanned the shoreline. He had a white shield on his back, and he was carrying a long spear with an odd shape that Jolan recognized from somewhere, but couldn't quite place. The man trudged onto the beach while the others remained in the boat.

Jolan almost didn't recognize the man because of his short, wildly cut hair. But those rough features and green eyes were unmistakable, as were the blue bars running down each cheek.

"That's the Flawless Bershad," Jolan whispered.

"Dragonshit. It's just a somewhat tall lizard killer."

"No. I've met him before."

"Don't believe you."

Jolan thought back to that day in Otter Rock. The boy who'd woken Silas Bershad from that chair in the inn was a stranger to Jolan now. A kid who didn't exist anymore.

Jolan looked at Willem. "Fine. Let's make a wager, then."

"What are we putting up?"

"If I'm right, then you need to stop drinking so much."

"If you're wrong?"

"Then I'll brew you a hangover tonic every day for a moon's turn so you're more comfortable while you drink yourself to death."

Willem weighed that by taking a sip from his canteen.

"Deal."

Jolan looked back at the shoreline. Bershad was scanning the ferns. Sniffing like a wolf on the prowl.

"We should probably announce ourselves carefully," Jolan muttered. "Don't want to surprise him and get—"

"Come on out, kid," Bershad called, looking directly at him. "The warden, too."

Willem shrugged. "Don't think you need to worry about catching that one off guard, kid."

Willem stood up first, dusted off his knees, and headed down to the beach holding his arms out at his sides—palms facing the dragonslayer. Jolan followed a stride behind, suddenly nervous about what was going to happen.

"That's far enough," Bershad growled when Willem was about ten strides away. "Where you from, warden?"

"Bale's Glade."

He grunted. "Deep gloom, eh? You're a long way from home."

"Seems we all are."

Bershad looked at Jolan for a few moments. Sniffed again.

"I remember you. You're the alchemist's apprentice from Otter Rock. Woke me up to go kill that Verdun."

Jolan glanced at Willem. Smiled. "Yes."

Bershad scrutinized this information.

"Only reason you'd be waiting on this beach in the middle of nowhere is if you're also the one who sent the pigeon."

"That's right."

"Best you talk to Ashe."

"Ashe? Queen Ashlyn?"

Bershad didn't respond. Just motioned to the people in the ship. Three of them hopped out and came over. One was a dark-skinned woman wearing leather armor and carrying a rapier on her belt. The other was a short Balarian with twitchy fingers.

And the third was Ashlyn Malgrave, queen of Almira.

Alive. And standing in front of him.

Jolan went down on one knee without thinking. Willem stayed where he was.

"Don't bother with that," Ashlyn said, motioning for him to get back up. "You're Jolan?"

"Yes, my queen."

"And you?"

"I'm the motherfucker who opened this coastline for you," Willem growled. "And I lost my entire crew making it happen. So where are the rest of you? Where's the Papyrian navy?"

"There is no Papyrian navy anymore. There is just us."

"But that's not enough," Jolan said. "That's not nearly enough."

Bershad gave a grim smile. "Probably not."

APPENDIX

GREAT LIZARD PHYSICAL EVALUATIONS AND SPECIMEN REQUIREMENTS FOR CONSTRUCTION OF THE BALARIAN ARMADA OF SKYSHIPS

Compiled by Osyrus Ward, Royal Engineer of Balaria

(Specimen quality evaluations are ranked on a scale from 0–10, with 10 being the most desirable, and 0 being useless.)

Naga Soul Strider

Bone Strength: 9.1
Bone Weight: 8.6
Hide Quality: 10
Scale Quality: 5.2
Oil Quality: 6.1
Tooth Count: 42
Harvesting Difficulty: 9.2

Specimens required for Armada: 45

Notable Anatomy for Construction

- *Bones strong, but also heavy. Viable for primary support beams only.*
- *Wing leather optimal for skyship sails, since the Nagas have adapted to withstand powerful sea cyclones.*
- *Tip of tail is extremely sharp and lightweight. Superior weapon. But each Naga only possesses a single barb. Not scalable for the ballista design. Will stockpile barbs for later projects.*
- *Seafaring behavior and island habitats make harvesting time-consuming and difficult. Initially engaged a Lysterian whaling outfit on a long-term contract, but the morons were obliterated whilst trying to slay a mating couple.*
- *Will use backchannels to manipulate Papyrian government into cutting more writs and transporting dragonslayers from across Terra to execute them.*

Gray-Winged Nomad

Bone Strength: 9.9
Bone Weight: 1.3
Hide Quality: 4.1
Scale Quality: 5.4
Oil Quality: 8.4
Tooth Count: 36
Harvesting Difficulty: 9.8

Specimens required for Armada: 30

Notable Anatomy for Construction

- *Bones are perfect for the construction of wings: Strong enough to support a one-hundred-meter wingspan, yet light as sparrow bones. Incredible.*
- *Hide and scales unremarkable.*
- *Wish the gray devils weren't so hard to catch. Chased one beautiful specimen halfway across Terra in the prototype skyship—burning substantial fuel—but the stubborn bitch never landed. Eventually forced to abandon hunt.*
- *Filling quota will be difficult. Plan to substitute with Green Horn specimens as necessary.*

Dunfar Sand Strider

Bone Strength: 2.1
Bone Weight: 3.3
Hide Quality: 9.7
Scale Quality: 1.1
Oil Quality: 2.7
Tooth Count: 68
Harvesting Difficulty: 2.7

Specimens required for Armada: 930

Notable Anatomy for Construction

- *A poor quality specimen apart from the hide, which is exceptional.*
- *Hide possesses extremely potent insulation properties. Expect this is from the extreme desert heat during the day, but frigid cold at night.*
- *Ideal for levitation sacks—better insulation yields higher fuel efficiency.*
- *Harvesting is easy. A blessing, given the high quota required.*

Ghalamarian Stone Scale

Bone Strength: 10

Bone Weight: 10

Hide Quality: 1.7

Scale Quality: 10

Oil Quality: 2.1

Tooth Count: 24

Harvesting Difficulty: 10

Specimens required for Armada: 2

Notable Anatomy for Construction

- *A flightless behemoth. Unparalleled heft and weight, which limits applications to skyships.*
- *Scales noteworthy. Each scale can be heated to 3,500 degrees without degrading the structure, and retains 90 percent of that heat 72 hours later. Superior method for sustained dragon oil combustion. Makes coal look like cow dung.*
- *Harvest is extremely dangerous. Nearly lost my life collecting the first specimen that I used for testing. Will submit writs on them until some dragonslayer gets lucky and brings me the second.*

Ghalamarian Green Horn

Bone Strength: 5.2

Bone Weight: 4.9

Hide Quality: 7.7

Scale Quality: 6.2

Oil Quality: 5.1

Tooth Count: 48

Harvesting Risk: 3.1

Specimens required for Armada: 1,000

Notable Anatomy for Construction

- *Bones are relatively unremarkable in terms of strength, but their pliable nature make them ideal for hull construction.*
- *Easy to kill, and available in high numbers in the Ghalamarian wheat fields. Their bones will be the nondescript and uniform elements I use to build the Armada.*

- *Currently negotiating a contract with the king of Ghalamar to eradicate the species from his lands on the condition that 95 percent of harvested materials go to Emperor Mercer's treasury, and thus to me.*
- *Leather is surprisingly supple. Made a jacket for personal use.*

Yellow-Spined Greezel

Bone Strength: 7.7
Bone Weight: 4.3
Hide Quality: 10
Scale Quality: 4.4
Oil Quality: 10 (highly toxic)
Tooth Count: 44
Harvesting Risk: 9.3

Specimens required for Armada: 5

Notable Anatomy for Construction

- *Needled spines highly valuable as tools that are required for building the engines, as well as surgical tools for general experiments.*
- *Toxic oil can be refined for medical purposes, and may help prevent seizures in my latest specimens. Not directly applicable to the Armada in its current form, but if new developments are made with the organic power supply, this will become vital.*
- *Reduced required specimens from 10 to 5 due to complications. My first hunting party was exposed to the venom and popped their own eyes out after suffering powerful hallucinations. Such feeble meat sacks.*

Almiran River Lurker

Bone Strength: 9.6
Bone Weight: 2.1
Hide Quality: 3.4
Scale Quality: 1.1
Oil Quality: 1.9
Tooth Count: 318
Harvesting Risk: 8.3

Specimens required for Armada: 3

Notable Anatomy for Construction

- An inferior specimen in all ways except those wonderful and numerous teeth, which I require for the high-intensity gears powering the rotors.
- Difficult to fish out of the Almiran riverways. Four of my laboratory assistants were eaten during our first attempt. One of them was actually competent, too.
- Plan to hire some backcountry Almirans from the gloom of the Dainwood to assist. Apparently, the muddy barbarians know a clever trick.

Red Skull

Bone Strength: 10
Bone Weight: 6.3
Hide Quality: 4.9
Scale Quality: 5.1
Oil Quality: 2.8
Tooth Count: 36
Harvesting Risk: 10

Specimens required for Armada: 30

Notable Anatomy for Construction

- Skull cap can be scooped clean of brain matter and retrofitted as a combustion vat that never cracks or deteriorates. A vital component for each engine.
- Bones, scales, and skin all capable of superior melding with metal and machinery, ideal for connective joints and engine room apparatus.
- Calculations require one specimen for each skyship. Unfortunate, given their extreme aggression.
- Anticipating heavy losses. Have asked the Emperor to budget for an 80 percent casualty rate of the hunting platoons we are dispatching to the Razorback Mountains.
- Considered outfitting them with a modified design of the prototype armor I abandoned on the island, but decided against it. The materials and time required to construct the armor is more valuable than a few thousand soldiers.

Common Thundertail

Bone Strength: 8.3
Bone Weight: 9.1
Hide Quality: 5.3
Scale Quality: 4.8
Oil Quality: 3.2
Tooth Count: 56
Harvesting Risk: 4.6

Specimens required for Armada: 120

Notable Anatomy for Construction

- *Tail spikes of fully grown adults are ideal for propellers, but must be carved into an appropriate shape, which is painstaking. Exploring updates to the stationary Acolyte design to expedite the process.*
- *Otherwise, this a common, all-purpose specimen that can fill gaps in the construction quotas as needed.*

Papyrian Milk Wing

Bone Strength: 2.3
Bone Weight: 5.2
Hide Quality: 4.1
Scale Quality: 3.3
Oil Quality: 10
Tooth Count: 48
Harvesting Risk: 4.3

Specimens required for Armada: 2,000

Notable Anatomy for Construction

- *Specimen's oil yields are by far the most potent and efficient of the great lizard breeds. If the Green Horns are the bones of the armada, the Milk Wings are the fuel.*
- *Cannot risk a return to Papyria personally. Too much exposure to Okinu's dreadful widows.*
- *Will cut writs under a large network of proxies so as not to attract unwanted attention from the Papyrians. Expect 10 to 20 years before stockpile is complete.*

Ghost Moth

Bone Strength: 5.9
Bone Weight: 7.4
Hide Quality: 2.1
Scale Quality: 9.4
Oil Quality: 8.9
Tooth Count: 18
Harvesting Risk: 1.1

Specimens required for Armada: 100

Notable Anatomy for Construction

- *Despite the fact that the prototype skyship was built exclusively from Ghost Moth parts, their bones are not a preferred source for mass production. Too much weight, not enough strength.*
- *Scales ideal for armor prototype, but that project is on indefinite hold.*
- *Breed still of interest due to a unique network of capillary tissue that produces electrostatic heat, which warms their blood and allows them to survive frigid climates.*
- *Electrical charge extinguished upon death. Can be rekindled with chemicals, but the original and full potency is lost. Exploring alternative techniques for recovery.*
- *In his infinite wisdom, Emperor Mercer has approved the above quota based on this speculative value and the low harvesting risk. Given the stockpile of tissue already in reserve from prior projects, this will give me quite the surplus for experimentation.*
- *Even a modest breakthrough would alter the trajectory of all future projects. Moreover, it would alter the trajectory of the world.*

ACKNOWLEDGMENTS

I would like to thank my agent, Caitlin Blasdell, and my editor, Christopher Morgan. Without their advice, insight, and wisdom, I would have had a series of nervous breakdowns instead of completing this book. I would also like to thank Desirae Friesen, Laura Etzkorn, Molly Majumder, and the talented team at Tor, as well as Bella Pagan, Georgia Summers, and everyone at Tor UK.

Thank you to my family. For this one, I must thank my father in particular, for fielding a large number of very odd and specific questions about synthetic organs and how to treat trauma injuries with limited supplies.

Once again, I owe a great debt to Lola, my brave and stalwart German shepherd, who slept at my feet while a large portion of this book was written and came up with all the good ideas.

And most of all, thank you, Jess Townsend. I couldn't have done it without you.

ABOUT THE AUTHOR

————

BRIAN NASLUND is an American fantasy author based in Boulder, Colorado. He grew up in Maryland and studied English at Skidmore College in New York. Brian first started writing about dragons to escape the crushing boredom of his incredibly long bus commute. When he's not writing, he's usually griping about video games on Twitter; hiking with his dog, Lola; or whitewater kayaking in the mountains. The last activity makes his mother very nervous. You can connect with him at briannaslund.com.